JULIAN SUMMER

KING
COTTON

Matador
9 De Montfort Mews
Leicester LE1 7FW, UK
Tel: (+44) 116 255 9311 / 9312
Email: books@troubador.co.uk
Web: www.troubador.co.uk/matador

ISBN 10: 1-905886-48-9
ISBN 13: 978-1-905886-48-7

Typeset in 11pt Stempel Garamond by Troubador Publishing Ltd, Leicester, UK
Printed in the UK by The Cromwell Press Ltd, Trowbridge, Wilts, UK

Matador is an imprint of Troubador Publishing Ltd

District
Rotation Plan
no... 7

KING COTTON

To all the J's, with love...

"Though with the North we sympathise
It must not be forgotten
That with the South we've stronger ties
Which are composed of Cotton"

Punch, 1861

I

Richmond, Virginia – June, 1861

The tall, barrel-chested man stood in front of the full-length mirror, dressed only in his shirt and drawers, and examined himself. He turned his head to the left and then to the right noting that the few grey hairs at his temple had recently multiplied and now seemed to be moving southward down the line of his luxuriant and hitherto dark whiskers.

He looked down to where the fussy little Frenchman knelt at his feet busying himself beneath the long tails of his shirt.

"Have you not finished down there yet?" he inquired irritably.

"One second, M'sieur, I am nearly done with you." The Frenchman ran his hand up the inside of Commander James Bulloch's leg as far as his groin. "*Ah, bon – à la droite.*" He rose to his feet, rolling his tape measure around the back of his hand with a practiced flick of the wrist. "I can 'ave your uniform ready the day after tomorrow," he said, jotting down some numbers in a small notebook.

"The day after tomorrow?" The colour rose in Bulloch's face. "I should say not! I have an appointment with the President himself tomorrow morning at eleven. Do you wish me to attend in my dressing gown? Do you wish me to tell him that my sorry state of undress is entirely due to the slackness and indifference of Richmond's leading military tailor – who is, furthermore, a foreigner, clearly a war profiteer and probably also a spy?"

The Frenchman assumed that most Gallic of poses, his shoulders hunched and hands raised, palms upwards. "But what can I do, M'sieur? We are so busy, with the war and all the uniforms I must make. For tomorrow morning I would 'ave to work all night long!"

"Then that is what you shall do," the big man said with some finality. "I shall return at ten tomorrow morning to collect my uniform and it will be the worse for you if it is not ready."

Bulloch left the tailor muttering, walked two blocks along Main Street in an easterly direction and paused outside a shop which advertised its trade on a swinging sign by the single word "Guns". He looked in the window and admired the rows of sleek dark oiled revolvers that were displayed on a red velvet cloth. Then he pulled the old and heavy Remington from its worn and stitched holster at his waist. He looked at the bubbles of rust that marred the bluing of the barrel and sighed. Clearly having come to a decision, he holstered the gun and entered the shop.

"Oblige me by showing me some revolvers, if you would be so kind," he said to the shopkeeper, who dutifully produced four different models from a glass-topped display case. "Two Colts," he said, "the 1860 Army Model, which is a .44 and the 1851 Navy Model. She's a .36. Then we have a Remington .44 – similar to the Colt, but perhaps not so well balanced. Lastly, this one, which is a Starr – also .44, but double action. Lookee here". He picked it up and pulled the trigger several times, which rotated the cylinder and cocked and released the hammer in one motion.

Bulloch took the Starr revolver and drew a bead on a framed photograph that hung on the opposite wall. He pulled the trigger. "Heavy gun. Seems hard to hold the target as you fire. Let me look at the Colt – the Navy one." Again he drew a bead on the photograph. He cocked the gun by pulling back the hammer with his thumb and sighted along the barrel. He lowered the gun, hefted it in his hand a couple of times and then took it over to the light, to admire the engraving of a ship on the cylinder. "I like this one," he said, "but it only fires a small ball. Will it stop a man?"

"In his tracks," the shopkeeper replied. "Sure, a heavier ball will do more damage, but there's no man alive who'll take a .36 in the body and still keep coming at you. More accurate too, and lighter. We sell a lot of these."

"Very well, I'll take it. Powder and caps too. Now, what's that little pistol there?" He pointed to a revolver that seemed to be a miniature of the one he had just bought.

"That one," said the shopkeeper "is also a Colt. It's the Pocket Model – a .32. Hasn't either the range or the punch of your Navy Model but she's a good little weapon to have about you nonetheless."

Bulloch picked up the little gun, slipped it into his trouser pocket where it lay flat with hardly a bulge and nodded. "This one as well," he said.

The next morning he was back at the tailor's at precisely ten o'clock by the chiming of the bell tower on Capitol Square. The tailor, who had dark circles below his eyes, beckoned him into the fitting room and helped him into the grey uniform. First the trousers, held up by suspenders. Then the high cut waistcoat, and lastly the double-breasted frock coat with turned-back lapels and brass buttons bearing the inscription 'CSN'. Bulloch fastened the belt, from which hung the new revolver already loaded with the brass caps snugly seated on their greased nipples. Lastly he pulled the black-visored cap down onto his brow and stood back to admire the effect. The well-cut jacket emphasised the width of his shoulders and the narrowness of his waist. "Good," he said nodding, "very good."

The tailor fussed around him, flicking dust from the shoulder boards and pulling down the long skirt of the coat. "This is the first I 'ave made of these," he said. "Very few naval officers around 'ere, I suppose."

"Very few naval officers altogether," said Bulloch. 'And very little navy,' he thought to himself.

It was a source of considerable regret to Bulloch that most of the officers and men with whom he had served in the pre-war United States Navy had sided with the North and had taken their ships into its service. But as a native Georgian he had seen little option but to return South and to offer his services in the defence of his homeland.

He paid the tailor, counting out the new and unfamiliar Confederate dollars into the outstretched palm, noting that the ink came off the bills and stained his fingers as he counted. He nodded to the tailor and adjusting his peaked cap low on his forehead, he stepped out into the street.

Outside he set off at a brisk pace to walk the short distance to the Customs House building that Jefferson Davis, newly elected President of the Confederacy, together with his ministers, had occupied as their temporary offices. As he strode down the crowded pavement he attracted admiring glances from many of the women he passed; some of these were ladies, out shopping with their Negro maids, where a momentary flutter of the eyelids from

3

behind a fully extended fan indicated more than a passing interest. To these he would nod, tap the brow of his cap with his forefinger and mutter "Ma'am"; others were from professionals, plying their trade with low cut bodices and swirling skirts, where the looks were more lingering and suggestive. He could not of course openly acknowledge the clear invitation in the raised eyebrows or pouting lips but he did promise himself that, if his meeting with the President went well, he would reward himself later with just such an attractive and willing companion.

Upon his arrival at the Customs House, he was shown into a small and airless ante-room, where he was invited to wait. He sat down and placed his cap on his knees. The silence was oppressive. Even the distant rumble of carriage wheels on the stone cobbles outside was muted by the closed shutters and heavy velvet drapes. A solitary fly buzzed lethargically. In an adjoining room a clock chimed and then the silence settled again.

As midday approached, the heat in the room intensified. The gilded legs of the chair creaked as Bulloch shifted uncomfortably on the brocade seat, easing first one buttock, then the other, from the sweat-dampened serge of his uniform trousers. As the wait lengthened, so his nervousness grew and he wondered yet again about the reasons for his urgent summons to Richmond.

He had received the letter just four days earlier, as he breakfasted in the oak panelled dining room of his home in Savannah, Georgia. The maid, Ruby, had brought it in on a silver tray and had then bobbed a curtsey and left. He had seen right away the letters 'CSN' embossed in gold on the back of the envelope and had immediately torn it open and looked to the signature. It was from Stephen Mallory, whom he had known slightly in the Florida Keys some years back; Bulloch remembered a squat, heavily bearded man with sharp blue eyes and a good deep laugh. He and Bulloch had sat together in the shade, sipping rum and lime juice and smoking cigars as they watched the Negroes clambering up the steep gang planks of the anchored ships, sweating under their heavy loads.

At that time, Bulloch had been in command of a coastal survey ship, charged with mapping the Florida coast for the United States Navy. He remembered the boredom of the unvarying routine to this day and hoped fervently that Mallory would instead recall Bulloch's time as the Commander of a frigate during the Mexican war rather than his later, more pedestrian activities, when it came to

4

allocating him a new command. For although Mallory had then been a mere port official, his subsequent rise to prominence had been swift and he had even served a term in Washington as a United States senator before returning south at the outbreak of war. His letter to Bulloch had come on the headed paper of the Secretary of the Navy and formally requested him to present himself to his Commander-in-Chief, in Richmond, at his earliest convenience. At the end, in his own hand, Mallory had written *'James – I am looking forward to renewing our acquaintance. The President is anxious to meet you as well.'*

"If they give me command of a ship," he said to his wife, Harriet, "I may be gone for some time." She had looked at him crossly, her lips pursed, as if the war was merely another excuse for him to shirk his duties as a husband and a father.

"Very well then," she said, finally, giving her grudging approval to his departure. "If you have to go, I suppose you must. Just don't go getting killed on me, James Bulloch, there's too much to do around here, for a woman on her own."

As he was about to climb into the trap, which would take him to the station, she had thrust her father's old sword into his hands. He had looked at it and tried to find the words to thank her, but she had already gone back inside and the door had closed behind her.

Bulloch had much time to consider the meaning of his summons as the train chugged slowly across the marshy lowlands of coastal South Carolina and then northward into the thick forests of pine, oak and dogwood that crowded the sides of the track for mile after impenetrable mile. He knew that his chances of command of any serious blue-water fighting ship were slim at best and yet he could not conceive of any other reason why two such important individuals might wish to see him.

The sudden sound of laughter broke into his reverie. He saw the door handle turn and then the smiling face of Stephen Mallory appeared. He had put on weight and his face was fuller than Bulloch remembered, while his spade-shaped beard was flecked with grey but the piercing blue eyes, which now regarded Bulloch with such keen interest, were as clear and bright as ever. "So, there you are Commander Bulloch. Welcome to Richmond. Let us not keep the President waiting." He opened the door wide and beckoned Bulloch to follow him.

They walked out into the corridor and then across the hall into a large room with a long oak table, at the end of which sat a man with a thin aesthetic-looking face, a long aquiline nose and high cheekbones. He was clean-shaven except for a small, tufted, almost goatee beard, that protruded from below his chin, and he wore his dark and wavy hair oiled and brushed severely down.

Bulloch recognised President Jefferson Davis immediately, came to attention and saluted briskly. The President coughed slightly and waved Bulloch to a chair saying "Forgive me for not rising Commander, but you find me temporarily indisposed. Now, Stephen," the President turned to Mallory, who had entered behind Bulloch, "we have much to do, so may I suggest that we start. The floor is yours."

"Thank you, Mr President," said Mallory. "Now Commander, you will have been wondering why we have asked you to come here today. Let me explain. First, by way of background, I shall give you some facts. The overall population of the North is, as you well know, vastly greater than our own, especially when it comes to men of an age to bear arms and we exclude, of course, our coloured folk. This means that they have the ability to field five armies to each one of our own. Then, let us look at our respective resources. Our wealth is principally based on agriculture – theirs on manufacturing. True, we will not starve, but they have many times the number of factories we do and access to an almost unlimited pool of European gutter trash to run their damned machines. Did you know that the state of Massachusetts alone produces more manufactured goods in one year than the whole of the Confederate States combined?"

Bulloch shifted in his chair. This frank and brutal appraisal was greatly at variance with the public perception. Since Fort Sumpter had fallen to the South in April, the men had been hurrying to enlist, fearful in case the fighting should end before they saw action. The feeling was strong in the South that right was on their side and that this was a war of liberation from an oppressor, who sought to impose its own views and narrowly defined standards of morality upon them. Well, to hell with them! The British had found out in 1776 that these were not a people to be dictated to by some foreign power! Now the militias were massing again under the same battle flags, which depicted a coiled rattlesnake and the legend 'Don't Tread On Me'. As for being out-numbered, well, their enemies in the North were, in large part, the result of an exodus from Europe's slums. Men, driven from their homes by poverty and starvation, who could neither ride, nor march, nor shoot. While against them stood country boys, born to the saddle, who could take the eye out of a squirrel at a hundred yards, led by the flower of the American officer corps – every one a graduate of Westpoint or VMA.

"I know what you are thinking, James," Mallory continued, "but all the valour in the world is useless if your enemy is armed and you are not – and we are desperately, desperately short of guns and weapons of all types. So the question is, how will we procure these weapons and the other war materiel that we need? Well, first, of course, we will turn what factories we can to war production. Tredegar, here in Richmond, is already producing several heavy artillery pieces each day. We have also removed the machinery from the arsenal at Harpers Ferry – right under the noses of the damned Yankees I might say – and we will shortly be producing our own Springfield rifles, here in the South. And there are other factories and foundries as well but they will not be enough. So we will need to go abroad – to England, France, perhaps Spain. Anywhere we are welcome. But here again there is a problem. We need to get the guns we buy back to this side of the Atlantic, but we have no navy with which to protect the merchantmen, who will undoubtedly attract the unwelcome attention of the Union fleet – your old comrades, James. And then there is the blockade. The Union Navy has thrown a cordon round the mouths of our best deep water harbours – Wilmington, Charleston, Savannah, New Orleans, Galveston, Pensacola and Mobile. They seek not only to prevent war supplies from coming in, but also to cut off our exports and so starve us of the money we need to finance the war."

"And this is their mistake," the President interjected, speaking slowly and with a frown. "For in blockading us, they have cut off England and France from their only source of cotton and I do not believe that these countries will accept this situation. Not for long, anyhow. Both their economies, but particularly England's, are dependent on our cotton for a major part of their industrial output. Without it there will be unemployment and hunger. Mills will close, their owners will go out of business and the banks' loans will become worthless. These dire effects will be felt across the entire country and will bring ruin to many men of influence – even to some who sit in the British Parliament itself. As a consequence, Palmerston, their Prime Minister, will come under considerable pressure to ameliorate the situation. He can only do this by breaking the blockade and that will mean war with the North. Seward, Lincoln's new Secretary of State, has threatened this explicitly and in this matter, at least, I do not believe that he is lying. But, for the moment, they are playing a waiting game. The cotton shortage has not yet begun to bite and so they will defer any decisions that might lead to a confrontation until they are forced to take them. And until that time, we are on our own." The President nodded at Mallory to continue.

"So, James, what we now need is a number of fast, modern, well-armed ships, as raiders that will harry the Union merchant fleet. This will damage their trade and will force them to remove ships that now blockade our ports, in order to protect their commerce. So at the same time, we hurt them where they feel it most – in their pocket books – and we enable our own ships, and those of other foreign friends, to pass freely in and out of our ports. D'you see?" Bulloch nodded.

"Good. Now this is where you come in. We want you to go to England, as the agent of the Navy and commission ships of this type – or buy them, if any can be found that will suit our purposes. I know that this will take you away from home for months at a time but I cannot over-emphasise its importance to our ultimate victory in this war and to gaining our freedom from the yoke of Northern domination." He smiled at Bulloch. "So James, tell me what you think – will you do it?"

Bulloch's heart sank. He had wanted a fighting command, instead of which he was being offered the job of an agent, a clerk at best, a spy at worst. Where was the honour in that? Where was the chance for glory or even promotion? And promotion, particularly if accompanied by an increase in pay, would have gone a long way towards easing Harriet's grief over his prolonged absence. Money was always an issue in the Bulloch household, as Harriet's insistence on maintaining a large house with three servants, which she considered to be appropriate for a lady of Savannah, put a severe strain on the family's finances.

Bulloch became aware of the lengthening silence in the room. "Mr Secretary," he said, "I had allowed myself to believe that I would be given command of a warship – even though I am aware that our Country has little in the way of such commands to offer. But to act as a mere purchasing agent seems … well … so very …"

"Dishonourable?" The President frowned, drawing his brows together severely and pressing his lips into a thin line. "I do not think so. I do not see any dishonour in undertaking a role so crucial to the survival of our Country. In wartime, Commander, we are all called upon to perform tasks and accept responsibilities that, had we our druthers, we would rather turn away. I myself did not accept the role of President gladly or happily. But I suppose that I am as well suited as any man to the burdens of this Office – as you are to the role we are now asking you to play. But let me help you a little. First, the rank of Captain will be yours upon acceptance. And secondly, if you are successful, as we believe that you will be, then these ships will need officers to command them. With your experience in the Mexican war, you will be an obvious candidate for such a command. But no ships, Commander, means no Captains. Do I make myself clear? And do not think for one moment that this will be an easy assignment. You will be opposed. And when the Union agents discover what you are about, they will use every means at their disposal to frustrate your ambitions. You may well be in personal danger Commander Bulloch."

"That is why we need you, James," Mallory continued. "You are one of the few really experienced Naval Commanders that we have and your unquestioned bravery makes you ideally suited for this dangerous and challenging assignment. So what do you say?"

※　　※

"Well, you were right," said the President. "Flatter his ego and promise him a captaincy of one of the new raiders and he will roll over like a dog wanting his tummy tickled. Wasn't that what you said? But tell me, truthfully, is he really the right man for this – he was not our first choice, if you recall."

Mallory shook his head. "He is clever, resourceful and determined. Very determined. But subtlety is not his long suit and he tends to lead with his chin. He is also vain – I mean did you see his whiskers? My god! It may be fashionable but they stuck out a full six inches from the side of his face. So I don't suppose, with his profile, that our activities will go unnoticed for very long. But, on the other hand, if things become difficult then there's no man I would rather have in this position."

* *

It was early evening, but the sun was still warm on his back as Bulloch strolled down Carey Street in the direction of the docks and the naval yards to see which ships might be in port. Gone was the new uniform, packed with care and considerable regret, into a trunk, with tissue paper between the folded cloth. In its place, he wore a long black frock coat with a maroon silk waistcoat and a top hat of moleskin, set squarely on his head. In his hand he carried a cane, which he twirled reflectively in his fingers as he walked. "Get rid of the uniform," Mallory had said when they met later in his office, "you won't be needing that for some time. You are now a man of commerce, engaged in the legitimate purchase of goods abroad, which you intend to re-sell here in the South at a considerable profit. Act like a wealthy businessman. Not too wealthy, of course, as our funds are severely limited. But stay in a good hotel. Eat in restaurants. Be seen around town. Act the part ... but James ..." and he raised a finger in warning, "keep very close about your real business. The President was right. When they find out what you are up to – as they shall – you will be in danger."

As Bulloch walked on, the houses on each side of the street became lower and their fronts narrower, and boards replaced glass in the windows. The cobbles beneath his feet gave way to hard-packed and dusty earth. Above the door of one house he saw a sign, which hung drunkenly from a rusty nail. It read: "Ma Kelly's Bar and Gentleman's Club." He ran his tongue around the inside of his mouth, feeling the thirst in his dry throat. Cautiously he pushed open the door and, stooping to avoid knocking his hat on the lintel, stepped down into a low, dark, smoke-filled room that stank of stale beer and unwashed bodies.

The vile atmosphere nearly drove Bulloch back out the door and into the street, but his need for whiskey propelled him across the uneven and rough planking of the floor towards the bar. Behind this, a woman of elephantine proportions, wearing a soiled pink dress, was polishing a glass by spitting into it and rubbing it with her filthy apron. Apparently satisfied with its cleanliness, she set it down on the bar top and fixed Bulloch with a baleful stare.

"Yep. Whadya want?" she asked, clearing her throat and spitting onto the floor behind her.

"Well, ma'am, you can start by getting me a beer," he replied, "and I'll have a whiskey too. But none of the rot gut that you serve your regulars, mind." He jerked his thumb over his shoulder to a table at which two men were slumped, face down, one with a line of drool leaking from the corner of his open mouth and pooling on the table top.

The woman opened her mouth, revealing a line of blackened and rotting stumps of teeth and emitted a high-pitched cackle. "So ye don't want no rot gut, eh? So what'll it be then, friend, 'bust-head' or 'tangle-foot'?" She stopped laughing and lent across the bar pushing her face close enough to Bulloch for him to smell her sour breath. "Whiskey's ten cents a glass – take it or leave it, it's all the same to me."

He took the beer and whiskey to a table, drinking first one then the other. He banged the empty whiskey glass down for a refill, and drank that when it arrived. It was God-awful but it did what whiskey was supposed to do. It took the sharp edges off everything. He lit a cigar, sat back and reflected on the day.

Neither flattery nor even the promotion to Captain would have been enough to persuade him to accept this assignment, but it was the offer of a command on one of the new raiders that had convinced him, as he knew that it would probably be the only way in which he would ever fight this war from the poop deck of his own ship.

Later, as he had sat with Mallory, poring over the blueprints and designs for the bark-rigged steam sloops that he would be commissioning in England and discussing their armaments, the mission had begun to excite him for itself and not just for what it might lead to.

They had then discussed money and how the shipbuilding programme was to be financed. Mallory had handed him sight drafts drawn on the Charleston head office of the banking firm, Fraser, Trenholm to a value of two hundred and fifty thousand dollars. "That's around fifty thousand pounds at today's rate of exchange", Mallory had told him, "enough for one ship."

"One ship?" Bulloch had reddened. "I thought I was to commission a fleet of these things! How will we pay for the rest?"

"More funds will become available over time," Mallory had replied, but to Bulloch he looked anything but certain. "And when you get to Liverpool you are to contact a man by the name of James Spence. I will write to him and inform him of your imminent arrival. He has been highly successful in raising funds for the war effort by the issuance of bonds on the London Stock Exchange. He should be able to assist you financially. You may contact Spence through Charles Prioleau – a charming man, of my acquaintance and a native of Charleston. He manages Fraser, Trenhholm's office in Liverpool. See that you send him my warmest regards when you see him – which will be soon, James." Mallory stood up to stretch his back and ambled across to the window, lifting the blind and staring out at the busy street outside. He turned back, clearing his throat and continued. "These matters cannot wait – you under-stand. Time is not on our side. I have booked a passage for you on the *North American*, a steamer which makes the Montreal to Liverpool run in seven days. She leaves on the twenty-fifth. You'll ride north, sticking to the back roads, as far as Washington. When you get there, sell the horse – um…pretend you've had a bad run of luck at cards – then take the train to Montreal. You'll have to change in New York, maybe over-night there. It adds to the risk, but it cannot be helped. You will have to write to Harriet and inform her of your departure, because there is insufficient time for you to return to Savannah. I am sorry James, I know that she will be upset."

'Upset' thought Bulloch, 'she will be furious.' But deep down he was glad that he would not have to face the shouting and the tears that would inevitably follow the news of his departure.

Mallory clasped Bulloch by the hand and looked deep into his eyes. "Good luck James, and may God be with you."

Bulloch stubbed out the butt of his cigar in the empty whiskey glass and stood up. "Not going so soon are ye, my lovely?" shouted the obese barmaid, her clay pipe still clamped between her teeth. "Why don't'cha stay awhile – maybe step in back with me, if ye've a mind – I kin give ye a fine time." And she scooped up her sagging breasts in her calloused hands, proffering them to Bulloch, who stepped back, involuntarily, his eyes widening in alarm. The barmaid cackled and spat.

Bulloch half walked, half ran to the door, ignoring the hoots of laughter from the regulars, flung it open and launched himself into the street, immediately pulling in deep breaths to clear both his lungs and his thoughts of the foul atmosphere of the bar.

But as he walked back towards the Spotswood Hotel, he started to laugh and soon found that the idea implanted in his mind by the fat barmaid had begun to take root. His thoughts turned to Daphne's, a real 'Gentleman's Club', in the Tenderloin district where curvaceous and scantily clad ladies were always eager to accommodate a gentleman's desires. He wondered if the mulatto girl was still there and, whistling to himself, set off at a brisk walk.

II

Liverpool – July 1861

It was shortly after dawn on a fine summer morning in early July, with the mist still clinging to the calm dark waters of the Mersey, as the Allan Line steamer *North American*, out of Montreal, slowly made her way up-river against the tide. The gulls swooped and dived for edibles of an indeterminate nature among the floating detritus of the great port, their cries audible above the clatter of the pistons and the asthmatic wheezing of the ship's boilers.

As the Albert Docks hove into sight, the pilot ordered the helmsman to decrease speed and took the wheel for the docking manoeuvre. Bulloch could see the steam-driven cranes looming over the edge of the wharf like vast birds, pecking cargo from the open entrails of the waiting ships. The great city with its sturdy buildings of brick and stone seemed to him to reflect the character of its inhabitants – solid, square, plain and unemotional. But the spires of the churches and ornate work on the fascia of the port buildings and Harbour Authority, also spoke of a wistfulness and a fancy that could exist beneath the ponderous exterior.

However, as the ship drew closer to the shore, the grime encrusted on the buildings became steadily more apparent, as did the piles of spoiled cargoes that dotted the wharf, black with their attendant swarm of flies. Dark smoke belched from the numerous factory chimneys, which jutted up into the soot-laden sky, and a pall of yellow sulphurous smoke hung over the city like a cloud.

The Mersey, this close in, was brown and thick with sewage, its water scarcely visible beneath the multitudinous forms of floating refuse created by the city's near half million inhabitants. Bulloch, standing at the rail, hatless, the breeze ruffling his long hair, was mesmerised by the view. Liverpool, he knew, was the largest port city of the greatest industrial power in the world. The empire it controlled spanned the globe and the tentacles of its commerce drew back goods and profits beyond measure to those who organised and financed its trade. He could hear the city from the water, he could certainly smell it, but above all he was immediately aware of its vibrancy and life.

The process of disembarkation proceeded smoothly. Bulloch walked through the long customs shed, where a fiercely moustachioed customs officer with a red face gave his papers a cursory glance before waving him on.

At the end of the hall a crowd was waiting. Friends and relatives stood on tip toe for glances of their loved ones, jostling for space with bowler-hatted porters, hansom cab drivers in capecoats, pick-pockets, prostitutes and vendors of all description. The noise was deafening, but from close-by he heard his name being called by a young man with unruly blond hair sticking out from underneath an old, but clean silk top hat.

"Mr Bulloch... do I have the honour of addressing Mr James Bulloch?" he yelled, moving his mouth closer to Bulloch's ear.

"I am he. And you are...?"

"Of course, forgive my manners, I am James Spence. I have received a communication from our friends in Richmond asking that I meet you and put myself at your service. But let us leave this bedlam forthwith...I am near overcome by the noisome odours of our people!"

He grabbed the larger of Bulloch's portmanteaux and hurried out of the shed to a waiting carriage, where a grumpy looking driver sat idly, flicking his whip at the broad rump of the horse that stood between the shafts, its head lowered in silent resignation.

They got in and closed the door and sat back on the damp and musty velvet cushions.

Spence stuck his head out of the window and yelled: "The Queen's Hotel, driver, as quick as you ever can." Then he turned to Bulloch. "Welcome to England, Sir. I am pleased to have found you, for I received only last evening a package from the Captain of a fast clipper ship, which must have overtaken yours at sea. It contained instructions regarding your good self and enclosed this letter for you." He handed over a heavy buff envelope, sealed with wax and the crest of the Department of the Navy.

"I do, in truth, thank you for meeting me Mr Spence. You have saved me the trouble of seeking you out, for I was given your name by Stephen Mallory, the Secretary of our Navy. But first, if I may, I would like to ask you a question. I am curious as to why you involve yourself in my country's affairs. I detect from your accent that you are English and yet our present disagreement is an internal one, as you know, between our States."

"Indeed, it is an obvious and important question. You see, I am a merchant and I have taken on the direction of my late father's business. He passed away last Michaelmas. Our House has always traded with your country – indeed the principal trade that we have – had – is in cotton, out of New Orleans and Charleston. I am well acquainted…" he paused, and ran the top of his tongue over his lips, "indeed somewhat too well acquainted, if truth be told, with the banking house of Fraser, Trenholm. They have extended a considerable quantum of credit to my firm against the purchase and shipment of cotton that, alas, currently sits on the docks in Charleston as my ships are unable to get past the blockade and into the port. Messrs Fraser, Trenholm have suggested that my bills will not be called in, provided that I can be … of service … in certain matters, to themselves and to some of their clients. When this war has been won by the South, as I am confident that it will be, and in short order I'll be bound, why, then I shall collect my cotton, repay my loans and salvage my business. Meanwhile, I run a few errands and even make a crust or two by selling bonds issued by your Government to wealthy cotton brokers and the like…you have many supporters here in Liverpool, you know!"

"Well, that is good and I am sure that your assistance will be invaluable to me in what I must achieve here … although I commiserate with you on the circumstances which have brought us together. Now, tell me, what do you know of the purpose behind my visit to England?"

"Only that you are here on behalf of your Government and that there are certain items which you need to purchase – not what those items are, nor from whom they should be purchased." He smiled.

Bulloch sat back in the carriage seat, as it bounced over the cobbles, jolting its passengers every time a wheel found a pothole in the street. He was on the one hand pleased that this amiable young man had been sent to help him, but at the same time he doubted the strength of Spence's commitment to their cause. However, Mallory clearly trusted this Englishman, so Bulloch decided to take him at face value – for the moment at any rate.

They parted at the hotel and Spence left with some regret, to return to the red ink in the ledgers at his office, with its bare floorboards and idle clerks.

Bulloch breakfasted on kidneys, bacon and a strange rice and fish dish, called Kedgeree, which he washed down with several cups of indifferent coffee. He then lit a cigar and set off on foot to find the offices of W. C. Miller and Sons. In the letter from Stephen Mallory were instructions to interview the proprietor of this modest-sized family-run firm of shipbuilders so as to ascertain their willingness to construct a ship to his order and specifications, at a fair price.

After repeated delays, caused by losing his bearings in the narrow and filthy streets around the dock area and, after failing to understand the directions he was given by a cloth-hatted passer-by with a broad Liverpudlian accent, Bulloch finally found himself at the base of a wooden staircase that ran up the side of a black timber warehouse.

A brass plaque bore the inscription: 'W. C. Miller & Sons, Shipbuilders – Proprietor: William Miller, MP.' He walked up the staircase and entered the door at the top, finding himself in a large gloomy room, lit only by skylights set into the sloping roof. These were blackened by soot and admitted little daylight, hence the necessity for the oil lamps which hung from the tarred beams at irregular intervals, emitting smoke from their untrimmed wicks. In and out of the gloom moved figures, carrying ledgers or bundles of rolled blueprints, while along one wall stood a line of clerks at high desks, writing in heavy volumes with pens, whose nibs they frequently dipped into brass inkwells.

One of the clerks, a cadaverous individual with sunken cheeks and receding oiled hair, put down his pen and approached Bulloch. He rubbed his hands together making a dry, rasping sound.

"May I be of any assistance to you my good sir?" he intoned in a thin nasal voice. "You have perhaps an appointment with someone?"

"No, I have no appointment," replied Bulloch, looking down at the clerk with barely concealed disdain, "but I wish to see Mr William Miller. Be so good as to tell him that Mr James Bulloch of the … from America, wishes to see him."

"Oh no, he won't see nobody, not without an appointment, he won't. Not since he's become our Member of Parliament and all, he's become ever so grand. You'd best be getting along now. Write. Yes, that's it, write and request an appointment. Goodbye."

Bulloch felt the blood rise in his face, helped by the constriction of the high, tight collar of his shirt.

"Listen to me, and listen carefully, for I will tell you but once – go and tell your Mr Miller that I require him to build a ship for me and that I intend to pay him handsomely for the privilege, which will be entirely his. Tell him that I will see him within two minutes or I will leave and place the order with Lairds."

At that moment the door of the glass-fronted office at the end of the huge room was flung open and a short, portly figure came forward, his heavy footfalls banging noisily on the bare boards. "That will do, Mr Groat, thank you. Now who is using the name of that pissant Laird in my company office?"

"James Bulloch, at your service sir," said Bulloch, stepping forward and bowing in the English manner. "Come with some business for you, if you've a mind to take it".

"Miller never says no to business – so long as there's a profit in it." He chuckled. "And so long as its legal – or so I am obliged to say out loud, now that I am a Member of Parliament, newly elected, sir – for this very constituency of Liverpool. But come into my office, do, so that we may discuss this business of yours in more comfort. Groat, come with me. The rest of you, back to work. You have all been idle these five minutes past and you will work five minutes after hours today. Time is money and your time is my money and I won't have you wasting my money." He turned and stamped back towards the office leaving the now fawning Groat to usher in Bulloch with little repeated bows and waves of his hand.

In the office was a huge leather-topped desk with ornate brass work on its legs, depicting buxom women in classical poses. Miller sat down heavily behind the desk in a large winged chair, which Bulloch immediately guessed had been raised to disguise the diminutive stature of its occupant.

Miller flipped open the top of a heavy gilt box and chose a cigar. He pushed the box across to Bulloch and waved his hand. "Go on, help yesself. They's finest she-roots from Burma, they is. Expensive too. Put a couple in your pocket for later as well, why don't you. Now tell us about this business of yours – and don't worry about young Silas Groat here, you can speak in front of him. He's my chief accounting clerk, he is, and knows nearly as much about my business as I do myself – don't you Silas?"

Bulloch took a cigar. "Well Sir, I am recently arrived from America ..."

"Which part? North or South?"

"Why sir, the South."

"Thought as much. I can hear the accent of the plantations in your every word – but pray proceed."

"As I said, I am recently arrived from America – from the Confederates States of America. I represent a loose affiliation of merchant venturers, based in Richmond, Virginia. My partners and I require a ship for our cross-Atlantic trade. Had we the capability to construct such a ship back home, we would certainly have commissioned one, but unfortunately, at this present moment we lack the resources so to do. Hence my visit to your country." Miller visibly relaxed. He sat back in his chair and beamed, disclosing uneven tobacco stained teeth.

"D'ye have the plans already?" he enquired.

"I do." Bulloch opened the leather wallet he had been carrying under his arm, selected a folded plan and spread it out across the desktop.

Miller rose to his feet and bent over the blueprint, running his fingers along the lines and muttering to himself. After two or three minutes he looked up at Bulloch, his small dark eyes unwavering. "How many guns do you expect her to carry?" Bulloch looked surprised. "Guns? There are to be no guns – this is to be a merchantman, as I have said."

"Rubbish – if you'll pardon me, sir. I've been building ships since I was a lad – started as a caulker's mate in Her Majesty's Naval Yards at the tender age of eight. I've built every manner of ship afloat and this ain't no cargo-carrier. Look at her lines. She's a greyhound she is, fast and low – sail close to the wind as ever a ship can – and with twin screws. There's not enough room in her holds for cargo to pay for a ha'penny ride 'round the harbour. So how many guns d'ye want and where d'ye want 'em?"

Bulloch felt an immediate pang of disquiet in his stomach. Should he trust this man? Probably not. But, then again, the contact had been suggested by Mallory, in who's view there were not more than two, maybe three, yards in Liverpool capable of carrying out the work they wanted. And this little man was clearly greedy – for money and for position. These were things that could be used to keep him on the level. Bulloch decided to proceed.

He nodded. "Very well, sir, it seems I have no option but to trust you. Let us talk about guns. She should carry as great a weight of metal as she may, in broadside. Fore and aft she will be fitted with rifled guns, deck-mounted on swivels, probably of Armstrong's patent. The guns will be mounted at a later date and not in this country, so as not to offend the neutral sensibilities of Her Majesty's Government. You should however fit the platform and the runners for the swivel guns and the rings and reinforcement for the broadside guns – here, here and here," he said stabbing the plans. "Now sir, we Americans are known for our direct talk and you are a man of business, so you will forgive me for being blunt. When can I have this ship and what will she cost me?"

Miller's eyes narrowed. "As to when, I should think nine months from today, say next March at the latest. And as to how much …" He looked at Silas Groat, who leaned across and whispered in his ear. Miller frowned "It seems our Mr Groat here wants to bankrupt me and drive myself and Mrs Miller into the workhouse," he said. He bared his teeth at Silas Groat who swallowed, his protuberant Adam's apple bobbing up and down his scrawny neck.

"I am a fair man Mr Bulloch, and I will make you a fair price. Shall we say sixty thousand pounds?"

"In dollars that would be …"

"Oh no, Mr Bulloch, none of your homemade dollars here, no sir, thank you very much! We don't take nothing with Mr Davis' face on it – no disrespect meant, mind you. You can pay me in pounds Sterling, or gold if you've a mind, and I'll discount the price for it – or even in Northern dollars if you must, but then at a premium. What do you say?"

Bulloch finally worked out the enormous sum in dollars. He winced. "If you will forgive me, Sir, but I do not believe that to be a fair price. I should not expect to pay above forty thousand pounds for a ship of this type, not even fully rigged and sailed. If you cannot do better than that sir, I will have to go and see if Mr Laird can improve."

"Piss on Laird and shit on him too!" roared Miller, banging his fist on the table. "You'll get no satisfaction from that bastard, I can tell you, he's tighter than a fish's arse." Miller had risen to his feet and drops of spittle flew from his lips. He sat down again. "fifty thousand pounds. It's my last offer, take it or leave it – half now and half on completion."

Bulloch knew that fifty thousand pounds was a very full price and he was tempted to stand up and walk away. But on reflection he considered it better to pay over the odds, secure the commission and pander to the man's greed. He extended his hand. "You have a deal, Sir, although you strike a hard bargain."

They shook hands, Miller suddenly calm again, a broad smile creasing his round face. He turned to his clerk, "Get us some champagne and quick about it." Silas Groat scurried off to do his master's bidding.

"Now Mr Bulloch, I would guess that one ship's not the full extent of your Country's needs at this time. Would I be right?" He sucked heavily on the 'she-root' until the end glowed and smoke obscured his face.

'Aha' thought Bulloch, 'here's the bait.'

"You would indeed be right, Mr Miller, but you and I have but this one ship to discuss at this moment. If matters progress satisfactorily, then, perhaps, we can discuss other commissions."

"I see, yes, I see. Very well then, one ship at a time. And things will be satisfactory, more so indeed, for at Millers we pride ourselves on delivering the best founded hulls on the Mersey – and in double quick time." He paused. "But if we're to do business together, then my name is William, and my friends call me Bill." He smiled, with all the warmth of an attacking shark. "That's what my friends call me, but there's precious few of them. The others call me Bull, on account of my being a little rough in my ways." He looked Bulloch straight in the eyes as he spoke.

The champagne arrived, which was warm and cheap. They toasted each other and to a long business relationship and finally to the new commission, which was to be called the 'Oreto', after an Italian ship that Bulloch had once seen in Montevideo harbour.

As soon as possible Bulloch left. Walking down the stairs from the gloomy attic offices, he thought to himself that he had rarely met such a thoroughly dislikeable individual.

Bulloch anticipated sending a message to Stephen Mallory that evening, advising him of the commission and the costs involved and he would recommend that the next order be placed with another shipwright, such as Lairds, thus putting the two firms into competition, so as to keep them both keen and honest.

* *

After his departure from the office, Miller called Silas Groat back in. He frowned as the clerk stood in front of him shuffling from one foot to the other, his hands clasping and unclasping in anxiety. "You're a fool Groat" Miller barked, "and ye'll never be half the businessman I am, nor even a quarter. You said, 'ask him for fifty thousand pounds and settle for forty thousand pounds – well, I'm ten thousand pounds richer by not following your advice." He sneered. "And that's more money than you'll ever see in your lifetime. Now do something useful. Follow the Yank. Tell me where he goes and who he sees, what he has for breakfast and what colour his shite is. I want to know everything about him – and his credit too. Now get out and stop wearing down my carpet."

Groat fled from the room and returned to his desk. There he paused and glared at the other clerks, who quickly lowered their eyes. Then he slipped his hand into the well of the desk and removed a straight razor, which he palmed and dropped into the inside pocket of his shabby black jacket, before slipping quietly out the door.

Bulloch returned to the hotel, where he composed a letter to Stephen Mallory setting out the day's events, and another to Harriet.

He found the letter to his wife hard to write, and his unwillingness to express insincere sentiments made it sound cold and formal as he read it back to himself. Had he been in love with her at one time? Perhaps, yes, in the early days of their marriage, when she was full of life and anything seemed possible for the young couple. True she had hardly been a great beauty even then, but she had nonetheless been a handsome young woman, with piercing blue eyes and a strong jaw that spoke of a determined and even single-minded nature. However, after their son Henry died from typhoid at the age of seven, the light seemed to go out of her eyes. Bulloch had reacted to the news, which hurt him physically like a blow to the heart, by hugging his girls to his chest, as they clung to him, wailing. Harriet, on the other hand, had locked herself away in her room, where she spent a day and a night on her knees in prayer. She emerged on Sunday, in time for church, dressed in the black clothes that she continued to wear from that time.

"It's God's will," she had said to Bulloch, angry that he would not accompany her to church, "and there's no point in crying – it won't bring him back." And with that she had left the house and closed the door and Bulloch felt all the affection that he had once held for her, draining out of him, like blood from an arterial wound.

Harriet had become increasingly plain as she approached middle age – indeed she seemed to wear her drab clothes and permanent frown as evidence of her piety. She attended the nearby Baptist church daily and spent much of her time in charitable works among the poor whites of Savannah. It seemed to Bulloch that whatever warmth or kindness there was left within her, was all given to the homeless, sick and needy and there was none left over for him – or even for their own daughters, whom she treated in a polite but distant manner.

He smiled at the thought of Martha and Jessie and opened his pocket watch to look at the small and indistinct sepia photograph of the two of them, sitting side by side at the piano, that he had attached to the inside of its cover.

Bulloch picked up the pen and concluded the letter by asking Harriet to pass his fondest love to the girls and to say how much he missed them.

There was a knock at the door. "Who is it?" he called.

"It is I, James Spence, have you forgotten, we are to dine?"

"Oh my apologies James, indeed," he shouted through the door wiping a tear from the corner of his eye. "I was miles away. Let me throw some water on my face and I will see you downstairs in the lobby momentarily."

"So tonight, my friend," said a very dapper James Spence who had changed out of his frock coat with the frayed cuffs and shiny lapels, into evening tails and white tie, "tonight I will show you Liverpool – at least the better parts of our fair city. It is not London, not by any measure, but there are still places where Gentlemen can go for a night out." He glanced at Bulloch, raising one eyebrow, but received neither encouragement nor dismissal.

Bulloch was still dressed in his day clothes – indeed in the same clothes he had put on that morning aboard the *North American*. It was not the custom at home to dress for dinner in such a formal manner – not even in Charleston – and thus he owned no evening-wear. His suit, bought in Richmond shortly before his departure, was of a fashionable cut in Virginia, and yet seemed baggy and even dowdy among the sharper dressed inhabitants of this cosmopolitan city. He resolved to use some of the money entrusted to his care to outfit himself anew, reasoning that someone improperly attired would stand out and draw attention to themselves.

As for young Spence's carefully worded invitation, Bulloch was tired after the long crossing from Montreal, although the seas had been calm and he had slept well in the swaying cot. But then again, ten days at sea with all-male company and ship's galley cooking did give a man certain appetites. He smiled at his companion. "Very well James, let us see what Liverpool has to offer and I am sure that it will shine in comparison to the very basic fare of my home-town."

First they stopped at *O'Neill's*, a pub patronised by the local Irish community, but also by gentlemen, slumming. Bulloch was introduced to that dark syrupy beer, called stout, which they drank standing up at the bar, while eating whelks and other rubbery morsels of shell fish in a sharp vinegar.

Then they walked the length of Dale Street to Green's Chop House, a large well-lit establishment, where they sat in a booth with a starched white tablecloth and gas lamps hissing above them. The waiters, who wore striped aprons, brought them some dark soup, with a strange spicy flavour, called muligatawny, followed by chops, kidneys, liver, sweetbreads and brains, all grilled, with boiled cabbage and fried potatoes. To accompany the mountain of meat and offal they drank two bottles of a very intense Hermitage and then sat back, wiping their greasy fingers and lips on the huge napkins that had been tied around their necks.

As they lit their cigars and sipped their port, Bulloch felt a warmth towards this tousle-haired young man with the easy smile and decided to confide in him. He related the day's events and described his feelings towards 'Bull' Miller.

"Well, you are right there," said Spence after a little thought. "He's a mean one and no mistake. He's from very humble origins, of course, self-made and very rich. He's got a bad reputation in this town, with rumours abounding of his somewhat unsavoury business practices. Some even say that he has had some of his erstwhile business partners done away with – those who knew too much and threatened to talk. Nothing proved, of course, but the Mersey keeps her secrets all right. I'd be very careful of him if I were you James. Now, his reaction to Laird's name is interesting. Of course there's competition between them, naturally, as they are in the same business, but I suspect it goes further than that. Lairds are the largest shipbuilders on the Mersey. Founded by the father of the current firm's head, John Laird. So they're old money, by comparison at least, and they've had time to buy themselves a measure of respectability. Laird became the Member of Parliament for Birkenhead, where his yard is, and so of course Miller had to become an MP as well."

"How did he do that, with his reputation?"

"Oh that wasn't difficult. He is one of the two members for the City of Liverpool. You have to understand, James, that here you can only vote if you own or lease a property above a certain value. We don't hold with your so-called democratic principles, thankee very much. Anyway, much of the City of Liverpool is industrial and much of it is comprised of slums – and very dark and pestilential places they are too. Well, Miller's a big landlord here and so are a lot of his cronies – all voting men – and naturally they want one of their own to represent them. Not some outsider who might start to ask questions about why the new housing regulations are being ignored and why they're still building more of these courts at the back of the houses, where they pack a family into one tiny room with no water or light. Filthy places they are and rife with disease. You don't live long in some of Mr Miller's prime dwelling houses, I can tell you!"

"So then, if I take my next ship to Laird's, I cannot expect our good Mr Miller's thanks?"

"Indeed you cannot! In fact you can expect that he will react quite badly."

'So be it,' thought Bulloch, 'for I simply cannot put all my eggs in one basket'. "But enough of business, James," he said, "why don't you show me what Liverpool has to offer in the way of after supper entertainment."

They left and walking slowly in the warm summer evening, soon came to a tall brick house on Castle Street. Spence rapped on the door with the silver head of his cane. A Judas window shot open and a bearded face with a hooknose jutted out.

25

"Ah, Mr Spence, why, what a pleasure to see you again! Your ships have come in, of course, and you are here to pay off your gaming debts. Surely that is it?"

Spence reddened considerably. "No ... I ... that is ..."

Bulloch stepped into the line of sight of the face and said, "I am Mr Spence's guest and I should like a game. I believe my credit to be sufficient."

Dark moist eyes regarded Bulloch from under heavy lids. The Judas window slammed shut and a few seconds later they heard the sound of bolts being pulled and the door was thrown open. As they entered, their interlocutor stepped back and Bulloch could see that he was a well-built muscular man and clearly a Jew from his features and his shiny black skullcap.

"Please," said the Jew "any friend of Mr Spence's...". He tailed off and gestured towards a door at the end of the hall, also iron-studded and bound like the street door.

Through this they entered a different world. The noise was intense. The rattle of roulette wheels, the thump of dice on green baize, the cries of triumph, the groans of dismay and the popping of champagne corks, merged into a cacophony of sound. At the same time the smells of sweat and perfume and the strong odour of tobacco from the many cigars combined to assault the senses.

Bulloch laughed out loud. He turned to Spence to congratulate him on his taste, but found that he was not at his side. Instead he saw him by the entrance door, against the wall. The Jew had him by the neck and was going through his pockets. Bulloch moved towards them to remonstrate, but the Jew, seeing him coming, released Spence and backed out of the room, his head bobbing with frequent bows.

"He has my money, James," said Spence despondently, his mouth pulling down at the corners. "I know that I am in his debt, but really the man is the most frightful cad. It was only a few guineas I was carrying, for a hand of cards or two, and perhaps half an hour upstairs with one of these exquisite ladies." He waved his hand around the room, gesturing at the various women, all fashionably dressed, some of whom were playing at the tables, while others hung on the arms of gentlemen in evening dress, as they gambled.

"The ones playing are shills," Spence whispered. "They play for the house and they are seen to win to encourage the real punters. The others will be trying to get their escorts to bet more heavily."

Bulloch nodded. "Thank you for the warning. Nonetheless I feel like trying my luck at some cards. I don't suppose there is a poker table?"

"Not really an English game, James, old boy. Sorry."

"Twenty-one then, or Chemin de Fer. Whist at a pinch. Ah, I think I see Shimmy, as we call it, being played over there. What will you do?"

"Unfortunately I am now somewhat embarrassed due to the quick fingers of yonder Jew. Perhaps, although I hate to mention it, you could see your way clear to…" He tailed off.

"Would five guineas be enough?"

"James, you are a gentleman," Spence cried delightedly, "You Southerners are very much the right sort. Very nearly English, if you don't mind me saying so!"

"No I don't mind." Bulloch laughed, "I take any compliment, rare though they may be, in the spirit in which they are given."

He walked over to the table in the corner where two smartly dressed men were playing cards from a wooden shoe, together with a strikingly beautiful woman, with slightly dark skin and luxuriant black hair piled up on her head. 'A quadroon, possibly an octoroon' mused Bulloch. He sat down next to her and smiled.

"May I join you?" he enquired politely.

The men nodded. The woman turned to Bulloch and showed him her even white teeth. "Of course, Sir. It would be a pleasure." She swayed slightly closer to him, so that he could smell her perfume, which was a heady scent of lilies and, at the same time her knee came lightly into contact with his own.

"*Huit, à la banque,*" cried the dealer, adjusting his green eyeshade. The two gentlemen players, who had six and seven respectively, folded their cards, muttering.

Bulloch's neighbour flicked her hole card face upwards with a long varnished nail. "*Neuf, la Grande*" she said, smiling at the dealer, who proceeded to count out a pile of dark green chips before sliding them across the table with a long-handled wooden pusher.

From the very start, Bulloch had seemed to be in luck. Against the banks seven, he would be dealt a natural eight, while he frequently topped the bank's 'petite' with a 'grande'. The pile of chips in front of him grew and the two male players stopped to watch. At this point however, the pressure of his neighbour's knee against his own started to become more insistent and, after a time, he found his interest in cards waning. He rose to his feet, nodded to the dealer and pocketed his winnings.

His neighbour looked up at him from under her long eyelashes. "You are not going already, I hope, sir. Why, the evening is still young."

"Only as far as the bar, lovely lady, as I am parched from all this play, but I would be honoured if you would join me in a glass of champagne."

She looked up at him, one eyebrow raised, a small smile playing at the corner of her deep red lips. She glanced at the dealer, who nodded very slightly, before proffering her hand to Bulloch.

At the bar they sipped cold champagne from tall glasses with fluted stems. She looked at him with her large brown eyes and leant forward until her breasts rested lightly against his chest. He breathed in deeply, savouring the musky scent of the feminine sex beneath her perfume. His mouth dried. She took one long-fingered hand and gently stroked his whiskers.

"Why sir, what prodigious fine whiskers you have. I do love a man with large appendages." He coloured and after a short pause said in a husky voice, "I would really appreciate the opportunity of getting to know you better Ma'am." She looked at him quizzically and raised one eyebrow.

He said, "A poke ma'am, I am talking about a poke."

She laughed, throwing back her head. "Then you should have said so sooner sir, and we could be drinking this fine champagne in bed. Come with me." She took his hand and led him towards a low door beside the bar. They climbed a narrow staircase that came out onto a landing off which several doors opened. She turned the handle of one and went in, beckoning for Bulloch to follow. The room was small but cosy, warmly lit by gas lamps in red silk shades. In the grate, a small coal fire glowed. Against one wall stood a brass bed with a bright, chequered gingham coverlet and a stack of white linen pillows. Beside the bed, on a small marble top table stood an ice bucket containing an open bottle of champagne and next to it, two glasses.

The dark haired woman held out a slim hand, which Bulloch took. "Before we fuck, sir, I believe that it is customary to introduce oneself. I am Marise."

"And I am James," Bulloch replied hoarsely.

"Good," she said, "now stop talking and undo me."

Later, a happy and tired James Bulloch reappeared through the low door. The room had emptied, except for a few hardened players. He looked around for Spence. Spying a man sprawled in a large armchair, asleep, his top hat pulled down over his eyes, he kicked the outstretched feet.

"What, what… oh, it's you James, what time is it? Three o'clock, my God man, you must be insatiable! We must get you to bed …to sleep this time! We have a meeting tomorrow morning at ten sharp, at the offices of Fraser, Trenholm. We will be meeting one Charles K Prioleau, a strange cove, but a decent chap nonetheless. One of yours – from Charleston I believe. He's their money-man here in Liverpool."

They parted at the door and within minutes Bulloch was back at the Queen's Hotel, where he fell into his bed, exhausted, and was asleep immediately.

The next morning he woke refreshed, having slept deeply. While he shaved his chin, he thought of Marise and promised himself that they would repeat their encounter of the previous evening.

Having breakfasted, he called for a cab and set out for 10 Rumford Place, the Liverpool offices of Fraser, Trenholm.

After rapping on the newly painted black door with the heavy brass knocker, he was admitted by a butler in a tailcoat, who showed him into the hall and invited him to be seated in a deep and comfortable-looking leather armchair.

He glanced through the latest *Punch*, laughing at the depiction of a gangly Abraham Lincoln as a barefoot rail-splitter, before the butler returned and led him up the broad staircase to the first floor and flung open a set of double doors.

As he entered, a dapper little man with a pointed moustache and brilliantined hair, rose and came out from behind the desk, his hand extended.

"My dear Captain Bulloch," he drawled in a strong southern accent, so that the effect was of 'Mah deah Captain', "I am so very glad to make your acquaintance. Permit me to introduce myself. I am Charles Prioleau. I manage the Liverpool office for Mr Trenholm. May I have the honour of introducin' these two here gentlemen – Mr James Spence – who I do believe that you already know, and Captain Edward Anderson, also of Savannah, Georgia, currently on attachment to Army Headquarters in Richmond."

A tall, slim man with swept back grey hair and a neatly trimmed beard rose to his feet. Bulloch shook his hand warmly.

"It is indeed an honour Captain Anderson, for although I don't believe that we have ever met, I voted for you when you were standing for mayor of our fine city."

"Why Captain Bulloch, thank you kindly for that courtesy. I now find that I am dealing not only with a colleague from the Navy, but also one of my electorate. I must be very careful with you, sir, indeed I must," he said, wagging his finger and smiling.

Prioleau invited his guests to be seated and then turned to the new arrival. "Captain Bulloch, before you arrived we were discussing the sordid but inevitable subject of money. Now I understand from our Mr Spence here that you have, very commendably and right off the bat, commissioned an armed cruiser from our new Member of Parliament. That is correct?"

"It is Mr Prioleau," replied Bulloch, somewhat annoyed at James Spence discussing his business behind his back. He glared at Spence, who met his look with an untroubled gaze.

"And, may I ask, Captain, as to the financing plans for your purchase?"

Bulloch hesitated. "Come now, Captain, you are among friends."

Bulloch opened his leather wallet and removed a thick buff envelope. This he handed to Prioleau, who sliced it open with a silver-bladed letter opener, removed the contents and carefully unfolded the sheets onto his blotting pad. His fine dark eyebrows rose as he considered first one sheet and then the next.

"Why Captain, you are indeed in funds," he exclaimed.

"I am aware of that fact Mr Prioleau, and it is clearly essential that you, as the manager of this branch of this Banking House, know that also. However, I fail to see why we are discussing matters of a confidential nature, in front of an audience."

"Captain, Captain, please calm yourself. The fault is entirely mine for not introducin' our 'audience' in a fuller and more appropriate manner. You see, Captain Anderson is sent here by Army Headquarters to buy guns – as you have been sent to buy ships – with only the slight variation that Richmond has not seen fit to equip Captain Anderson with sufficient funds to complete his purchases. Mr Spence here plays an invaluable role in assisting such purchases by raising money for our cause through the sale of bonds, backed by our Government.

"We were discussin', when you arrived, the fact that the proceeds of the most recent four per cent bonds, organised by our Mr Spence here, amounted to some five hundred thousand pounds. Subscriptions were, unfortunately, slower than had been anticipated. Now after commissions and costs we are left with around four hundred and seventy thousand pounds. A goodly sum you would say and so it is. However, Richmond has declared that all but twenty thousand pounds of that is earmarked already and must be repatriated at once, to assist with paying the troops and so forth.

He sipped his water, then continued. "Now, as Captain Anderson will tell you himself, he has already spent all of that twenty thousand pounds and has still over half of his requirements left unfilled."

Captain Anderson cleared his throat. "That is correct. But although I have been quite successful so far, in that I have bought some seven thousand Enfield rifles and various other equipment, I have had to use all my available funds. At this point, vendors of war materiel are in a fine position. They ask exorbitant prices and demand a high proportion as a down payment. Why, only last week I contracted for five thousand rifles from the London Armoury Company when the Yankee purchasing agent, to whom they were originally committed, was unable to produce the cash deposit. I upped the price by ten per cent and put down half in gold." He frowned. "But now I'm cleaned out and given the time it takes between order and delivery, I'm desperate for more cash so we can get the guns ordered and production started before its too late. Time is not on our side Captain – I am sure I do not have to tell you that."

Bulloch nodded. "I may be able to help. You see, I have just placed drafts in front of Mr Prioleau for around fifty thousand pounds." Prioleau nodded. "Now the ship I have commissioned from Miller's yard, will cost all of that, but I have only to pay half at this time. If I can commission a further ship from one of Miller's competitors without any down payment, then I will have the use of the remaining twenty-five thousand pounds for the next nine months. I am seeing a Mr John Laird in a few days time and will know then whether this is the case, but given the nature of competition, I believe that it may well be. Under these circumstances I would be prepared to advance say, twenty thousand pounds to Captain Anderson so that he can order further guns for our army – provided," and he paused and looked sternly at each of the others in turn, "provided that you can absolutely guarantee me that I will be repaid before the final installment becomes due to the charming Mr William Miller."

They all turned to James Spence, who, looking uncomfortable at being put on the spot, shrugged and made a face. "I feel confident that I will be able to float at least one more issue of bonds in the next nine months. Getting the allocation of the proceeds from Richmond, on the other hand, s'not really my call. Edward, how do you see that?"

"If I can't get another twenty thousand pounds before next spring, then I am wasting my time here and will demand a posting to a line regiment. You have my word Captain – you will be repaid, one way or another."

"Good, it's settled then," Prioleau said quickly, before Bulloch could change his mind. "Captain" he said, "we have reason to be grateful that there are those amongst us who are not concerned by petty inter-departmental rivalries but are prepared to act solely for the benefit of the Cause. We thank you. Your Country thanks you."

Bulloch warmed to the praise, but was already mentally drafting a letter to Stephen Mallory requesting more funds. To Captain Anderson he said: "So now you have a further twenty thousand pounds to complete the Army's purchases, have you given thought as to how the materiel will be transported back home."

"I had thought to charter a vessel and certainly to accompany the cargo myself."

"Perhaps. But let me reflect on it. It is possible that we may have to buy a ship, because I fear that owners will be reluctant to accept a charter when the cargo is mainly guns, bound for a theatre of war and needing to run a blockade before arriving in a friendly port. You see, no insurer would give them cover for such a voyage and thus they would have to contemplate the loss of the entire value of their ship. So, if we could buy a ship, which could also be of ultimate service to the Confederate Navy, why then we would be killing two birds with one stone. When do you think that you will have your purchases completed and the cargo assembled?"

"That is hard to say. Production is slow and the foundries are weighed down with orders. You see, not only are we and the Federal purchasing agents active buyers, albeit with little ready cash, but there are also many individual buyers – merchant adventurers, looking to take delivery of guns and sell them on to the highest bidder at inflated prices. That is a long way of saying 'several months'. Perhaps by October or November, if we are lucky."

"Then I will start to make enquiries immediately concerning an appropriate ship. Mr Prioleau, provided my meeting with Laird goes well, you may disburse my funds as we have discussed and I will be writing to Secretary Mallory, today, requesting an increment. Now is there further business that we all need to discuss at this time?"

The following week, on one of Liverpool's rare fine clear mornings, Bulloch emerged from the hotel at eight-thirty, having already breakfasted. He hailed a hansom cab and got in. The cabby's red face appeared through the hatch in the roof and Bulloch told him to go directly to the Prince's Pier.

At the Pier he bought a ticket and then boarded the steam ferry for Birkenhead. Across the river, Bulloch set off on foot at a leisurely pace. He admired the new brick town hall with its large clock face before turning and walking slowly along the riverbank. Before long he saw the tall fingers of masts in the distance, grouped as thickly as trees in a forest and shortly afterwards he came to the limestone quays that were the beginning of Laird's shipyards – known as the Birkenhead Iron Works. What a difference to Miller's mean little office in the South Docks! Here there were no less than eight ships in varying stages of construction. Three-masters and two; some with screws and others with paddle wheels; schooners, barks and clippers. While all over the hulls swarmed the shipwrights, caulking with hemp and tar, hammering in nails, hauling on ropes and banging hot rivets into steel plates with giant hammers. The noise was deafening, but for Bulloch the scene was magical. Here he would have his ships and as many as they needed!

Now, with a more purposeful stride, he set off towards the elegant mansion with the Doric columns that housed the company's offices. He was greeted at the door by a butler, to whom he explained that he was very early but hoped that Mr John Laird would be available to see him.

He was only kept waiting a few minutes before a tall man of late middle age, but clearly fit and wearing a magnificent set of white whiskers, came quickly down the wide, marble-banistered staircase. He extended his hand in the American manner and smiled.

"My dear Mr Bulloch – or perhaps I should more correctly address you as Captain Bulloch – how glad I am to see you, you are most welcome."

"Why thank you Mr Laird, thank you, but Mr is the appropriate title at this moment."

Laird raised one bushy eyebrow. "Very well, Mr Bulloch, let us proceed upstairs to my office, where I shall introduce you to my sons. I shall be retiring from the shipbuilding business at the end of this year, d'ye know, as I am away too often these days in London, especially when Parliament is sitting. The Boys will be taking over from me, but you'll be in safe hands with them. They're good boys!"

The 'Boys' turned out to be men in their thirties, called William, John and Henry. After the introductions were made they all sat around the large mahogany table and drank Brazilian coffee from fine Sevres porcelain cups. Bulloch then produced a large blueprint plan and started to unfold it on the table, whereupon the 'Boys' quickly pushed the coffee cups out of the way to make space.

John Laird senior stroked his whiskers as he examined the drawing. "Is this the same as Miller is building for you?" he enquired politely.

Bulloch contemplated Laird evenly. His intelligence is good, he thought.

"Yes, much the same. I did explain, I recall, that we are looking for a number of fast sloops of around one thousand tons displacement, for our transatlantic trade."

The bushy eyebrows rose again. "I see. I think, however, Mr Bulloch, it would be better if you were able to take us into your confidence completely. You see, we are all supporters of your cause here. None of us want the damned riff-raff Yankees winning this war and spreading their so-called democracy all over the globe, do we? I mean, universal male suffrage, eh? Whatever next – I suppose women and blacks voting! Can't be done, Mr Bulloch, can't be done. Then they've gone and cut off the cotton trade – and that means less business all round and fewer ships on order – not that we have anything to complain about at the moment, but we don't want this war to drag on for too long do we? No, Mr Bulloch, you should consider yourself to be among friends here."

While his father had been speaking, William Laird had been lightly sketching on the blueprint with a pencil. "Mr Bulloch, Sir, as one friend to another, may I be so bold as to venture a suggestion? Now, we can equip your ship with two, three hundred horse-power engines, to our own design and cast them in our own foundries. That will give you ten, twelve knots maybe in this hull. But we need only one funnel, not the two in your design, and more positioned amidships, like so. This will enable you to set a forward rifled gun here on a raised platform, with a wider arc of fire – so – and the aft gun on a traversing carriage here, firing with either broadside or directly astern. What do you say to that?"

"Excellent, really excellent thinking young man! But can you tell me also where I can acquire these guns?"

John Laird senior spoke. "We can cast the broadside canons here, as they will be smoothbores, but for the rifled guns – I would recommend that you fit Blakeleys – we will have to go outside. In the past we have often used Fawcett and Preston. They're good and don't ask too many damn-fool questions. In any case we'll need a cover story – I suggest that the ship has been commissioned by the Spanish Navy. Perhaps she is to be in service, patrolling the Cuba Straits. We'll name her something Spanish. Henry, what was the name of that Latin filly you so much admired at Derby's ball last season, eh?"

"Umm, *Enrica*, I think father." The young man looked embarrassed.

"You know damn well what her name was! Very well Mr Bulloch, she's the *Enrica*, until you name her different. To us, though, she'll be Hull 290 and may God bless all who sail in her!"

"Amen," chorused the 'Boys'.

"Now, Mr Laird." Bulloch cleared his throat, "forgive me for being direct, but I believe that we have still to discuss the price."

Laird's eyes twinkled. "I'll charge you five percent less than whatever Miller charged you, and she'll be better built, to a better design, with first-class materials and more powerful engines."

Bulloch laughed. "In which case Mr Laird, I will owe you forty-seven thousand, five hundred pounds when she is delivered to me and if she's as good as you say, then you'll have other orders from us besides."

"The price is agreeable, Mr Bulloch, but might I request a payment of half in advance. It is usual in such commissions, you know." Bulloch shook his head. "Among friends, Mr Laird, such deposits are surely not necessary. You may, should you wish, enquire of Fraser, Trenholm as to my financial status, but I speak for my Government in this matter and my credit is their credit."

"Very well, Mr Bulloch, very well. You drive a hard bargain but I have a notion that you are to be trusted."

Bulloch was shown to the door, and was taken back across the river in a private steam launch owned by Lairds. He was elated and immediately went to his hotel room to draft a report to Stephen Mallory.

Later that day, Silas Groat reported the visit of Bulloch to Laird's shipyard and how he had observed Bulloch and Laird shaking hands on the steps of his mansion, very friendly like, and how Bulloch had come back across the river in one of Laird's private ferries.

Miller listened without interruption, but his face reddened and a vein throbbed visibly at his temple. When Groat had finished, Miller smashed his brutal, scarred fist down onto the desk, knocking over an inkwell and spilling the dark ink onto its fine leather surface. He said nothing, but sat back down and breathed deeply. When he had sufficiently composed himself, he said, "that Italian chappy, Mr Groat, you know, the one what wrote that book I read…"

"Machiavelli, Mr Miller?"

"Aye, that's the one," he said. "Revenge is a dish best served cold – well, we'll have our revenge and it will be cold. For now, you stay after Bulloch – I still want to know what he's up to and who he sees. But I've got plans for him alright don't you worry! When the *Oreto's* finished, we'll take his money and more if I can get another order out of him. Then it's the river for him with some chains for company! And that ship of Laird's will never sail – not if I have anything to do with it, anyhow. So you keep your eyes and ears open – I want to know everything about that ship – see if you can get one of Laird's shipwrights to take a bob or two from us, on a regular basis like, for information. Go to it Mr Groat." He returned to his papers as calm as he had been before he had heard news of Laird's commission, his hot anger spent. But determination had set his jaw and his eyes were as cold, dark and pitiless as the Mersey on a winter's night.

The following day, Bulloch went to London by train, looking for a ship to carry Anderson's guns through the blockade, having found none for sale in Liverpool.

The journey from Lime Street station to Euston Station took some five hours. During this time he was able to admire the English countryside as it flashed by – so neat and tidy, with its open fields and carefully trimmed hedgerows and so unlike his native Georgia where the flat coastal swamps gave way to thick forests and arid grasslands. Perhaps there were parts of America that were like England, but he did not think so. The English had worked their land for hundreds of years. They had tamed it and bent it to their will. The land of his country was wilder and less enclosed. Bigger of course, and emptier, with that fine sense of disorganisation and lack of boundaries that defined the spirit of the Confederacy. The train stopped to allow further passengers to board, and Bulloch bade a hearty good day to a parson travelling with his young daughter. They exchanged a few pleasantries until the whistle blew and the train continued on its way to London.

Bulloch glanced up to see that he was being keenly observed by a man of some forty years of age with thinning fair hair, wearing small round spectacles and dressed neatly in clean, but clearly very old and patched clothing. He nodded his head, acknowledging the scrutiny.

"You will forgive me for staring sir, but 'ave I detected from your manner of speech that you har a foreigner in these 'ere parts?" asked the man.

"That is correct. I have recently arrived from America."

"Pray do tell sir – from which part of America do you come, if I may be so bold as to enquire?"

"Why do you wish to know?"

"Just curiosity, sir, just curiosity, even though I knows it killed the cat. Ha! You see, if I may be permitted to introduce meself, I am Josiah Wetherspoon and I 'ave the 'onour to be the Representative of the Manchester Cotton Workers Union. As such, I am deeply interested in the goings on in your country and your war is of much current concern to my members."

"Because of the cotton shortage, you mean, caused by the Yankee blockade?"

"Ho, no sir – well not directly any hows, seeing as there's no cotton shortage to speak of, although as God is my witness, if the war goes on, there surely will be. No, sir, there's no cotton shortage on account of 'ow the 'arvests of '59 and '60 were prodigious abundant and 'ow the mill owners, God rot 'em, bought and over-bought. So now the greedy sods are putting my members on short time, using the war as an excuse to jack up prices, while they unload all the finished cotton goods that they've 'ad cluttering up their warehouses these two years past at a great profit to themselves. But among the working men there's awful 'ardship already, sir, and it's going to get worse if this sad war continues, you mark my words."

Bulloch nodded in agreement. "Well, I and all correct-minded folk hope, like you, that this war will soon be over. It is a sad war that pits brother against brother and it was not of our doing."

"Then you must be from the North, sir!"

"No, indeed I am not!" Bulloch's brow furrowed. "Why would you say such a thing?"

"Because of slavery, sir. Because of the keeping and of the using of your fellow man as an animal. That cannot be right sir, indeed it cannot."

"This war is not about slavery! It is about the rights of individuals to self-determination. It's about freedom from Government interference and freedom of trade. Of all people, you English should understand that. This slavery issue has been built up by our enemies to discredit our Cause and its damn nonsense because there are slave states who have sided with the Union and you don't see any sign of those slaves being freed, do you?"

"And do you own slaves, sir, if I may be so bold as to enquire?"

"Well… I … yes, that is, my wife does – although we refer to them as servants. They live and work in the house and are well fed and well treated. There's many a city slum dweller that's a sight worse off than they are."

"That's as may be, sir, but thems what live in our slums is there of their own choosing and there's no way on God's earth that you can justify that awful state to me, nor to any of my members! They'd as soon starve as support your lot they would. Now I'm sorry I started this conversation, but I cannot continue with it – indeed, I cannot." And with that he lapsed into silence and held up a well-thumbed copy of *Uncle Tom's Cabin* in front of his face.

'So that's where he gets all his nonsensical notions from,' thought Bulloch, who was nonetheless much concerned at the intensity of feeling that seemed to be directed against the South. 'I will spell this out in my next letter to Mallory, for I do not believe that they understand how powerfully emotions are running here among working men!'

On Spence's recommendation, Bulloch stayed at Morley's Hotel on Trafalgar Square and dined on oysters at Bentley's and the following night, on beef at the Angel. It was on his way back to the hotel on the second evening, that he became aware of a figure that seemed t o be dogging his footsteps. He would stop and thirty or forty yards behind him, a man would also stop and then turn away or duck into a shop doorway. Bulloch found him again the next morning, reading a paper on the pavement opposite his hotel. When he boarded the train back to Liverpool that evening, the man was still there, boarding the same train, two compartments behind.

He was, as far as Bulloch could see, of a stocky muscular build, with a short neck and was clean-shaven, except for a drooping moustache, which gave him a somewhat melancholy appearance. He invariably wore a brown suit, with a high-buttoned waistcoat and a black bowler hat, except when it rained, which it did often, and then he would don a rubberised canvas riding coat.

Bulloch became increasingly angry at the persistence of his shadow and determined to confront him. As they disembarked from the train in Liverpool, Bulloch set off rapidly, ignoring the rain that was sweeping across the city from the Mersey and strode purposefully up Lime Street towards the Adelphi Hotel. A quick glance over his shoulder told him that his tail was about forty yards behind, and walking as fast as his short legs could carry him in an effort to keep up. Bulloch smiled. He turned left suddenly, just before the Hotel, strode up the hill, turned next right and ducked down behind a wooden coal store. He drew the Colt .32 Pocket Model from inside his jacket, cocked the hammer, admiring the precise 'click' that it made as the lugs locked into place. He breathed deeply and slowly so as to steady his aim. He did not have long to wait. His shadow appeared at a run, much out of breath and dashed past where Bulloch squatted in the shadows. Bulloch lashed out a foot, catching the fellow completely by surprise and pitching him head first into a puddle of water, which was black with coal dust. The man yelled with surprise, but before he could get to his feet Bulloch was on him, pulling him onto his back, then straddling him, and pinning him down in the dirty water with his considerably greater weight. He placed the barrel of the loaded revolver against the clearly very shaken man's forehead and said:

"Now who the hell are you, and why have you been following me all this time? Talk, damn you, or I'll blow your brains out all over the street."

"Who am I? Who are you? Why have you attacked me in this manner? Now let me up right away or I will call the Peelers," the man stammered in reply.

"Nice try, but not good enough. I've seen you in London, outside my hotel and on the train. You've been following me and I intend to find out why." Bulloch felt inside the man's jacket with his left hand, while holding the revolver steady in his right. In the inner pocket he found an old and battered wallet. In it was a folded five pound note, a stamp, a locket of hair tied with a ribbon and a card identifying the owner as Matthew J McGuire, Detective, of 15 Lower Chambers, Scotland Road, Liverpool.

"So, Mr McGuire, in whose employ are you currently detecting?" Bulloch ground the barrel of the revolver into the powerless detective's forehead, cutting the skin with the sharp foresight.

"All right, all right, let me up and I'll tell you. I'm being paid to follow you, not to get killed."

Bulloch stood up, pulled McGuire roughly to his feet and pushed the dripping detective up against the wall, holding him there with a forearm against his throat. "You were saying...?"

"Yes, all right, all right. I am employed by the Ignatius Polacky Detective Agency. We have been hired by Mr Thomas Dudley – he's the United States Consul here in Liverpool – got a real posh office over on Water Street. Anyway, he's paid me five pounds a week to follow you, see where you go and report back to him. That's all, nothing else."

"I see, yes, well, that is what I expected." Bulloch stepped back, lowering the gun.

"You won't tell him, will you? Tell him as how you spotted me and I 'fessed up as to who I was working for, will you? I need the money, see," he said glumly. "The fight game's not what it was. Bantam weight champion of Liverpool, that's me – in '53 and '54," he pointed to himself with his thumb and stuck his chest out in an attempt to reclaim an iota of his lost dignity.

"No, I won't tell him. What's the point? He'd only replace you with someone else and I'd have to go to all the bother of spotting him. Not that that would be difficult, if he's as bad as following a man as you are."

McGuire looked hurt. "Go on with you now," said Bulloch. "I'm going back to my hotel – the Queen's Hotel as you should know. I shall be dining there and I won't be leaving until tomorrow morning at around ten. No doubt I will see you then."

The detective sighed, picked up his wet and dirty bowler and replaced it on his head after a half-hearted attempt to brush off the worst of the soot and grime. He walked off, back the way he had come, limping slightly.

'So' Groat thought to himself, as he slipped away home to his dark, cold attic, 'there's a turn-up for the books. Nothing for a week, 'cept he's down the shops spending money like it was going out of fashion, then its off to Laird's, with them two close as love-birds, followed by London, down at the docks, up the Isle of Dogs and bought a ship he did. Overpaid most likely too. Then there's that detective fellow' and here he permitted himself a rare chuckle, 'stuck out like a wart on a whores face he did, and got a jolly good beating for it. Serves him right. Lot here for Mr Miller. He'll be pleased as punch. Give me a bonus I shouldn't wonder. Mebbe not. Still, he'll let me back in the office now, anyhow.' But as he climbed the rickety, uncarpeted stairs to his attic, Groat paused. 'Perhaps our Mr Miller doesn't need to know everything,' he thought. 'About the detective, yes, but not as how our man's quick on his feet, handy with his fists and's got that little pistol in his pocket. That's for me to know, 'cos you can never be too careful with Mr Miller and this might just come in handy.' Pleased with the thought, Silas Groat clambered under the damp blankets fully dressed and fell asleep with a wan smile on his thin lips.

Later that week, Bulloch was awoken by the sound of shouting and cheering in the street below. He ran to the window and flung it open, wearing nothing but his flannel nightgown.

"What's the ruckus, boy?" he shouted down to the newspaper seller, who was waving papers in his hand and shouting some gibberish.

"There's been a great battle, in America, sir – the South done beat the Yankees hollow at some place called Manassas."

III

Washington – July, August, September, 1861

❧ ❦

The sun was well up in the sky and, even though it was barely six, the humidity of the Washington summer was already well in evidence. The porters, leaning on their trolleys, indolent in the heat, watched silently as the over-night from New York puffed and clanked its way into the station. Clouds of steam billowed across the platform, as the train finally came to a rest with a screech of breaks and the clatter and thump of its carriages as they banged to a halt against their resisting buffers.

Out of the first open door leapt an elegantly attired woman who appeared to be in her late thirties, with a small black leather bag in her hand. Behind her, nervous of the big step, a small girl of about eight hesitated.

"Oh do come along Rose," said her mother, impatiently beckoning to her daughter. The child took a deep breath and then jumped, landing on both feet with a shout.

The mother grabbed her daughter's hand and began pulling her towards the exit, walking as quickly as her fashionably narrow skirt would permit, the daughter running to keep up.

She ignored the blandishments of the porters and the cries of "carry your bags for a dime, lady!" and went straight to a waiting cab.

"Quick," she said, "take me to the corner of 13th and I Street."

In the coach she is hugging herself in excitement and anticipation, and rocking backwards and forwards on the seat.

"Oh Mama please do be still," says the girl, whose sleepy eyes and dishevelled hair speak of a night on the train and little interest in her toilet. Her mother, on the other hand, although she has dark smudges below her eyes, is clearly alert and in a fever of excitement.

Indeed, she had been trembling since the news – the wonderful news – had reached her in New York the previous day. She had been returning from the docks, after seeing her older daughter Leila off to San Francisco, when she became aware of people running in the street. Several horsemen galloped past them down 3rd Avenue, spurring on their mounts while groups of sombre faced men began to gather on the pavements, reading from broadsheets. A whiff of panic was discernible in the heavy air.

She had leaned out of the carriage and had shouted to one of the groups of men in order to attract their attention. When an individual approached, she had asked him what the cause of the commotion might be. He looked up at her, a worried expression on his face.

"Well Ma'am, there is news of a bloody defeat – McDowell's been whipped by the Rebs at Manassas and has fallen back on Washington in disorder. Rumours say that there's a hundred thousand Rebs on his tail and that Washington's threatened. It's a disaster and no mistake."

"Yes, yes of course it is," she had almost shouted back at him, quite unable to keep the smile off her fine features. The man watched, frowning, as the carriage drove off, the horses whipped into a fast trot, with peels of exultant laughter audible in its wake.

"We've done it, we've done it," she said to herself. "Oh Beauregard, your name is right, you are a beautiful man and when I next see you, I'll show you just how I feel about you!" She hugged her daughter, who was sitting staring at her, her eyes wide with alarm at her mother's unusual and unseemly outburst.

"We are going home my darling, right now, we are going to catch the train home. Everything is going to be all right – you will see!" She hugged her again.

Now, only eighteen hours later, she is home in Washington and running up the stairs of the stoop of her narrow brick house and shouting to her maid, "Lucy, Lucy, where are you child? Come down and let us in."

It is not Lucy who answers the door however, but a good looking man, tall and slim with a moustache and a small pointed beard. He smiles broadly and takes her hand, leading her into her own house. Once inside and out of the view of the street, he puts his arms around her, hugging her to his chest.

"Oh, Rose, you marvel. You've heard the news, of course?"

"Only the barest outline. I was in New York seeing Leila off to California, but tell me more – tell me everything."

"It's a great victory. We thrashed 'em, taking fifteen hundred prisoners and capturing twenty-eight artillery pieces and many, many rifles and quantities of stores. McDowell's boys broke and ran and all the fine citizenry of Washington who had gone to watch their boys whip 'Johnny Reb' and who were eating picnics – I tell you, Rose, they were eating their picnics and sipping their wine on the banks of the Bull Run, why, they were trampled in the rush and they had their carriages and horses stole by the runnin' troops and they jes' had to walk back! Ha!"

"I am so very happy, Michael, and so happy that we – you, I, all of us were able to contribute to this wonderful victory."

"You especially Rose...and before I forget..." he looked around furtively and then produced a folded note from his pocket, which he pressed into Rose's hand. She opened the note and read:

Our President and our General direct me to thank you. We rely on your further information.
The Confederacy owes you a debt.
Thomas Rayford.

Tears welled up in her eyes, which she brushed away with the back of her hand. She folded the note and put it into the pocket of her skirt.

The man frowned and looked worried. "Rose, you should not keep that note. Especially not now. They know that word had gotten to Beauregard of McDowell's movements, and they will be looking for us. It's not safe. You must think of yourself, and little Rose as well."

She sighed. "You are right, of course." She tore the note in half and then tore it again, before flinging the pieces into the unlit stove and slamming its black metal door.

"So Michael, were you with Beauregard?"

"I surely was – and Joe Johnston – until this morning. Johnston's got twenty thousand men and wants to march on Washington at once. Beauregard's for it too, of course, but Davis is prevaricatin'. He thinks that we could smash ourselves on Washington's forts and then get chased all the way home with our

44

tails between our legs. He – the President – wants plans of their forts, he wants to know how many troops – militia included – they got for the defence of Washington and where they are. Anything else, any idea of their signals or alarms would be of real help too! Then he's gonna make up his mind about the attack. You see Rose, it's a big step from defending Northern Virginia from an invader, to besieging his Capital. It's got more political ramifications than a dog's got fleas. So he needs our help bad."

"All right." She frowned, forcing her tired brain to think. "Maybe I know a way. There's this Captain..."

He laughed. "Why Rose, there's always this Captain or that General or the other Senator. You are a wonder!"

"I don't do it because I like it," she snapped, the exultation that followed the news of the victory was suddenly replaced with the leaden weight of the knowledge of what she still had to do and how much still depended on her. "You think I like the fine ladies of this town calling me a whore and a roundheel behind my back? And not always behind my back, either!"

"No Rose, I'm sorry, I didn't mean it that way, you know that. You also know that I love you Rose and I'd do just anything for you."

She smiled a little sadly and stroked his face with her gloved hand.

"I know Michael, but it seems the time's always out of joint for us. Perhaps when this is all over......... and now, if you will excuse me, I'm dog-tired and I need a bath. We'll talk later. And Michael..." he turned, half way through the door, his hat in his hands "...will you tell the others to come by...just as soon as they can."

He saluted. "Colonel 'Empty', Ma'am, at your service."

*   *

That morning in another part of town, two men sat facing each other across a large mahogany desk.

One was a portly figure in late middle age, grey-haired and bearded, but with a clean-shaven upper lip. His eyes were focused on the untidy and shabbily dressed man, who perched on the edge of the chair opposite, clutching his bowler hat on his knees.

"Well Pinkerton, I thank you for coming at such short notice."

The man nodded, shifting on the chair, easing his backside, which ached from many hours in the saddle.

"You come highly recommended you know. McClelland says you're the sharpest detective he's ever met. Not that I suspect he's met many, but that's McClelland for you! Also, I understand that you were responsible for getting the President out of Baltimore alive, earlier in the year. Is that so?"

Pinkerton took a deep breath and wiped his hand down his dark and heavily bearded face, feeling the tiredness well up in him. "Aye, I done that, sir," he replied in an accent still strong from his native Glasgow. "Ye know I was reet pleased to save the wee man's life." He laughed at his own joke – the President being some one-and-a-half feet taller than himself.

The older man did not laugh. "I asked you to come here Mr Pinkerton to see what you can do to put a stop to the flow of sensitive military information that seems to be reaching the Rebels. You are an accomplished detective, or so I am led to believe, and I would assume this to be well within your capabilities." Pinkerton snorted.

"Washington's more full of holes than a Swiss cheese. Ye have more supporters of the Rebel cause here than honest citizens – why, if ye just went out into the park and arrested ten joes ye'll net five spies, I'll be bound."

The older man flushed red, unused to being on the receiving end of sarcasm. "You seem to take this very lightly for such a serious matter, Mr Pinkerton. We have hundreds of our boys dead, and thousands wounded or captured because bloody little Pierre Gustave Toutant Beauregard knew just how many men McDowell had and just where he was going to put them. This has to stop," he shouted, banging the flat of his hand on the desktop and causing the many pens and pencils to leap into the air.

"I'll take ye seriously, when ye give me reason to do so and not before. Now ye want me to rid this town of all its spies and I tell ye it canna' be done. But if I get the men and the authority, I'll go after the ring that gave away yer battle fer ye and they'll swing before the year's out. That's a promise." He sat back.

"Very well, Mr Pinkerton, that seems as good a place to start as any. You'll have the men and you'll have the power to search, arrest and detain on suspicion. We have suspended habeas corpus and there are no public trials and no appeal. If we can prove their complicity to a military tribunal, they will be locked up for as long

46

as we deem expedient. If we catch them red-handed in the act of passing on information, they will die. Satisfied?"

Pinkerton nodded.

"Verra well Mr Scott, that will do. And for this I'll report straight to you as the Assistant Secretary of War but to no other, mind. And don't ye worry, I'll get yer men fer ye, no doubt I will."

"And women, Mr Pinkerton, and women."

*   *

Rose Greenhow was taking tea in her parlour on the first floor of her house and fanning herself to get some relief from the stifling heat. There was a knock at the door and Lucy, her maid, entered.

"Pardon Ma'am, but Miss Mackall has come to pay her respects." She bobbed a curtsey. As she stepped back a young woman swept into the room and pulled off her bonnet freeing the golden curls beneath. She ran across to Rose and plumped down next to her on the sofa, flinging her arms around her neck, and kissing her several times on the lips. "Oh Rose, my Rose, how I've missed you – how I always miss you when you're away."

"Now Lily, it was only a few days!"

The young girl looked sulky, which did not improve her somewhat plain appearance. Her face, while not ugly, was improperly proportioned for beauty, the eyes being slightly too close together and the nose slightly too broad across the bridge. Nonetheless when she smiled, the whole blended together in a passably attractive manner and she now smiled and kissed Rose again.

"Lily, you musn't. What if Lucy came in?"

"I don't mind, Rose."

"Yes, but I do. And I have enough problems in this town, with people talking, without that!"

"Without them saying that you have a young girl as your lover." She tried to look coquettish, but only achieved a somewhat perplexed look. Rose laughed.

She put her hand on Lily's arm and said gently, "Lily, my sweet, we are really not lovers you know."

Lily looked hurt and stuck out her lower lip. "But, those things we did", she blushed slightly at the memory, "that meant so much to me and I ache, I ache to have your hands on me again and to feel your body pressed against mine."

Rose leaned forward, stroking Lily's hair and, picking up the hem of her heavy silk dress with the other hand, she pushed it up her thighs. Lily's breath quickened, the colour rushing to her cheeks as Rose's hand moved up to her waist, and untied the blue ribbon which secured the top of her voluminous cotton drawers. Rose slid her hand inside feeling the coarse hair of Lily's crotch, her fingers probing, stroking and finally pushing up inside her. Lily gasped, pushing Rose's hand away.

"Not like this, Rose," she seemed close to tears as she pulled her dress down, "like it was before."

"That's what I mean, Lily. That's what women do to love each other and more besides. We just held each other in bed, for company and kissed. That's all. I like you Lily, I really do, but my life is as complicated as it can get right now and I don't think that an affair with a beautiful young girl would make it any simpler."

Lily laughed, wiping the tears away with her handkerchief and sniffing. "Well I love you Rose, and if that's what women do together then that's what I want to do with you. I'd die for you Rose, you know that."

"Now silly, what's this talk about dying?"

"I know what you do Rose and I know how dangerous it is. And it's not just me who knows, everyone does."

"Everyone?"

"Why Rose you are so indiscreet. Always mouthing off about States Rights and your admiration for Mr Davis and such things. There are those who openly call you 'Rebel Rose'."

Rose sat back, shocked. "It's true Rose, you must be more careful. And if I were you, I would look behind me when I'm out walking, just to see if, you know, there's anyone following, or taking a bit too much of an interest."

"Very well then my dear, why don't we go and see. That will prove what nonsense you are talking!" They both laced up their bonnets and stepped into the street, opening parasols as they did so, against the strong afternoon sun. They walked together, arm in arm, the full length of 13th Street, turning left at the corner into K Street, where they paused and looked back down the way they had come. Two men, both wearing bowlers stopped abruptly and developed a sudden interest in a window box. At the next corner, 14th Street, they stopped again and again the same two men turned away, feigning disinterest. At last, returning to Rose's front door, they turned and waved happily at their shadows, before re-entering the house.

Inside, Rose's cheerful demeanour vanished instantly. "You were right Lily, thank you. I must be more careful. My God, this house, if they ever search it, there's enough incriminating evidence here to hang me five times over. Lily, you can help me. She ran to her bureau and started leafing through piles of paper. "Take these, and these – and this also. Rip them up and we'll burn them in the stove. What else, dammit, what else?"

The two ladies ran in and out of the bedroom and then back into the parlour or the dining-room, with occasional cries from Rose indicating that some crumpled message or half-written communication had been found poking from the well of her desk or lying out in the open on her dressing table. She retrieved the papers that were still essential to her and the cipher given her by Captain Thomas Jordan, when he had recruited her, before the start of the war. These she assembled and tied into a leather portfolio, which she placed on the top shelf of the bookcase in her parlour.

'There,' she thought, considerably more relaxed. 'That's better. Now where are those matches?'

*   *

The hot dry spell broke suddenly as August drew to a close with a torrential downpour of tropical proportions. The huge drops of rain smashed against the pavement, sending clouds of spray up to knee height. All around, the thunder roared and the flashes of lightning illuminated the prematurely dark early evening sky.

The watchers outside Rose's house were drenched to the skin within seconds and ran to take shelter below the stoop that led up to the front door. Here, they felt that they would be out of the line of sight of those within the house and yet be able to see a person leaving, should anyone be so foolish as to venture out in this storm.

And there they waited, with rain drops coursing down the inside of their necks and soaking them through to their woollen undergarments. Detective Ascot's hat, shoddily fabricated from cardboard, had melted in the rain. As a result, the brim suddenly detached itself from the crown and fell down around his eyes, much to the amusement of Detective Corroon, who laughed loudly enough to be heard above the storm. "Something funny, Detective?

Something verra funny is there?" shouted a voice from above. They looked out of their temporary shelter up at the squat menacing figure of Alan Pinkerton who was dressed as usual in a baggy ill-fitting black suit, which now sodden from the rain, clung to him tightly, emphasising his powerful muscular frame.

He came round the back of the stairs and squatted down, joining the other two detectives in their shelter.

"So, how goes it lads? What have ye ter report?"

"She knows she's bein' followed, sir", said Detective Ascot.

"And not through our fault at all," joined in Detective Corroon.

"Aye and it must be the fairies that told her, ye incompetent useless fools. I'ffin I'd had yer in Baltimore ye'd be dead now, cut up and castrated by them Blood Tubs, murdering bastards that they were…" He stopped abruptly, raising a finger to his lips, as footsteps suddenly became audible climbing the steps. A man cleared his throat and knocked on the door. Pinkerton risked ducking his head out and caught a glimpse of a soldier, an officer, entering the house, a bouquet of flowers over his arm.

"I must see him," muttered Pinkerton, scuttling on all fours, like a crab up the steps, but the windows on each side of the door had their blinds drawn and were too far away for him to reach out and peer through. He ran back down.

"Here you two, redeem yesselves. Kneel down and I'll stand on your shoulders. Then I should be able to see into that room up there."

He kicked off his shoes and clambered onto the back of the uncomplaining detectives. As Pinkerton rose to his full height the base of the window came level with his eyes. He carefully reached in and twisted one of the closed slats of the blind, until it was suffi-ciently open for him to peer into the room itself.

Inside he saw the soldier, a Captain he could now detect, leaning over a map which was held open at its corners by a variety of glasses and cups. The Captain was pointing with the index finger of a hand, which also held a newly lit cigar. Hanging on his shoulder and looking at where he pointed was Rose Greenhow, her hair up and pinned with a tortoiseshell comb. She had lightly rouged her face and in the lamplight Pinkerton thought that she was the most beautiful woman he had ever seen.

He drew a sharp breath, aghast, both at her beauty and at the blatancy of the act of her treachery that was laid out before him like a tableau. His fury, though, was reserved for the Captain, who had now clasped Rose in his arms and was kissing her passionately. Arm in arm they left the parlour and Pinkerton clambered off the back of the swaying Detective Ascot and sank to his haunches in the damp dark space below the stoop.

They waited there in silence for the better part of an hour. Then the door opened above and someone made to depart. There were noises of kissing and murmured endearments and then heavy footsteps descending to the street.

Pinkerton peered out to see the Captain striding off in a southerly direction, and whispered "Ascot, you come with me, but stay well back. We'll follow this bastard, find out who he is, then pinch him. You, Corroon, whatever your name is, stay here and observe, with yer damned eyes open for a change."

He moved off down the street, staying close to the houses and skipping from shadow to shadow, moving swiftly through the yellow glare of the gas lamps in the street. He quickly became aware that he had forgotten his shoes as pebbles and small shards of broken glass assaulted the soles of his feet, but it was too late to return, so he shrugged off the pain as he had done so often in the past and persevered.

In this manner the two detectives dogged the footsteps of the Army officer down several streets, deserted in the rain and up to the doors of a military establishment at the corner of 15th Street and Pennsylvania Avenue, close to the White House. This was guarded by one lonely sentry wearing a sodden cape in an effort to keep off the rain, the brim of his kepi pulled well down over his eyes.

Pinkerton approached the sentry. "Which barracks are these, Private, and what is the name of the Captain who just entered?"

The sentry kept silent, having been ordered not to speak to passers by, but he shifted his feet and wondered if the powder in his rifle was still dry enough to fire.

At that moment the iron studded doors of the barracks were flung back, suddenly flooding the street with light. Four soldiers, their rifles lowered, bayonets fixed, ran out followed by the Captain, who had until now been the prey rather than the predator. "Arrest these men Sergeant," he yelled and the four soldiers obediently surrounded the two sodden detectives, menacing them with their bayonets. "You'll have to come with us, sors," said the Sergeant in a heavy Irish accent, "and you'll no be giving us any trouble now, will you, or it'll be the worse for you, so it will!"

Pinkerton and Ascot were marched into the barracks, through a guardroom where a group of soldiers played cards and smoked, along a dark corridor and down a flight of stone steps. At the bottom was a row of cell doors, made of iron with reinforcing bars for extra strength. In the middle of each door was a little shutter, though which the guards could keep an eye on the inmates.

The detectives were thrown into separate cells and the doors slammed shut with a reverberation that echoed down the empty corridor and bounced off the damp stone flags.

Pinkerton slumped down on the filthy straw palliasse and put his head in his hands. He looked up as the shutter banged open and a disembodied eye examined him briefly, before it snapped closed again.

"Oh God," he thought, "this is goin' to be verra difficult and verra embarrassin' to explain." But he had recognised the Captain as one John Ellwood, of the 5th Infantry, assigned to the Provost Marshall's Office in whose cells he now sat. Worst of all, he suspected that the map that Captain Ellwood had been showing to Rose depicted the Washington defences and that this information was even now on its way South.

After half an hour, the door opened and a Private armed with a rifle beckoned to Pinkerton, who was by now shivering uncontrollably in his wet clothes. He was taken up two flights of stairs and into an office, where Captain Ellwood sat behind a long pine table on which lay two Colt .44 Dragoon revolvers, the handles pointing towards the Captain. The Private, who took up his position behind the Detective, thrust Pinkerton into an upright chair facing the desk.

"What is your name?" the Captain asked, frowning.

"Allen, sir, E J Allen."

"And what Mr Allen, were you and your friend doing following me? And where are your shoes?"

"We were never following you sir, no, we were just on our way home, in the same direction, maybe as yourself, so it may have seemed we were following you. And my shoes, well they were just shoddy Chicago manufacture and they just fell to pieces in the rain. That's a fact."

"So you are from Chicago, Mr Allen?"

"Aye." Cautiously.

"And what are you doing in Washington? Are you not involved with the war effort?"

"No sir. I represent a firm of barrel makers. We hope to have business supplying the War Department."

"So, you are a war profiteer, eh? With no love for your adopted country, unwilling to fight for her, in her hour of need?"

Pinkerton coloured and bit his lip. 'Fight for her? Unlike you, you damned traitor – you don't fight for your country, you just fornicate for her'! He said nothing.

"Very well Mr Allen. You may join your friend in the drunk tank. We'll see if a few hours there will loosen your tongue. Take him away, Private."

They went back down the stairs where Pinkerton was shoved at rifle point into a long room with floor to ceiling bars that divided the communal cell from the guards, who sprawled in chairs, chewing tobacco and spitting their brown saliva at the prisoners for sport. As the Private was about to leave, Pinkerton grasped the young man's lapel.

"Listen friend, your Captain Ellwood is in big trouble. Do yesself a favour, see, and take a message from me to Thomas Scott, the Assistant Secretary of War. Ye'll find him at home at this hour. Tell him that Mr Allen and Mr Ascot are locked up here and to come and get us out, sharpish, mind. There'll be a reward in it for ye too, if ye hurry."

The Private looked perplexed and broke away, frowning. Pinkerton turned back, becoming aware for the first time of the appalling smell, mainly of urine and vomit that permeated the large cell. On the floor, sitting or lying, were upward of a dozen men all in an advanced state of inebriation. A bucket, overflowing with excrement sat in the corner, the drunks having positioned themselves as far away from this as possible.

'My God, what a terrible reek' he thought. Then out loud he said, "Ascot, where are ye?" One of the fellows raised his head and Pinkerton could just barely recognise Ascot's features, with one eye swollen shut, a bruised cheekbone and a bleeding lip, which he dabbed gently with the cuff of his jacket.

"What the hell happened to ye then?"

"I got beat up," he mumbled thickly. "I called the Sergeant a stupid Mick and he and the corporal hit me with their rifle butts, and it hurts like hell."

"Well ye shouldn't have insulted the man then, laddy. Ye know what those damned Micks are like. Fight you for a dime they will. Anyhow…" he squatted down and lowered his voice, "I hope we won't be here for too long."

* *

At eight o'clock, after a night of little sleep and great discomfort, Pinkerton was standing with his face pressed against the bars in an attempt to breathe in some less putrid air. The Irish Sergeant entered the corridor, with a shout of "Atten-shun!" The guards leapt to their feet, straightening their jackets and fastening their buttons.

"Get me the prisoners Allen and Ascot," he yelled at the top of his voice.

* *

Scott looked at Pinkerton, his eyebrows rising. He sniffed.

"It has to be said, Pinkerton, that you smell as bad as anybody can. No offence mind but I'd be grateful if you would move your chair further back from my desk … and tell me what happened."

He listened in silence, frowning, occasionally taking notes. When Pinkerton had finished, he looked very serious. "We must act without delay. Mrs Greenhow's house must be searched immediately. If evidence is found incriminating her, she should be arrested. Keep the place under surveillance and have anyone who comes, followed on their departure. Arrest them if they are seen passing on anything or acting in any way suspiciously. We can always apologise later. But Allan…be careful with Rose Greenhow…she has many powerful friends and even ranks one Senator at least, to my knowledge, among her…intimate admirers. And you leave Captain Ellwood to me!"

Pinkerton stood. "Yes sir, I'll get on to it right away. And I'll be circumspect around the lady."

"Oh and one more thing…perhaps a bath and some fresh clothes first. It wouldn't do to convey the impression that the Department of War employed hobos who couldn't even afford a pair of shoes!" He opened his mouth and laughed loudly, to

Pinkerton's discomfort, as he retreated hastily closing the door.

Two hours later, a freshly bathed Allan Pinkerton, his beard and thick dark hair neatly combed, walked up the steps leading to the door of Rose Greenhow's house. With him were the two detectives and a detachment of regular army troops. He paused on the top step and flicked some dust from his lapels before ringing the bell. He was unsure as to the reason for his nervousness – whether it was the simple act of the arrest of a notorious traitor or whether there was a deeper underlying cause relating to the extreme attraction he felt for this dark, sensual, and obviously promiscuous lady. The thought of sex with Mrs Greenhow made his mouth go dry and his hands trembled at the image of her unclothed body beneath his.

Since an early age, his mother, a fierce Presbyterian woman with a vicious slap, had drummed into his little head the evils of the flesh and the consequences of dalliance with loose women. To his Mother, any woman who was not married from an early age, who did not remain at home spinning, and who was clothed in other than a tightly buttoned dress of black serge was a 'loose woman'. And loose women were the agents of the Devil himself and the gateway to hell and eternal damnation lay between their legs.

So now he was about to arrest and bring within his power a woman, whom he believed to be truly loose and who was at the same time extraordinarily beautiful and alluringly dangerous.

The maid interrupted his reverie. "Good afternoon, Sir, is Mrs Greenhow expecting you?" She looked startled at the large group of men, several in soldiers' uniforms, who were gathered on the steps.

"No, but we're coming in anyway," he said, brushing past the maid and entering the hallway. At that moment Rose Greenhow appeared at the top of the stairs. "What is it Lucy?" she called.

"Why Ma'am this man just forced his way in."

"Mrs Greenhow – my name is Pinkerton. I've come with a warrant to search these premises."

"On whose authority do you do this?" she enquired, slowly descending the stairs, a small smile playing on her lips.

"On the authority of the Government you have betrayed."

She paused, struck by the enormity of the situation.

"What is it Mama?" little Rose called from upstairs.

"Nothing to concern you, my dearest, just some nasty men

come to arrest your Mama."

"Enough of that Mrs Greenhow, now if you'll go to your room, I will place a guard outside your door. You may have your daughter with you." He turned to the rest of his men and said, "Get inside you lot, quickly now, we don't want to alert her accomplices. Ascot, you stand by the door. If anyone comes – anyone mind – you grab 'em. And be careful, they may be armed."

Rose sat in her room while from downstairs noises came of moving furniture, slamming drawers and books being opened and then flung onto the floor. She had already hidden the portfolio, containing her most important papers, under her pillow and had put her small derringer and the cipher in the tops of her stockings, held in place by lace garters. But she was equally aware that she had never found the matches the other day…

She brightened, turning to little Rose. "Would you do something for your Mama, my precious?"

* *

At the far end of the street from Rose Greenhow's house, Michael Thompson, the self-styled 'Colonel Empty' had just appeared, walking rapidly. He had collected a copy of the plan of Washington's defences late the previous evening and, after he had successfully lost Detective Corroon, had passed this on to one of the young girls they used as couriers. She was even now sitting in a railway carriage on a long and circuitous journey to Richmond, the information on tightly rolled strips of paper hidden in her neatly pinned hair.

He was hurrying to tell Rose that more details of the artillery emplacements were needed and that another encounter with Captain Ellwood was going to be necessary. As he approached Rose's house however, he stopped and listened, because he had heard a little girl chanting from the tree that grew close to the house.

"Mama's been arrested, Mama's been arrested, Mama's been arrested" the little girl sang over and over. A small crowd had gathered below, all laughing and pointing at the branch on which little Rose sat, swinging her legs and enjoying the game and the resulting attention, immensely.

Michael Thompson quickly crossed the street and continued on without a pause or a glance behind. He had a lot to do: people to alert in Washington, including the other members of the Ring; and messages to send to Richmond, warning them of Rose's arrest and the possible seizure of their cypher.

Back at the house, little Rose had finally been removed from the tree, by a burly soldier who had climbed a ladder up to the branch and had dragged the little girl off, kicking and screaming, to a chorus of boos and whistles from the crowd, who had then gone about their business, leaving the street deserted.

As a result, Lily Mackall was unaware that anything might be amiss as she came quickly up the steps, holding her beige cotton dress with its hooped skirt away from her feet thus displaying her neat buttoned boots. She rapped on the door with the handle of her parasol and turned to look back down the street. The door opened, but before she could turn, a large pair of arms in dark blue serge, grabbed her from behind and dragged her into the house, her involuntary scream echoing in the stillness of the mid-afternoon.

"Mr Pinkerton, we've got another one," called Detective Ascot. Pinkerton ran into the hall. He saw the burly soldier, grappling with a small but fierce looking young woman, who was shouting "let me go you brute," and trying to stamp on the soldier's feet.

"Let her go, Private. Now Ma'am," turning to Lily, "who are ye and what do ye want here?"

"My name is Lily Mackall. I am a close friend of Mrs Greenhow and I demand an explanation! Why have I been manhandled by this ruffian? Who are you and more to the point, what are you doing here?"

"My name is Pinkerton, Ma'am. I am in the employ of the Department of War. I have just arrested Mrs Greenhow on the charge of spying and at this moment we are detaining all callers at this house on suspicion of being accomplices of a known spy. Now, I am afraid that you will have to be questioned before you will be permitted to leave."

"Oh" said Lily in a very small voice. "Oh dear." Then louder, "may I be permitted to see Rose...Mrs Greenhow?"

"Aye, but ye will need to submit to a search before and after seeing Mrs Greenhow. We cannot have her communicating any further with her Rebel friends! Now we have here a female prison warder, a Miss Van Mulder, who will carry out the search."

A heavily built woman, with the faint trace of a moustache on her upper lip, came forward and took Lily by the arm, leading her into the parlour.

Twenty minutes later, Lily was shown into Rose's bedroom, where she sat on her bed, reading to little Rose.

"Oh Lily," she jumped to her feet, "how wonderful to see you, I am so glad you came." Then she looked down at her feet, "but I have been arrested Lily, you were right, they were on to me. I have been so stupid," and she started to cry.

Lily cradled her in her arms, and little Rose hugged her round the knees.

"Were you searched by that dreadful woman with the moustache?" asked Lily.

"Thankfully not. But I have hidden the cipher in my stocking tops. Do you think that she will look there?"

"Undoubtedly. You must find another place Rose. She seems to enjoy looking under women's clothing – as I do," she added quietly with a wink.

Rose cleared her throat and looking sideways at her daughter said, "now, tell me what that horrid little man Pinkerton and the soldiers were doing downstairs."

"They were lifting all the contents of your stove out very carefully and Pinkerton was on his knees on the rug trying to put together the pieces of those letters and whatever, that we ripped up the other day – that you said you were going to burn," Lily said in a rush, looking accusingly at Rose. There was a silence. "Oh Rose, what will you do?"

"I don't know Lily. I really don't." She suddenly looked frightened. "You don't think they …" she lowered her voice. "You don't think they hang women do they?"

"No Rose I'm sure they don't, but they will lock you up. However, if they find anything directly linking you to Manassas, then, well, it could be bad Rose. They are still very angry about that."

"There's nothing Lily. I am sure about that, not concerning Manassas anyway."

Lily looked at Rose, her brow furrowing. She walked to the window, to Rose's desk and bent over the pink blotter, that sat in the middle of the desk. After a moment she started. "Rose, I can see the word Manassas here on your blotter!"

Rose blanched. She picked up the blotting paper and tore it in half. "Unfortunately Lily I am unable to offer you any tea, but they say that blotting paper can be quite delicious..." The two women smiled at each other and started to nibble on the two halves of the pink blotter, watched by little Rose, who laughed and clapped to see two grown-ups behaving so childishly.

It was midnight before Lily was allowed to leave and then only after submitting to a further search by Warden Van Mulder. Although she had been forced to strip to her camisole and bloomers and had had to wait while her clothes were carefully inspected, the Warden going over each seam with her short blunt fingers, there had been no attempt to search her undergarments. This was as well, for she now carried a message for Michael Thompson in a carefully worded code, hidden in a very intimate place, warning him of the situation and asking him for help.

Rose was not allowed to dwell on her situation alone for too long.

Pinkerton knocked on the door and entered. "Mrs Greenhow, I trust that ye are as comfortable as possible. Ye have dined satisfactorily?" he enquired politely, turning his ever-present bowler hat around and around in his fingers as he spoke.

"Thank you Mr Pinkerton, quite satisfactorily."

"Ah, good." He looked to where little Rose was sleeping on a pile of cushions, partially covered by her mother's bedspread. He took a couple of steps forward. "May I?" he asked, gesturing to the end of the bed, furthest from where Rose sat.

She looked a little startled, then nodded. He sat and she edged away from him along the bed, until the wall barred her further progress.

"Now Mrs Greenhow, I do not need to tell ye that ye are in a great deal of trouble. I have pieced together several letters to and from rebel sympathisers, some containing information of a military nature. Ye are a spy and ye'll be convicted as such. Of this there is no doubt."

Rose remained silent, looking at her hands that were clasped together in her lap. She did not dare to let herself speak, for her instinct was to round on this little man, who perched so insolently on the end of her bed and tell him to his face, that yes, she was a spy and that she had and would continue to do anything she could to preserve the freedom of her beloved Country and to defeat its cruel oppressors.

He moved along the bed a little closer to her. "Mrs Greenhow, have ye given thought to yer future and to that of yer daughter?" He licked his fleshy lips, pushing the straggling hairs of his moustache away with his thick pink tongue. She shuddered, but continued to say nothing. "Because I may be able to help you there, Mrs Greenhow. Y'see, it is possible that ye may be able to stay on in this house. Under guard, of course, not being able to leave. Now if I support this very lenient approach, then yer imprisonment and that of yer daughter, may not be that unpleasant, especially, given the egregious nature of yer crimes, that is." He moved closer to her down the bed.

"On the other hand. On the other hand, Mrs Greenhow, were I to take a contrary position, were I to demand a harsher regime, one more fitting to yer crimes, then there is a cell waiting for ye and yer daughter in the Old Capitol building and a dark and sorry place that is too."

She groaned involuntarily. She knew the Old Capitol building, which had been a rooming house before it became a prison. In fact, she had spent some of the early years of her youth there, when poverty and early widowhood had driven her mother into the city and away from the farm, which she had been unable to keep up on her own.

She squeezed her eyes shut, hot tears of anger leaking out from behind her closed lids.

Pinkerton continued. By now he was sitting close to her and he had placed one hairy-backed hand on her thigh. He spoke quietly, his accent even more pronounced than usual. "Mrs Greenhow, to tell the truth, I find you a verra attractive woman, verra attractive indeed. If we could … get to know each other better … if we could…" He slid his arm around her waist, but she suddenly and violently pulled herself away.

"Don't you dare touch me you filthy little man – and get your hands off me – now! You must know that I will never submit to your unwelcome advances."

Pinkerton drew back, surprised and hurt. "But ye do yer dirty business with all and sundry, ye hurr, I've seen ye, with that damned Captain Ellwood for a start."

Rose drew herself up to her full height. "What I have done with Captain Ellwood – and with others – I have done for my Country. I do not consider myself to be a 'hurr'," she mimicked his accent, "but if I were to let you make love to me now, just to ease the condition of my imprisonment, why, then I would be a whore. Now get out of my room and leave me alone."

A red-faced Pinkerton stumbled from the room, slamming the door behind. At the foot of the stairs he came across Detective Ascot. "Get a prison wagon. Get it here now. And take that treacherous bitch and her whelp to the Old Capitol building and lock them up in the darkest cell ye can find and don't allow them any visitors or any communication with anyone from the outside."

'We'll see how much she can take of that before she changes her damned tune,' he thought to himself.

IV

Holyhead to Savannah – October, November, 1861

❧ ❧

The *Jolly Tar*, an old and ramshackle inn, was perched high up on the slope of the large hill that overlooked the harbour at Holyhead. So steep was the incline on which the inn had been built that it seemed in imminent danger of joining the granite boulders and the other scree that dotted the coarse grass below and spilled down as far as the old harbour wall.

Pace, pace, turn. Pace, pace, turn. Each time as Bulloch came abreast of the bow window, he would stop and gaze anxiously out to sea, before turning again. But each time that he looked, he would see the same thing. Line after line of white crested waves, driven in from the Irish Sea by a severe north-westerly gale, racing across the outer harbour and smashing against the mole, sending spouts of grey water into the air and coating the dark stone with spume.

The wind howled and occasionally a particularly strong gust would send a cloud of smoke and sparks from the guttering fire into the room, while the rain lashed continuously against the ill-fitting panes of the leaded windows.

It was barely four in the afternoon, but already it was getting dark. And that meant another wasted day, because Bulloch knew that John Low was too experienced a seaman to attempt bringing the *Fingal* into harbour at all in this weather, let alone at this hour, with the light fading fast. And he was only too aware that each passing day increased the risk of their discovery by the same Yankee agents, who had up until now dogged their every movement and whom they had only thrown off with the greatest of difficulty to arrive in Holyhead, undetected.

The stakes were high, because next to the *Jolly Tar* was an old wooden barn, which contained crate after crate of rifles, some fifteen thousand in number, together with revolvers, swords, gunpowder, uniforms, medical supplies – and four cannons. All of these had been purchased over several months, with considerable difficulty and at great cost. They were covered in tarpaulin and lashed down with ropes both to keep them dry from the rain that dripped incessantly through the warped timbers of the barn as well as to protect them from prying eyes. Were the guns to be found, they would certainly be impounded by the British authorities until the end of the war, with potentially disastrous consequences for Lee's army in North Virginia.

✳   ✳

Bulloch had purchased the *Fingal*, a two-masted iron-clad steamer in September for seventeen thousand five hundred pounds. At eight hundred tons, she had been designed for the rough waters of the Irish Sea and was almost brand new. She was exactly what they needed to transport the guns to Savannah and the price had been reasonable. Except that he had no money. Bulloch's loan to Edward Anderson had left him with precious little even to live on, especially after purchasing a new suit of clothes. For his part, Anderson had spent every penny of the loan, even using the last four hundred pounds on two million percussion caps. Frequent letters to Stephen Mallory and to Judah Benjamin, the newly appointed Secretary of War, requesting, even begging, for more funds were met with prevarication and finally exasperated refusal, as their political masters sought to slice ever more finely their budget cake, made up as it was with devaluing dollars.

Mallory could not see why Bulloch had 'lent' twenty-five thousand pounds to the Army and had been openly hostile to the idea of financing the purchase of the *Fingal* to transport the weapons. Benjamin simply told Anderson that no money was available at that moment and that he would simply have to wait until Spence could raise more from European investors. So they went to see Prioleau together.

The dapper little man had greeted them warmly and had served coffee scented with chicory in small demi-tasse cups that looked ridiculous in Bulloch's large hands, together with *langue du chat*, which he found delicious. After the initial pleasantries had been dispensed with, they had informed Prioleau, somewhat disingenuously, that they were authorised by their respective departments to seek a loan of eighteen thousand pounds from Fraser, Trenholm as the 'Depository of Confederate Funds Abroad'.

Prioleau had hummed and hawed, but had finally consented and had produced a draft the next day, which he handed over against their signatures.

"The five hundred pounds is for living expenses," Bulloch explained to Edward Anderson, as he pushed the heavy bag of sovereigns into the inside pocket of his new dark grey worsted frock coat, which was at the same time both elegantly understated and fashionable. Anderson decided not to gripe about Bulloch's 'living expenses', given the generosity of his earlier loan to the Army, but he might have done had he known that two hundred and seventy pounds had gone straight to Isaac Kopa, the Jew who owned the gambling house on Castle Street, to meet some unfortunate recent losses and a further twenty-five pounds had been spent on the antique sapphire ring that now graced the middle finger of Marise's right hand.

"Woo, James, it is so beautiful," she had said, kissing him wetly. "Come to my room right now, so that I can say thank you properly." He had smiled at his own reflection in the mirror on the ceiling above her bed as he lay there naked, watching her head bob up and down over his groin, confident that he would soon be able to repay the odd pound or two that he had spent less than entirely directly for the benefit of the Confederate States of America. One big win, that was all, and meanwhile …

* *

The door of the snug banged open, the sudden draught flaring the embers of the fire, sending sparks flurrying into the room. Edward Anderson stalked in, shaking the rain from his hat, his clothes soaked and his boots making squelching noises as he crossed the uneven brick floor.

"Anything?" enquired Bulloch.

"No, thank God, there's not a soul around. I woke up the two Miguels – they'd gone to sleep, for God's sake, under a canvas sheet – and made them reload their revolvers with dry cartridges. Other than that – nothing – I guess we must have finally shaken them off."

Bulloch nodded. They had journeyed together from Liverpool to London by train and had then crossed from Euston to Paddington Station by hansom cab, forcing the cabbie to drive at speed down narrow streets, and make sudden turns in order to throw off any pursuers. However when they had boarded the train at Paddington, bound for Bristol, they were both frustrated and concerned to see an individual, who seemed vaguely familiar, come running down the platform. He flung open the door and jumped into the last compartment, even as the train started to pull out, the clouds of black smoke belching from its funnel and billowing across the glass roof of the station.

At Reading, both men had left their compartment and had walked down the platform, re-boarding the train at its far end. The occupant of this last compartment had watched their advance down the length of the train with some obvious consternation, before ducking his head back in through the window. As they entered, he snatched up a copy of the *Times* and held it in front of his face.

The only other occupant of this compartment, a vicar, had smiled and nodded but said nothing. The four men travelled in silence as far as Newbury where the vicar alighted, bidding them all 'good day'. As the train gathered speed, Bulloch reached across and took the newspaper out of the man's hands.

"Wh… wh… what do you want?" he had stammered in an accent that clearly identified him as an American.

"You, my friend," replied Bulloch, "we want you." He had grabbed the man's right arm, while Anderson had taken his left. The man struggled furiously but Bulloch was able to hold onto him with one large hand, while he opened the compartment door with the other. By this time the train was travelling at some speed, racing along an embankment that rose from the lush green meadows on each side.

"Be sure to give my best regards to President Lincoln," Bulloch said, laughing, as they propelled the hapless man out through the open door. They saw him fly through the air, his legs and arms cartwheeling furiously, until he hit and bounced off the gravel that formed the side of the embankment, then rolled several times before finally coming to a rest on his back in the meadow grass below.

"Do you think he's dead?" asked Anderson.

"Do you care?"

"Not really. He wouldn't be the first I've killed."

"Me neither."

"Well then, let's drink to him anyway." Anderson unscrewed the top of a silver flask and they both drank deeply from the strong spiced rum it contained.

*　*

"He won't come today then?" Anderson asked.

"No, not today. He's probably well out to sea, giving a wide berth to the coast in this wind, lying to. Assuming he left Greenock on Thursday, he would have been here yesterday, if it weren't for this storm, God dammit! Still, at least I doubt anyone's followed the *Fingal*. That's one good thing about the weather."

They dined alone in the snug, too worried to converse much and then retired early.

At 6 a.m. Bulloch awoke with a start as the door to his room was flung open, banging against the wall behind. A young man wearing oilskins stood dripping in the doorway.

"John, is that you? What in God's name is going on?" Bulloch said, sitting up in bed.

"We've got trouble, James. We sank a ship. By accident. The wind dropped in the night to ten knots, still from the Nor'west and I decided to risk entering the harbour at dawn. But the damned fog came up and we couldn't see a thing. We're under steam and blowing the whistle to warn other shipping, but there's this damn Austrian coaler, called the *Siccardi* or something – Captain probably drunk – and we hit her amidships and she goes right down. Just like a rock James – you should have seen it – it was the damndest thing. Anyway, we've picked up the crew, no-one's dead – but the harbourmaster's been woken and wants to inspect the damage."

"Blast and damn. And the *Fingal*, how is she?"

"A buckled plate or two, really nothing."

Bulloch sat up in bed and rubbed his hand over his unshaven chin. 'Why oh why did everything have to be so damn difficult' he wondered. 'Still, no going back now.' "Alright then, this is what we'll do," he said to John Low as he swung his legs out of the bed.

"Get the crates onto the lighter and get the loading started. I'll go to the Harbourmaster's office, see if I can head him off and buy us time. I want to be loaded and away from here by noon – at the latest. Promise the dockers double if they load us in time."

He dressed hurriedly and walked swiftly to the Harbourmaster's office that occupied one of a row of small cottages, which abutted the quayside. He went through a doorway so low that he had to stoop, and entered a room full of arguing men. The Harbourmaster, wearing a blue uniform and naval cap, had his hands in the air and was shouting "Gentlemen, gentlemen, if you please ..." The Captain of the *Siccardi* and two of his officers wrapped in blankets, but still obviously wet and cold, were shouting in German, and gesticulating wildly, but not making themselves understood to the Harbourmaster, who was becoming increasingly annoyed at their noisy foreign behaviour.

Bulloch's arrival, which seemed to fill the low-ceilinged room to capacity, caused the argument to subside. In the silence they all looked at him expectantly. He introduced himself to the Harbourmaster and then turned to the Austrians and said in fluent German:

"*Entschuldigen sie mir, aber veilleich Ich kan sie hilfen.*" (Excuse me, but perhaps I can help you). "My name is Bulloch" he continued in German, "and I am the owner of the *Fingal*, the ship which collided with yours this morning."

The Austrians were so relieved to be understood that they greeted Bulloch warmly, in spite of his admission of ownership of the vessel, which had, in their words, loomed silently and swiftly out of the fog, giving no warning, before neatly slicing their ship in two and sending it and its highly valuable cargo to the bottom. It was a miracle that no one had been killed – at this they all crossed themselves – but there were many injuries and all this would add to their claim for compensation.

Bulloch listened silently frowning and nodding. He then stood up and with a broad and, he hoped, engaging smile, invited all present to breakfast at the *Jolly Tar*, at his expense. The Harbourmaster was delighted.

They breakfasted on chops, sausages, black pudding and fried potatoes, accompanied by strong coffee and weak ale and, in the case of Captain Apponyi, several hot rum toddies. Bulloch glanced surreptitiously at his watch. Nine-thirty already. Excellent. They continued their discussions of liability and compensation after breakfast, in the snug. Bulloch agreed reluctantly, after a prolonged negotiation in German, to compensate the Austrians in full. This called for more drinks.

It was now ten-thirty, and the Harbourmaster was becoming increasingly insistent on going out to the *Fingal* to inspect the damage first hand, while the Austrians had retired happily to the rooms they had taken, with much shaking of hands and bowing. They would have been considerably less happy had they known that Bulloch had neither the wherewithal to compensate them, nor any intention whatsoever of so doing.

The dingy, weighed down as it was with the Harbourmaster and Bulloch in the stern, made slow progress, the lone oarsman sweating as he heaved against the tide, a steady stream of profanities passing from his lips. As their boat neared the *Fingal*, which was anchored in the outer harbour, they could see the feverish activity of the crew who swarmed over the ship, winching up case, after case from the bobbing lighter, and stowing them in the hold.

"You are still taking on cargo, sir?" asked the Harbourmaster.

"Well, yes" replied Bulloch. "We hope to leave as soon as possible, now that everything is agreed."

"Oh dear me no, sir! I'm afraid that won't be at all possible. You see, all sinkings must be investigated thoroughly and reported to the insurers and the legal documents drawn up and signed and surety provided for the compensation and so forth. Could take weeks."

"But we can't wait weeks," Bulloch blurted out, unable to disguise his concern.

"Why ever not? Is your cargo perishable? And what exactly is your cargo, if I may be so bold as to enquire?" The Harbourmaster surveyed the mound of cases and barrels that still covered the deck with mounting suspicion.

Bulloch thought quickly. "It's er, it's medical supplies. Bound for Montevideo where they have a bad outbreak of Yellow Jack and are in sore need of assistance. They cannot wait. Thousands will die."

"And what exactly is that, sir?" The Harbourmaster pointed, frowning, to where a large object, wrapped in canvas, secured with rope, was being winched into the air from the deck of the still heavily laden lighter. Though masked, its shape was both sinister and obvious.

"It's a cannon. We have to travel some dangerous waters and must be able to defend ourselves. The ship itself is not otherwise armed – as you can see. We will mount the cannon once at sea."

The Harbourmaster, who seemed satisfied by this response, grunted noisily as he heaved his bulk out of the small boat and up the slippery steps to the deck. The crew watched fearfully as each wave that rocked the ship threatened to propel him into the still rough sea. At last, red in the face and panting he planted his feet on the deck and drew a deep breath. Lieutenant John Low saluted him and then whisked him away on an inspection of the ship. Bulloch whispered, as he left, "slowly John – stretch it out as long as you can."

By the time the inspection had finished it was after mid-day. The cargo had all been loaded, but was by no means stowed away or even secured.

The Harbourmaster emerged from the main cabin smoking a cigar, accompanied by the Lieutenant. "You have all been most helpful, I will say that." He nodded at Bulloch. "And now, may I suggest that you up-anchor, enter the inner harbour and tie-up against the quay. I will complete the paperwork and we will try to get you under way as soon as possible – inside a week if we can. What do you say?"

"Well, if we have no choice, then I suppose that is what we must do," Bulloch replied, catching the looks of alarm from the Lieutenant and from Edward Anderson, who had up till then been directing the loading of the cargo. "But may I suggest that your man rows the dingy back to shore and that you stay on the *Fingal* and pilot us into the harbour?"

"My pleasure indeed," said the Harbourmaster, who had not been looking forward to a return journey down the slippery and narrow steps that hung from the *Fingal*'s side.

The *Fingal*'s boilers were already fired-up and soon the anchor chains were clanking around the steam-driven capstans and down into the chain lockers.

Bulloch watched as the dingy rounded the mole, entered the inner harbour and vanished out of sight. He took Edward Anderson by the arm. "Like in the railway carriage, Edward," he whispered out of the corner of his mouth.

Anderson smiled. "Very well James, but I don't want us to make a habit of this."

69

The Harbourmaster was standing next to the Lieutenant, who had the wheel. The two men approached quietly from behind, grabbed an arm each and propelled him at a run, across the deck and through an opening in the rail where he plummeted straight into the sea with a high pitched scream. He hit with a splash and vanished, but soon surfaced spluttering, bobbing in the waves, his hat and cigar gone.

Bulloch leaned over the side. "A little swim, I am afraid sir, but I am told it is good for the constitution."

He turned, laughing, to the Lieutenant, who was also laughing, along with the rest of the crew, who lined the rails. "Take her out Mr Low, if you please, full speed ahead."

No sooner had they rounded the heads and were making for the open sea at full speed, than Lieutenant Low knocked on the door of Bulloch's cabin.

"Excuse me Captain, a word if you please." Bulloch looked up from the log which covered the three days since the *Fingal* left Greenock. He nodded.

The Lieutenant sat. He was a young man, only in his mid-twenties, but a veteran seaman nonetheless. He was Scottish by birth but had served as a midshipman in the Union Navy and passed as a Lieutenant before he was twenty. When the war had broken out, he left Annapolis, where he had been stationed and travelled south to Norfolk, to enlist in the Confederate Navy and fight for his adopted Country. Mallory had liked him and had sent him to England to help Bulloch, but he was now deeply concerned that his first command had nearly ended in disaster. He sat, unshaven and looking despondent.

Bulloch saw the anxiety on the young man's face and smiled. "Don't worry John, you have done well. I am particularly glad that you managed to leave Greenock and avoid detection. My worry was that you would arrive with the whole British fleet in tow!"

"We left at the dead of night, sir and one of the dock-side snoopers will have woken the next day with a sore head, if you know what I mean!"

"Good – very good. And don't worry about that Austrian coaler. That was not your fault and no harm has been done – to us anyway. And now Mr Low, set a course for the Azores, if you please."

"Just one thing more, Captain. We left Holyhead so suddenly

that we had no opportunity to take on water or victuals, beyond what we had already. By my count, we have two barrels of water, fifty pounds of flour and twenty pounds of salted pork to last fifty men for seven or even eight days. We are going to be mighty hungry and thirsty by the time we arrive in Terceira, sir."

"Then hungry and thirsty we will be, Mr Low, for I am not going to risk an encounter with another ship just to take on provisions. Rig the canvas awnings and pray for rain!"

Seven days later, after a crossing of fair winds and calm seas with no rain, the lookout perched in the cross-trees atop the mizzen mast called out in a voice that croaked for lack of moisture "land ahoy!" The crew ran to the side and saw, in the distance, a small break in the horizon. They cheered, throwing their caps in the air.

"Thank God for that," Bulloch rasped through cracked lips. "I was getting ready to drink my own piss I was so thirsty," he said to Edward Anderson.

The *Fingal* took on as much in the way of water and supplies as they could in the limited time available, including live chickens, which were stored in cages on the deck. Early the next day they steamed out of the little harbour of Porto Praya and turned due west.

The next eight days they encountered strong head winds, which delayed their passage to Bermuda. The *Fingal* had insufficient coal to remain under steam for the whole crossing and thus was at the mercy of the winds, which required them to tack and tack again. The sea had become rougher as well and a nasty swell kept Edward Anderson to his cabin. Bulloch, all sympathy, offered him hot tea and lemon, a sound drink for sea-sickness in his experience, but Anderson merely groaned and turned his face to the cabin wall.

On the last day, the wind died and the seas became calmer. Bulloch summoned the crew onto the deck and addressed them: "We will shortly be entering St George's harbour on the island of Bermuda, which as you all know, is British territory. We have been and will continue to fly the British flag and our papers identify us as an English ship, out of Liverpool, with medical supplies for Montevideo. It is essential that you maintain this story as you go about St George's for the purpose of re-supplying the ship. However, in order to minimise the risk of our true purpose being discovered, there will be no shore leave on Bermuda and I will not

71

be issuing any pay until we arrive in Savannah."

There was considerable muttering among the crew at this news, for the bars and brothels of St George's were rightfully famous. Bulloch was adamant, however, not only to preserve the secrecy of their voyage, but also because he had absolutely no money to pay the crew with, the last of his depleted funds being earmarked for new supplies and especially for coal.

As the *Fingal* steamed into St George's harbour, the Union Jack fluttering from her masthead, the sun broke through the clouds and warmed the men who stood muttering in disconsolate groups around her deck.

They dropped anchor and lowered the launch. Bulloch, Anderson and Low were rowed across by six sailors under the command of a midshipman, all of whom seemed determined to extract a petty revenge by flicking drops of seawater from the ends of their oars at the officers.

They arrived at the dock and Lieutenant Low went to report to the Harbourmaster and the customs officials, while Bulloch went to negotiate the purchase of coal and Edward Anderson swayed unsteadily into a bar, looking for the first meal in a week that he would actually be able to keep down. Around one hour later, Bulloch and the Lieutenant joined him at the bar, both commenting on how the now empty platter of beef steak had brought back the colour to his sunken and sallow cheeks.

As they spoke, a man seated a nearby table, stood and walked across to them. He raised his hat politely and asked if he might join them. He introduced himself as Franklin Gregg, a merchant from San Francisco.

"So nice to see some fellow Americans," he intoned nasally, stroking the tips of his upswept moustache, "the English are all right – in small doses – but they're as tight as a crabs ass – you never get nothing out of 'em." He smiled broadly showing one gold tooth. "Now what are all you Southern boys doing with that British ship over there, if you don't mind me asking?"

Bulloch looked carefully at their new companion, immediately sensing that there was something not quite right about him.

"Mr Anderson and I are taking passage to Montevideo," he replied. "We are doctors, accompanying the medical supplies that we carry. They have an epidemic down there that has been raging for months now and we are going to see what we can do to help

72

them. Mr Low is the first Lieutenant of the *Fingal.*"

"Why, how nice" continued Franklyn Gregg, "for you all to meet up so far from home and to travel all together in this way. You must have so much to talk about, what with the war and all that. But I really mustn't take up any more of your time. Just to point out though, as a little warning, that right over the horizon is a fifty-gun Union steam frigate. She's waiting for the *Nashville* – that's that paddle-wheel steamer over yonder." He pointed off into the harbour to where a low grey ship with heavily raked funnels rode at anchor. "The *Nashville*'s a blockade runner, a good one too, but she don't dare come out of harbour, because if she does, she'll be sunk and sooner than you can say it." He looked steadily at the three men standing facing him at the bar. "And if you're not what you say you are, why sure then, you'll get sunk too. Good day to you, Gentlemen." He lifted his hat and walked out of the bar.

"God damn!" exclaimed Edward Anderson, throwing his straw hat onto the ground, "he's a damned Union agent, he must be – they're like flies on shit those people – and he suspects something."

"Whether he is or he isn't," said Bulloch, "we've got two things to worry about; the British and their damned neutrality seizing the *Fingal*, and that Union ship – if she exists – being warned of our presence in Bermuda. Either way, we must expedite our departure. I will go and see what I can do to hurry up the coaling and we'll meet back on board later."

It was a very despondent Bulloch who climbed the steps of the *Fingal* in the late afternoon, as the sun was sinking low over the buildings of St George's. "That bastard Gregg," he reported to Edward Anderson, "he's only gone and spread the story that we're a slaver – and the darkies have refused to coal us. We're stuck until we can persuade them otherwise. We dare not attempt to run the blockade with sail alone."

"What are we to do?"

"For the moment, Edward, I do not know. Maybe in the morning. Right now I have some serious drinking to do. Mr Low, break out the rum, double rations to the crew. And you Gentlemen, I would be pleased if you would join me in this bottle of Glenlivet, which I have been keeping for just such a moment, when its life-saving properties can fully be appreciated."

The next morning dawned clear and bright. Bulloch's head was pounding and he felt sick, but during the night, as so often happened, an idea had come to him. They would send the ship's tender to the coaling depot, bring two or three of the Negro workers to the *Fingal*, show them around, give them a good meal and send them back, happy and convinced that she was not a slaver.

The tender left, but returned half an hour later with no Negroes. "They won't board" said the Midshipman. "They's sure convinced as to how we're a slaver and that they're going to be chained up below decks and taken off to work on a plantation. No go, I'm afraid, Sir."

Bulloch shook his head. He felt his temper rising. "Bosun!" he yelled, "arm the men, we're going to get some coal." The cutter and the launch put out together packed with as many men as they could carry. Bulloch sat in the stern of the cutter, looking grim, his pair of English Adams revolvers, a gift from Edward Anderson, stuck in his belt. Down the length of the boats, between the rowers, were loaded rifles, covered with canvas.

As the boat drew up to the coaling depot. Bulloch leapt out, followed by his men, rifles at the ready. He drew his revolvers and cocked them.

"Hey, you, boy," he called to the first Negro he saw, who was humping a sack of coal on his back, "where's the boss-man?"

"He be up in de office, sah," muttered the negro, sulkily.

Bulloch ran up the stairs to the office and kicked open the door, followed closely by Edward Anderson.

A very fat balding man sat behind the desk, a napkin tucked around his neck. He had frozen, a chicken leg half way to his mouth and his jaw now hung open, revealing the semi-masticated fowl within his pink maw.

"What ... who ... what do you want?" he spluttered, chicken slivers flying from his wet lips.

"I want my coal, Goddammit!" growled Bulloch.

"Well you can't have it," said the fat man, trying to establish his authority by pushing himself upright in his chair. "We don't hold truck with slavers here – no sir, we do not." He shook his head for emphasis, his greasy chins wobbling in unison.

Bulloch advanced on the desk, an evil gleam in his eye. "Listen here my fat friend and listen good. We're not slavers and that's a fact. You've been listening to some damn lies put around by our business competitors to ruin us, but that just won't do! No, sir!

The way I see it, you have two choices. You tell your darkies that there's been some mistake and you load us up with coal, right now and you take payment in full, in gold." He dropped a small, but heavy leather bag onto the desk, which clinked appealingly. "Or," and he cocked one of the heavy Adams revolvers, pressing its barrel against the fat man's forehead, "I blow your brains out all over your desk and the darkies still load the coal, but at gun point. What do you want to do?"

The fat man licked his lips, slowly extended a hand with surprisingly long slender fingers and picked up the bag of coins, which he weighed reflectively in his palm. He raised the other hand and gently pushed the barrel of the revolver away from his head. "A pleasure to do business with you Sir," he smiled broadly "and I hope that there will be other occasions upon which we may extend our mutually profitable relationship."

With a huge grunt the fat man pushed himself to his feet and waddled onto the veranda of his office. He shouted to the foreman below, a huge Negro, who sat motionless in the shade of a tree: "Jefferson, these men no slavers. You go fill ship, quick as ever."

"Yassir, boss." The foreman turned and shouted to the other blacks in Swahili. They cheered and immediately sprung to work. "I promise dem rum if dey quick," he said to Bulloch, who nodded and said to him: "you can give me some sacks of anthracite as well as the usual sea coal."

"Why boss, they some reason why you doan wanna make smoke from yo chimney?" He grinned showing a long line of perfect white teeth.

"Just get me the coal," Bulloch snapped, "and keep your damned questions to yourself."

The following day Bulloch met with Captain Pegram of the *Nashville*. They went to considerable lengths to avoid being seen together, knowing that this would increase the level of suspicion directed at them both. In the end, both Captains met in a secluded bay, one arriving by water and the other by land, greeting each other with a warm handshake.

Captain Pegram confirmed that the Yankee agent Gregg's threat of a Union frigate was real and explained that she had chased the *Nashville* right into British waters off Bermuda, before breaking off the pursuit for fear of the guns of the harbour forts. The *Nashville* was built and registered in England and financed by

Manchester industrialists, keen to take advantage of the high prices that their goods would command in Southern ports. After three successful runs of the blockade, the ship-owners broke even on their initial outlay and everything after that was pure profit. The *Nashville*, Captain Pegram had said, proudly tapping his chest, has made eight successful runs to date and she's homeward bound to Liverpool with cotton and tobacco".

They discussed their strategies for leaving Bermuda and avoiding the Union frigate. In the end they agreed to wait a day or two, to see if one of the storms, so prevalent at this time of the year, would blow up out of the Atlantic. Should this happen, they would both leave together, after dark, one turning South and the other North, burning anthracite for reduced smoke and hope that one, if not both, would thereby avoid capture or destruction.

The *Nashville*, being purpose built as a blockade runner was the faster ship, but her two short masts meant that sail was of little real use except in an emergency. And being designed for evasive manoeuvres in estuaries and shallows, she drew less water and was consequently far less stable in high seas.

Bulloch asked Captain Pegram: "and have you put into Savannah of late? Do you know anything of the strength or disposition of the blockading fleet?"

"I fear not, for we find Charleston an easier port for our activities. However..." he paused reflectively, "I have a pilot on board, a man named Makin, who knows Savannah well and has been there recently. I can let you have him, if you wish, for he is merely ballast on our homeward journey. Leave him here in Bermuda on your return."

"Why that is uncommon civil of you, Captain," exclaimed Bulloch, "I had been intending to take the *Fingal* in myself, but a pilot who knows Savannah is welcome indeed – the harbour approaches are not the most simple at the best of times and with enemy ships guarding the channels through the reef, these are anything but the best of times."

They parted, Bulloch watching enviously as the *Nashville*'s tender pulled out of the bay, Captain Pegram sitting in the stern, with his cap raised in salute. Bulloch mounted the bony grey mare he had hired for the day and set off wearily up the rocky shoreline, the wooden saddle tree biting into his sore buttocks through its thin covering of worn leather.

The next three days they waited. Bulloch remained in his cabin, in a state of considerable anxiety, concerned that Gregg, the Union agent, might be able to convince the British authorities to move against the *Fingal*. Shore leave remained cancelled and the crew and officers became increasingly irritable with their enforced idleness and their overcrowded quarters, while only a few hundred yards away the docks swarmed with activity and the narrow streets of the harbour beckoned enticingly with their promise of every type of lascivious pleasure.

When they woke on the morning of the fourth day, 6th November, the weather situation had clearly changed. The glass had been dropping throughout the night and by dawn the temperature had fallen sharply as the direction of the wind had shifted to the North. A stiff breeze was blowing across the harbour mouth and heavy clouds scudded through the sombre sky. As the day progressed the weather worsened. White tops were clearly visible on the waves outside the harbour and, inside, the wind was whipping spray into the faces of the sailors who lined the decks of the ships, looking apprehensively out to sea.

As night fell, a long boat set out from the *Fingal*. Watchers on the *Nashville* could see her riding up and down on the swell, making scant progress against the wind and the running tide. At last she pulled up along side and a very wet midshipman ran up the ship's steps. "Captain Bulloch's compliments, sir, but the *Fingal's* boilers are just fired and he is looking to head out to sea as soon after eight bells as possible."

Captain Pegram nodded. "Very good, young man. We are making steam already and will be close behind the *Fingal* as she leaves. And, Midshipman."

"Sir?"

"My compliments to Captain Bulloch and tell him that I wish him and the *Fingal* the very best of luck."

Once clear of the harbour the *Fingal* took the full force of the gale, heeling over, her masts dipping towards the sea, before turning due south and running before the wind, the smoke from her funnel streaming ahead of her. She signalled to the *Nashville* and then was alone on the storm-tossed sea. A little later Bulloch thought he heard the sound of gunfire far off to the North, but could not swear to it.

The next day dawned fine, the gale having blown itself out

over night. The *Fingal* dowsed her boilers and unfurled her sails, turning due west for Savannah, the Union Jack flapping at her masthead.

The two, four and a half inch Blakeley rifled cannons were winched up from the hold and screwed to their deck mountings. The smaller guns likewise. The crew were kept busy filling shells and loading cartridges with powder. During the course of the afternoon barrels were thrown over the side and the Blakeley guns were fired for the first time. After several misses the barrels were finally struck and disintegrated into a shower of splinters. The crew cheered but Anderson looked glum.

"I surely hope we don't have to fight our way into Savannah," he grumbled. "This lot couldn't hit a barn door with a shot gun."

That night they celebrated Edward Anderson's birthday with two chickens from the coop on the deck and a bottle of wine. The conversation around the table in Bulloch's cramped cabin was muted by tension, and they retired shortly after dinner had been cleared.

Unable to sleep, Bulloch put on his coat and went on deck. He approached Lieutenant Low, who was quietly chatting to the Boson, who had the wheel.

"How now John?"

"Hello, sir. Couldn't sleep?"

"No. A little apprehensive about tomorrow, perhaps."

"I'm sure we'll be fine, sir. Have you agreed our approach with the Pilot?"

"I have. We both agree that the Warsaw inlet is the best. One has to know it well and there's precious little room for error or we'll be on the reef. But the blockade ships won't follow us in there. After a while, we'll be under the guns of Fort Pulaski and then we'll be safe."

"And the Pilot knows it well enough?"

"He says he can even do it at night. I doubt that! But we will be in his hands tomorrow and I hope to God that he's as capable as he thinks he is."

"Amen to that."

Bulloch went back to his cabin and slept fitfully. He was woken before dawn with coffee and dressed carefully in his uniform, which was severely creased and crumpled from the length of time it had been folded and packed in a trunk. Edward Anderson and John Low were already on deck, as he emerged from the companionway. Also in uniform for the first time in months, they saluted as Bulloch approached.

"Good morning, Gentlemen. Have you seen Makin?"

Lieutenant Low turned to the Gunner's Mate, who was polishing one of the Blakeley's and said, "Merriweather, go and rouse the Pilot and tell him that the Captain requests his presence on deck, right away, if you please."

"Aye, aye, sir." Minutes passed and finally Merriweather returned, staggering, his arm around the Pilot, who was clearly too drunk to walk unsupported.

"My God, the man's drunk," said Bulloch, grabbing the Pilot and shaking him. "You bastard, you worthless piece of dog shit, how could you do this?"

"Ah… ah… ahm alri'… ah can pilot thish ship, shober o' drunk. S'not a problem."

"Bosun," yelled Bulloch. "Get buckets of water and douse this man and get the cook to prepare a gallon of strong coffee and see that he drinks it – all of it. When I get him ashore…."

Dawn broke and the yellow sun rose majestically out of an empty sea. The lookouts, posted at the mastheads, anxiously scanned the horizon for any sign of the blockading squadron.

From the mizzen tops, a cry. "Ship ahoy to starboard, looks like a frigate, sir." Bulloch snatched up a telescope and put it to his eye. It was a frigate, a fifty gun, wooden-hulled sailing ship, lying completely becalmed in the still air, for the breeze had dropped as the sun rose. She carried every sail available, including her royals, but each one hung limp and lifeless. That she had seen the *Fingal* was clear when her gun ports banged open and her starboard guns were run out, but this was a mere display of bravado as she could not bring them to bear on the distant *Fingal*. Instead, she ran signal flags up her mast to alert the other members of the blockading squadron to the presence of an intruder, but these too were left flaccid by the total absence of any current in the air. Finally she fired a signal rocket in the direction of the *Fingal*, which was already past her, having engaged her propellers, and was now making for the smudge of land on the horizon.

Soon the *Fingal* was making eleven knots, her top speed. Her bows cut through the deep blue water like a blade, leaving in her wake a long white line of churned water to mark her passage. In the still air, the smoke from her funnel, even reduced as it was by the use of anthracite, hung like an accusing finger pointing at the ship as she ran for the coast and the safety of the reef.

The Master was swinging the lead and calling the depth, "...seven fathoms, six fathoms, five fathoms, four fathoms..." "Stop engines," yelled Bulloch. "Three fathoms, two and a half fathoms..." The *Fingal* had almost ceased to make any headway, when a grinding noise and a juddering brought her up abruptly. Members of the crew, who were not holding on, were suddenly pitched to the deck.

"Engines, full astern," Bulloch ordered and, there was another scraping noise and then she was free. "I think," said Bulloch, wetting his dry lips, "I think that was the outer edge of the Warsaw reef. Now, how is that damned Pilot?"

"If you please, sir, he's sobered up a lot," an able seaman replied.

The Pilot was sitting on a canvas chair next to the wheel. He looked terrible and his hands shook as if with St. Vitus' Dance, but he was clearly more sober.

"I'm sorry Captain," he mumbled, not looking Bulloch in the eye. "I'm really very sorry. But I'm better now and I can get you in. We struck the western edge of the reef. The channels over yonder" – he gestured with his hand – "about half a mile. It's only twenty yards wide. When we're in, we can do no more than one or two knots at the most if we're to make the turns. We'll be at the mercy of any ships that are waiting for us on the far side but, if they haven't seen us yet..." he shrugged.

Bulloch grabbed the Pilot by his dirty shirt collar. "I ought to kill you now, you wretch. If you put us on the reef, so help me, you will die and it will not be from drowning." He released the pilot. "Now do your best, and may God have mercy on you if you fail, for I will not."

The shaken Pilot started giving instructions to the helmsman and the *Fingal* gently eased her way into the channel. After two turns, a thick bank of fog that they had seen rolling across the sea like an enormous down quilt, enveloped the *Fingal*, cutting off all view of the distant shore.

"Can you find the channel in this?" asked Bulloch.

"It makes no difference," replied the Pilot. "The channel is not marked anyway and we are too far out for any landmarks to be accurate guides. That is why I said I could do it at night."

"Then this fog might be the saving of us yet."

The next thirty minutes were some of the most agonising in Bulloch's life. The calling of the lead, the Pilot's hoarse instructions to the helmsman, the hiss of the water beneath the hull, the thrumming of the engines below their feet – all these sounds were clear as a bell to Bulloch, as he stood right in the bow, his hands on the rail, leaning forward, his eyes attempting to pierce the enveloping fog. Behind stood the crew, the men of all watches on deck, motionless.

After what seemed an eternity, a seaman coughed behind Bulloch.

"Begging your pardon, sir."

"What is it?"

"The Pilot says we're through the channel, sir."

A loud cheer went up from the crew.

A voice boomed from off the port side: "What ship goes there? Identify yourself, or be fired upon."

"Silence," hissed Bulloch, "silence." To the Bosun: "all engines, stop."

All the noises ceased and an eerie silence enveloped the *Fingal*. The Pilot had passed out after his exertions, and began to snore. A seaman gagged him with his own handkerchief.

The voice called again: "what ship is that? Identify yourself." Suddenly one of the cockerels in the coops by the base of the funnel, convinced that dawn was making a re-appearance broke into a strident "cock-a-doodle-do!"

"Jesus wept," muttered Edward Anderson who was standing just beside the coop. He plucked the offending cockerel out and wrung its neck, which broke with a snap. Hardly had the limp and lifeless bird hit the deck before several other cockerels, possibly as a lament to their dead comrade, burst forth with cries of "cock-a-doodle-dooooo!"

"Full speed ahead!" yelled Bulloch to the Bosun. "Get us out of here. Man the guns, all men to their stations!"

The engines slowly rose to a crescendo as the *Fingal* surged forward in the water. Off in the fog a gun fired, the flash visible through the gloom, then another and another, but none of the shells came anywhere close to the *Fingal*.

"My God, James, but I envy the Pilot," said Edward Anderson

through gritted teeth. "Drunk and asleep, that's what I would like to be."

At that moment the *Fingal* burst from the fog. About half a mile away on the starboard beam lay a heavy Yankee steam frigate, a forty gunner, at anchor. Fort Pulaski, which guarded the entrance to the harbour, was four miles beyond her.

"No choice," Bulloch growled. "Steady as she goes. Take us around the frigate, helmsman, outside cannon range and then head straight for the fort.

Luckily the *Fingal*'s emergence from the fog bank had taken the heavy frigate completely by surprise. The deck was a flurry of activity as the engines were fired, the capstans began to pull up the anchors and the guns were loaded and run out.

Steaming at eleven knots however, the *Fingal* had already passed the stern of the frigate, while her anchors were still not clear of the water and thus her broadside guns could not be brought to bear. The rifled cannon on her afterdeck, though, swung onto the *Fingal* and fired, a jet of flame leaping from the end of the barrel. The shot screamed harmlessly overhead. The second shot was closer however, clattering through the rigging and sending a shower of broken spars on the deck below. One sailor was felled, his skull crushed by a falling block, but there were no other casualties and the third shot fell short.

The *Fingal* raced on towards the fort, which sat, squat and square, its many guns jutting out like bristles in a beard. One gun fired, its ball bouncing harmlessly on the water towards the *Fingal*, before sinking.

"My God, the flag," shouted Bulloch, "raise our flag."

The 'Stars and Bars' broke joyously from the masthead and flapped tautly in the breeze. A cheer broke out from the fort as they passed under its guns. Bulloch drew himself up to attention on the deck and saluted the fort, the exhilaration of victory rising in his chest.

The *Fingal* entered the north channel of the Savannah River and after four miles came into the harbour itself, its quays now lined with the people of Savannah, all cheering, and moored abreast of the city, at the foot of Whittaker Street.

V

Savannah and Richmond – November, December, 1861

❧ ❧

The party ran on through the day and into the night. They had been carried on the shoulders of the cheering townspeople to the Mayor's residence, who greeted them in his silk dressing gown, a lit cigar already jutting from his beaming face. The Mayor hugged his predecessor and gallantly referred to him as "Mayor Anderson" in the impromptu speech of welcome, which he delivered from the marble steps of his colonial-era mansion.

The people of Savannah, seeing the metal cladding of the *Fingal* and the deck-mounted cannons, believed her to be an armoured war-ship sent to deliver them from the imposition of the Yankee blockade. Their joy was only somewhat muted by the truth, especially when the contents of her cargo became generally known.

A long line of swaying army commissariat wagons carried away the guns and other supplies to the City Arsenal and within hours the *Fingal*, until recently the scene of so much fevered activity, was deserted other than by the solitary figure of a lone watchman.

The jubilant crowd, which grew as the morning progressed, surged, through the streets, waving flags and singing *Dixie's Land* and other patriotic songs. Bulloch and Anderson were soon separated, Bulloch being carried into a saloon by a crowd, which included many of the *Fingal*'s crew. The grinning barman lined up shot glasses of whiskey down the length of the bar and Bulloch did his best to consume them to the rhythmic clapping of his crew.

After half a dozen shots, he held up his hands. "Enough for me boys – see what you can do!" The sailors crowded around the bar, which was soon awash with spilt whiskey, elbowing each other and jostling to get at the once-in-a-lifetime opportunity of endless free drinks.

They went from saloon to saloon, from bar to bar and hotel to hotel, each of which competed with the last in bestowing the fullest measure of their civic gratitude and pride on their sailors, who had run the blockade and delivered all those guns into the eager, but empty, hands of their brave young soldiers.

So it was, that in the late afternoon, there entered into the much drink-befuddled brain of Captain James Dunwoody Bulloch an errant thought regarding his wife and children, whose entire existence he had temporarily forgotten in the celebrations that followed their arrival. He was at that particular moment, nuzzling the soft, deep and highly perfumed cleavage of a bar girl, named Clara, at the Southern Belle Saloon & Gambling Parlour on East Broad Street. The thought of Harriet and the Girls brought a severe pang of guilt and sobered him for long enough to extricate himself from the silken depths of Clara's bosom, stagger to his feet and, with a mumbled apology, lurch out through the swinging doors into the nearly deserted streets.

It was starting to get dark and a brisk wind had come up from the river, blowing the litter of the day's celebrations – papers, torn buntings, discarded hats, cigar buts, the odd shoe – in cascades down the gutters. Bulloch suddenly felt very tired as the adrenaline of the past few days and weeks drained from his system. He was also aware that he had not eaten since the previous night and the day's consumption of whiskey on an empty stomach was beginning to make him nauseous.

He swayed as he walked, placing one foot with great care in front of the other, pointing himself in what he believed to be the direction of home. Twice he stopped to be sick, throwing up almost neat whiskey, which burnt his nose and the back of his throat, fouling his shoes and the ends of his uniform trousers. Finally, unshaven, stinking, with bleary and watering eyes he arrived at his own house in Charlton Street, climbed the steps to the front door, holding on tightly to the wrought-iron balustrade and beat upon it with a clenched fist, while supporting himself on the lintel with an outstretched arm.

The noise of his banging reverberated around the house and echoed in the empty hall. Silence returned. His brow creased in perplexity and again he hammered on the door. Finally, from deep within the house, he heard a voice calling. It was Martha, one of the house servants, an elderly Negress with almost white hair, who was coming up the stairs from the ground floor, muttering and cursing under her breath, which was coming in short pants from the exertion. "I's a comin', I's a comin', doan go knockin' down de door." Bulloch heard the sound of bolts being drawn and finally the door opened a crack. "Who dat? Wat you wan' mistah? They's no-one heah. Not now!"

"It's me, Martha. Don't you recognise me?"

The eye peered at Bulloch. "Lord's sake! It's de massa!" She stepped back, flinging wide the door. Bulloch unbalanced, almost fell into his own house. He managed to get to an armchair in the hall and sank into it gratefully, with a deep sigh.

"I'm home, Martha and it's good to see you." He looked around, perplexed, seeing through the open door the dustsheets that covered the furniture in the parlour. "Martha", he said slowly, his mind numb, "where is Mistress Harriet and where are the children?"

Martha stepped back, both her hands going to her mouth.

"You doan know, do you? Mah po' lamb, you doan' know!"

"What, Martha, what don't I know?" Through the alcohol, Bulloch sensed that something was very wrong and felt fear grip his stomach.

"Why Massa ... I doan' like to say ... it's not rightly my place ... de Mistress ... she wrote you a letter an' all ..."

Bulloch, becoming increasingly anxious, pulled himself to his feet with an effort and placed a hand on her shoulder. "Martha, just tell me what has happened."

Martha looked at her feet, twisting her fingers together as she spoke. "It was, I guess, mebbe... ooh... mebbe tree, fo' weeks ago, dat de Mistress come in to de servants quarters. She kiss me an hug me an say 'Martha, I gotta go 'way.' Then she frees us all ... God bless her ... and gets into a pony trap with dis soldjah. Marcel, he put de tings in her trunk, holdall, hat boxes – everyting in de back of de trap and dey jest go off down de street, turn de corner and I never sees her no mo'. Later dat same day, her sistah, she come from Atlanta, she spend a lot of time wid de Girls – and Lord, dey is cryin' and little Flora, she jest weepin' her tiny heart out all ober de place. An den dey is sayin' 'Goodbye Martha', we's off to stay

85

with Aunt Abigail and we see you soon fo' sure and den dey is gone. Marcel, he gone North, mebbe to fight and Ruby ... she workin' in de town now ... she a ho'. An I sit here all by misself, till you come long. Heah..." she held out a crumpled letter, which she had retrieved from the folds of her skirt... "dis de letter she wrote."

He took the letter and sat back down heavily. He inserted his finger under the flap, tore open the envelope, removed the one folded sheet and, with a trembling hand, read:

My dear James,
By now you will have heard of my departure from this house which, I must tell you, is also from your life.
   It has become quite clear to me that whatever affection, or even love, that we may have had for each other at one time, has over the years slowly evaporated until there is nothing left but a memory. Perhaps this is my fault. I know that since God, in His Wisdom, took our beloved Freddy from us, I have neglected the physical duties of our union and I believe that this may be the reason why you have so often strayed. Nevertheless I feel that I cannot continue to live in this meaningless and barren state and now that I have met another, a God-fearing man, with whom I believe that I may have one more chance of true happiness, I am determined to end our sham of a marriage. The children have gone to my sister Abigail in Atlanta, who will bring them up in the way of the Lord.
   It is my fondest hope that you will, in time, find it in your heart to forgive me.
   Harriet.

The paper fell from his loose fingers and fluttered to the floor. He sat there stunned, motionless, unable to comprehend the full import of its contents.

'She has left me,' he thought, 'left me, her husband ... just walked out and left me ... and abandoned our children ... the bitch ... the goddamn shit-faced bitch, I'll find her and I'll ...,' but he couldn't think what he would do or what he would say when he found her. Instead, it occurred to him, that he would kill the man she had absconded with. He turned to Martha. "Tell me about the man ... what was his uniform like?"

"It was grey sah, jess like yo's ... ceptin de hat, witch was black an' had dis big yella feather ting comin' out de top."

'Ah, cavalry' thought Bulloch, "and did they say where they were headed ... anything at all?"

"Marcel ... he heard de man say dat dey wuz gonna spen' a few days in Richmond befo' he gotta go join his Regimen' in de Nort' and fight de Yankees ... say Massah, is it true dat de Yankees gonna come heah an rape ebbeybody? Cos if it true, den I gonna put my best dress on!" She flung back her head and cackled loudly, showing the two teeth that she still retained in her upper jaw.

"Did they say anything else Martha, anything at all? Think, please, it's important."

She frowned, furrowing her brow with the effort of thought. "Mebbe one ting ... dey was arguin' bout de Mistress goin wid him to de Army ... an' he was sayin' dat de Gen'ral, Old Joe his name, de Gen'ral didn' like no wimmin in de camp an such..."

'Old Joe... Joe Johnston' he thought... 'Now all I need is to find the cavalry in his command and I have him'.

"Thank you Martha" he said, bending forward and kissing the diminutive Negress on her lined forehead.

"Why Massa ... ceptin' I doan have to call yew Massa no mo' ... tho I doan rightly know what a body'd call yew ... so Massa ... kin I be getting' yew summat to eat ... not dat deys much ... ceptin' eggs ... an some ol' bacon what I cant chew wid no teet ..." But Bulloch's head lay on his chest, the deep rumble of snores coming from his open mouth, as his consciousness finally surrendered into the embracing arms of sleep.

Early the next day he rose early, eating eggs and fried bacon with Martha, before bidding her a fond farewell and leaving her money for her wages – an idea she thought unnecessary but quite charming. He went to the *Fingal*, packed his valise, carefully placing the Adams revolvers at the bottom and left for the station, once more the elegant gentleman in the well-cut frock coat and silk top hat.

The journey was endless. Bulloch was forced to change trains twice and then there were delays and re-routing to give way to trains bringing reinforcements and supplies to the Army in Northern Virginia.

In Richmond, Bulloch was easily able to discover Old Joe Johnston's whereabouts, as he had just fought a successful action at

Balls Bluff down the Potomac from Harpers Ferry and was even now encamped outside Leesburg.

Again Bulloch caught the train North, sharing a carriage this time with a contingent from Mississippi, whose fellow regiment had just fought so well at Balls Bluff.

"Shoo," said the Captain, "I heard how the Yankees ran and jumped right off the cliff into the river and how our boys jes' stood there and picked 'em off, one by one … like shootin' fish in a barrell …'cept more fun. I surely wish that I had been there," he added wistfully.

Bulloch sat and stared out the window for most of the journey, the landscape outside seeming strangely crude and foreign after the well ordered fields and orchards that he had observed on his many train rides in England.

The train finally puffed and clanked its exhausted way into Leesburg, coming to a halt in the little brick station, whose platform was stacked above head height with all manner of crates, boxes and cartons. Chickens and ducks ran, clucking, among the feet of the disembarking soldiers, while beyond the station, vast pens held herds of lowing cattle and grunting swine.

Beyond the noise of the farmyard, there was audible a more sinister sound – the moaning of wounded men in pain. For down the line, waiting for the train to take them home, there lay row after row of stretchers, on which lay the victims of the recent fighting, with bandaged heads, limbs and torsos visible above the brown army issue blankets.

Bulloch left the train, struggled his way down the crowded platform and emerged into the dusty street of the little North Virginian town, until recently an unheard-of and unvisited speck on a map in some cartographer's office. He looked down the street and was rewarded by the sight of a small troop of cavalry, under a sergeant, trotting towards him. The horses' hooves kicked up little clouds of dust, that would soon turn to thick greasy mud at the advent of the winter rains.

He hailed the Sergeant, stepping out into the road and raising his hand. "Whoa, Sergeant, a moment if you please."

The troop reluctantly reined in their horses, coming to a stand-still just in front of Bulloch. The Sergeant leaned down from his horse and carefully ejected a thin stream of brown saliva onto the ground near Bulloch's foot. "Whaddya want?" he growled, clearly unused to any interaction with civilians, other than helping them to part with their livestock or animal feed and clearly believing them to be a somewhat unnecessary sub-species, to whom courtesy was neither owed nor given.

Bulloch restrained himself, aware of the Springfield rifles in leather saddle-holsters and the Colt Army Model .44s which most of the troopers carried thrust into their belts or sashes. "I am looking for a cavalry unit – stationed hereabouts, with Johnston. They wear plumes – big yellow plumes in their hats – do you know of any such?"

"Mebbe I do and mebbe I don't. Who's asking anyhow?" The Sergeant looked suspiciously at Bulloch.

"My name is Anderson and I am a Captain … with the Provost Marshall's office in Richmond …", he said, already aware of the weakness of both his question and his explanation … "I am looking for an officer … travelling with a woman … possible case of abduction … and you will call me 'sir', even though I am out of uniform, Sergeant."

"Yes sir," said the Sergeant, throwing an exaggerated and somewhat mocking salute. "You'll be looking for the Virginia Light Cavalry, the Third I think, with them yeller plumes … but as to women … not with the cavalry … no sir. Stuart don't hold with women in the camp … says they mess things up." He sniffed. "Reckon he's right at that." He saluted again, a mere wave of the hand, before kicking on his horse and, brushing Bulloch out of the way, led his troop off down the street.

Disconsolate and unsure of how to proceed, Bulloch wandered into the only saloon that the town offered, to find it nearly empty.

He ordered a whiskey and as an afterthought, a steak, aware that he had not eaten since leaving Richmond. He drank two whiskeys before having an idea. He said to the barman: "If, er, there were women – soldiers' wives – with a unit that didn't accept them in camp – where might they be, d'you think? Is there a hotel or some women's encampment?"

The barman shook his head. "Only hotel's this one and we've got no women here … that's anyone's reg'lar wives anyhow …" He grinned showing tobacco-stained teeth below his ragged moustache. "But they kin be yor wife for an hour or two ifin you've got a mind fer it – and two dollars, of course." He leered at Bulloch, winking suggestively.

"That's not what I'm looking for. I am looking for … my sister

... who's here with ... her husband ... with the Virginia Light Cavalry ... but I don't know where to start looking for her."

"Try the field hospital, why don't you. There's any number of ladies as is working there, as nurses and such ... not that I'd call 'em ladies fer doing that kind of work any more 'n I'd strictly call them whores upstairs ladies ... still, you know what you're doing, I guess."

Bulloch nodded. "Good. Good idea. After I've eaten, I'll go and see if she's at the hospital.

"Go before I ate if I was you," mumbled the barman. "You kin smell the place more 'n half mile 'way, what with all them rotting legs an' all. Be a shame to lose yer dinner right after payin' fer it."

Nonetheless Bulloch ate, chewing the old and tough steak until the pieces were just small enough to be washed down with whiskey. Then he set off to find the field hospital. An enquiry directed him to the outskirts of town, where, as the barman had suggested, he could smell the sweet cloying odour of rotting flesh long before he could see the hospital itself, which was composed of only half a dozen long low tents. Again, that weird keening noise, the half human, half animal sound of pain and distress could be heard, and it sent shivers down Bulloch's spine. He approached the largest tent and raised the flap.

He saw Harriet right away, but did not recognise her. She sat on the edge of a wooden camp bed, holding the head of a wounded soldier in her lap, stroking his hair and smiling reassuringly into his wild eyes which stared out of a face riven by pain and fever. Occasionally a great retching cough would rack his emaciated frame and he would bring up gobs of blood mixed with sputum, most of which would splash onto Harriet's stained blouse and skirt, missing the rolled bandages which she held hopelessly to his mouth.

"My God," Bulloch mouthed silently, finally recognising Harriet, in spite of the dried blood smeared on one cheek and the wisps of dirty hair falling from an untidy bun. "Harriet ... is that you?"

She looked up and, seeing Bulloch, shook her head. "Why have you come? What do you want with me?" Bulloch was, for the first time in his life, speechless.

"Have you come to kill him? Is that it?" When he didn't answer, she laughed mirthlessly. "So like you, so full of sound and fury. Well you're too late. He's been dead and buried these two weeks past, God rest his soul. Yankee sniper got him when his troop was scouting the enemy on the morning of the battle. Only a handful of our boys killed that day and he had to be one of them. It was a punishment. A punishment from God, for my sins." She started to cry, hugging the dying soldier's head tighter in her arms. "He has always tested me … tested my faith … and I was sorely tempted to doubt Him when he took our Freddy … but I see it now … I see that I have done wrong in his sight … putting my own happiness above my duty to God … and so I have been punished and I beg his mercy and forgiveness for my sins every hour of the waking day…."

Bulloch gently unfolded her arms from around the soldier's head, revealing his ashen features, composed in death. He helped her to her feet and led her out of the tent and away from the over-powering stench of sickness and decay. She clung to his powerful forearm, her thin and dirty fingers plucking at the fine material of his sleeve as she stumbled along at his side. It was a time before either spoke. At last he said: "So Harriet, what now? What will you do now?" She wrinkled her brow. "Why, I will follow the Army of course, nurse the sick and wounded, see if I can find redemption in serving God's will among the needy." She shrugged. "These past weeks I have seen so much … suffering … so much more than I thought possible that I cannot return to what was before."

"But what about our children? Surely they need a Mother? Will you desert them too?"

"I see others who need me more. I believe that God has shown me the way to my salvation. I must do His work."

Bulloch covered his eyes. "Harriet, you are and you always were a fool. You see the hand of God in your own damned failings and, frankly, I think you have been made … mad with grief … at the death of your lover … ." At this she made to protest, but he silenced her with a raised finger. "Whether you leave me or not is of little consequence, for as you said in your letter, our marriage had become a sham. But I will soon return overseas and even after that, I will still be a Navy man, at sea for months at a time. The children need at least one parent they can rely on. Your sister Abigail, kind woman though she is, has four children of her own. I cannot believe that they will get the care or affection that they need in that house."

"My sister is a God-fearing woman. I have provided for their upkeep and she will bring them up in a devout and pious household. She has promised me that."

"Your mind is made up?"

"It is." She raised her chin and stared defiantly at him.

"Then you are a sad woman, Harriet, lost and alone. In truth, I hope you find your God and I hope He is all you seek. Goodbye."

He turned and walked away, surprised by the tears that welled up in his eyes and ran down his cheeks.

'Damn, damn, damn', he thought to himself. 'The damned bloody woman' and he punched himself repeatedly on the thigh. 'Why am I crying?' he asked himself and at that moment couldn't answer his own question. Perhaps he still felt some residual affection for her, perhaps it was wounded pride, perhaps he missed his girls and worried for their future. Perhaps it was all of these.

"I will pray for you," she shouted at his retreating back.

✻   ✻

Two days later Bulloch was back in Richmond. He sat across the desk from Stephen Mallory and smoked one of his fine Jamaican cigars, rolling it between his fingers, savouring the mellow smoke, which he blew gently from his pursed lips. Mallory studied him carefully through his gold-rimmed spectacles, noting the change in the man since their last meeting. Bulloch had lost weight and seemed somehow less robust. He frowned and looked away to hide his concern.

"So," he said, after Bulloch had finished his report, "you are to be congratulated. You have done everything that we could reasonably have expected of you … and more. While it is true that you have exceeded your authority, lent and borrowed money that you had no right to, disobeyed and countermanded my orders," he raised a hand motioning Bulloch to silence … "you have nonetheless achieved a truly great success. The army is delighted with its rifles – and when the army is pleased, the President is pleased and indeed so pleased are we all that I am sending you back … to continue the good work."

"And what of the *Oreto*, Sir….. may I have her?"

"Have her, in terms of the command of her? No James, not the *Oreto*. It is too soon and I need you in England. You are my most valuable agent and it is possible that the situation will change markedly in the very near future. Things are very fluid at this moment."

"Fluid? How do you mean, sir ?"

"Have you heard of the *Trent*, James?"

"The *Trent*? No, I do not think so."

"Well, while you were at sea on the *Fingal*, the *Trent* – she is a British mail steamer of no great import in herself, which plies the Caribbean waters – was boarded by a certain Captain Wilkes, Commander of the *San Jacinto*, a Union 'tea kettle' of how many guns I know not. Anyway, there were two Confederate ministers who were travelling on her, bound for Europe – James Mason and John Slidell by name, who were forcibly removed and taken as prisoners of war to Washington. The British are furious, of course, claiming it's in breach of their neutral status, an insult to the flag and so forth. The reality is that it's a damned cheek and it's exactly the sort of thing that brought us to war with the British in 1812 and I wouldn't be at all surprised if it does so again. So, you see, we may soon have access to as many ships – proper war ships – as we can afford. But for the moment, James, I must have you in place. You are my man!"

Bulloch, annoyed but not surprised, paused for a moment to consider the implications of what he had just heard before speaking. "All of this seems very good news and I will, of course, return to England as you order. However, I must ask for your assurance that I be given command, if not of the *Oreto*, then of the *Enrica* … I must have a fighting command, sir, and it was promised to me. It is my due."

"I understand James, I understand. But you must be patient and you must not only follow the orders of your superiors, but also accept that what they ask of you will ultimately be for the greatest good of your Country. You, I, all of us must, during this period when we are fighting for our survival, for everything we believe in, for our very way of life, subjugate our own personal desires and ambitions to the exigencies of our young nation. Now, let us turn to the ever-present and never popular topic of money. How do we do, James?"

Bulloch shifted in his seat. This was the subject he least wished to discuss, but knowing that it would be raised, he had prepared himself carefully for it.

"Well sir, as you know, you disbursed two hundred and fifty

thousand dollars to me in the form of sight drafts, drawn on Fraser, Trenholm. In round numbers, this is fifty thousand pounds, out of which I have paid twenty-five thousand pounds to Miller, for the *Oreto*, and have lent a further twenty-five thousand pounds to the Army, under the signature of Captain Anderson. We owe another twenty-five thousand pounds to Miller, due on completion of the *Oreto*, which I anticipate will be in March of next year. Then we will owe forty-seven thousand five hundred pounds to Laird's for the *Enrica* when she is delivered, which I have been promised for July. Lastly," and here he cleared his throat, "I was a signatory to a loan of eighteen thousand pounds which was the purchase price of the *Fingal*. I believe she has now been renamed the *Atlanta*."

"So" said Mallory with a frown, "to recap: you have spent the two hundred and fifty thousand dollars provided you and so long as our loan is repaid by the good Secretary Benjamin, we are currently indebted or obligated, to the tune of a further three hundred and twenty five thousand dollars. Is that correct?"

Bulloch scratched his head working on the mental arithmetic, "Umm … yes … I believe that to be correct."

"Very good. We need more ships, James. More cruisers, but also blockade-runners. Like the one you saw in Bermuda – the *Nashville*, didn't you say? Draws only eight feet I understand. Ships like that. So, I can authorise a further five hundred thousand dollars. You will have considerable expenses to meet arming and equipping both ships we have currently under construction and you may need to deposit funds at the time of commissioning of the new ships – although Laird did not seek such a deposit which was commendable – very commendable. You will give him my personal thanks, won't you James?"

"I will sir." He looked relieved at the direction the conversation was taking.

"Oh and James…"

"Sir?"

"How have you been living? I mean do you have sufficient for your everyday purposes?"

"Well, ah … yes. Although our dollar has been decreasing somewhat in value and I have many travel … and other … expenses … and so I am often a little constrained."

"We can't have that James. You must draw on your funds as you need them … for your own living expenses and so forth. With

94

a full accounting, of course."

"Of course," Bulloch echoed dryly.

He returned to his room, sat down at the desk and penned three letters. One to each of his children and one to Abigail, their Aunt. To his children, he wrote of his love and deepest affection, explaining that he had seen their Mother, that she was well but would not be returning home at any time soon. Instead, she was working to ease the suffering of the wounded in the army hospitals – an admirable vocation, for both its humanity and for the support it lent to their Cause. Lastly, he told them that he would soon be going abroad again, and that he regretted very much being unable to travel to Atlanta to see them, or to spend Christmas with them, but that he would return in the Spring bearing gifts, and would visit them at that time, without fail. He again picked up his pen, dipping the nib's tip into the brass inkwell and tapping the excess ink onto its glass rim. He sighed deeply and began to write to Abigail.

My dear Abigail,

I have recently come from a small town in Northern Virginia, named Leesburg, undistinguished in all respects except that it is the temporary headquarters of our Army and its Commander, General Joe Johnston.

I met with your Sister, my Wife, in Leesburg and I feel that I must accurately report to you of her condition. I have to tell you that her companion, Captain Rufus Graham, was killed in the fighting around Balls Bluff and I fear that this has turned her mind.

When I saw her she was working in the field hospital, tending the wounded and carrying out many duties, which I firmly believe to be quite unsuited to a woman of Harriet's background and upbringing. Furthermore, I believe that the whole atmosphere of an army hospital is having a most dele - terious effect on her already nervous and emotional state. Abigail, I must say to you that I fear for her sanity if she remains where she is. You should go to her and try to persuade her to come to Atlanta to be with you and the children. She will listen to you, even as she pays no heed to me.

As for my children, you have kindly taken them into your home. I understand that you have some funds from Harriet, which will, I trust, cater for their needs for the present. I have today, however, given instructions for our house in Savannah to be sold and for the proceeds to be held by the law firm of Fagan & Whalley in Atlanta, and to be applied for the benefit of my children. This will ensure that they are not a financial burden to you or your household.

Abigail, my children are very dear to me. Although I must go abroad again tomorrow, you should understand that I value their well-being and happiness above all else in this life. I hope and believe that you will grant to them the same measure of love and consideration which you bestow upon your own children.

I will be returning to these shores in the Spring and will look forward keenly to visiting you in Atlanta and to seeing you and my children again at that time.

With my best wishes to you and your family, for a Happy Christmas,

Your brother-in-law

James Bulloch

Early the next morning, he left the hotel and took a trap to the docks. There he boarded a paddle steamer which took him down the James River as far as Norfolk, where he would join the *Magpie*, a British vessel bound for Liverpool.

VI

London and Liverpool – January, February, March 1862

꙳ ꙴ

The small fire flickered feebly in the grate, failing miserably to dispel the damp chill of the January morning, which pervaded every inch of the palatial office. The gloom was only partially relieved by the hissing gas lamps, which were suspended on chains from the high vaulted ceiling, around which rubber hoses were wound in a serpentine manner. The burning gas threw off an eerie yellow light that rendered sallow the sunken cheeks of the office's elderly and only occupant.

He was seated at a mahogany desk of sufficient magnitude to dwarf his stooped and narrow frame. The old man leaned forward, and in his anxiety to decipher the spidery script of the letter that lay before him on the blotting pad, seemed to devour the very words from the page. Finally he sat back, grunted with satisfaction, and unclipped the *pince-nez* from the bridge of his nose.

There was a knock at the door and his secretary, a tall young man from a good but recently impoverished family, entered.

"My Lord, if you please, Sir George Lewis is here to see you."

"Very good. Be so kind as to show him in." He dismissed his secretary with a wave of his hand and then, looking up at the new arrival said, "Ah, George, there you are. Come in, come in." He rose to his feet and propelled his visitor, a man who stood a full head higher than himself, towards one of a pair of green leather wing-backed chairs that crowded the small hissing fire.

The visitor sat down heavily and then leant forward holding out both hands to the fire in an attempt to warm them.

"Beastly cold out, Johnny. Not much warmer in here, if you don't mind me saying so. They keeping you on short rations of coal, what?"

Lord Russell smiled, his full-lipped mouth stretching on each side to meet the heavy whiskers which framed the narrow face.

"I am glad you came George. I have good news. I have just received this morning a letter from Lyons in Washington dated the 29th ultimo. He informs me that they have released the Confederate commissioners – Mason and Sidell – and while we are still two furlongs short of an apology, it looks as if the immediate threat of war has receded somewhat – for the time being at any rate. He enclosed a letter from Seward informing him of the decision. Here, have a look at it. See if you can make anything of it. It's all legal mumbo-jumbo if you ask me, justifying just about anything, but it does have one or two interesting points." He passed across the same letter, which he had been studying so carefully a moment earlier.

Lord Russell sat back watching the shadows cast from the fire as they danced on the ceiling, and reflected on how close they had just come to war. Had Her Majesty not requested Prince Albert to re-write the carefully drafted ultimatum to the United States, toning down its bellicose language and demands for an apology that he knew would never be forthcoming, they would be at war by now. War had to come of course, he was sure of it – it was only a matter of time. The Americans could not be allowed to re-unite the two halves of their country. They would be too strong and their navy, which was almost as powerful as Britain's already, would be a threat in all the world's oceans. Britain's sea routes to its empire would be at risk! Unthinkable! But this had to be done carefully. His hand could not be seen in this too directly. Gladstone was with him, but Palmerston wavered and the others, they were for the North. All emotional claptrap, this slavery business, as if it mattered a damn over here. The supremacy of the British Navy protecting the trade routes to our colonies – that was what counted. But this would be a long game, and the first rubber had only just been played.

Sir George Lewis looked up from the letter, which he had angled at the fire to increase its legibility. "I see what you mean. I follow his argument just up to the definition of 'contraband' and then he loses me. Does it matter?"

"Not really. The only important thing is that he describes the *Trent* as a 'neutral ship'. That means that he regards our declaration of neutrality as a fact, much though it annoys him, and as a consequence the South must therefore be a belligerent nation, not a rebellious region. This has implications for our discussion on recognition at next week's Cabinet meeting."

"If you recognise the South, there will be war. Of that I am sure."

Russell shrugged. "Of that we are all sure. But there are many steps betwixt and between and many other matters to be considered. Have you spoken to Gladstone of late?"

The younger man shook his head.

"He'll tell you what's going on. Up north there's a million unemployed from the mills already. That goes up to two million when you count those on short time. Two million, George, I tell you, there will be riots this winter. And all because of the damned blockade."

"The French must be feeling the pinch too."

"Indeed they must. Though Froggy's got other fish to fry at the moment, what with his Mexican adventure and so on. Left us and the Spanish behind in Vera Cruz, dontcha know and legged it off to Mexico City, all on his own! Damned rash if you ask me, but Napoleon seems to want to recreate the empire lost by his illustrious uncle and sees this as a golden opportunity. Lincoln and Seward don't like it one bit apparently, flies in the face of their so-called Munroe doctrine and don't forget Mexico's got a damned long border with the United States. Even if they did beat the South – which I have to say is looking increasingly unlikely – they'd have us on the northern border and Monsieur Frog on the southern. Bit of a rum do for chaps who are always on about how much they despise the old European powers, what? Anyhow, getting back to the point, there's a limit on how much we are going to put up with just to keep Lincoln and his chums happy. We can't have our people starving, George, now can we? Not just to keep the Yanks happy."

"You are right, of course, I can see that. We can all see that. Let's just hope that it doesn't have to go that far. As Minister of War I know how unprepared we really are. Most of our stuffs left over from Russia and some of that came from Waterloo! We've got damned few steamers and no ironclads to mention. The Yanks wouldn't be a push-over for us at all!"

"Not alone, perhaps. Which brings us back to Napoleon again. Anyway, we'll keep it under review and chew it over next week in Cabinet, eh?"

The westerly wind howled in from the Irish Sea and blew flurries of snow up Water Street. Bulloch sat shivering in the back of the coach, as its thin and despondent horse trudged slowly up the hill towards his lodgings. He had spent Christmas on the *Magpie,* dining alone with the Captain as the other passengers were confined to their cabins by sea-sickness and the fierce Atlantic swells. Although, after a few days, the enforced idleness had begun to chafe, he nonetheless enjoyed standing at the fo'csle rail, his feet planted firmly on the pitching deck, watching the waves rushing along the ships side as she ran before the wind.

His landing in England had unfortunately coincided with the arrival of a particularly cold spell, with temperatures dropping well below freezing at night and remaining there throughout the day. The skies were permanently overcast and the dim daylight blended seamlessly into dusk and then night as early as four o'clock in the afternoon. It was a grim and depressing welcome for one more used to southerly climes, to warm breezes and long days even in winter time.

Bulloch had taken lodgings, shortly before his departure in November in Canning Street, paying six month's rent in advance. Now as he pulled up outside the door and paid off the driver, the head of his landlady appeared above the basement steps.

"Oh Mr Bulloch, I am glad to see you. I had given you up for dead, I had. Lord's sake, you being gone these two months and more, a body's got to worry! Now come in do, and warm yourself." She ran back down so as to open the front door and let him in. Soon Bulloch was sitting, shivering still, in front of a gas fire, in the small but cosy sitting room of his suite. He looked around and was pleased to see his belongings still in place – and carefully dusted. The bottle of Glenlivet was also there, on its silver tray, with the two cut crystal glasses. He filled one half way to the brim and swallowed the fierce spirit. Immediately he felt a rush of blood to the face and the shivering started to subside. He relaxed, swirling the whiskey around the glass, which he cupped in his two hands.

'Now,' he thought to himself, 'where do we go from here? The first visit should be to Millers. I want to see the progress of the *Oreto* – she should be really taking shape by now – and I think I'll offer him the commission of a gunboat. Something small, but something to keep him interested. Need to talk to him about the *Oreto's* cannon as well.'

* *

"She's a beauty ain't she?" Miller was so heavily wrapped in coats and scarves that he looked like a large ball, wearing a top hat. The incongruity of this had made Bulloch want to laugh and he had been forced to hide his mirth by coughing theatrically into his handkerchief.

The *Oreto* lay in the graving dock at Toxteth, her hull complete, her engines and boilers installed. The masts lay alongside, waiting to be raised. Bulloch was pleased and showed it with a wide grin.

"You should be able to take her out for sea trials by mid-March and we can have her ready for final delivery by the end of that month. Told you she'd be on time didn't I?"

"You did, Mr Miller, you surely did and I am very pleased. In fact, I am prepared to discuss another commission with you, but why don't we return to your office. I must confess that I find the cold wind in your country quite paralysing."

They sat across Miller's desk, the plan of the *Alexandra* laid out between them. "She's a shrimp – no'wt but a shrimp." Miller finally said, fixing Bulloch with a steely gaze.

"Well, I do agree that she is smaller than the *Oreto*, but we have needs for many ships, both large and small. And do not underestimate the significance that she will have to my Country and our Navy."

"And, if I may enquire, will you be commissioning other vessels at this moment?"

"That, Mr Miller, is none of your business and, furthermore, if I may say so, it is an impertinent question."

Miller looked back down at the plans, frowning.

"I'm a blunt man, not well-educated like and I speaks as I finds. No offence meant, Mr Bulloch. We'll be pleased to build your ship. But you should know that we've had snoopers a-plenty round 'ere, all interested in 'oo the *Oreto's* for. Most of 'ems just rubbish. Busybodies like. We throw them in the dock if we catch 'em. But of late we've had some official types, up from London.

Had one of your Yanks with 'em. Course we told 'em nothing. But they'll be back, I fear."

Bulloch nodded. He had been expecting an increased level of surveillance and even diplomatic pressure after the *Fingal's* successful arrival in Savannah, which would surely have been noted by Federal spies. He had accordingly consulted an eminent Liverpool lawyer, a Mr F.S. Hull, on the Foreign Enlistment Act of 1818, which would be the legislation they would attempt to use against him. He had been told, quite categorically, that provided the ships were not armed when they left British waters, then they could not be seized under the somewhat convoluted provisions of the Act. He explained this to Miller, who grunted his approval.

"Nonetheless, we can't be too careful can we? I've 'ad papers drawn up, saying as how the *Oreto's* an Italian commission, from a firm what trades with Palermo. I've left 'em lying around my desk for anyone to see who wants to. Not that I don't trust this lot," he gestured with his thumb to the outer office, where the clerks continued to scribble in their heavy ledgers, "seeing as how they knows what would 'appen to 'em if they was caught. Broken legs – at best – and life on crutches is an awful big price to pay for crossing me, don't you think?" He looked up at Bulloch meaningfully, who returned his stare without blinking.

*   *

That night Bulloch dined with Charles Prioleau at his house in Abercrombie Square.

As he climbed the stairs to the drawing room, a young blond-haired woman of great beauty wearing a hoop-skirted dress of lilac organza, came out onto the landing to greet him and took his hand lightly in her gloved fingers.

"You must be Captain Bulloch. I am so pleased to meet you. I am Mary Elizabeth Prioleau and it is an honour for us to receive a genuine hero into our home."

He reddened, partly from the close attention of this fine looking woman and partly from the warmth of the house after the chill of the night air. Up close he was able to admire her flawless skin, her clear blue eyes and the line of her neck as it rose gracefully from the lace collar of her dress.

"Why Mrs Prioleau, you must be thinking of someone else, I am sure. I am but a simple Navy Captain."

She raised one eyebrow coquettishly. "Simple, Mr Bulloch? I think not. But we shall see. Now come and say hello to Charles and meet our other guests."

She introduced him to a heavy set man, who owned a local mill and to a well-dressed, rather foppish individual who explained that he was a cotton broker.

"You are among friends here," Charles Prioleau said in his ear as he guided him away from the others. "In fact you can even stand on that chair and sing *Dixies Land*, should you have a mind to. Now, I must first congratulate you on the voyage of the *Fingal*. Your Country owes you a great debt, for at this moment she would have neither the weapons nor the ship were it not for you." He leant towards Bulloch, lowering his voice and coming close enough for Bulloch to smell the violet cashews on his breath. "However, whilst we are on the subject of debts and if you will forgive my lapse of manners in mentioning such a delicate subject on a social occasion, I seem to recall that you have a small one outstanding to Fraser, Trenholm. When, do you think, it might be convenient for you to settle this matter?"

"At the exact same moment that Captain Anderson repays me the twenty-five thousand pounds that he owes – which you will recall I lent him at your urging – and not one moment sooner."

Prioleau frowned, his finely curved dark eyebrows drawing together across his lined brow.

He was about to say something more when at that moment his wife arrived to rescue Bulloch. "You have met my wife, Mary Elizabeth?" he enquired, his countenance lighting up at the arrival of the woman he clearly adored.

"I have indeed had that honour."

"Then perhaps, Mr Bulloch, you will do me the honour of escorting me in to dinner?" she murmured, taking his arm and placing her hand on his forearm.

At dinner he was seated to the right of Mrs Prioleau, which put him opposite the cotton broker, who was most anxious to quiz him about the progress of the war.

"You see, Mr Bulloch, it's a funny old situation here. We all support the South, course we do. We don't want that bunch of rabble-rousing democrats kicking your Southern Gentlemen in the pants do we? Yet Mr Hardcastle here", nodding in the direction of the mill owner, "he's doing very nicely from the cotton shortage, laying off his workers, cutting wages and still with plenty to sell from his warehouses. And I'm broking cotton parcels on the Flags, watching the price go up as the shortage starts to bite and the speculators move in. Making a pretty penny too, I can tell you! So we're not keen for this war to be over too soon – not that it will be in any case, I suspect. Sounds harsh, I'm sorry, but that's the way it is."

Mrs Prioleau intervened quickly, sensing Bulloch's anger at the blatancy of the cotton broker's self interest. "Mr Quick and Mr Hardcastle are two of the largest contributors to the fund I am raising to help the Confederate wounded. They have both been most generous…" she said, her voice trailing off towards the end.

"I'm glad to hear of it," Bulloch said through clenched teeth. "However, it would be so much better if Mr Quick and Mr Hardcastle were actually able to see where their money was going. If they could actually go to a field of battle and see the wounded laid out for the surgeon. Do you know Mr Quick, that if you are shot anywhere on the torso, the stretcher-bearers often don't even bother to pick you up. It's a rather unpleasant system of prioritisation called 'triage'. There's nothing they can do for you in that case, you see, because you are going to die anyway. If it's an arm or a leg, they just cut it off – maybe you survive as a cripple, maybe you die of shock or of gangrene – but on the torso, you just lie there, slowly bleeding to death, hoping that you die before the vultures start to pick at your eyes or the fires get you – yes, the fires, caused by exploding shells. There's many a poor wounded soldier, that can't even crawl, who gets roasted alive on a battlefield. And the smell…"

"I think, Mr Bulloch, we have all got your point," interrupted Hardcastle. "Don't forget we didn't start your war – all we're saying is that it's a fact that's helping some of us financially – and we're giving some of what we've made back to help the wounded, which we think is only right and proper."

"I understand" said Bulloch after a moment's pause, "and I apologise, but it's awful hard to see young men dying and others getting rich out of it." He paused for a moment to regain his composure. "But tell me about the mill-workers. I met this man on a train a couple of months ago who claimed to represent them. He said that they supported the North on account of the slavery question and that no amount of hunger or unemployment was going to change that."

Hardcastle shook his head. "That seems to be what they think. Of course, there's some scurrilous rags about, what are trying to stir them up, making out the war is about class – your posh southern landowner trying to keep down the workers, be they black or white – or some such nonsense, which has got them awful het up. Why, only the other day, one of these socialistic types threatened to burn me out if I didn't open the mill full time! I gave him short shrift, you can imagine – fired from my employ and blacked him in the rest of the industry too! That'll learn him to threaten me!"

The conversation moved on to lighter topics but Bulloch remained detached from the discussion. After the plates were cleared he smoked a cigar and drank a brandy with the men, before excusing himself, complaining of a coming cold and headed down towards the front door. He was struggling into his heavy top coat when Mary Elizabeth appeared at the top of the stairs.

"Not leaving us so soon are you Mr Bulloch?" she enquired, one eyebrow raised, descending the staircase so lightly that she seemed to float down.

"If you will excuse me Ma'am, I have some minor ailment which is dogging me. I fear it has made me a bore. It is better that I administer a number of patent remedies in the confines of my own lodgings, rather than subject your guests to my long face any further."

"Nicely said, Mr Bulloch." She took one of his hands in both of hers. "But I hope that you will come and see me again – perhaps to take tea – when you are feeling better." She graced him with her radiant smile and Bulloch felt his knees go weak.

"Indeed I would be most honoured, Ma'am." He bowed and left the house for the dark and damp streets of Liverpool.

After only a short walk he found himself heading in the direction of the gambling house on Castle Street, all of a sudden eager and excited – both for Marise and the cards.

He was disappointed immediately by the former, who was hanging on the arm of a portly balding figure in evening dress. She waved to Bulloch over her escort's shoulder and blew him a kiss, but only shrugged when he took out his watch and pointed to it.

So he sat down at the Faro table, called for a brandy and started betting heavily against the bank on both splits and cases. Before long he had lost the one hundred pounds of chips that he had cashed on his arrival. He felt, rather than saw, the Jew, Isaac Kopa, by his elbow.

"Good evening, Mr Bulloch, a word in your ear if you don't mind. In my office, please. It won't take a moment." He stood up, sighing heavily and followed the Jew, whose broad shoulders were encased in a maroon velvet smoking jacket that was several sizes too small. On his head, tilted to one side, he wore a matching velvet cap, with a long dangling tassel.

Upstairs, in the cramped office, Bulloch sat down on a plush upright chair and accepted a brandy. The Jew pulled up another chair and sat down opposite him, so close that their knees almost touched. "Now, Mr Bulloch, you know that you are one of the most regular and esteemed patrons of our little Club and that we do value your custom very highly. Indeed we do. But Mr Bulloch, there is the small matter of an outstanding debt due to myself and to my Mother, who was, bless her, very upset – nearly had to be hospitalised – when she heard that you had left the country. Anyway, you are back now, safe and sound it appears and we are both ever so pleased. So may we now settle up and clean the slate, so to speak?"

"I seem to remember paying you two hundred and seventy pounds just before I left." Bulloch crossed his legs and sat back, increasing the distance between himself and the Jew.

"Indeed you did, Mr Bulloch, indeed you did, and we were very grateful for it, don't think that we were not. However, at that moment you did owe us nine hundred and thirty pounds seventeen shillings and six pence and then you lost a further one hundred and fifty pounds that same night, bringing us, as of this moment, to a total owing of eight hundred and forty three pounds three shillings and six pence, including our usual two per cent monthly interest charge, of course."

Bulloch's jaw swung open. He had no idea that the sum had become so large. Fortunately he had the drafts given him by Mallory, but he was reluctant to deposit them with Fraser, Trenholm unless Prioleau should simply help himself to eighteen thousand pounds, before the Army had re-paid their loan.

After a moments reflection he said to the Jew "You will have your money Mr Kopa – and before the week is out. I am in possession of bank drafts for sums greatly in excess of what I owe you and as soon as I have negotiated these, you will be repaid in full."

"Thank you so very much. My Mother will be so pleased. But is there anything that I can do to assist you in the encashment or deposit of your monies. I have many good acquaintances who are in the banking profession, with houses of considerable repute and handsomely capitalised as well."

"I will consider it Mr Kopa, and let you know. In the meantime, I would like to return to the Faro table, but I seem to need a small extension to my credit. You can add that to the amount outstanding."

*   *

The table in the Cabinet Room at 10 Downing Street was long and highly polished. Silver candelabra with frosted glass shades had been placed at regular intervals down its considerable length. Two men sat at the table, the thin stooped figure of Lord Russell, the Foreign Secretary and an even older man, with untidy white hair and untrimmed whiskers, which reached down to his chin. The older man was talking, his head nodding and his rheumy-pouched eyes fixed on the backs of his hands, which rested on the table.

"So you received Mason, eh Johnny? I am not sure how wise that really was."

Russell waved a long thin hand in dismissal. "It was in my home, so it was not official. Frankly, Prime Minister, I can't see what difference it makes."

"None, unless Seward finds out. Then he'll be ranting and raving and threatening war and I'll have to go to Windsor and see the Queen again and you know how I hate that. That damned Castle's as cold as a meat safe! Anyway, what's he like, that Mason fellow?"

"Not impressive." Russell shook his head. "A large man – very large head, even larger nose, untidy, rather noisy – common fellow. I rather felt that their President Davis could have done better. Still, he gave me an enormous stack of reports and statistics showing that the blockade isn't effective and that therefore we were legally justified in ignoring it. I've sent all this to Parliament and I think we should give it a good airing."

"Perhaps we should." Palmerston sighed. "It's all such a worry, though. What's new on the military front, if anything?"

"Not a great deal. They're still in winter quarters in the East. Further West the Federals have just taken a couple of Forts, called Henry and Donelson, in Tennessee. Don't know how important they are really, even though Nashville will probably fall. But I expect it'll be a bit of a morale booster for the North – after the drubbing they took at the end of last year, they need one. Make them more likely to push on and see it through I expect." He paused and began again somewhat hesitantly. "You know, Prime Minister, this war is not going to be over soon. And we are going to have to do something about it sooner or later."

Palmerston shook his head. "I don't want war Johnny. I really don't. Don't forget I've fought the Yanks before. In fact I was Minister of War in 1812 and I can tell you, they sank plenty of our ships before we got them under control. Burnt Washington, though! Hah! That taught 'em."

Russell raised his eyes to the ceiling. "I know, Prime Minister, I believe you have told me before. However, I have just received a note from my man in Paris. He understands that Napoleon is becoming increasingly concerned about the situation – they have as many out of work as we do. Apparently, Napoleon has already proposed to Lincoln that he try to mediate some sort of settlement with the South, but needless to say, he was shown the door pretty sharpish. I now understand that he may be willing to take things a little further – provided we're on board, of course."

"But we're not. On board that is. Not now, at any rate. Let's wait and see, Johnny. Particularly, let's see how things go when the spring campaigning starts up. If the South continues to dominate the battlefield, then Mr Lincoln may be forced to negotiate with them. If not, well, things may be over sooner than we think."

Russell sucked his cheeks but said nothing. "Oh and Johnny, one other thing ..."

"Yes, Prime Minister?"

"This Adams fellow ... Charles Adams ... you know, the United States Minister. Says he's been trying to see you but you've been ... ah ... unavailable? Keeps on coming round here and bothering me. Do me a favour, there's a good chap, he's upstairs now, in the drawing room, if you please. Pop in on your way out and see what he wants, why don't you? Till next week then."

Russell sighed and stood up. "Until next week, Prime Minister." He climbed slowly up the stairs, holding the wooden banister and humming a little tune to himself. 'Really, this Adams was such an infernal nuisance. Always complaining about this or that, always threatening, always cajoling. Still, when all was said and done, he was, at least, well-spoken and clearly intelligent – a credit to his country – pity President Davis didn't have Adams instead of that farmer, Mason.'

Russell entered the drawing room through the double doors, closing them behind him with a barely audible click. Adams looked up from the copy of *Punch* that he was reading.

"Why, Lord Russell, what an unexpected pleasure." He bounded to his feet and crossed the room, his hand extended. Russell took it in his own, somewhat diffidently and allowed it to be pumped up and down by the beaming Adams.

They sat and Russell cleared his throat before speaking. "I understand from Palmerston that you wish to see me. Well, here I am, at your disposal, but pray do be brief for I have other matters, of a pressing nature, to attend to."

The smile vanished from Adams' patrician features.

"Very well, I will come straight to the point. I have information that the Rebels are building warships in Liverpool. This is contrary to the Foreign Enlistment Act of 1818. What do you intend to do about it?"

"You have proof of your accusations?"

"Documentary proof, no, not as such. But there are several ships under construction and one nearing completion at Miller's yard in Toxteth. Again I ask, what do you intend to do about it?"

"In the absence of proof I can do nothing except to carry out investigations of our own, to see whether what you have told me is both correct and actionable." He shrugged. "I am very familiar with the Act to which you refer, but I must warn you that it is not a particularly outstanding example of the draftsman's skill. There are many clauses which are open to interpretation and there is a paucity of precedent to aid in definition and distinction. Should your enemy be so foolish as to sail an armed warship down the Mersey under his own colours, in broad daylight, then the matter of the crew's arrest and the ship's impoundment would be quite simple. However, the complexity of the situation increases exponentially with every derogation from these conditions. I hope I have made myself clear?"

"You have made yourself abundantly clear. You will do nothing to prevent your country from becoming a supplier of weapons of war to one side in a dispute in which you are a self-professed neutral. I must communicate this without delay to Mr Lincoln and Mr Seward." He got to his feet, but made no attempt to leave.

"Tsk, tsk, tsk ..." Russell wagged his finger at Adams. "Really Mr Adams, you do go on so. You heard exactly what I said and know exactly what I mean. We will carry out our own investigations, particularly at Miller's dockyard, you can be sure of that. In the meantime, should your agents uncover any written evidence, hard evidence, which will stand up in a court of law, then you should bring it to my attention without delay. Hmm?"

Adams nodded. "Very well Lord Russell, we will play it your way ... for the moment. May I wish you a good day." He inclined his head just enough not to be considered rude and departed.

Lord Russell remained seated for some time before pushing himself upright using the arms of the chair and slowly walking across the drawing room, a small, stooped figure with an uneven gait.

*　　*

February turned to March with no discernible improvement in the weather. Bulloch was as busy as he had ever been, spending more time with Miller than he liked, supervising the final fitting-out of the *Oreto*. In early March he and Lieutenant Low took the *Oreto* down the Mersey and into the Irish Sea for the first of her sea trials. She handled well, cresting the tops of the tall waves, before plunging down the far side, to emerge again with hardly a shudder. She was clearly well-founded, shipping very little water and while she sailed a point further off the wind that he would have liked, she was nonetheless a fine ship and well-suited to her purpose.

The engines, from Fawcett, Preston & Co, ran a little rough and Bulloch felt that there was some leakage of steam, which caused the fluctuation of the needle in the pressure gauge. Otherwise both he and Lieutenant Low enjoyed their day at sea and were sad to return her to port.

As her bow eased through the lock into Toxteth Dock, Bulloch saw a small group of men standing talking, their heads close together so as to hear each other above the whipping wind, which flared the skirts of their long dark coats, baring their trousers to the rain.

Bulloch tapped Lieutenant Low on the shoulder and shouted in his ear: "We have company. I am going below and I'm going to stay there. After we tie up, you remain on board until the crew leave, then you go with them. Hopefully you'll draw some of them off. If you're stopped, don't answer any questions except to say that you are an employee of Miller's and you don't know who the owners are. All right?"

Lieutenant Low nodded silently. Bulloch slipped down the companionway onto the lower deck and went into the unfurnished Captain's cabin, where he positioned himself by a porthole, which gave him a clear view of part of the dock. He could just see the group of men who, seeking shelter, had now retreated under the overhanging first floor of one of the red-brick warehouses that lined the dock.

After a while the noise of running feet and shouted orders subsided and, although he could not see the gangplank, he assumed that some of the crew had already left. He waited a further half hour and then, quietly opening the porthole, he cautiously looked out, craning his neck so that he could see down the length of the ship. The dock was deserted and it seemed that all of the watchers had departed. Suddenly there was the flare of a match from the deep shadows and he knew that at least one remained. He smiled grimly and, moving as quietly as he could, opened the door to the cabin and stepped out onto the main crew deck, slipping past the mess tables that swung gently from their ropes as the ship rocked in the wind.

Before ascending to the upper deck, he glanced down the companionway to the hold and was amazed to see a moving light.

"What the hell!" he said out loud, instantly regretting it as he groped in his waistband for the Colt .36 Navy Model, which he now carried with him at all times. His hand closed on the smooth wooden butt of the revolver, but as he tugged the long barrel clear of his belt, he took a heavy blow to his right shoulder, which paralysed his arm and caused him to drop his pistol onto the deck with a clatter.

Bulloch moaned out loud as a kick to the back of his knees pitched him headlong down the companionway. He fell, bruising his hip painfully on the steps, before landing heavily on the deck below, which knocked the air from his lungs. He struggled to a sitting position as a second man, who had been crouched over a

111

lantern ran for him, brandishing a billy club. Bulloch waited until he was close, then swung his foot up, catching the assailant a mighty blow in the groin with the toe of his heavy seaman's boot. The man collapsed to the deck, howling and clutching the injured part with both hands.

The first man was coming down the companionway as fast as he could, but not being a sailor, he misjudged the height of the deck above in the dark and hit his head hard on one of the low beams as he came. This gave Bulloch time to clamber to his feet, groaning as he put pressure on his bruised leg. He picked up the dropped billy club in his left hand, his right still being numb from the blow to his shoulder, and struck the man who was still writhing on the deck, his hands pressed between his legs. The blow was delivered to the back of his head with the full force of his anger and the man instantly ceased all movement and lay still.

The man from the upper deck jumped the last few steps, landing heavily and squared up to Bulloch. In the dim light of the dark lantern, which threw only a narrow beam, Bulloch could see that he was a rough dock type, wearing a check shirt with a red bandanna, while his patched trousers were held up with a rope belt. He had drawn a knife, which he now tossed from hand to hand in a thoroughly expert manner. He grinned, his teeth bright in the lamplight and suddenly lunged forward, the knife blurring with the speed of its motion. Bulloch leaned over to his right and the knife sliced through the left side of his coat, painfully scoring his ribs. He backed away, the man with the knife following, the blade held low and flat. Bulloch backed up to the lantern and as he did so an idea occurred to him. He gave the lantern a hard kick, sending it flying against a bulkhead, which extinguished it, plunging the deck into complete darkness.

Bulloch ducked into a stall designed to hold livestock and waited. After a moment's silence there came a muffled curse from well forward as the docker banged into some hard object. Bulloch slipped off his boots, and moved silently down the length of the ship towards the noise, feeling the inner planking of the hull with his right hand. The arm was now movable, although feeling had also returned to his shoulder, which sent shooting pains down his side and across his back as he walked. He hoped that it was not broken.

Ahead he heard the scrape of a hobnail on planking and then he saw, very faintly, the shape of his attacker, outlined for a moment in the dim light that came down the forward companionway from the deck above. He took two steps and swung the billy club from side to side. On the second swing he made contact. The docker yelled and Bulloch was now able to position him exactly, striking at his head and face ferociously with the club until the man fell. Bulloch leapt on to him, feeling for his head so as to continue the beating, but there was no point. His fingers encountered blood, in considerable quantities, leaking through the thick hair, below which he felt a soft and spongy area of the skull, which was a clear indication of its fracture. The man was dead.

Bulloch got to his feet breathing heavily, found the lantern where it had been kicked and re-lit it with a match from his pocket. As he swung it around the deck he saw something in the space below the companionway steps that made his blood run cold. He stood stock still, the fury welling up in him like a tide, the gall bitter in his mouth. For in the yellow glow of the lantern he could easily discern a pile of burlap and old caulking, soaked in pitch. The two men had intended to fire the *Oreto,* his ship!

Bulloch climbed painfully to the deck above and opened one of the gun ports on the side away from the dock and secured it. Then, grunting with the effort, he dragged the two men, one by one, up the companionway and manhandled them until they hung with the upper half of their bodies out of the open port. He then lifted their feet until they vanished out through the side of the ship, each of them falling into the water with a splash.

Bulloch retrieved his gun and returned to the main deck. Out of the porthole he saw the glowing ember of a cigar under the warehouse which identified the continued presence of the watcher, seemingly oblivious to the drama that had just taken place.

Keeping below the rail, Bulloch climbed down the steps on the far side of the ship and lowered himself into the freezing water. The sudden shock of the immersion completely took his breath away, but also numbed the pain. Holding his gun clear of the water, he swam around the ship, sculling with his good arm, until he reached a ladder at the river end of the dock. Here he climbed up and ran quickly into the shadows below the warehouses. He moved cautiously forward, stepping lightly in his wet stockinged feet, until he saw the burning tip of the cigar and smelt its pungent aroma. He walked silently up to the smoker, undetected until he cocked the revolver with the thumb of his left hand and said through clenched teeth, "you have only seconds to live. I suggest that you make your peace with your maker."

*   *

"So what did he say then, the bastard?" Bull Miller was in a fever pitch of excitement and anxiety, pacing around his office, clasping and unclasping his hands.

Bulloch had called on him at his offices first thing the following morning, having spent an uncomfortable and sleepless night. A doctor, known to his landlady, had set his shoulder, which was dislocated rather than fractured and had stitched the knife wound across his ribs, tutting all the while. The doctor had given Bulloch four drops of laudanum in water for the pain, but although this made him drowsy, sleep would not come. The events of the past few hours continued to appear beneath his flickering eyelids as he replayed them over and over again. Yes, he had killed before and yes, he had been subjected to a vicious and unprovoked attack by assailants who clearly would not have balked at his murder. And yet one of the men he had tipped into the water had still been alive and he would have died by drowning, inhaling lung-fulls of filthy water, panicking, retching, suffocating.... Bulloch sat up, his heart pounding, his eyes wide in the darkness. Death by drowning. 'My God' he thought, 'when my time comes, don't let it be death by drowning.' So it was that he was tired, stiff and sore and walking with a pronounced limp, his arm in a sling, when he entered Miller's offices. Bulloch recounted the tale, leaving out nothing and was amused as Miller's reaction changed from concern, to fury, to unconcealed admiration.

"He confessed that he was none other than Thomas Dudley, the United States Consul in Liverpool." Bulloch recounted. "I felt unable to gun him down where he stood, although I would much have liked to. He is a man of some stature and with heavy political connections. I feared that his death at this time would only serve to attract even more attention to our plans and could even result in direct intervention by the British authorities."

"On which subject," Miller interrupted, "you should know that they was 'ere yesterday. The authorities that is. Two posh types from London and an escort of local Peelers. Wanted to know all about the *Oreto,* they did, God blast 'em. So I showed 'em the

114

papers, what say as 'ow she's Italian. Then they wanted to see my bank records. 'Course I refused, but I'm affeared they'll be back. With a warrant. Then I shan't have no choice, see, me being an M.P. and all. They'll see that your draft was drawn on Fraser, Trenholm and while that don't prove nothing, it'll make my I-talian story look pretty thin. What then?"

Bulloch rubbed his forehead with his one good hand, feeling the tiredness well up inside him. "Well, first of all, we play for time. You should get the boilers and engines checked over double fast and we'll try to have her out of here before they return."

"Yes, that's the thing. Have her well out to sea before they can come back," Miller said doubtfully. "One more thing though. We don't dare arm her now. Not after this. I had thought to put the cannon in her hold. As ballast like. Now I think they should go separate."

Bulloch smiled. "Way ahead of you Mr Miller. The cannon, rifles, powder and shells are already loaded onto another ship and she is even now at sea, on her way to the rendezvous, where she will lay up and wait for the *Oreto*." This was not strictly true, but the ship had been purchased a few days earlier and the armaments would shortly be loaded at Hartlepool, after which she would head out to sea at all speed.

'Blimey,' thought Miller, 'this is a sharp one and no mistake. And a killer too. Maybe I should revise my plans for him, seeing as how he could be horrible dangerous to take on. Still, we can't let that bastard Laird get off scot-free. But I think I know a way to scupper him and keep my own hands lily white.'

To Bulloch he said, smiling broadly: "a smart move, if I may say so, very smart. Alright then, let's pick a date. Say, twenty-ninth of March at the latest we should have her ready for sea. We'll have her boilers and engines gone over with a fine-tooth comb and have her fully furnished, stocked and provisioned. I'll hire a crew for you as well." Then he paused. "Oh, and just one more thing...if I might have the remaining payment of twenty-five thousand pounds before you sail off in her … no offence meant, Mr Bulloch, but I don't want you picking a fight with some Yankee warship and her going down with all hands, if you know what I mean."

Bulloch looked at Miller's pug-like face, wrinkled in concern at the thought of losing his twenty-five thousand pounds and nearly laughed. Getting himself under control he said,

"Don't worry Mr Miller, you will get your money when I get my ship – in perfect order and fully fitted out. But don't concern yourself with the crew – I already have one."

*　*

Bulloch rested up for the next two days in severe pain, before rising from his bed and going to call on Isaac Kopa at his gambling club on Castle Street. It was past noon, but the Jew had clearly only just risen and was sipping coffee, wearing a silk brocade dressing gown, his feet in pointed yellow mules.

"Why Mr Bulloch, what a pleasure to see you, as always. To what do I owe this honour?" He then noticed Bulloch's drawn and haggard appearance and his arm supported in a sling. "Oh Mr Bulloch, what has happened to you? You were discovered in a compromising situation by an enraged husband, don't tell me?"

Bulloch laughed, but then stopped and winced as this pulled at the stitches on his ribs. "Something like that Mr Kopa. Now, may we talk business, or have I arrived too early in the day. Should I come back later on?"

"No, no, not at all. Any time is the right time to talk business, especially profitable business. Pray continue."

Bulloch frowned. "Well you remember the other day when we were discussing the matter of my small outstanding indebtedness to you and your Mother…."

"Not so small now, as it happens."

Bulloch frowned. "Well, anyway, you mentioned that you had contacts with a good, reputable, safe banking house? I would like an introduction, if you would be so kind. I need to deposit some funds and to make one or two payments, including to yourself, of course."

"No trouble, no trouble at all. I will write a letter of introduction right away to my dear friend Louis Sassoon at the Liverpool & County Bank. He will be able to assist you with all your financial transactions."

Bulloch took the hastily scribbled note and thanking the Jew warmly, made to leave.

"Oh, Mr Bulloch, one more thing … that small matter … it is now one thousand seven hundred pounds fifteen shillings and six pence – I fear you were unlucky the other night."

"I fear I am always unlucky in your establishment, Mr Kopa," Bulloch replied grimly.

As he left the Jew's establishment, Bulloch cursed himself, more determined than ever to win back the money without delay. As a man of scrupulous honesty, the idea of misappropriating Confederate government funds, which were in any case in desperately short supply, was a complete anathema to him. He had and continued to, rationalise this to himself as a short-term loan to help him over a period of bad luck. And like most gamblers, he believed in his own luck and moreover that no losing streak, however severe, could go on forever. Had Bulloch been able to enter the club at that moment, however, he would have been considerably less sanguine. He would have seen the Jew checking the small lead pellets that were carefully spaced around the roulette and faro wheels and positioning the cards, whose edges were finely trimmed by razors, in the shimmy shoe, ready for that evening.

The next days Bulloch spent largely with Lieutenant John Low, discussing the last minute details, including the hiring of the crew, which was going well. They had been told that the ship was bound for Cuba on her maiden voyage, to take on a cargo of molasses and rum. In fact, she was bound for Nassau, where she would meet with the *Bahama*, which carried her cannon and shot and where she would pick up her Captain, John Maffit and be commissioned formally as the *C.S.S. Florida*. At that time the crew would be offered the opportunity of signing on for a very different type of voyage, with significant opportunities for sudden enrichment or equally sudden death. Bulloch then planned to take his leave of the *Florida* and embark on a packet for Richmond, to meet again with Mallory in order to persuade him that the *Enrica* should be his to command as well as to visit his children in Atlanta.

The twenty-ninth dawned fair, with a pleasant westerly breeze. Bulloch had boarded the *Oreto* the night before and had slept in the Captain's cabin, enjoying his first deep and untroubled sleep for weeks.

Miller came aboard early and took one last tour of inspection, expressing himself satisfied with the *Oreto's* condition. Bulloch presented him with a draft for twenty five thousand pounds drawn on the Liverpool & County Bank.

"They finance a considerable volume of trade with Palermo and Naples – and Genoa as well, for that matter."

Miller graced him with a rare smile, revealing his yellow and uneven teeth. "As I said Mr Bulloch, you are a smart one. It's been a pleasure doing business with you, it really has. May I wish you a successful maiden voyage and a speedy and safe return. Oh, and take my advice and don't go with none of them poxy whores in Havana – the Cuban drip is the worst – I should know!" He scampered down the gangplank and with a wave of his top hat, was lost in the crowd that thronged the dockside.

The hawsers were cast off and, with a blast of the ship's whistle, the *Oreto* engaged her propellers and eased out of the dock. By the lock to the river stood a solitary figure wearing a long dark coat. As the *Oreto* eased her way through, he looked up, finding Bulloch with his eyes and raised his top hat, holding it above his head with an extended arm.

"Who's that?" Lieutenant Low enquired.

"That, Mr Low, is Thomas Dudley, the United States Consul in Liverpool." He raised his hand cutting off the Lieutenant's immediate question. "It's a long story, but suffice it to say, I spared his life and he may be expressing his gratitude."

The *Oreto* gathered speed as she steamed down the Mersey, her engines running as smoothly as silk and was soon lost to sight as she rounded the point by Wallasey and entered the Irish Sea.

VII

Washington and Richmond – April, 1862

❧ ❦

Rose sat on the cot, hugging herself, her knees drawn up to her chest. She could feel the boards of the narrow bed through the thin mattress and its meagre ration of worn, grey, army blankets. Little Rose lay on her cot, facing the wall, asleep and still, except when another bout of coughing wracked her emaciated frame.

From time to time Rose would get up and feel the girl's forehead, anxious in case the fever had returned. She rearranged the blankets, pulling them up to the little girl's neck, tucking them in around her narrow shoulders.

With the arrival of April, the weather had improved substantially, which was a blessing, given that their cell was unheated and while the small barred window set high up in the wall let in some light through its grimy panes, it also managed to admit the cold and damp winds that blew off the Potomac.

It had been a long six months since the night that she and little Rose had been taken in the locked prison wagon up to the forbidding front of the Old Capitol building.

She had felt her heart stop as they drove through the heavy wooden gates which closed behind them with a crash, that echoed in the empty courtyard, overlooked by the many small barred windows.

Pinkerton had visited the next day. He nodded with satisfaction as he inspected her cell.

"Ye can get out of here any time ye want to, lassie. Just tell the guards and they'll come and fetch me." He winked at her before leaving, the cell door slamming behind him. The noise of the heavy iron bolts being thrown reverberated down the bare corridor outside and in the ensuing silence, Rose broke down and wept, clutching her daughter tightly in her arms.

Since that day and admittedly with some relief, she had neither seen nor heard from Allan Pinkerton. And yet as the door to her cell was suddenly flung open, banging back against the wall, there he stood, dressed in his usual shabby black suit, his bowler hat pulled well down onto his ears. His beard was longer, less well trimmed and he looked tired.

"May I come in?" he enquired politely, but then entered her cell without waiting for a reply. He walked over to her cot and looked down at her, noting the flecks of grey in her hair and the drawn pallor of her cheeks.

"I trust I find you as well as can be expected?"

"Perfectly well, thank you Mr Pinkerton," she replied with as much conviction as she could muster, determined not allow him even the merest glimpse of her loneliness and despair.

He reached out and stroked her hair, which was coarser than he remembered. She permitted him this intimacy without moving, but when his hand moved to her cheek, she flinched and he withdrew it, frowning.

"Ye continue to reject me, Mrs Greenhow. Why is that? Am I that much more repulsive than the others?"

She shook her head, but did not answer him.

He continued: "I have always felt a deep sense of admiration for ye and for the risks which ye took in furtherance of a cause in which ye believed, no matter how mistaken that cause may be. Y'are a brave woman Mrs Greenhow, of that there is no doubt. And yet I wonder if ye really have the right to impose the results of yer bravery on yer bairn, over yonder. Not been well of late, I understand. Tsk, tsk." He shook his head. "As I told ye before Mrs Greenhow, I can improve yer situation for ye, and for yer bairn and it won't be anything ye haven't done before."

She looked up at him, with the utter contempt that she felt expressed clearly on her features and with such loathing in her eyes that he stepped back, as if slapped.

"Well, it doesn't really matter anymore," he muttered under his breath. "Ye are free to go anyway."

Rose heard the words, but only barely and in any case did not believe them, assuming this to be another ruse by Pinkerton to force her into his bed, so she remained silent and did not react.

"Did ye no hear me, ye stupid bitch? The high-ups have done some deal and ye are free to go!"

"Truly?"

"Aye. Although I'll be damned if I know why. If it had been up to me, I'd've hung ye as a traitor and a spy. At least I'd've seen ye rot in here for the rest've yer days. Now get up yer bairn and pack yer things. There's transport for ye at the gate and ye are going to Richmond to be with the rest of yer damned Rebel friends." He turned to walk out of the cell, but paused at the door and stared at her from behind lowered lids. Finally he took a deep breath and said: "Ye haven't heard the last of me, Mrs Greenhow. One way or another, ye haven't heard the last of me."

*   *

It was mid-April by the time Bulloch arrived in Richmond. He had landed at Norfolk only five days after bidding the *Florida* a fond farewell, watching sadly as she steamed out of Nassau on her first cruise, fully armed and with almost the entire crew that had signed on in Liverpool.

From Norfolk, he had taken the train, arriving in Richmond from the South, through Petersburg. He had been amazed and alarmed at the extent of the fortifications that had grown up around Richmond – trenches, forts and batteries protected by earthworks, all manned by militia that, on closer inspection, seemed to be comprised mainly of schoolboys and their grandfathers.

The atmosphere in Richmond had changed noticeably as well and the heady euphoria of the first days of the war had evaporated in the harsh light of repeated battles. Instead, the diminished number of civilians on the streets had a worried, tense look – the forced smile, the quick hollow laugh – while everywhere he looked, Bulloch saw men in uniform, marching in column with rifles on their shoulders, the stamp of their new boots resounding on the cobbles. He smiled proudly, recognising Enfields in the hands of one detachment, their locks still glistening with the manufacturers original grease.

He arrived at the Spotswood Hotel with his portmanteau, and went up to the unattended reception desk, banging the bell for attention with the flat of his hand. After a minute or so, a harried looking individual, clean-shaven, with a round pink, perspiring face came out.

"Yes?" he enquired brusquely.

"I would like a room, please – number 108, if it is free."

"We have no rooms at all, Sir. Not 108, not any. They are all taken. You can't get a hotel room in Richmond, not these days, not for love nor money."

Bulloch frowned, staring at the clerk below knitted brows. Slowly he took a roll of dollar bills from his pocket and counted off two singles, which he pushed across the desk.

"And your shinplasters won't fix it neither."

Bulloch sighed. He peeled of a $5 bill and pushed it to join the two singles.

"Been out of town for long, have we, Sir?" said the clerk. "You wouldn't believe the price of things these days. Butter's 75c a pound, coffee's $1.50 and sugar 'n salt, why you can't hardly get them at all and, like hotel rooms, they're awful dear when you can."

Bulloch flicked through the diminished roll and took a $20 bill from the centre. He pointed to Jeff Davis' face on the front and said, "I'm seeing him tomorrow. I would hate to have to tell him that the clerk at the Spotswood Hotel was unimpressed by his likeness."

The clerk smiled, collecting all the bills and slipping them into his waistcoat pocket. "I am, as always, a great admirer and loyal supporter of the President. Now, for the moment you can have my room – until something better comes up, that is. Here's the key, it's on the top floor, turn left as you come up the stairs – oh, and if the cat's been sick again, you can open the window."

The next morning Bulloch set out for his meeting with President Davis, which this time would take place at the Confederate White House, a mansion which had recently been purchased for the President and his family as a residence and an office. Bulloch strolled up the grassy slope in front of the Capitol, which shone blindingly white in the sun, with its tall Doric columns fronting the portico under which senators and congressmen from the Southern States mingled or stood in groups conferring earnestly. He raised his hat to the equestrian statue of George Washington as he passed and, crossing Broad Street, walked up 12th to where the White House stood on the corner of Clay Street. It was an imposing building, the home of a wealthy merchant, but smaller and less pretentious than some of the more recent town houses built by the nouveau riche.

Bulloch was admitted to the hall, where he admired the faux marble paint work before being shown into the ornate and fussy sitting room, which was over-furnished with chairs and sofas in burgundy brocade to match the wine red velour of the wallpaper. This time, however, he was hardly kept waiting at all, but was both surprised and flattered when the President came directly out of his office, smiling warmly and gripped Bulloch by the hand, shaking it vigorously.

"Well done my boy, well done. You will be delighted to know that the *Florida* has already drawn blood – there's a Yankee whaler that she burnt and a Boston clipper taken as a prize. And all down to you. Well done indeed."

Bulloch was beaming from ear to ear. He looked over the President's shoulder and saw Stephen Mallory, who nodded, quietly applauding.

"But please do come in." Bulloch was ushered by the President into the dining room, which was also used as an office, especially when his health was poor. A man rose to his feet as Bulloch entered. He was short and plump, with curly dark brilliantined hair and a neatly trimmed beard, which rimmed a round face with a sallow complexion.

"May I present Mr Judah Benjamin, our new Secretary of State." Bulloch shook the plump and slightly damp hand, which held his own lightly between its thumb and fingers.

"… And Mrs Rose Greenhow … lately returned to us from a lengthy period of incarceration in Washington. Mrs Greenhow, in addition to being an old friend, has, in the past, provided us with much information relating to enemy troop positions, that has been invaluable to our Cause." The President smiled at Rose, who met the President's warm gaze and courteous words with a graceful incline of her head.

Bulloch was immediately taken by Mrs Greenhow. She looked a little tired, perhaps a little thin, but she was nonetheless a very handsome and attractive woman with a powerful presence. Bulloch was also immediately aware of her breasts which were of a sufficient size to be clearly visible as they pushed out the pale green silk of her frilled blouse, which was tucked neatly into the small waistband of her long beige riding skirt.

"I have heard so much about you, Captain Bulloch." She extended a hand with long, elegant fingers, which he took in his own and kissed lightly. The other men laughed.

"My God," Mallory wheezed through a cloud of cigar smoke, "send the man to Europe and look at the fancy manners he comes back with."

Bulloch reddened slightly, but could not take his eyes off Rose. He found himself hoping that there was no 'Mr Greenhow', but quickly put the thought out of his mind as he sat down at the table, where the President indicated.

"When did you leave England?" the President enquired.

"On the twenty-ninth of last month, Mr President, and I have been travelling ever since, really without pause. I am sure that I am well behind the current state of affairs. What is the latest on the war, if I may ask?"

The President frowned and sat back in his chair, steepling his fingers. It was then that Bulloch noticed the changes in the man since their last meeting. Jefferson Davis had aged. His dark, neatly trimmed hair had receded somewhat from his brow, emphasising the angular appearance of his face, while the exhaustion and the demands of his office were visible in the dark rings below his eyes and the gauntness of his sunken cheeks, below the prominent cheekbones.

"A lot has happened this spring," he said after a reflective pause, "and I cannot pretend that all of it is good. In fact, in this company, I will admit that there have been setbacks. For a start, there was Shiloh. You have heard of Shiloh?"

Bulloch shook his head. The President continued. "The Battle of Shiloh took place earlier this month on the Tennessee River, by Pittsburg Landing, in the southern part of that State." He paused, as if gathering his strength. "It was truly a terrible slaughter and at the end of the day, it is hard to say which side had the better of it. We both proclaimed victories, of course, but they were left in possession of the field – although they suffered more casualties than we. Thirteen thousand on their side to ten thousand, seven hundred on ours – out of around forty thousand men on each side that took part in the engagement. And sadly for us General Johnston was killed. He bled to death on his horse – a ball from a Yankee sharp shooter got him in the leg. We will sorely miss him."

Bulloch recoiled. He had never heard of a battle where the numbers of dead and wounded were so high. The other two men in the room shook their heads, looking grim, while Rose Greenhow put her hand on the President's arm, as if to lend him strength.

"Then, well, most importantly, McClelland has finally come out of hiding and has brought his grand 'Army of the Potomac' all the way from Washington, by water, to land it on the York Peninsula. He is there himself and they have placed Yorktown under siege. Ironic isn't it? We are using many of the same old earth works that the British used so many years ago. Let us pray to God that the outcome is not the same on this occasion."

"Amen," murmured Mallory, under his breath.

"McClelland seems to have upwards of one hundred thousand men with him and he plans to march up the peninsula and lay siege to Richmond. You should know that Joe Johnston has brought his Army down from the line he held on the Bull Run, and General Jackson will reinforce him with his troops from the Shenandoah Valley. Meanwhile I have given overall responsibility for the defence of Richmond to General Robert E. Lee, in whom I have the greatest confidence.

'Old Granny Lee', thought Bulloch, while keeping his face impassive. 'The King of Spades? Well, maybe he was the right man for the job, given how much digging there was going to be'.

"And last of all," the President said, pursing his lips, "I am afraid that you will not be using Savannah again to bring in cargoes of guns from England."

"Savannah has fallen?"

"No, no Captain Bulloch, do not alarm yourself, please. Although Fort Pulaski has been taken – and therefore the harbour is beyond our reach."

Bulloch reflected happily on the fact that his children were no longer in Savannah and congratulated himself on the speedy sale of his house that had followed their departure.

"So that is how matters stand at this moment. And that is why your activities in England and those of our other people there are so crucial to our efforts to emerge victorious from this terrible war. Secretary Mallory will talk to you later about the details, but we want you to go back to England and commission several 'rams' for us – steel hulled steam frigates, modelled on the *Virginia* which, as you will have heard, sank three Union warships at Hampton Roads last month."

"Furthermore," he continued with barely a pause to draw breath, "I want you to work closely with James Mason, our Commissioner in London, who is active on the diplomatic front in his attempts to secure recognition for our Country. He can be of assistance to you, possibly in the area of helping to raise further funds for your activities or at least in terms of providing intelligence, gathered through his network of agents. This is where Mrs Greenhow comes in. She will be going to England with you and will be based in London where she will be co-ordinating the activities of all our European agents. She will be your primary contact point for Commissioner Mason. I am sure that you will agree that it could be compromising for a diplomat to be seen hob-nobbing with one, such as yourself, who has, I understand, ah, achieved a certain notoriety over recent months." The President saw Bulloch's frown and hurriedly continued... "Only insofar as Charles Adams, the Union's Minister in London, has correctly identified you as a Confederate agent and the guiding hand behind both the *Fingal* and the *Florida* – about which he is, apparently, highly vexed. Mason believes that Adams has voiced his concern to Palmerston, the Prime Minister who, while fence-sitting as usual, may just be encouraged to do something about your activities. Hence I urge you to take the greatest care to ensure that nothing prevents your next ship from sailing. Bye the bye, what are we to name her?" He turned to Mallory.

"The *Alabama*, Mr President, if that's agreeable to you."

"A fine name, a fine State. Yes, quite agreeable, thank you, Stephen."

"And Captain Bulloch, should you find that the atmosphere in Britain becomes unconducive to the execution of the commission of our 'rams', then you should feel free to use Mrs Greenhow to contact John Slidell, our commissioner in Paris. He informs me that the French are a thoroughly venal lot, who will do almost anything if bribed appropriately."

Bulloch glanced up at Rose Greenhow, to find her studying him with a quizzical expression on her face. He caught her eye but she quickly looked away, suppressing a small smile that danced around the corners of her mouth. He continued to examine her fine features and this time when their eyes met, neither looked away. He grinned broadly, but she gave a little frown, indicating that the President's office was an inappropriate venue for flirtation, but this soon melted away and was replaced by a frank and open gaze that seemed to promise much.

In fact, she was thinking that this tall, heavy-set man with the striking set of whiskers was a highly unsuitable candidate for any mission involving tact, diplomacy or discretion in any measure. True, he had dark blue eyes which twinkled when he smiled, and was to some degree attractive, but every emotion was writ large upon his prominent features and she could not believe that his passion or his temper were ever fully under control.

For his part, he was entranced by Rose Greenhow. She had that rare magnetic quality that attracted him immediately and elevated him to a state of near breathless anticipation when he found his admiring looks being returned in such a forthright manner.

"Mr President, a question for Captain Bulloch, if I may?" Rose said, neatly cutting off the President's monologue and Bulloch's reverie.

"Eh?" said Bulloch, coming back to reality with a rush.

"Captain Bulloch, could you tell me what is the level of activity by Federal agents in England? And does it currently pose a threat to the achievement of our objectives?"

"Eh? Ah, yes. That is …" he floundered, his thoughts racing this way and that. "Er … the … Consul in Liverpool … um … Thomas Dudley is his name … he's … he's running several agents, some of whom tried to burn the *Oreto* … the *Florida* that is. We are followed often in Liverpool and always when we venture up to London. It hasn't affected us overly much… as yet … but they will keep on trying and I am sure that they will be seeking to bring pressure on the politicians to clamp down on us."

"And, how is it that your activities are so well known that they can be clamped down upon, may I ask? I would have thought that you would have cloaked your shipbuilding within layers of obfuscation and falsehood, so that they would be invisible to enemy agents."

Bulloch frowned and glared at her. 'What's the damned woman doing?' he thought to himself. 'She's trying to show me up – in front of the President – the witch!'

"Perhaps this can be discussed later … with Secretary Mallory," intoned the President, who had been watching this verbal exchange, and the non-verbal which preceded it, with some amusement. "And now I believe that the Secretary of State may have some information which relates to a scheme for raising a really very significant quantum of funds from Europe – that I know will be of interest to you." He turned to Judah Benjamin, signalling him to proceed.

"Ahem." The Secretary of State cleared his throat. "The details are still some way from being clarified I am afraid – I feel that it would be premature, if you don't mind. Perhaps in one or two month's time?"

The President nodded. "In which case, lady and gentlemen …"

*   *

Later that day Rose sat in Stephen Mallory's office and sipped tea from an elaborately glazed, bone china, tea service. She dabbed the corners of her mouth with the small silk square provided and said, "really Stephen, I cannot see where your confidence in this man derives from."

Mallory looked at her evenly. 'The lady doth protest too much…' he thought, but said: "It is like this; men are similar to horses – many will perceive the obstacles in their path and will be brought to a standstill by them, refusing the jump; others, the few, may jump those fences, but even they will always refuse at some point, when confronted by a fence that their reason tells them is too high to jump or too broad to go around. Bulloch, on the other hand, is one of a rare breed of men who simply does not accept the existence of obstacles – he does not see them and thus crashes straight through them when, inevitably, they do occur. He is absolutely single-minded and very brave. I do not believe that others could have accomplished a fraction of what he has done to date. So, Rose, do not judge him harshly especially for a lack of subtlety, when you do not yet know him. He is a complex man and is far more cunning than you give him credit for."

Rose was surprised at this eulogy, especially coming from Stephen Mallory whom she had always considered to be both reserved in his praise and taciturn in his manner. She said: "Very well, Stephen – I have always respected your judgement and accepted your advice." But inwardly she remained highly sceptical.

"Now Rose, there is one more thing." Here Mallory sighed deeply and looked uncomfortable, crossing his legs and adjusting his cuffs before he spoke. "You should know that Captain Bulloch has, from the very start, wanted command of a fighting ship. In fact, while I have never expressly promised him such, he has been led to believe by no lesser a person than the President himself that, provided ships are built as a result of his activities in England, then

128

one of these vessels will be his to command. Now, I know that he did not really expect to be given the first, the *Florida* but he did have his heart set on the *Alabama* – a ship, which I understand, has been most lovingly built, from the finest materials, entirely to his own specifications." He paused. "Earlier this afternoon, I had the uncomfortable duty of informing James Bulloch that the Captaincy of the *Alabama* had been awarded to Rafael Semmes – a naval officer of considerable experience and reputation. He was … crest-fallen … to say the least. Now, I tell you this by way of back-ground and so that you can understand that what I tell you next, I do not say lightly." He took another deep breath. "I am a little concerned about Captain Bulloch's handling of the monies with which we have entrusted to him. There. I have said it. Are you surprised?"

"Why, of course I am surprised. You build up the valiant Captain as an officer of capability, determination, and fortitude and then you strike him down as an embezzler and a thief. You have evidence?"

"No, I have no evidence, I have only a bad feeling. He is very vague in accounting for some thousands of pounds, which I admit is only a small part of the funds at his disposal, but then again there is a worrying report from Charles Prioleau, whom you will meet. He is the manager of the Liverpool branch of Fraser, Trenholm, the Charleston-based banking house, you know? He acts as a sort of unofficial clearing house for our financial activities in Europe. Anyway, he has informed me of a most concerning development. Apparently our Captain Bulloch refuses to repay a debt owed to his firm and has gone so far as to deposit the funds, which are all earmarked for the ships that he has commissioned, with a different financial institution. Bulloch says that this is to avoid Prioleau helping himself to repay the loan, but Prioleau believes that there may be a more perfidious explanation. He believes that … ah … Captain Bulloch may have gambling losses. Apparently he does frequent one particular gambling den … it's all very worrying, I must tell you. You see, I have known James for many years and he owes his current position to my recommendation and thus the situ-ation is even more difficult for me than it might otherwise be. And that is why I have been telling you all this, Rose. I would like you to … investigate these rumours to see if there is any substance to them. No one must know, of course, other than you and I – and I must beg you to be as careful and as discreet in this matter as you ever can be. He is already not a particularly happy man and he is very valuable to us. Were he to find out that we were investigating him, then he could react in a very ... unpredictable ... manner. He has a bad temper and can be violent when aroused."

Rose sat back, astonished at these revelations. "Why, Stephen, of course I will see what I can find out ... and you have my assurance that I will be the very soul of discretion and will only communicate with you personally. But I must tell you that I am not comfortable with this assignment."

"I would not expect you, or any reasonable person, to be comfortable with the idea of ... spying ... on a comrade-in-arms. But we must do what we must do."

"Where is Captain Bulloch now?"

"He has gone to Atlanta to see his children. His wife left him recently ... it's an awful story ... ran off with a cavalry officer, who was killed at Balls Bluff. She has become somewhat peculiar, I am led to believe. She now works as a nurse in the military hospital ... up there ..." he pointed out the window, on "Chimborazo Heights." He shook his head, "We have so many wounded boys ... but it is still not a fitting activity for a woman of her upbringing and position in society."

"Oh, and being a spy is, I suppose?" asked Rose innocently.

* *

Ten days later, Rose met Bulloch again, on the platform of the station in Richmond. She was elegantly attired in a hooped dress of burgundy velvet, with black silk frogging and a matching bonnet, tied below the chin. Bulloch saw her, raised his hat and inclined his head. "My dear Mrs Greenhow, what a pleasure. I had hoped to see you again before leaving – or are we to travel together? I do hope so."

He looked calm and rested. She extended her hand, petite in a lace fingerless glove, which he took lightly in his. 'No kiss this time,' she thought. 'Shame. But I do admire his manners'. "Yes, Captain, we are to travel together, all the way to Liverpool. Although you will find my conversation very dull I am sure, perhaps we can pass the time at cards. You do play cards, don't you Captain Bulloch? I myself am very fond of whist."

They boarded a train of the Richmond and Petersburg line, which puffed and clanked its way over a long iron railway bridge that spanned the James River. Below they could see 'Belle Isle' the inappropriately named island where three thousand Union prisoners of war eked out a thin and miserable existence.

The train continued south for several miles, before turning eastward to Petersburg, and on to Suffolk and then Norfolk.

As the train pulled into Norfolk, a scene of great chaos greeted them. Boxes and cases of all shapes and sizes were carelessly piled and stacked here and there, all over the station and its yards and the streets and areas beyond. Soldiers, with guns at the ready, guarded the piles of supplies, but some were asleep in spite of the clamour and the bustle, while others lay on their backs in the sun and chewed quids of tobacco, occasionally spitting gobs of brown saliva onto the platform.

Down on the docks the situation was as bad, if not worse. Small boats which flitted in and out of the docks, were quickly filled to capacity with all manner of goods, before setting off up the Elizabeth River, while stevedores laboured with derricks to load the piles of waiting cargo into the holds of the larger ships.

"What is going on?" Bulloch asked a sturdy overseer who held a long whip, which he occasionally flicked at one or other of the group of Negroes in his charge, when he perceived a lessening of effort on the part of that individual.

"They's Federal gunboats at the mouth of the Elizabeth, they is," mumbled the overseer, rotating his wad into the corner of his mouth to improve his diction. He spat. "Rumour is that they's Yankees on the far bank of the James too and that Norfolk can't hold. They's plans for e-vacu-ating us. So we's getting out fust." He spat again. "Get on yer lazy nigger." He flicked the whip and nodded happily at the yell it produced.

Bulloch took Rose by the arm and guided her through the melee, elbowing aside those who through carelessness or design sought to block their way. He kept a close eye on the Negro porter who struggled along in their wake, bowed under by the weight of Rose's trunk and her several cases of assorted sizes, all in matching pig skin. Towards the end of the dock they saw the *Golden Plover,* a two-masted schooner that was due to take them to Bermuda, where they would board a steam-powered passenger ship for the remainder of their journey to Liverpool.

Surrounding the *Golden Plover* was a crowd of well-dressed individuals, both men and women, gesticulating and shouting. On the deck, looking down at them with studied disinterest was the Captain. He was leaning on the rail, his cap pushed to the back of his head, smoking a short clay pipe, which from time to time, emitted a small pungent cloud that was instantly whipped away by the on-shore breeze.

Bulloch pushed his way through the crowd, ignoring the shouts of 'mind where you're going!' and 'oh really!' and 'have a care there!' which were directed towards him from the well-dressed throng, all of whom were trying to attract the Captain's attention and some of whom waved handfuls of large denomination dollar bills, the better to do so.

When he arrived at the front, Bulloch shouted up at the Captain, "I say, Captain, my name is Bulloch ... I and ... my friend ... have reserved cabins on your ship ... to Bermuda. May we board?"

The Captain looked at Bulloch. "You may not. All previous bookings are cancelled. We's gonna auction the cabins agin, jes as soon as I'm ready. So stand yer ground and git ready ter bid." Rose looked at Bulloch with anxiety. "What are we going to do?" she shouted in his ear, so as to be overheard above the surrounding cacophony.

Bulloch looked up and down the dock in exasperation. "Aha ... just wait here," he shouted back, "I won't be long" and he shouldered his way out through the crowd, before setting off back the way they had come, at a run, the tails of his coat flying out behind him.

After a few minutes, the Captain took a belaying pin and banged it on the rails, several times. The crowd fell silent. "Now," he said, "the auction's gonna start. What we'll do is ter auction the cabins first, one by one like – there's six of 'em – then we'll get onta the shared spaces, on the lower deck and last of all, the deck places, for those of ye with less cash like. Now what am I bid fer ... what the hell ..." He stopped and looked beyond the crowd to where a column of ten sailors, with rifles at the port, bayonets fixed, jogged behind an officer, who blew a whistle as he approached. Next to the officer was Bulloch, his revolver in his hand.

The crowd parted as if by magic and those on its outer edges started to drift away, unwilling to have their unpatriotic and cowardly behaviour witnessed by the military.

"What's going on here?" demanded the officer, as he came abreast of where the startled Captain stood.

"I was just sellin' cabin space I was. Nuttin' wrong with dat, eh?" replied the Captain, spitting.

"Other than its obvious immorality, no. Unless of course the cabins were already sold that is – in which case it is fraudulent conversion and war profiteering," said the officer who had been a lawyer prior to volunteering, "punishable with imprisonment and confiscation of the relevant goods – namely this ship."

"Orright, orright," said the Captain, clearly rattled, "keep yer shirt on. Your friend 'ere and his missus", he winked at Rose, "can come on board. They can 'ave their cabins – if I can sell the rest. Fair do's?"

The officer looked at Bulloch who shrugged. Bulloch, Rose and the porter climbed the gangplank which was lowered for their access, as the auction re-commenced and the volume of the crowd rose once again.

Later, as Rose sat on the swaying cot in her cramped cabin and the *Golden Plover* edged out into the James River, catching the swell that came in from the open sea, she thought about Stephen Mallory's description of James Bulloch. 'Yes,' she thought, 'he does go straight through all obstacles, like a ... like a ...' She groped for the correct simile ... 'like a bullet through butter. And he does grow on one. I shall have to be careful not to become too fond.'

VIII

Liverpool and London – June, July, 1862

అం ఈ

The *Golden Plover*, which had taken them on the mercifully short crossing from Norfolk to Bermuda, had provided cabins whose dimensions permitted the swinging cot barely twenty degrees of lateral motion before colliding with the movable partitions on each side. And to make matters worse, there was room for only a single sea chest, without blocking the route between the cot and the door. Rose had the difficult and humiliating task of climbing over her piles of baggage each time she entered her cabin, which caused her to curse and swear in a very unladylike manner.

This was audible to the crew and the other passengers through the partitions, which being no more than thin sheets of pine, let through every sound. Bulloch would bid Rose 'goodnight' from his own cot and then lie awake until her heavy breathing turned into light snores, at which time he would relax and drift off to the soothing melody of the creaking of the ship's planking, the gurgle of water below the hull and Mrs Greenhow's nasal lullaby.

The toilet arrangements were also far from satisfactory as there was but one internal head for all the passengers, while the crew used the communal head with its direct ocean drop. Bulloch gave up using the single passenger's facility early during the crossing as one of the female passengers seemed to enjoy occupying this dark and humid cell for extended periods and no amount of loud coughing or muttered imprecations were successful in shifting her.

The *Maid of Derry*, on the other hand, was a purpose built passenger liner that ran from Bermuda to Liverpool and provided large, light and airy cabins, with fixed cots and plenty of storage room. The weather was fine, the wind fair and Bulloch and Rose spent much time together, either walking the deck, playing cards, or just talking. Bulloch found himself opening up to Rose, as the days passed, confiding in her about his wife and children and his sadness at the recent turn of events and even of his bitter disappointment at Mallory's gift of the *Enrica's* Captaincy to Rafael Semmes.

For Rose, the sea air and enforced rest had a thoroughly beneficial effect on her constitution, weakened as it had been by the months of prison hardship. Her face filled out again, the wrinkles mostly vanishing, except for the faint smile lines around her violet eyes which, if anything, added to rather than detracted from her overall beauty, and her hair regained its original fullness and lustre. She would take Bulloch's arm as they promenaded the small area of deck available to the passengers, swaying lightly against him as the gentle swell propelled her first in one direction, then the other.

If a larger than usual wave caused her to stagger, he would clasp her around the waist to prevent her from falling and briefly luxuriate in the weight of her body against his chest. And so the days passed. On their last evening aboard before reaching Liverpool, the weather had worsened somewhat as the liner rounded the South of Ireland and entered St George's Channel. The passengers were invited to dine with the Captain, but many declined as they were feeling unwell. Bulloch and Rose, however and two other couples enjoyed the full measure of the Captain's hospitality – the men staying on at the table after the service had been cleared to consume port and brandy with their cigars, while the ladies withdrew to the stateroom.

After the dinner finally broke up and the men went their separate ways with many a handshake and back-slap of intoxicated good-fellowship, Bulloch went to look for Rose and found her sitting alone, in the corner of the stateroom with her back to the other ladies, who were playing cards.

"Why so solitary Rose?" he asked, placing a hand lightly on her shoulder. She looked up at him and saw that her eyes were brimming with tears.

"How now, my dear, what is this?" He sat on the arm of her chair and took her small, lightly boned hands in his large, scarred fists.

"Oh, just feeling sad, James. Missing my girls… wondering what they are doing … just that sort of thing", she replied, dashing away the drops with the back of her gloved hand. And then, for no particular reason, she told him about her arrest and imprisonment and about the persistent importuning of the dreadful Allan Pinkerton. Bulloch was shocked and said so, but he looked so serious and self-righteous that she laughed, unused to seeing him in the ill-fitting guise of a gentleman. Her laughter clearly surprised him and he looked so startled that she again laughed. "Look, you are a wonder James, you have completely lifted me out of my brown study. Now it is getting late so I would be obliged if you would escort me back to my cabin."

At her cabin door, he waited while she fumbled with the key, but when she had unlocked and opened the door, she turned around to bid him 'goodnight' only to find him standing very close to her. He put his arm around her waist and, putting his lips close to her ear, said: "Rose, Rose I have so enjoyed these past days and weeks spent in your company and you know that I find you very attractive." He paused. "Rose… I … would very much… like … to …", but she placed two fingers against his lips, preventing him from finishing his sentence.

"I know exactly what you would like to do – James," she said in a kindly manner, smiling at him, but shaking her head. "But it is not to be. We must work together and I fear that things … may be complicated enough, without our becoming lovers. Now, back to your cabin my friend, and sleep soundly for tomorrow we arrive in England and we have much to do." She kissed him lightly on the lips before propelling him out through the open cabin door and shutting it quietly behind him.

'Damnation', he thought, as he trudged heavily down the corridor to his own cabin. But the rejection had been so nicely and kindly done that he could not really mind and in that last little and really unnecessary kiss, there had been some promise for the future. Or so he told himself and the idea cheered him so that he fell asleep smiling.

The next day Rose was all business and bustling efficiency throughout their disembarkation. She left him to catch the train to London with a quick wave of the hand and a small smile. "Stay in contact," she shouted from the window of the cab as it pulled away from the kerbside. He raised his top hat in salute and nodded.

*   *

Since that moment he had divided his time between Laird's and the gambling club on Castle Street. His welcome from Marise had been ecstatic. She had flung her arms around his neck, kissing him noisily before pulling him through the low door by the bar and up the steep and narrow wooden staircase. The first time they had not undressed at all. Bulloch had merely pushed her onto her back and lifted her skirts, grunting with satisfaction at finding her drawerless, before unbuttoning his trousers and roughly entering her. That coupling had lasted scarce minutes before coming to a climax that left both of them panting and dishevelled. On subsequent occasions the pace had been more leisurely and the undressing more decorous, but Bulloch's mind had also strayed from his olive-skinned partner to Rose, from whom he had heard not one word.

His reception from the Jew, Isaac Kopa had been nearly as warm, given that Bulloch had cleared his £1,700 debt prior to his departure. The Jew had instructed the dealers and the shills that Bulloch was to win – not too much of course, but just enough. And win he did. And thus the first few weeks after his return were happy days, with winnings jingling in his pocket and frequent visits to Marise's bedroom and all the while the sun shone and the news of the war from across the Atlantic changed for the better and remained good.

Old 'Granny' Lee had combined the small and divided armies of the Confederacy at Richmond and, taking command, had attacked McClellan's superior forces and had attacked them again and again, all the while driving the enemy back down the Peninsula, often with terrible losses to his own troops. In the end, McClellan's grand Army of the Potomac had retreated as far as Harrison's Landing, on the James, where it had gone to camp, awed by the aggressiveness of its foe and convinced as to their numerical superiority.

*　　*

John Laird rose as Bulloch entered the boardroom, whipping his spectacles from his nose and hiding them in a cupped hand. Young Mr William, who had been accompanying Bulloch on a tour of the nearly finished *Enrica*, followed him into the room.

"And so, Mr Bulloch, how do you find her … how do you find Hull 290? A fine ship, is she not?"

"Indeed, Mr Laird, she is that," replied Bulloch, looking somewhat wistful. "But more than that, she appears to be a marvellously well-founded ship. I am impatient to put her through her paces. When can I have her? What do you say?"

Laird and his sons beamed at Bulloch's enthusiasm. "Another few days... perhaps on the nineteenth, we can schedule a sea trial? Would that suit?"

"Indeed it would, Mr Laird ... and I will be in a lather of anticipation until that day. Now, if we may be seated, there is another matter that I wish to discuss with you."

Laird, father and sons, sat down across the table from Bulloch and watched attentively as he carefully unfolded the detailed plans of a ship, which were finely etched on waxed paper. He smoothed the creases with the palm of his hand before turning the paper around and sliding it across the finely polished table.

The Lairds sat forward, while the two boys, who were seated at the extremities of the table, stood and leaned over for a better view. After several moments silence Laird looked up, his piercing blue eyes below the bushy, white brows, holding Bulloch in an even gaze before returning to the plan with a "hmmm..."

After a further while, the boys returned to their seats, while John Laird senior sat back in his chair and, resting his elbows on the table, steepled his fingers and tapped them lightly against his mouth.

"It won't be easy, Mr Bulloch".

"And that is because ...?"

"And that is because, Mr Bulloch, as you very well know, Hull 290 has attracted, and continues to attract, a considerable degree of attention, from a variety of sources, both official and unofficial. But we have our story fairly well worked out and we also have some friends ... in positions of influence. Now, this unwelcome attention is in spite of the fact that Hull 290 could, just, at a stretch of the imagination, be an armed merchantman. Unlikely, but possible. This 'thing', Mr Bulloch, on the other hand, is a war ship – and nothing else could she ever be. I do not know that ... our friends ... will be able to keep the wolves from the door in the face of such blatancy. Why, she even has a seven foot iron ram on her prow and ... turrets ... to protect her guns."

"Not 'she' Mr Laird".

"I beg your pardon, sir?"

"Not 'she' … 'they'. I am ordered to have two such ships built and it is my strong preference to have them built here, in your yards. However, should you be unwilling …"

"No, no Mr Bulloch, let us not be hasty. I was merely pointing out that this may be an enterprise which is not entirely without risk. I am sure that we would wish to extend our mutually satisfactory relationship, but there are other matters to be considered. I would like to reflect on this further, together with my directors. Perhaps we could discuss it again, say, on the 19th? Hmm? I will accompany you on 290's sea trials. Indeed, I wouldn't miss them for the world. We can talk then."

* *

The Foreign Secretary, Lord Russell, sat at his magnificent desk in his palatial office, completely dwarfed by the scale of his surroundings. He was hunched forward in his chair, sitting with bowed head and rounded shoulders, oblivious to the noise of carriage wheels on the cobblestones below his open windows and to the insistent rapping on his inner door. At last he looked up. "Come," he said, his husky voice barely above a whisper, but sufficient for his secretary, who had his ear pressed firmly against the wood, waiting for just such a response to his request for admission.

"Well?" said the old man, barely stirring in his chair at the flustered and hurried entry of his young secretary.

"Well, my Lord … it is Mr Adams … he is still here."

"Oh drat! I suppose I shall have to see him then. Really the man is such an infernal nuisance. Show him in Stainforth, if you'd be so kind."

Lord Russell was barely half way to his feet when a veritable whirlwind blew in through his door and charged across the sumptuous rugs towards the desk, huffing and puffing, perspiring heavily, with tails flying out behind him and his right hand extended.

"So kind, Lord Russell, so very kind. Please do not rise on my account."

Lord Russell paused, a momentary flicker of annoyance crossing his angular features, before he straightened with somewhat of an effort and accepted the outstretched hand. He waved Charles Adams to one of the upright and intentionally uncomfortable chairs that fronted his desk and then sat back down himself.

"So, Mr Adams, to what do I owe this pleasure … if I cannot guess that is …?"

"Well, I am sure that you may be able to guess. Of course, I wish to discuss, again, the warships that are being built for our enemies, by British shipyards. The last one, you may be interested to know, which was constructed at Miller's Yard in Liverpool, is now called the *Florida*. The Confederate Steam Ship, *Florida*, that is. She has already destroyed several unarmed merchantmen and has cost their owners dear both in terms of lives and property." He paused, waiting for a reaction, but receiving none, continued. "Now my agents tell me that the other big one, which is being built at Lairds, is nearing completion. I have a sworn affidavit from their foreman that she is designed to carry eleven guns, that she has waterproof ammunition magazines and that platforms have been screwed to her decks for pivot guns. Really, I ask you, what does that look like? And yet, and yet I take this affidavit … the written proof, which you informed me was a prerequisite for official action … I take this to the office of the Collector of Customs in Liverpool and what do they do? I will tell you what they do, my Lord – they do nothing. They maintain that this is insufficient evidence and they do nothing. Bah!"

"Calm yourself Sir, calm yourself, or you will suffer an embolism," Lord Russell quickly interjected, raising both hands, alarmed at the purple hue of his visitor's face and the line of spittle which was forming around his lips. Adams collapsed back into his chair with a gasp and drew in several ragged breaths.

"So," he continued, after sipping at the glass of water proffered by the hovering Stainforth, "I have come both to express our extreme unhappiness with this state of affairs – to register a formal complaint, if you will – and to inform you as to my next course of action." He paused both for effect and to draw breath. "I intend now to seek a written opinion from Robert Collier which, coming from the Judge Advocate of the British Fleet and, I suspect, the greatest authority in this country on maritime law, may encourage or indeed compel you to a course of action that you otherwise seem unwilling to pursue."

"My dear Adams, you must do exactly as you see fit," Lord Russell murmured, his face impassive, but his mind already considering the implications of going against an opinion of Collier's. 'Then I would really be out in the open', he thought, 'and it's too early for that. But should he opine against us, there are always other opinions than might be sought. Oh yes, and getting these can be damned time consuming'.

To Adams he said: "and was there anything else …?"

"Just the one small thing – there seems to be a motion before Parliament, to be debated on the nineteenth, which has been proposed by William Lindsay – a Tory, I believe. It contemplates the recognition of the Confederacy as a sovereign state and seeks to push Britain into the role of mediator in our internal struggle." He leaned forward. "You must understand Lord Russell, that your country's mediation is neither sought after nor welcomed and that formal recognition of the Confederate Rebels will lead, inevitably and, may I say, regretfully, to a state of war between our two countries."

Lord Russell smiled thinly. "So both you and Seward have told me before. And yet I do not know why you would threaten us with a war that you cannot conceivably win. Why, I have only today received the news that your General McClellan has been thrown back from the gates of Richmond and is retreating in some disarray down the York peninsula. Is that not so?"

"Not entirely, no."

"Well, whatever the details, he has been turned back – or to put it another way, the Union has suffered yet another military reverse at the hands of its smaller and less industrialised adversary. Is *that* not so?"

Adams pursed his lips but said nothing, frowning at the backs of his hands.

"And this motion of Lindsay's, Mr Adams … he is, as you correctly point out, a member of the Conservative Party and thus he is neither part of, nor is he supported by, Palmerston's ministry, to which I belong. Is that clear? Now is there anything else Mr Adams…?"

After Adams had left, Lord Russell relaxed, leaning his head against the soft leather of the chair back. 'Much to consider from that', he thought. 'If Lindsay can carry Parliament, which he should be able to with this latest news – and with the information I have supplied him – then we are on the way. But first I must shift Palmerston and for that we will need one more convincing victory…'

The nineteenth of July dawned clear and fine, with just a few small clouds, high in the sky, scudding before the Sou'easterly breeze, which blew steadily at fifteen knots. "Capital weather, Mr Bulloch, capital weather! Permission to come aboard?" Bulloch leaned over the rail and saw John Laird standing, hat in hand, with all three of his sons at the bottom of the gang-plank amidst the organised chaos of their yard

"By all means," Bulloch shouted to be heard above the noises of riveting and caulking, "come aboard. We are nearly ready to cast off and must proceed without delay if we are to catch the tide on the turn. I intend to sail her down the river and out to sea but then to return by steam." He was totally absorbed for the next while in the preparations for their departure.

Lieutenant Low took the wheel as they eased down the river under only their topsails. As they entered the Irish Sea and turned with the wind, Bulloch ordered the large fore and aft sails, the jibs and trysails to be unfurled. He stood on the poop-deck, one hand on the rail, one behind his back in a fist, his heart ablaze, as the wind caught the sails, bending the long masts of yellow pine and singing through the iron rigging. The *Enrica* picked up speed and was soon whipping along at a good ten knots, the spray flying, as her sharp prow cut through the water.

Bulloch looked around to see Laird by his side, the wind streaming his whiskers out behind him, and said, "she's a fine ship Mr Laird, you've done us proud."

* *

The Members filed into the Commons chamber, taking their appointed places – the ministers on the Government front benches, the leaders of the Opposition facing them across the chamber, both with their backbenchers arrayed behind them. There was a hubbub of noise from the many raised voices as Members stood around in small groups, earnestly conferring or speculating loudly with their neighbours on the outcome of Lindsay's motion. A hush fell briefly as a loud altercation erupted from the visitor's gallery, where a large man, with prominent features and long swept-back hair could be heard shouting, "if goddamn Moran is allowed down on the floor I'm not sitting up here with the rest of the goddamn peons."

Lord Russell looked up briefly and then turned to Gladstone, who sat to his right. "It's that fellow Mason making all the noise. Frightfully uncouth – I may have mentioned it." Gladstone nodded. The altercation died down and Mason reappeared below the visitor's gallery with a friend. Both took seats along the row from Benjamin Moran and glared at him. Moran took no notice until Mason rolled his wad of tobacco in his mouth and spat a large gob of brown saliva onto the floor, at which point he winced and looked away.

The Members had little time for further consideration of the expectorational habits of the Confederate Commissioner before the Speaker, resplendent in wig and gown, called the House to order. "The House recognises William Lindsay, honourable member for Sunderland," he cried and a small man, with thinning grey hair, clutching a bundle of papers, rose diffidently to his feet. On the Government front bench, Lord Palmerston, the Prime Minister, who was sprawled untidily, with his legs apart, tipped his top hat forward to cover his eyes, folded his arms across his chest and sighed deeply.

*   *

In the engine room, two Irish stokers, black with coal dust except where the sweat had cleaned their skin in thin stripes, shovelled laden spadefuls of sea coal into the roaring red maws of the furnaces that heated the boilers of the twin engines of Hull 290.

The *Enrica*, now under a full press of canvas, still ran before the wind in a Southerly direction, with the lightness and grace of a swan. On deck members of the scratch crew, who were not actually busy working the ship, together with her builder, his sons and her new owner, stood in awe of the grace of this craft.

When the steam pressure had risen to the appropriate level, Bulloch gave the order for her propellers to be lowered from the well into which they retracted while the ship was under sail alone, so they could be attached to the drive shaft. The speed rose slightly and then some more. "How fast?" Bulloch yelled at the Master who swung the lead, holding it between his wet fingers and counting. "Thirteen and a half knots, Sir," he shouted back with a huge grin on his face.

The sails were taken in and the *Enrica* turned North, back towards the Mersey, running on engines alone. Their speed dropped considerably as she now moved against both wind and tide. Bulloch found Laird below decks giving final instructions to one of the carpenters and shook him warmly by the hand. "I can find no fault, Mr Laird, you have a very happy customer. And now, if you are ready, I would like to discuss our other business."

"By 'our other business', Mr Bulloch, I assume that you are referring to Hulls 294 and 295?" Laird smiled as he said this, all the while propelling Bulloch into the *Enrica's* cabin, his hand on his elbow.

When they were seated, he continued. "We feel that provided there are no unforeseen delays, 294 can be ready for sea trials in March of next year, while 295 will be one or two months behind her sister. Is that satisfactory to you?"

"It is, Mr Laird, it certainly is. However, this might be an appropriate moment to discuss how we may prevent 'unforeseen delays'. I believe in this context that you refer to the risk of impounding or seizure by the British Government?"

"I do."

"Well, in the first instance, we must take some comfort from the fact that there has been no action taken so far. I am advised that we have the law on our side and thus I do not expect any officially sponsored disruption, unless, of course, there is a marked change in policy. As regards unofficial action ... well you should clearly maintain a very high level of vigilance within your yard. Secondly, there is a debate in Parliament today – indeed as we speak – which may change the stance of your Government substantially in our favour. And lastly, I have a plan on which we may fall back, should events move against us."

"Would it be appropriate to enquire as to the details of this plan?"

Bulloch shook his head. "Should it become necessary, Mr Laird, you will be the first to know."

*   *

William Lindsay had been on his feet for over an hour already, sometimes mumbling, sometimes shouting, striking at the air for emphasis with his papers crumpled in his fist, oblivious to the ones that escaped and fluttered to the floor to lie among the general litter of a long parliamentary session. Some Members emulated Palmerston, but actually slept, while others talked openly among themselves. Occasionally, at some point of Lindsay's, which was delivered in both an audible and a coherent manner, one or more of the Members would shout "hear, hear," but these were infrequent and gradually the House began to empty.

Sensing that he was losing his audience, Lindsay paused in his tirade against the Union and its bully-boy tactics and chose to sum up crying loudly, "I, like every Englishman who is honest with himself, must, in his heart, desire the destruction of the American Union which is too great a power. England should not let such a power exist on the American continent," and promptly sat down.

Lord Russell covered his face with his hands to hide his emotions. 'This man must be the greatest fool in Christendom', he thought. 'I have done everything short of writing his speech for him and yet not only is his delivery of the weakest kind, but he concludes with that statement, in which he quotes me verbatim and which is the only part of his speech that he has got right. And yet I would not have had him say that for the world, for it is not only utterly irrelevant to these proceedings, but it is a notion of the most inflammatory kind.'

Both Moran and Mason sat bolt upright at the conclusion of Lindsay's speech and even glanced at each other fleetingly before Moran slumped back on his bench and Mason spat tobacco-stained saliva onto the floor vehemently, scowling all the while.

Other speakers followed, The Emancipation Society Secretary, Patrick Taylor, who was deeply pro-union, could not be heard above the shouts and jeers from the Conservative benches, while Lord Adolphus Vane-Tempest provided a comic turn by attempting to support Lindsay, while excruciatingly drunk and finally falling over backwards into the row behind him.

At last the uproar subsided and an air of expectation entered the chamber. Sensing that the moment had arrived, Palmerston pushed his hat back from his face and slowly rose to his feet.

Ever the wily politician, his skills of oratory honed by count-less debates, his fine wit and sharp intelligence undimmed by the years, he eloquently dismissed the call for intervention as being premature when Southern independence was not yet firmly and permanently established.

He went on to chide the House for its temerity in assuming a role in decisions that belonged to his Ministry and to his Ministry alone. "My Government must and will maintain the discretionary power to decide what can be done, when it can be done and how it can be done," he concluded and sat down. The packed house remained silent for a moment and then the Members broke into loud applause, rising as a man to their feet, with cries of 'bravo!' and 'hear, hear'.

Palmerston strode out of the Chamber towards the Lobby, his Ministers in his wake, among them Lord Russell, walking slowly, his face calm and impassive.

I X

Harrison's Landing, Virginia – July, 1862

≈ ≈

The Grand Army of the Potomac was camped on a sandy point of land that protruded into the James River. Row after row of white tents, which provided shelter to over eighty thousand men, gave to a distant observer the impression of order. But closer to, the chaos of an army in a confined space became apparent, exacerbated by the heavy summer rains that had fallen intermittently for almost a month and at that moment still came sweeping in from the river to lash the shore. Miserable sentries hunched beneath their sodden capes while the remainder of the army sheltered in their tents, whose canvas was so thin and worn as to provide almost no barrier to the rain at all.

Around the tent city the earth had been churned into a brown viscous fluid in which some of the heavier artillery pieces had become irretrievably stuck, together with their caissons and even, in some cases, their teams of mules. These poor animals, having sunk into the mud up to their withers, could not be extricated and had had to be shot even as they thrashed in the mire, braying in panic.

The rotting flesh of the mules and the unburied dead on the surrounding hillsides and the decaying amputated limbs, which were piled outside the field hospitals, combined with the over-flowing latrines to create a stench that nauseated the encircling Confederate cavalry, even up-wind of the camp.

During the previous three weeks since the cessation of the fighting, the badly wounded had mainly been taken off down the river and returned to the relative comfort and cleanliness of army hospitals in Washington. But the hospitals at Harrison's Landing

147

continued to fill from diseases of every type, brought on by the filth, the wet and heat. Closed wounds wept and opened, sores erupted and suppurated and limbs disappeared as repeated amputations sought to stem the encroachment of gangrene into the body's core. The mosquitoes swarmed and sang, replete on the blood of the soldiers and their animals that packed the narrow area of land. Malaria swept through the encampment and together with typhus, typhoid and dysentery carried off more men than had the guns of Lee's armies in the seven days of battles around Richmond.

Now the army was shrinking as regiment after regiment was ordered onto transports and sent North to join the Army of Virginia, under the command of John Pope, which was now encamped in country that was dryer, cleaner and safer. Their morale, as they marched through the heavy mud, with bands playing and arms swinging was in direct contrast to the thousands that remained, slouching sullenly in groups or sitting dejectedly in front of their tents, playing cards and smoking.

Nonetheless the morale of the remaining troops was higher than that of their commanding officer, General George B McClellan, who had, until that morning, commanded the largest and best equipped fighting force that had ever existed on the American continent. An army which had recently been blunted and driven back by the repeated and savage attacks of a foe that could barely muster half their strength.

McClellan sat slumped in a chair, in the parlour of an old white clapboard farmhouse, an open newspaper in front of him, from which he had just learned of his replacement by General Henry Halleck as General-in-Chief of the land forces of the United States. How he cursed Lincoln! How he despised him for his weakness and his cowardice in not informing him of the termination of his command to his face. How he loathed the Republican courtiers who surround the simple backwoodsman President, always whispering and second guessing, while pretending expertise in matters military, whereas in reality their ignorance was as broad as their incompetence was profound.

McClelland also cursed the weather, the mosquitoes, General Lee and Allan Pinkerton – the latter because it was on his advice and using his intelligence apparatus that McClelland had stalled for so many days, waiting for reinforcements and had then advanced so slowly to meet an enemy that he believed to be his numerical superior. Pinkerton had seen regiments, brigades, divisions – even corps – where in fact none existed and were it not for him and his fallacious advice based on fictitious troops, why, he George McClellan, might even now be sitting in Davis' chair in the Executive Mansion in Richmond, instead of which…

For his part, Pinkerton had just received an exemplary dressing down, before being dismissed and being told to get out and leave for Chicago without delay. He, too, sat in his office in the parlour of a small homestead, where he used the dining table as a desk. There was a loud knock on the door.

"Come in", he shouted.

The door opened, revealing a tall, thickset man in a tattered, faded blue uniform with long black unkempt hair and a large bushy beard. His size was such that he filled the door frame completely and the two guards who followed him with rifles at the ready, bayonets fixed, were invisible to Pinkerton, who seemed startled by his visitor. The man entered, followed by his guards and stood dripping on the rug.

"You sent for me," he said addressing Pinkerton in a strong, guttural German accent.

"Yes, indeed – ye must be Sergeant Kurz. Come in now and seat yesself." Pinkerton waved away the guards and nodded to an upright chair opposite his desk. The German crossed the room, walking slowly with small steps, the shackles that linked his ankles clinking as he came. He sat down and rested his strong hands with their stubby brutal fingers on the tops of his meaty thighs and said nothing. Pinkerton picked up his file and read from it, not for the first time. Occasionally he would look up and stare at the German, who remained quite still, looking impassively at a spot on the wall.

The background of this man was interesting. Born twenty-nine years ago in Prenzlau in the Kingdom of Prussia, he had emigrated to the United States after the deaths of his parents, while he was only fourteen. He arrived in New York and shortly afterwards found a job as a blacksmith, the trade to which he had been apprenticed back in Prussia. He worked hard and diligently and on attaining his majority, was taken on as a partner by his erstwhile employer and fellow countryman. They expanded the business to include a livery stable, which both cared for the horses and carriages of the wealthy and rented them out to visitors. In the years before the war they prospered, but immediately after

Manassas, Kurz had surprised his partner by the sudden announcement that he was going to enlist and fight for the unity of his adopted country. His partner was distraught, but Kurz would not be swayed and after a while his partner ceased in his attempts to dissuade him as he knew that trying to change Kurz's mind when it was made up, was a futile endeavour.

Kurz enlisted and, to his pleasure, was sent west, after some rudimentary training, to join Franz Sigel's German brigade. Here he displayed a natural talent for shooting with great accuracy and this, combined with his ability to remain completely still for protracted periods, led to his selection as a sharpshooter. In the early days he carried his regulation issue Springfield rifle-musket but lamented its lack of accuracy at anything much beyond 500 yards. However at Lexington in late 1861 he had the fortune to come across a rebel sharpshooter, who was poorly concealed among some rocks. He broke the rebel's neck with his bare hands and took his British-made Whitworth rifle with its built in telescopic sight, which extended his range dramatically – to twelve hundred or even fifteen hundred yards. He killed dispassionately and indiscriminately – both officers and enlisted men, not only of the infantry, artillery and cavalry, but also supply wagon drivers, stretcher-bearers, cooks and priests. He would kill from hides, carefully chosen and well camouflaged, at extreme range. The bullet would arrive before the sound of the shot, either snuffing out the life of the victim instantly or causing hideous wounds from its large calibre soft lead ball.

His effect on the morale of the enemy, who, up till now, seemed to have a monopoly on the arcane skills of sharp shooting, was dramatic. So much so that Gottfried Kurz was promoted to Sergeant and requested to train a special group of sharpshooters. Reluctantly he agreed, but before he could start, a surprise enemy night march at the battle of Pea Ridge in Arkansas cut him off and left him behind Rebel lines. He was captured by a company of skirmishers and beaten severely, for sharpshooters were the most feared and hated of all the enemy. Finally, they placed his right hand on a boulder and smashed his fingers with their rifle butts, marvelling that he neither cried out nor begged for mercy.

Pinkerton looked up and considered the badly set, crooked fingers of the right hand, splayed, as if for inspection.

"Can ye shoot with that?" Pinkerton pointed to the hand.

"Maybe." He flexed the stiff fingers. "But not as well as before."

Pinkerton returned to the file. After capture, Kurz was taken by train, a journey lasting three days in cramped cattle wagons, without food or water, to Richmond. There he and the new Union prisoners, who had survived the journey, were herded across an iron bridge onto Belle Isle.

The camp at Belle Isle was no more than an open area of land, dusty in the Summer, muddy in the Winter, surrounded by a three foot deep ditch, which also served as a latrine and beyond that a four foot high earthen wall. On the far side of this stood the guards and, positioned at regular intervals, old smooth-bore cannons loaded with canister faced inwards, their barrels at maximum depression. There was one rule: cross the ditch, known as the 'deadline' and the guards would shoot to kill.

There was no shelter from the rain or from the sun. Some soldiers dug shallow pits and used sticks and their great coat to create a shelter from the elements, but most just endured until disease and the poor diet gave them release. Once a day the guards would beat a drum and, at the signal, the prisoners would move to the back of the enclosure. An old door would be put down across the ditch and the daily rations of stale bread, and a cauldron of weak soup would be carried into the compound. Any dead from the previous day would be carried out and buried beyond the berm, usually after a rigorous bayoneting to deter those who saw this as a potential avenue of escape.

Kurz did not get ill and he did not starve. Shielding his broken hand in his pocket he would be first at the rations, grabbing all he could and defending what he saw as his prerogative with vicious kicks that could break a bone on contact. In a place where a broken leg was a sentence of death, most were content to let the burly German take his fill. Others, who sought to challenge his actions, by ganging up against him, usually met an untimely end, often by strangulation in the night.

As McClellan's Army of the Potomac wound its slow and painful way up the York Peninsula during the month of May and the battles raged outside Richmond, so the guard detachments shrank in number and even the ancient cannon were removed to the outer perimeter defences of the city.

Just before dawn one day in late June, while the mist lay thick on the ground, the prisoners and guards were awoken by the noise of cannon-fire that no doubt signalled the start of yet another battle to the east of Richmond. The guards turned to stare at the flashes that illuminated the sky in that dark hour after the setting of the moon, wondering if this would be the final decisive battle of the war. Choosing his moment carefully, and staying low in the mist, Kurz sprang over the ditch, rolled across the berm and sprinted to the river. He made the water before being seen by a sentry on the bridge, who fired down on him, but the bullet splashed harmlessly into the water, missing his head by an inch. The current was strong and Kurz let it take him down the river, through the city. Below Richmond he came across barriers erected across the river to prevent Union warships from getting close enough to fire into the city, but these were not so closely constructed as to prevent one man from squeezing through.

At last, exhausted and freezing, Kurz climbed the bank only to be fired on by Union pickets, who saw this large figure looming out of the still-misty dawn. Happily, while a ball tugged at his sleeve, none hit and he was soon being fed bacon and corn bread around a fire.

Pinkerton closed the file. "You were not the only one to escape." A statement.

"So it would seem."

"And now I understand that the Provost Marshall has brought charges against ye for yer conduct while a prisoner and ye will face a court martial. Is that not right?"

"It is."

"Hmmm. Ye will probably go to prison for a long time. Ye may even hang if they can prove murder. What do you think about that?" Kurz shrugged.

"Ye seem indifferent. But I know you want to live. Ye are a survivor. What would ye say if I could give ye back yer freedom? Give ye another chance. Well?"

For the fist time a flicker of interest appeared in the German's dark eyes. "What must I do?"

"Kill someone for me. Kill an enemy of yer country. Kill a spy. That wouldn't be so hard would it?"

"No, I could do that."

"There are two other things ye should know. First, the spy is not in this country, but in England. Secondly, the spy is a woman. Does that change yer answer?"

"No. But what will I do after I have killed this woman?"

"I don't care. Just don't come back to America, that's all. Go home, go to Australia, go anywhere. I will give ye enough money to start again."

The German grunted, nodding his assent. Pinkerton reached under his jacket and took out a Remington .44, which he placed carefully on the table between them, the handle towards himself. "Take it," he said, "let me see what ye can do with that hand of yers." Pinkerton watched the broken right hand carefully but, until it was too late, failed to see the left hand shoot out, grab the pistol, cock it and aim it at his right eye.

Pinkerton was startled and a little flustered but was careful not to show it. "Easy there my friend – it's loaded. Now put the gun down again. I'd say ye have the job." The German paused for a count of three before releasing the hammer and replacing the gun exactly as it had been before.

"Now I am going to give ye some details and then I will explain to ye how ye are going to escape."

X

Liverpool and London – July, August, 1862

≫ ≪

Charles Adams sat in the same uncomfortable chair on the far side of the desk, facing Lord Russell.

"I came to tell you that I have Robert Collier's opinion." Adams proffered the heavy document, which was stitched together with scarlet silk ribbon.

Lord Russell ignored the outstretched arm and asked, intrigued, in spite of himself, "what does he say?"

Adams placed the document on the desk. "In his conclusion, he says that he could hardly conceive of a stronger infringement of the Foreign Enlistment Act. So, I must ask you, My Lord, will you now act?"

Lord Russell leaned forward, a particularly malevolent look in his rheumy eyes and tapped the document with a long yellow fingernail. "Before taking any precipitate action, I feel that it would be only prudent to obtain another opinion. I shall send this document to Sir John Harding Q.C. who is probably the leading 'Silk' on maritime law. We shall see what he has to say."

Adams sprung to his feet, his mouth agape; an angry flush suffused his patrician features. "The damned ship is nearly ready to sail – they were at sea only last week on trials – for God's sake man, if you prevaricate in this manner, she will escape."

"Do not raise your voice to me, Sir! You forget yourself! Now be seated, or I will have you shown out." Adams collapsed back into the chair perspiring heavily and mopping at his brow with a linen handkerchief. "I can assure you that Sir John will be asked to expedite the matter. I will personally write to him today and emphasise the urgency of a response. You must understand, Mr

Adams, that Her Majesty's Government cannot act against private property without the soundest of legal reasons in support – and were I to base such action on an opinion obtained by an interested party ..." he held up a finger to prevent Adams from interrupting ... "by an interested party, then I should expose the Government to criticism, which, under the circumstances I believe would be justified. Now, Mr Adams, if you will excuse me, I will begin that letter to Sir John Harding ... be so good as to send in my secretary, should you see him on your way out."

*   *

Having arrived early, Bulloch waited anxiously outside the house on Abercrombie Square until the appointed hour. Then he rapped on the door with the brass knocker. He was admitted by the butler who regarded him with a supercilious air, but deigned nonetheless to show him into the withdrawing room, where Mary Elizabeth Prioleau reclined decorously on a royal blue chaise longue.

"My dear Mr Bulloch, how very good of you to come," she said, extending a small lily-white hand, which Bulloch took and brushed lightly with his lips. He noticed then that there was the merest hint of a Liverpudlian accent remaining below the genteel upper-class drawl affected by Mrs Prioleau. When they had met over dinner he had not noticed it. Perhaps in broader company, especially with her husband's business associates, she took greater pains to conceal her humble origins, but now, in more intimate surroundings, she was less on her guard. Intriguing.

He sat opposite her, perched on the edge of a low and somewhat hard Chesterfield, as the maid served tea. He balanced the small cup and saucer on his grey worsted knee and nibbled cucumber sandwiches the size of butterflies and warm scones that were no larger than a plover's egg, spread thickly with raspberry jam.

He told Mary Elizabeth about the *Oreto* and his fight to save her from the arsonists, about Richmond and their journey by sea from Norfolk. She sat spellbound, occasionally interjecting 'no!' or 'truly!'. When he had finished his somewhat embellished tale, she placed one hand above her ample chest, fanned herself with a small ivory handled fan and said,

"Why, Mr Bulloch I do believe that you are the bravest man I have ever met. Not like Mr Prioleau" – she made a moue – "all he

155

ever talks about is money – and he doesn't seem to be very pleased with you Mr Bulloch – I don't know why. Have you two had words? Not over me, I do hope ..." She looked down coquettishly.

Bulloch cleared his throat, which was beginning to feel a little constricted and assured her that this was not the case. But he noticed that she had moved down the chaise longue, leaving space ... perhaps this was an invitation. Nothing ventured, he thought and swiftly rose from his chair and sat down close to her, but not touching. He angled himself towards her and said in a low voice: "I must tell you Mrs Prioleau, or may I call you Mary Elizabeth? I must tell you, how much I admire you, for your fine works in furtherance of our Cause ..." and detecting a faint but clear frown of annoyance continued quickly ... "and for your grace, elegance ... and your sublime beauty." He observed the light blush creep up her neck and continued, emboldened, first taking one of her hands in his and pressing it to his lips. "Oh how I want to hold you in my arms, to stroke your fine, long blonde hair, to feel you ..." but she did not wait for him to finish before launching herself at him, flinging her arms around his neck and kissing him firmly on the lips. He responded and they fell together onto the soft velvet of the seat. Bulloch started to undo the buttons of her blouse, pushing his hand inside and squeezing her firm breast through the light cotton covering of her camisole, feeling the hardening nipple below his palm. She reached down and grabbed at the front of his trousers and, finding the object of her interest already aroused, squeezed it gently. In quite a broad Liverpudlian accent she said: "lord luv us, you are a big one and no mistake ..."

Just then there was a gentle rapping on the door. "Ma'am, Ma'am" called the maid, "I can see the master coming up the stairs." Mary Elizabeth pushed Bulloch off her and began scrabbling with the buttons of her blouse, mouthing, "damn, damn". Bulloch shot to his feet and sat back down on the Chesterfield, just as Prioleau entered and stopped. He looked carefully at the scene before advancing, his hand extended. "Why, Mr Bulloch, what a surprise and ... what a pleasure, albeit an unexpected one. My dear," he said turning to his wife, "you should have told me!"

Mary Elizabeth had completed the refastening of all her buttons, bar one, but was flushed and flustered. Trying desperately to regain her composure she stammered ... "Mr Bulloch was passing ... he called to see you. I said he should wait ... as I believed that

156

you would not be long ..." she finished lamely, her eyes downcast.

"But my dear, do you not remember ... I said that I had to go to Manchester ... it is only by the merest chance that my meeting was cancelled and that I am home at all this evening. Well, Mr Bulloch, an opportune meeting indeed ..." Prioleau raised one perfectly curved eyebrow.

"Yes" said Bulloch glumly.

"And might I enquire as to the subject you wished to discuss with me? I had felt that our business dealin's were somewhat at arm's length followin' your engagement of the Liverpool & County Bank to transact your bankin' business. Is that not so? I should be truly delighted were it not so." He smiled evenly, meanwhile seating himself near his wife, in exactly the spot that Bulloch had occupied until just recently, crossing one elegant leg over the other and flicking an imaginary piece of dust from his knee.

Bulloch had, in fact, been intending to visit Prioleau in his office and to ingratiate himself with the fussy little man by repaying the £18,000 he owed Fraser, Trenholm out of the £25,000 that he had finally received from the Army's purchasing agent. This would leave him with sufficient funds to pay Laird £47,500 on the completion of the *Enrica* and to pay for the necessary cannon and stores to equip her fully. However the resultant balance of £22,500 was nowhere near enough to meet the down-payment that Laird required before starting work on the Rams.

Laird had explained, in the nicest way, that the risk of seizure was so much higher that his directors had only authorised him to proceed on the understanding that they received fifty percent of the amount due, up front. This came to £93,750, the price of one ship. Bulloch had written to Mallory asking to be credited with further money, but given the financial constraints under which the Confederate Government perpetually operated, he was not optimistic. The solution was to seek a further loan from Fraser, Trenholm which he knew he would not obtain until he had repaid the previous loan.

This Bulloch explained to Prioleau who nodded happily throughout, while Mary Elizabeth yawned obviously and fanned herself with irritated flicking movements.

"Why, Mr Bulloch, I am truly delighted that we can renew our business relationship and we will, of course, consider your proposal for a further loan most carefully, but if you will excuse me, I am puzzled ... why did you not chose to call on me in my office this afternoon?"

"Um ..." muttered Bulloch, looking desperately around the room for inspiration.

"My goodness – is that the time? I am so sorry, Mr Bulloch – my dear – but I had become so consumed by your discussions – ladies are so rarely permitted a glimpse into the fascinating world of commerce that you gentlemen occupy – that I had not been keeping an eye on the clock. And now it is nearly six and I must excuse myself. I am due at Lady Scrimgeour's at seven." Mary Elizabeth Prioleau rose to her feet, inclined her head slightly to the two men, who also stood, and swept out of the room.

"Well," said Bulloch quickly "I must be away as well. I shall certainly contact you to arrange a meeting, but whether or not this will be before I take the *Enrica* to the Azores, I cannot say. Until then." They shook hands and Bulloch almost ran down the stairs in his anxiety to be gone from the house.

Piroleau stood at the top of the stairs, watching Bulloch's rapid exit, tapping his foot and looking grim. 'This man is a fool', he thought. 'He makes love to my wife, in my house and then lies like a child caught stealing apples. Still, I am glad to have him back in the fold. Now I may get a better understanding of what he has been doing – but if he has not been straight as a die, then I will bring the heavens down upon him. Even then, he must still be punished for his ... bad manners ... as she must be'. Prioleau went into his study and took a short riding crop from his desk and, flicking it idly against his calf, went upstairs to his wife's bedroom.

Bulloch returned to his lodgings in a pensive mood. His landlady greeted him as he entered. "There's a lady come to see you Mr Bulloch. I've shown her upstairs. I hope that's alright?"

"It's fine," he replied. "You always have my permission to show ladies up to my rooms – especially if they are beautiful. Is she beautiful?

"I really can't say." His landlady managed to look prim and disapproving at the same time.

Bulloch knocked on the door of his sitting room and entered to find Rose Greenhow seated on his somewhat over-stuffed leather armchair, looking anxious and irritated.

"Why Rose, what a pleasure," he leaned and bent down to kiss

158

her forehead.

She jerked her head away. "There's no time for that, James, I have come to warn you. You must get the *Enrica* out of Liverpool and into international waters without delay. I have it on the best authority that Charles Adams has obtained a very favourable opinion from an eminent lawyer, which he is using to goad the Government into action. They will impound her James, if you do not get her out!"

"How long have I got?"

"I don't know. Days, hours, I really do not know. Adams met with Lord Russell two days ago. Russell has gone for a second opinion, but this will not delay matters for long, I fear."

"How do you know all this Rose?"

"It doesn't matter how I know this. Suffice it to say that we have friends within the Government and that this source is unimpeachable. But I will tell you where Adams is obtaining his information – it's from Laird's foreman. He has been bought!" Bulloch nodded, outwardly calm, but inwardly seething at the betrayal and worried by the extent of the information that Laird's foreman would have access to.

"Oh and one other thing. Adams has sent word to a heavy Union frigate, called the *Tuscarora*, which is currently in Southampton harbour, to get into position so as to intercept you on your departure, if he is unsuccessful in getting the Government to do it for him. The *Enrica* won't have any guns by then will she James? She'll be defenceless!"

"Against a heavy frigate, she would be defenceless in any case," he replied grimly.

"So, you are warned. I have done what I can do and I must be going now." Rose stood on tiptoe and kissed Bulloch lightly. She squeezed his arm. "Good luck, James" she said and then left quickly, getting into the Hansom cab she had kept waiting and driving off without a wave or a backward glance.

"Stupid man – stupid, stupid man. Why did he have to do this?" she asked herself. For, while she had been waiting for Bulloch, she had taken the opportunity to look through his desk, leafing quickly through the stacks of correspondence and invoices that were stuffed into its numerous pigeonholes, meanwhile keeping a sharp eye on the street outside, alert for Bulloch's sudden return.

She was quickly convinced from the many bills from tailors,

outfitters, jewellers and milliners, that Bulloch was living way beyond his own slender means and beyond those which Mallory would be prepared to allow him. Then, behind a sliding panel, which was too obvious to be accurately described as a secret compartment, she found the receipts from Isaac Kopa, totalling nearly £2,000, which she knew from the headings, could only refer to gambling debts. She was horrified that Mallory's suspicions had turned out to be correct, especially when everything she knew about Bulloch showed him to be a fiercely loyal and patriotic individual, prepared to suffer injury and even death in the defence of his Country. That such a man might stoop so low caused her deep distress, especially as she had, against all her better judgement, become really very fond of him. After much heart-searching on the train back to London however, she decided that for the moment she would do nothing, but instead would confront Bulloch with the facts when they next met and at least give him the chance to provide an explanation.

Bulloch left his lodgings shortly after Rose and crossed the river to Birkenhead, arriving at eight in the evening. He ran from the point where the ferry dropped him to the Georgian mansion, beside the Iron Works, where John Laird and his family both lived and had their offices. He knocked loudly and repeatedly on the door before it was answered by a footman.

"Yes, what do you want then?" the footman asked rudely.

"Who is it, Robert?" Laird's voice called out.

"Mr Laird, it's James Bulloch – I have to see you – now, if that is possible."

Laird came into the hall; a large napkin still tied around his neck and breadcrumbs in his whiskers spoke of an interrupted supper.

"Of course, come in, do. We were dining … will you join us?"

"I am afraid I don't have time, Mr Laird. I have heard that plans are afoot to seize the *Enrica* – 290 – and I need to take her to sea without delay."

Laird tugged at his whiskers, clearly agitated. "But, Mr Bulloch, I have one of her engines out – it was running rough as you heard the other day – she won't be ready for another week."

"I must take her out – the day after tomorrow at the latest – ready or not, one engine or two. Even that may be too late."

"Very well. I will have the men work on her all night. And the next if necessary."

"One other thing, Mr Laird. Your foreman. He has been

160

bought. He is the one who has been supplying our 'friends' with information. You should know."

"Then I will dismiss him this instant." Laird tore the napkin from round his neck and stamped his foot, so great was his agitation. "The damned man. I'll see he never works on the Mersey again."

Bulloch put his hand on Laird's arm. "Perhaps not. Perhaps it might be better if you told your Foreman that we were taking 290 out for a further sea trial on the twenty-ninth. Arrange for a normal scratch crew. Ask if they would like to bring their wives along. Why not? Put up bunting ... erect a canopy ... we'll have a buffet, champagne of course, a band. Make a jolly excursion out of it. That'll throw them off the scent. I'll arrange for a tender to follow us with ships' provisions ... enough to get us to the Bahamas... what do you think?"

Laird beamed at him. "I really must congratulate you Mr Bulloch. That is a capital plan, damme if it's not!"

*   *

The morning of the twenty-ninth of July dawned fair, with a gentle on-shore breeze. By nine o'clock the crew had arrived, together with their 'wives'. In some cases, where the sailors lived in Liverpool, these ladies actually were their wives – some were young, some were old, some merely looked old, but most clutched one or even two small infants, too young to be left on their own. Lieutenant Low and the Master, Matthew Butcher, stood by the gangplank looking disapprovingly at the squawking and babbling influx. In the case of the foreign sailors, of which there were plenty – from Spain, France, Italy and even Russia – they either came alone or brought whatever bawd or harlot they had woken with. All these were herded onto the foc'sle, even as an awning was being rigged on the afterdeck and trestle tables, covered with fine crisp white linen were laid out below to receive the buffet.

The band arrived and set up on the dockside, where they began to play a variety of music hall songs as well as patriotic tunes and marches.

By ten, most of the other guests had arrived – John Laird, with his wife and sons and their wives; Charles Prioleau, together with Mary Elizabeth, who walked stiffly without looking at Bulloch; the Spanish Consul and his wife, somewhat bemused as to the reason for the invitation and a smattering of port and harbour officials and their ladies.

The *Enrica* cast off and steamed gently down the Mersey with the tug *Hercules* chugging along behind. She made a fine sight, with gaily coloured bunting flapping from the masts and the band playing and the elegant ladies standing by the rails, waving at the onlookers who thronged the quays and ran along with the *Enrica* until her speed picked up and she left them behind.

The *Enrica* left the mouth of the Mersey, but stayed close to the Welsh coast, where Angelsey protected the ship from the breakers for which the Irish Sea was notorious. The buffet was laid out – cold hams and pressed ox-tongues, cold chickens, veal pies, eggs in aspic, lobsters and crabs, all jostled for space with gooseberry and rhubarb syllabubs, apple pies and cinnamon custard cakes. The champagne was icy cold and fizzed happily in the tall crystal flutes, while the faces became redder, the waistcoats greasier and the conversation louder.

On the fo'c'sle a somewhat humbler fare was served, but the tankards of frothing ale and small glasses of gin, with rich meat pasties and oysters created a similarly lively atmosphere. The band started up a jig and several Irish crew members treated their audience to a performance of flying feet and whirling and turning of that most Celtic of dances.

After lunch, when the dishes had been cleared away, Bulloch rang a bell and the assembled guests and crew fell silent. He leapt nimbly into the lower shrouds and said, in a loud clear voice:

"Ladies and Gentlemen – my thanks to you all for coming out with us today on our second sea trial. I hope that you have enjoyed the occasion and the light lunch that was provided" – some chuckles here from the fuller and more inebriated among the guests – "Unfortunately we have some work to do and must now take the *Enrica* further out into some rougher water, in order to prove her engines and her seaworthiness. As this will involve her staying out over night and in order not to inconvenience you all in this way, may I suggest that our guests might like to accompany myself back to Liverpool on the steam tug, *Hercules*, which is over yonder. I can assure you of a dry and easy transfer!"

He turned towards the fo'c'sle and continued, "should, however, any guests of the crew wish to remain on board, I can promise that the liquor will continue to flow, even if the level of accommodation may be a little crude tonight." A cheer went up from the assembled crew and their ladies, many of whom were already red in the face and swaying precariously.

Bulloch climbed down to scattered applause and searched out Lieutenant Low. "Now, John, you know what to do?"

"Yessir. We are to proceed under steam to Point Lynas and drop anchor. You will join us tomorrow, at first light."

Bulloch nodded. "God speed, John." He patted the young Lieutenant on the back affectionately.

It was slightly crowded on the *Hercules*, but the day remained fine, the sea calm, and the passengers continued to sip champagne and to be in good spirits. Bulloch found himself next to Mary Elizabeth Prioleau. "Good afternoon Mrs Prioleau, I trust that you are enjoying yourself."

She stared at him coldly. "Go away Mr Bulloch. Just go away and leave me alone."

Bulloch was startled. "Is there something the matter?" he enquired.

"Just go away. I do not want to be seen talking to you," she hissed, through clenched teeth.

He moved away from her, perplexed and a little concerned. Later he saw her husband put his arm around her waist and saw how she flinched. 'He has beaten her' he thought to himself – 'the despicable little runt, the cad … I'll …' but then he thought that anything he did would only make matters worse for Mrs Prioleau and there was always the loan to be considered. So he said and did nothing, studiously avoiding Mrs Prioleau until he wished her and her husband farewell at the top of the gangplank.

"Come and see me soon, Mr Bulloch", said Charles Prioleau, as he prepared to disembark. "We have much to discuss."

After the guests had all departed, Bulloch took a cab back to his lodgings on Canning Street, where he picked up his portmanteau, his pair of Adams revolvers, which were already loaded and £500 in gold – the latter from under the floorboards. Wishing his landlady farewell, he re-entered the cab and ordered the driver to take him back down to the dock where he intended to spend the night on board the *Hercules*. Just as the cab was preparing to pull away from the curb a small boy ran up and rapped on the front door. The landlady opened the door and took an envelope from the boy. "Wait, Mr Bulloch, wait" she called, waving the envelope, "there's a telegram for you." She leant in through the cab window and handed the small brown envelope to Bulloch, somewhat reluctantly it seemed, for she had never handled a telegram before and was now sad to part with it.

Bulloch took the telegram, thanked her and shouting for the cabbie to proceed, settled back in the narrow seat, tore open the envelope and read:

TUSCARORA HAS LEFT SOUTHAMPTON STOP PROBABLY HEADED QUEENSTOWN S IRELAND STOP BE CAREFUL STOP GOOD LUCK STOP R.

* *

Charles Adams danced excitedly from foot to foot in the dusty ante-room to Lord Russell's sumptuous and imperial office. Even in mid-summer the room was dark and the heavy velvet sofas seemed to extract the moisture from the very air, which they then conveyed to the trousers of those who sat upon them by a process of osmosis. The United States Minister was, in any case, in far too great a state of anxiety to sit. Five days had elapsed since his last meeting with Lord Russell and during that time he had heard nothing and had received no reply to his frequent notes requesting advice on the progress of Sir John Harding's consideration of Robert Collier's opinion. Finally, agitated beyond reason, he had decided to come to the Foreign Office and to wait outside Russell's office, until he was seen. The secretary to Lord Russell, had suggested that such a course of action was altogether improper and that it would be more appropriate if Mr Adams were to return home, where word would undoubtedly be sent to him when there was anything of note to report. However, Adams refused to leave and after further humming and hawing the secretary returned to penning a long letter in his clear copperplate, only occasionally fixing him with a baleful stare.

There was a gentle tap on the outer door. The secretary looked up and Charles Adams ceased his pacing. A messenger entered.

"Excuse me, sirs, but I have an urgent communication for Lord Russell, from Lady Harding."

"Thank you" said the secretary and took the proffered envelope.

"*Lady* Harding?" said Charles Adams.

The secretary knocked on the inner door and waited until summoned. He entered, with Charles Adams hopping in behind him in his wake.

Lord Russell and Sir George Lewis were leaning over a large map, their heads close together, Sir George pointing at some feature of particular interest.

"Excuse me, my Lord, but a communication has arrived from *Lady* Harding and I felt that, under the circumstances, I should interrupt you."

"Thank you, Stainforth," said Lord Russell, looking up. Then: "good god, what's he doing here?"

The secretary looked around, saw Charles Adams and extended both arms sideways. "Please, Sir, you should not have entered, you really must leave." Adams made no movement and the secretary looked over his shoulder for guidance. Lord Russell shrugged his narrow shoulders in annoyance.

"Very well, let him stay." Sir George Lewis carefully rolled up the map, but not before Adams had been able to see that it was a large scale depiction of Canada and the northern part of the United States.

Lord Russell took the letter, which the secretary had already slit open for him and read, his brows knitting together as he did so.

"How unfortunate. How very unfortunate."

"What is it?" Adams asked nervously.

"Ah, it seems that Sir John Harding was taken ill – with a stroke – that has paralysed him on one side. He … ah … never received my letter. Lady Harding opened her husband's correspondence only this morning, and found both Robert Collier's opinion and my request for his consideration thereof. 'Hmmm, so what to do now?' Lord Russell said, almost to himself, returning to his desk.

"You have no choice, my Lord." Adams blurted out rudely. "You must seize this ship at Laird's … if you do not, Seward will take this to be a hostile act. I cannot be responsible for the consequences."

Lord Russell blew out his cheeks and then gnawed his lower lip. "Very well. But impound, not seize. Just until further enquiries can be made into her ownership and another opinion can be obtained as to the law. Stainforth, take a letter."

165

"Perhaps, if I may suggest, my Lord, a telegram? Given how time is of the very essence."

Lord Russell regarded Adams with distaste. "Very well then, a telegram."

* *

The telegram caused considerable consternation when it arrived on the desk of Mr Price Edwards, the Collector of Customs in Liverpool. He was an elderly man, stout of build, with a florid face and thick white sideburns into which his moustache, yellowed from countless cigars, was lovingly combed. He scratched his shining pate, disturbing the few fine hairs that still clung desperately to that smooth dome.

After a while he arrived at a conclusion. He would reply to the signatory of the telegram who described himself as the Foreign Secretary, requesting clarification and at the same time seek instructions from the Home Office, which he acknowledged as his direct superior. Meanwhile, it would do no harm to call on John Laird, whom he knew well, so as to ascertain the status of the *Enrica*.

Shortly thereafter, the Collector found himself seated in the stern of a small steam launch, as it made its way across the river to Birkenhead. Facing him were six unsmiling customs officers, looking imposing in their blue uniforms and leather top hats, with their truncheons drawn and resting across their knees. Upon arrival at the Iron Works, the Collector made his way, slowly, to Laird's office, only to discover that he and all his family had gone out for the day. As he wheezed his way back to the docks, he saw his officers standing in a group, talking to a harried looking individual.

"Well, then" he puffed, "what have you discovered? Where's the *Enrica*?"

"If you please, Sir," replied one of the officers, "this 'ere gent is the Foreman. 'E says that the *Enrica*'s gone out on a sea trial with Mr Laird and 'is 'ole family and a party of nobs and gentry. 'E says as 'ow they'll be back tonight."

The commissioner was about to say something, when he saw John Laird senior, his wife and his family step out of one of their private launches and onto the dock.

"Ah, there you are," he called out, doffing his hat at Mrs Laird, who curtseyed in return. "I was told you were all at sea – ha ha." He laughed at his own joke.

Laird smiled politely. "My dear, you know the Collector, Mr Edwards," he said to his wife and then, "Price, what a pleasant surprise! Tell me, what can I do for you? It's not the brandy I've been running up the coast at night, is it?"

The Collector looked momentarily nonplussed, then he opened his mouth and emitted a wheezing gurgle, which Laird supposed was a laugh. "Good heavens, no, I should say not! Very good though Laird, capital, eh what! No, I've just received a most peculiar telegram from London – from the Foreign Office, no less – requesting me to impound one of your ships – the *Enrica*. Rum do eh! What do you make of it?"

"Rum indeed," Laird replied thoughtfully. "And I don't really know what to make of it. The *Enrica*'s at sea at the moment, on trials, won't be back till the morning."

"Morning eh? Not tonight? She decided to say out then?"

"Yes. Quite usual. There's a lot to do, making sure the engines are running smoothly and all her winches, pulleys and what-nots are all in perfect working order before she is formally handed over – and we get paid," he added under his breath.

"Who's she for, John? Who's gold are you taking on this one? Not a secret is it?"

"Dear me no! She's commissioned out of Spain, by the Government, through one of their agents, don't you know. Fine ship, if I do say so myself."

"Mo-ost peculiar. Can't think why the F.O. should want her impounded then. Still, I expect all will become clear soon. Sorry, John, but d'ye mind if I leave a couple of my boys here 'til she comes back – all official rot, I'm sure, but we can't say no to our Lords and masters can we? Eh, eh?"

Before dawn the following day, the *Hercules* cast off and steamed for the open sea. Six hours later she spied the *Enrica*, riding at anchor in deep water off Point Lynas. Bulloch came aboard, together with a dozen evil looking sweepings of the dock, who had signed up as additional crew. Bulloch called the somewhat hung-over seamen together and included their jaded wives and molls.

"Now men, hear this! The *Enrica*'s not going back to Liverpool. No, she's bound directly for the Bahamas. If you will sign on as crew, now, I'll pay you in gold, up front, £10 per man, all found, with your return passage paid for, should you not want to sign on again there. What do you say? Ladies," he bowed, "I'll give the money to you for safekeeping if you like and for your support, while your husbands are away!"

Loud cheering from the wives and cries of "go on Stan" and "take the offer yer rascal and sod off!" and "don't you dare say no." One by one the men stepped forward to the table where Lieutenant Low and the purser sat. Each man signed his name or made his mark and took his coins, which in some cases were ripped directly from their hands by some harridan, often with a filthy infant clutched to her sagging dugs.

The supplies were winched up and stowed in the *Enrica's* hold, while the wives and whores boarded the *Hercules* – the wives happily clutching gold, the whores merely angry, tired and sore.

Bulloch sat in the cabin with Lieutenant Low and worked out a course to take them west of the Isle of Man and into the Atlantic by the North Channel and the coast of Ulster – and in the opposite direction to where the *Tuscarora* was waiting for them, across the sea lanes of St George's Channel, in the South.

As the *Enrica*, now under sail and running before a stiff south-easterly, rounded the coast of Northern Ireland and approached the rocky promontory, known as the Giant's Causeway, a blue signal flare was fired from her deck. There was an answering flare from the land, which was partially obscured by the heavy rain, but soon a small sailing boat could be seen tacking out from the shore.

Bulloch took Lieutenant Low to one side. "John, I will see you in Terceira in a week or two. The *Agrippina*, with our cannon shot and other supplies left from Greenock yesterday and should be there ahead of you. I will now return to Liverpool, pick up Captain Semmes and his officers and set sail in the *Bahama* for the Azores, as soon as I can. Good luck to you!"

"And to you, sir." They both saluted, before Bulloch dropped over the side into the bobbing boat, which scudded off towards the coast at high speed, rocking precariously in the heavy seas.

*　*

John Laird sat at his desk and opened the letter, breaking the seal with his fingernail. Inside he found a note, written in haste:
    My dear John

*Thank you, as always! Please find enclosed a
draft, which should bring us up to date.
More later! In haste. J.B.*

He unfolded a banker's draft, drawn on the Liverpool & County Bank in the sum of £47,500 at the instructions of Hernandez y Hijos, shipping agents of Santander. He smiled broadly and called in his sons.

* *

By midday it was clear to a very worried Foreman that something was wrong. By three in the afternoon he was starting to become desperate and, when he saw the *Hercules* steam up to the Birkenhead wharf and start to disembark a considerable number of female passengers, he sprinted along the jetty towards her, holding on to his hat. Following him in a mob were a dozen or so customs officers, whose number had been augmented after the Collector had been told, bluntly, by both the Foreign and Home Offices, to comply with the request, without fail and without further delay. When the officers arrived at the *Hercules* they managed, with difficulty, to restrain two or three of the women, who were bound for the nearest pub for a serious wet, clutching their coins in their fists.

"Oh no," one of them said, "they's not coming back. Not fer months anyhow. They's gorn off ter sea." She expectorated heavily and grinned showing the blackened stumps of her teeth.

"Good riddance too," said another of the wives, a particularly scabrous old crone with a filthy baby under one arm.

"Paid us though!" said a third, "up front, in advance and in gold. Very generous if you ask me. It was that nice American gent wot did it. A proper gennelmun ee was."

Upon hearing this, the Foreman broke into a sweat and backed away, immediately losing himself in the crowd. He turned, running down the quay as fast as his legs would carry him, to catch the ferry across to Liverpool, leaving the customs officers at somewhat of a loss as to how to proceed.

When he arrived in Liverpool, the Foreman, making sure that he was not being observed, went straight to the offices of W.C. Miller & Sons in the South Dock area and climbed warily up the steps, looking behind him as he did so. He entered and slipped over

169

to the desk where Silas Groat stood leaning on its hard wooden top, surveying the other clerks disdainfully down his long thin nose, like a vulture.

"Ere, Mr Groat," he whispered.

"What do you want? Why have you come here? I told you never to contact me!" Groat hissed back at him, his adam's apple wobbling up and down his scrawny neck.

"I 'ad to Mr Groat ... only ... only ... 290 ... she's gorn!"

"Gone, gone where? Gone how?"

"Out on trials 'cept she ain't coming back. If you ask me it was all a trick – but either way, she's fully crewed and she's orf at sea! Thought you should know – soonest, like."

"Oh my!" Groat glanced over at 'Bull' Miller's office and licked his dry lips. "Oh my, his nibs is going to be very upset, oh yes he is. Very upset *indeed* I shouldn't wonder. You," he said to the Foreman, "you, get out of here – I'll speak to you later." He rubbed his shoes against the backs of his trouser legs to polish them and then walked with small steps across to Miller's office, glaring at any clerk who had the temerity to look up from his work. He knocked on the door.

"What!" yelled Miller. "Gone? Escaped? You bungling fool, Groat, you idiot, you incompetent ass. Can't you do anything right? You're fired – now get out of my sight! If I see you again I'll have you whipped!"

The clerks in the outer office could hear every word, such was Miller's volume. They looked at one another, smiling and nodding happily. There was more conversation at a lower volume from the office, then: "I don't care if your whole family starves to death, it's no skin off my nose – now bugger off before I call the Peelers and have you done for trespass!"

Groat emerged from the office, his ashen face wet from the two lines of tears that trickled down his dry cheeks. He took several items from his desk, which he put into a worn leather brief case and then walked slowly and dejectedly across the dusty floor-boards on his way out of the office.

"Goodbye, Mr Groat," said one smiling clerk. "Nice to have known you," said another. "Close the door after you," said a third.

*   *

In London, Lord Russell received the news by telegram, from the

Collector. He laughed out loud and called for his Secretary. "Funny how things sometimes turn out for the best, Stainforth, what? Now take a letter – the first is to the Prime Minister – and then one to Mr Adams. There's no urgency over delivering Mr Adams' letter, though. Tomorrow will do fine. I am at Windsor tomorrow, am I not, Stainforth?"

XI

Liverpool and London — September, 1862

❧ ❦

Bulloch had journeyed out to Terceira in the Azores on board the *Bahama* with Captain Semmes and his officers. Semmes was a small fussy man, fastidious in his dress and appearance, with waxed tips to his luxuriantly curled moustache and a quiff in the front of his still-dark hair.

On the twentieth of August, they arrived in Porto Praia da Vitoria, Terceira. The Agrippina was already there with the cannons and the stores, as was the *Enrica*, which had been in port for nearly ten days, still masquerading as a Spanish ship.

The three vessels put out to sea together almost at once and dropped anchor in the calm waters of Angra Bay on the lee side of the Island. The next days were a flurry of constant activity as the *Enrica* was fully loaded with provisions and her cannons were lifted onto the deck and, in the case of the swivel guns, bolted onto their rails and runners.

Four days later, in a brief ceremony, the *Enrica* was commissioned into the Confederate Navy as the C.S.S. *Alabama*. The officers and crew sang 'Dixie' and her guns fired for the first time, in salute. Bulloch did not delay. He ran his hand around her wheel in farewell, feeling the raised letters which spelled out "*Aide toi et Dieu t'aidera*", wished Semmes the very best of luck and, with a final salute, departed for the solitude of the homeward journey on the *Bahama*. Semmes did not delay either. Anchors were slipped and, with a blast on the horn, the *Alabama* set off on her first cruise, watched by a mournful Bulloch, who stood alone at the taffrail as she disappeared into the vastness of the Atlantic Ocean, her sails full and her masts braced, until there was only the long and slowly fading white line of her wash to mark her passing.

At the end of the first week in September, with England enjoying a late summer of fine weather and clear skies, the *Bahama* entered the Mersey under sail and shortly afterwards tied up at the Queen's Dock.

Bulloch disembarked unsteadily, unsure of his land legs, having been at sea for over five weeks. He was tanned, fit and he had lost weight from the plain and monotonous fare produced by the galley of the *Bahama*. He went straight to his lodgings and immediately flung open the windows to admit fresh air into the musty atmosphere of the small room. His landlady appeared shortly with a laden tray which she put down in front of him. Bulloch picked up the knife and fork and attacked the kipper with poached eggs, the kidneys and the black pudding, all of which he wolfed down, together with a pot of strong black coffee.

Much refreshed and replete from his breakfast, Bulloch turned to his stack of mail. Flicking through, he lit upon an envelope, post-marked London, which he was sure was in Rose's handwriting. He slit it open with a knife, still somewhat sticky with marmalade, and read:

Dear James,

It is imperative that I see you without delay. There are several matters which we must discuss and, for reasons that will be apparent when I see you, it is impossible for me to travel to Liverpool at this time. May I ask you to come up to London instead? Please let me know as soon as you return and have read this letter.

I am, etc,

Rose

Bulloch immediately drafted a telegram, suggesting that they meet at the Great Northern Hotel near King's Cross Station at four that afternoon, which he gave to his landlady, together with a shilling and asked her to take it to the post office. He bathed and shaved carefully, luxuriating in the unaccustomed experience of hot water. He then dressed in his newest and most fashionable coat, with a yellow high-buttoned waist coat, set his tall silk top hat firmly on his head and set off to Lime Street Station at a brisk walk, twirling his silver topped cane in his fingers and whistling 'Home Sweet Home' as he went.

He was somewhat irked to find that he had acquired a shadow shortly after leaving his lodgings, noticing the individual weaving and ducking his way down the street in a vain attempt to remain inconspicuous.

Arriving at the station, Bulloch bought a ticket for Birmingham, complaining loudly about the price, boarded the train and settled himself in the corner of a First Class compartment, holding the Times loosely in front of his face. He saw his 'shadow' glance fleetingly into his compartment as he walked past, before continuing on and getting into the next compartment down, slamming the door noisily behind him. Bulloch waited. Exactly on time, a whistle blew and the train's wheels started to turn, spinning at first, then suddenly finding their purchase on the smooth iron rails and jerking the carriages forward, as the engine puffed quantities of soot-laden smoke from its stack and the train began to gather speed.

Bulloch reached out through the window on the opposite side of the compartment to the platform, turned the handle and pushed open the door. He hesitated for only a fraction of a second before stepping out, holding onto his hat with one hand. The drop was three foot and the train was moving at nearly ten miles an hour. Bulloch landed heavily, but kept his footing, running with the train until he could safely stop. Then, he turned back to the station, clambered carefully up onto the platform ignoring an "ere, wot d'ye think yo're doin' then?" from a guard and went off to find the London train, all the while lamenting the scuff marks and dirt from the cinders that had soiled his shiny new boots.

On arriving in London, Bulloch went directly to the Great Northern and found Rose already ensconced in a corner of the lounge, a pot of tea and some small cakes on a tiered trolley beside her. She did not rise and at once Bulloch could see from her pallor and the sheen of sweat on her brow, that she was not well.

"Rose? Are you alright?" He bent down and kissed her lightly on the forehead, feeling the fever with his lips.

"Sit down James," she said in a low voice and, turning her head, nodded twice to a burly man, who was sitting by himself across the lounge, smoking a pipe, a newspaper open in front of him.

"Who's that?" Bulloch asked.

"One of my people. I don't go out by myself any more."

"Has something happened, Rose. Tell me."

"Well … it's all a little confused … but last week, I was returning home from the Theatre … we had been to a new production of *As You Like It* at the Queen's and had then dined at Sheeky's off the Charing Cross Road. I had such a short distance to go to my rooms in Longacre, a matter of yards only, that I sent Mason … did I say that I was with Mason? No, well, anyway I sent him off in his carriage and I walked. The night was warm, the area is well lit and it all seemed quite safe even though it was late and the streets were deserted. I was coming up to my front door, when I noticed this cab – a hansom – just waiting there, the driver up on top – he seemed to be asleep – and with the blinds drawn. I thought nothing of it and I had just opened my purse to find my key, when suddenly I heard a noise behind me and turned around. This must have saved my life, because the knife that was aimed at the centre of my back struck me in the side and was deflected by my whalebone corset – the first time I've ever actually appreciated that damned article of clothing! The blade, instead, cut across my stomach, but not deeply I'm happy to say. I cried out and my attacker, who was a very large and heavily bearded man, muttered something in a foreign language and then slashed at my throat with the knife. I recoiled, just in time, and raised my arm, which took the force of the blade across my forearm – cut quite deeply I'm afraid. Now before he could come at me again, I delved into my purse, which was already open – thank God I hadn't dropped it – and pulled out my Deringer, which I always carry. Only one shot, but I hit him, though not mortally, I fear. He clutched his arm, dropped his knife and leapt into the cab which drove off at speed towards Holborn. That's all really. I was bed-ridden for days and have had quite a fever, which is only just abating now.

Bulloch was silent throughout Rose's description of her ordeal, but inwardly he was angry with himself for leaving her unprotected and alone, even though she would have resented and resisted any attempt by him to act as her guardian. The full measure of his fury however, was reserved for her assailant, who was so base and cowardly as to attack a defenceless – well, almost defenceless – woman, with murderous intent, from behind and in the dark. "You have no idea who he was or where he was from then?" he asked, his voice reflecting his concern.

"None, except as I told you, he wasn't English … oh, and the knife that he dropped? It had Union Army markings on the blade."

Bulloch's mouth opened in surprise. "This is appalling! To sink that low … to attempt to assassinate … to murder … a woman! These people must have become very desperate indeed to stoop to such levels!"

Rose held up one limp hand, encased in a white silk glove. "It may not be that simple, James. Mason went to see Charles Adams after the attack. Adams was very disturbed and sent for Benjamin Moran, who controls their agents here. Moran denied the attack hotly and vehemently – and Mason believed him – which puts us back to square one. In any case, I am very careful where I go now and I take my friend here with me always – so I am probably safe enough."

"You must be careful Rose – very careful – I couldn't bear it if something … something else were to happen to you. As I told you on the boat … I have become very fond of you."

Rose frowned deeply at this last statement and eased herself in her chair, moving her wounded arm into a more comfortable position, which Bulloch could now see, as the wide sleeves of her coat fell back, was heavily bandaged.

"And, of course, I must congratulate you, James on the way in which you arranged for the *Enrica* to escape from Liverpool. Just in time too, I understand. It has, however, caused a great stink in Washington – and in London as well. I am told that Seward was furious and wanted to declare war on England but that Lincoln, who is not one quarter as foolish as many would believe, forbade it. Nonetheless Adams was running backwards and forward to Whitehall with letters of complaint. The papers here were full of it. And you've become quite a hero in Richmond, James, you know," she added thoughtfully.

Bulloch shrugged, feigning modesty, but inwardly pleased.

"Now, James, there is one other matter that we must discuss." Rose looked at the backs of her hands, which were clasped together in her lap. "And I … find … this … a very difficult subject to broach with you."

"Don't be shy – you know me." He smiled, but she continued to look down at her hands.

"James, I understand that you have run up considerable gambling debts. I am sorry to ask this … but I have to know … how have you managed to settle these debts? Where has the money come from?"

176

The blood drained completely out of Bulloch's face and a feeling of nausea grew in the pit of his stomach. "How do you know this?" he asked coldly.

"It doesn't matter how I know, only that I do. Indeed, I wish that I did not. However I must ask you again … from where did you get the money to repay your gambling debts? I must know, James. Will you answer me?"

"I will not! And I think that it is impertinent of you to ask. I still cannot think where … oh my God, you searched my rooms, while you were waiting for me that day … Rose! How could you have done that? I know that you are a spy and a woman and that this cannot be an easy marriage of conflicting sensibilities but, in the name of reason, Rose, what could have inspired you to do this?"

"I will tell you what inspired me to do it." Her lips pressed together in a thin line and her eyes flashed with anger. "While our Country is fighting for its very existence, while our boys are dying in their thousands and being buried in unmarked graves, while all that is going on, Captain James Dunwoody Bulloch chooses to misappropriate the funds with which he has been entrusted – funds which could be crucial to his Country's very survival – and to use them to subsidise his gambling and his whoring. Thank you Captain Bulloch, thank you very much indeed!"

Bulloch rose to his feet, his mind a whirlwind of conflicting emotions, bowed stiffly, mouthed "Ma'am" and left without looking back.

Rose sat there glumly for some time, before beckoning her companion over to help her to her feet and, leaning on him for support, slowly followed in the direction taken by Bulloch.

*   *

Stainforth, the ever-efficient secretary, knocked at the inner door and upon receiving a muted summons from within, entered clutching the morning post to his chest. Lord Russell looked up and sighed.

"The usual outpourings of mediocre minds again today I assume, Stainforth? The solipsistic rantings of delusional individuals? Tell me that there is one speck of gold among that pile of dross!"

"Actually, my Lord, I believe that there may be two specks of gold. I have taken the liberty of placing them on the top." He put the pile of correspondence in front of the Foreign Secretary, who continued to drum his fingers on the leather desktop, bowed and left.

The first letter was from the Prime Minister, Lord Palmerston. Lord Russell sat up and, applying his *pince nez* to the bridge of his nose, took the letter in both hands and held it close to his face. In truth, he was disappointed with Palmerston's prevarication over the American situation. Old Pam just would not get off the fence – too scared of his reputation being tarnished by a war that could be costly both in terms of men and money – particularly now that he was close to the end of his Ministry, the end of his political career and, in all probability, the end of his life – too scared of any mistake that might acquire the disapprobation of history.

Palmerston had asked for clearer signs that the South could and would win this war – as if it wasn't clear enough already! One more victory, always one more victory and then … and then nothing. When Russell went to him in August and had told him of the great Southern victory, won for the second time at Manassas – as if the first had merely been a dress rehearsal – and had shown him the Union losses of sixteen thousand together with prisoners taken: seven thousand; guns lost: three hundred and ninety; and small arms of all types thrown down by running troops: twenty thousand; he had agreed that the "Federals had got a very complete smashing," but declined to undertake any action that might be considered precipitant unless Baltimore or Washington fell into Confederate hands.

How could any action now be precipitant when Pope was in full retreat on Washington and McClellan, together with his 'invincible' army gone from the gates of Richmond?

He picked up the letter and read the usual polite enquiries after his health, and that of his family and then: "It is evident that a great conflict is taking place to the North-West of Washington and its issue must have a great effect on the state of affairs. If the Federals sustain a great defeat, they may be at once ready for mediation and the iron should be struck, while it is hot. If, on the other hand, they should have the best of it, we may wait awhile and see what may follow."

'We-ell,' thought Russell, 'so the old man has finally gathered up his skirts, bent his knees and is preparing to jump off the fence.

How interesting! But, North-West of Washington? What is Lee doing there? Indeed, what is there? Maryland? Pennsylvania? Why do all their places have such strange names? He called loudly for a map and picked up the second letter. This one was from Mason, the Confederate minister. He read:

My Lord,

I hope and trust that you will forgive the impertinence of this letter, but I remain, as you know, desirous of a further meeting with your good self, either on a formal, or on an informal basis should you prefer.

Rather than to discuss the generalities of our situation or to seek again the good offices of Great Britain as a mediator in our Conflict, I wish instead to make a gesture of Goodwill to the people of Britain, from their friends, the people of the Confederate States of America. Bearing in mind the very great hardship being suffered by many of your countrymen, I would like to offer you a parcel of one hundred thousand bales of cotton, at prices equivalent to those prevailing prior to the commencement of the blockade of our ports by Union warships.

It is my fervent wish that you accept this offer in the spirit in which it is intended – namely that of a gift, given freely, as between friends. I am, of course, at your complete disposal, should you wish to discuss the details of shipment and delivery.

I am, my Lord,
Your Obedient Servant,
James Mason

Lord Russell was a man of phlegmatic disposition and not at all given to displays of emotion of any kind. Now, however, his eyebrows rose nearly up to his receding hairline and he emitted a low whistle of surprise. One hundred thousand bales at six cents a pound, say, when the current price of New Orleans Middling was around eighteen cents a pound, that was twelve cents profit per pound ... and that was ... he pulled his quill from the ink stand fast enough to drop small blobs onto his desk and started to scribble on the back of one of his other letters ... a profit of ... $12 million or slightly under £2.5 million – a very tidy sum, which the Exchequer would find extremely useful. And one hundred thousand bales would put many of the labourers who, even now, were eking out a thin and miserable existence – in some cases actually starving – back into work in those dark satanic mills. This would make Palmerston and his Ministry look very good indeed – a point which would certainly not be lost on the Old Man! He chuckled and rubbed his thin hands together with a noise like the rustling of dry leaves and called out "Stainforth, a letter if you please."

*   *

Bulloch sat in the corner of the railway compartment, staring dejectedly out the window. He was more upset by his recent meeting with Rose than he could remember being at any time in his life, since the death of his Father. Harriet leaving him, Mallory giving the Captaincy of the Alabama to Semmes – both painful and humiliating, but as nothing to this. He felt betrayed by a woman for whom he felt a very real affection and, indeed, attraction, but beyond this, her words had cut him to the quick and had woken his dormant conscience out of its reverie and now he lambasted himself with the twin scourges of guilt and self-contempt.

When he arrived in Liverpool, he went straight to the Adelphi Hotel, into the long bar and ordered a whisky. He drank three straight tots before his hands stopped trembling sufficiently for him to light the cigar that he clamped between his clenched teeth. The whisky and the tobacco soothed him. Rose had over-reacted. She was in pain, it was only understandable, the amounts were not that large, they were only in the way of a loan, he was going to repay them when he could, it wasn't like he had stolen the money and look what he had accomplished in his short time here, those great ships, those guns and she searched his rooms, the bitch – who was acting dishonestly then, eh? He burped loudly, tasting the sour whisky in his throat, dragged on his cigar and called for the bartender.

Several whiskys later, Bulloch left the Adelphi and headed unsteadily off to Castle Street.

"Why, look who it is! It's the prodigal son returned, indeed! How very fine to see you again Mr Bulloch – I thought you had deserted us this time, for sure. Come in, come in do – Mother will be so pleased … as well as a certain young lady, I have no doubt." He winked lewdly.

Bulloch entered the gambling club – the heavy-set Jew, bowing and walking backwards in front of him.

"And what a fortuitous evening for you to have come, as well! Why, only yesterday, I was asked by some of our regulars to host a poker game – only ten per cent to the house, very reasonable you will agree, I am sure – and you have the great good luck to arrive just as it is starting. Should you wish to participate, I will introduce you to the other players. How does that sound?"

"Fine by me," Bulloch said in a voice made gravelly by the effects of raw spirit and tobacco on his vocal chords. "Lead on, Mr Kopa."

They climbed the staircase which led to the private apartment of the Jew and his Mother – whom Bulloch had never actually met and whose existence he secretly doubted – and went into a large room off the hall. Inside there was a circular green baize table, around which five men sat. They all wore evening clothes, although some had already removed their jackets, given the closeness of the evening and the stuffiness of the room, with its hissing gas chandelier and drawn velvet curtains.

Several girls were also in attendance, serving drinks and sandwiches, but wearing far less than in the more public rooms downstairs. One very buxom redhead, dressed only in her camisole and drawers, but with high buttoned boots, came across to Bulloch and handed him a foaming flute of champagne, making sure that she pressed her breasts, which were swinging freely inside the thin cotton garment, against his arm.

"Good evening Gentlemen," he said, accepting the champagne with a smile, "I don't know whether this is a private game, but I would surely appreciate the opportunity of playing. I am, as you may have guessed, from America. Poker is by way of being our national game and we pride ourselves on playing it pretty well."

"Really," drawled one of the seated men, rocking his chair back onto two legs and surveying Bulloch with a quizzical expression, "now that is interesting, isn't it Charles?"

"Come to teach us how to play, have you Yank?" asked the one named Charles.

"I hardly meant ..." Bulloch managed to get out before a third man, somewhat sullen looking, who had been frowning into his brandy, said: "If you've got the money, you can play. We put up £1000 each and play until either one person has won the lot or all the remaining players – all, mind – agree to stop. Those are the rules. Are you in?"

Bulloch looked over at Isaac Kopa, who nodded at him. "I'm in" said Bulloch and sat down at the empty place. The redhead brought him over a pile of chips, which she put down in front of him, one of her ample breasts grazing his face as she did so.

"All right Gentlemen," said Charles, "why don't we begin? Let's cut for dealer."

The luck of the cards moved around the table with one player momentarily gaining – all smiles and false modesty – before a losing streak would set in and another player would be seen to triumph fleetingly, before a particularly heavily bet hand, perhaps on five or seven card stud, would bring him down in turn. And so on, round and round.

Bulloch fared as well as any, winning a finely bluffed hand with a pair of tens against, almost certainly, a better hand, but losing badly later with three Jacks to three Queens. One player, a middle-aged doctor, who continuously mopped his pink and perspiring brow with an oversized handkerchief, was the first to lose his entire stake, having neither skill nor luck with the cards. He went and sat in a corner, where he could be seen muttering to himself and chewing his lower lip.

By midnight, the group was down to three, the sullen young man having rashly bet against two pairs showing in a game of seven-card stud, only to find that he was on the wrong side of a full house, Kings high. He left right away, bowing to the group and taking with him a petite blonde, who had, until then, been standing behind him massaging his tense neck muscles.

At two o'clock Charles went, losing £500 to Bulloch in a game of five card draw, nothing wild, where he overestimated the importance of two pairs and lost to Bulloch's flush in Clubs.

The remaining player, who had introduced himself as Ambrose Ampleside, was the scion of a Derbyshire land-owning family, lucky enough to find coal below their acreage and consequently a young man of some wealth. He had untidy fair hair and a somewhat prominent nose, but his overall good looks were marred by an almost permanent sneer, which expressed clearly the disdain that he felt when he was forced to consort with beings of a lower order. He played recklessly and with the luck that only comes to those who are indifferent to their fate and had won consistently for some time before the departure of his friend Charles. Each time that he held a winning hand, he would scoop up the pot greedily, saying "oh, hard cheese" to the losers, in a drawl, which elongated the vowels and emphasised his insincerity, before emitting a sort of braying laugh that sounded like "hwar, hwar" and made Bulloch clench his fists below the table in anger.

Around the time that Charles dropped out of the game, Bulloch, who had been drinking champagne steadily, was beginning to feel its effects. He had just over £2000 in front of him, while Ampleside had the remainder, being a little under £4000. Bulloch would dearly have loved to pull out and go to bed – with the redhead – taking his £1000 odd of winnings with him, but he knew that Ampleside would refuse and he did not wish to give him satisfaction by asking.

They played for another hour, winning and losing, with neither gaining the upper hand. Ampleside then became dealer and called for five-card stud, dealing a hole card to each of them, a Queen of Diamonds to Bulloch and a ten of Hearts to himself. Bulloch lifted the corner of his hole card and saw the Queen of Spades. Keeping his face impassive, he opened the betting at £10. Ampleside saw the bet and dealt two more cards, a Jack of Hearts to Bulloch and an Ace of Diamonds to himself. Ampleside bet £100, which Bulloch saw given the obvious nature of the bluff. Ampleside then dealt two further cards, a Jack of Clubs to himself and another Jack, of Diamonds, to Bulloch. Bulloch now had a pair of Jacks showing together with a pair of Queens, which were undisclosed. He felt confident against an Ace high and bet another £100, which Ampleside saw. The last two cards were dealt, a disappointing seven of Clubs to Bulloch and a King of Clubs to Ampleside.

Ampleside then asked for a break in order to visit the toilet. He slipped his hand down the front of his companion's camisole as he left the table and squeezed her breast hard, until she winced and tears formed in the corner of her eyes. Ampleside saw this and emitted his "hwar, hwar" laugh before sauntering nonchalantly out of the room, leaving his single card face down, with his brandy snifter on top of it. Bulloch stared hard at the back of the card, desperately trying to determine whether it was one of the two remaining queens which would give Ampleside the winning straight. The odds were considerably against there being three Queens out in ten cards, so he decided to bet, but modestly at first.

He hoped to draw Ampleside into betting heavily in order to try and bluff Bulloch into believing that he had one of the Queens.

Ampleside returned and took his place. Bulloch bet £100. Ampleside, after a pause, raised the bet by £500, which caused a gasp from those around the room. "Wot I'd have ter do ter get that, I wouldn't like ter think," muttered the redhead, blowing out her cheeks. Bulloch saw the increase and raised a further £500. "Three Jacks or two pairs" said Ampleside – "doesn't really matter which, though, to me … hwar, hwar" and raised Bulloch £1000, pushing the stack of heavy oblong chips into the growing pile in the middle of the table with a finger, whose nail was bitten to the quick. Bulloch paled. "I … don't … have … £1000 …" he said slowly, his tongue sticking to the top of his dry mouth and slurring his words, "why don't we just call it £700 and I'll see you?"

"We won't call it £700, old boy, because the jolly bet's £1000. If you haven't got the money, I suggest that you fold. No pay, no play, what? I say, what a card I am!" and then he collapsed with laughter at his own *double entendre*, slapping the table with the palm of his hand and rattling the stacked chips, the "hwar, hwar, hwar" putting Bulloch's teeth on edge. The Jew was suddenly at Bulloch's side.

"Another three hundred should do it, I would think Mr Bulloch, eh?" Bulloch took the chips with a muttered 'thanks' and pushed £1000 towards the already teetering stack of chips that took up most of the centre of the table. "See your £1000", he said flatly. Ampleside stopped laughing, narrowing his eyes and sucking in his lower lip. Then suddenly he smiled broadly, flipped over his card, and flicked it across the table to Bulloch.

"Queen of Clubs, so I win! Hard cheese … damned sorry – I don't think … hwar, hwar, hwar."

Bulloch's face set and he swayed in his chair. A further £1300 in debt to the Jew – what had he been thinking! Especially today, of all days. He got to his feet.

Ampleside, grinning from ear to ear, looked up at him and said: "not leaving so soon are we? Why don't you stay for a drink – on me as I don't suppose you can afford one now. Still, easy come, easy go, what?" He leered.

Bulloch's calm finally broke. He circled the table in two steps, pulled the young man up by the stiff front of his dress shirt and punched him with all his force in the middle of his face, feeling, with satisfaction, the nose break and the front teeth give way. Ampleside screamed a shrill, high pitched shriek, blood pouring down his face, and fell backwards across the sideboard, sending glasses, bottles and sandwiches flying. The rest of the room stood frozen in their places, like a tableau at Madame Tussaud's.

Suddenly the Jew was at Bulloch's side, holding a short lead-filled billy club. "Really, Mr Bulloch, there was no call for that! You lost fair and square. Now look what you've done. I could be closed down for this. Get out, and quickly, before the Peelers arrive and don't come back – except to repay your £1300 and I want that as soon as, or I'll be coming after you." He nodded twice, slapping the club into his open palm for emphasis.

Bulloch stumbled out of the room, to be met at the top of the stairs by the redhead, who had put on a long top-coat of beige linen and looked reasonably respectable, except for the heavy rouge and lip colour, which clearly advertised her profession. She held up a single £10 chip. "I took it out of yer pile when you weren't looking. I thought that if you won it wouldn't make no difference like, but if you lost, then you could still afford a fuck. Was I wrong?"

"No," said Bulloch, sighing deeply, "I guess you weren't wrong."

Back in the room, the doctor had helped Ampleside into a chair and held his perspiration-stained handkerchief to Ampleside's smashed nose, in an attempt to staunch the blood that flowed down his face and into his open collar. Ampleside put one hand to his face and started to feel his broken teeth, moaning all the while. As he did so, the doctor glanced down and saw the edge of a card protruding from Ampleside's cuff. Looking around to ensure that he was unobserved, he pushed the edge of the card back up the sleeve and out of sight. 'Better to have the Amplesides in ones debt than some penniless Yank,' he thought to himself, pleased that he might have a way of re-couping his losses before his wife found out.

＊   ＊

"So" said Palmerston, "seems this last battle was a draw. What was it called, Johnny? Oh yes, Antietam. Strange name. And the losses were extraordinary – twenty two thousand I'm told, in all. That's more than Waterloo! I mean, how long can they keep it up

185

for? It's bleedin' 'em dry – quite literally. Anyhow, Lee has limped back to Virginia, Washington's safe and so I don't see us doing anything right now – do you Johnny?"

"Well, Prime minister …"

"And particularly not now Johnny, just after Lincoln's Emancipation Declaration … I mean what would the people think – us wading in to support a group of slavers while …"

"With respect, Prime Minister."

"Yes, Johnny."

"Lincoln's *Preliminary* Emancipation Declaration only frees slaves in those states that are currently in rebellion. That means that slaves in the Northern States – and there are plenty in Maryland and Kentucky at least – are *not* freed. The newspapers – including the *Times* – feel that Lincoln is trying to stir up a slave revolt in the South – murder their owners in their beds and so forth – and that the whole thing's a pretty dire sort of last resort by a desperate man. So, my conclusion would be that the ghastly losses at Antietam demand that we should offer mediation, in the name of humanity and while this emancipation business may have muddied the waters somewhat, it has also shown Lincoln to be a pretty devious sort of cove."

Palmerston frowned, looking around the mahogany cabinet table, noting Gladstone's fervent nodding of support, but also the several heads shaking in unison, including that of Sir George Lewis. He licked his thick lips, like a snake tasting the air, the better to sense the direction of the prevailing political wind.

"Hmmm," he said at last, "the *Times*, you say, Johnny? Well then, so the question is still open. But I do think that, just for the moment, it should remain open. Y'see the North has to believe that it cannot win by force of arms before they will accept any form of mediation without declaring it to be a hostile act. Really, the whole matter is full of difficulty but I do believe that it can only be cleared up by some deciding events between the two contending armies. You do agree don't you, Johnny?"

XII

Paris – October, 1862

❧   ❦

The black and gold *barouche*, with a fine pair of sturdy geldings between the shafts, circled the Egyptian Obelisk, turned in through the gilded gates and ran smoothly up the long avenue. It passed between rows of marble statues of classical warriors in heroic poses and continued on towards the Palais de Tuileries, whose myriad windows blazed in the early morning sun.

Inside the coach, the Comte de Persigny lounged in a corner, his head resting against the silk cushions, his legs crossed, careless of the creases that he was causing to his immaculately tailored black frock coat. By contrast, his companion sat bolt upright, a battered leather wallet containing several loose leaves of paper open on his knee. He was clearly nervous and his lips moved silently as he tried to memorise the contents of one of the documents.

"Relax *mon ami*, you will find the Emperor a very open man, and highly receptive to your message. He will also be very impressed by your grasp of French, even if, like myself, he will also shudder inwardly at the way in which you choose to pronounce our mother tongue in Louisiana."

John Slidell frowned at his companion and nervously smoothed down his thick grey hair, which was receding from his brow, but which, as if to compensate, he wore long at the sides, completely covering his ears. "I have waited a long time for this meeting, as you know, Jean. It is our big chance and I cannot afford for anything to go wrong. You know that we are poorly received in England and I fear that matters there will only worsen. But if we can just encourage the Emperor to support us in some meaningful way – say through breaking the blockade or even, God willing, through recognition, why, then the entire situation of the war

187

would change markedly for the better." He smiled at his friend and tapped him lightly on the knee. "Don't think that I don't appreciate what you have done for us Jean – and indeed are still doing for us. *Le Consititutionel* is a far better and more widely read newspaper than Hotze's '*Index*' is in London and with influence that goes way beyond its circulation. Ah ... we are nearly here." He straightened his black stock, flicked dust off the sleeve of his jacket and prepared to alight as the carriage came to a halt. A footman, wearing a powdered wig, with a tailcoat and striped stockings reminiscent of the previous century, flung open the carriage door and stood to one side.

Together they walked up the long red carpet that ran across the gravel, up the broad marble steps and entered the palace through a pair of towering wooden doors, on each side of which stood a tall *cuirassier*, whose burnished breast-plates and plumed helmets were dazzling in their brightness. Once inside they were met by the Emperor's secretary, who bowed deeply and then ushered them quickly up a flight of broad stairs and into a small, but light and pleasingly decorated anteroom.

"The Emperor has a delegation from Rome with him at the moment," the secretary announced, raising his eyes ceiling-ward, "and these Italians, monsieur, they talk and talk ... still, I doubt that they will be very much longer and so, if you would not mind waiting a little ..." He positively ran from the room clapping his hands and shouting, "Marcel, Marcel, some refreshments for the Comte de Persigny, if you would be so kind."

In the event they waited for over an hour, due no doubt to the loquacious Italians. Slidell became increasingly nervous, jumping to his feet at each chime of the vast ormolu clock that sat on a side table and which depicted Napoleon I as the conqueror of Egypt, his hand resting on the head of the Sphinx, as if it were a favourite dog.

At last the Secretary re-emerged, putting his head around the corner of the door and beckoning. He took them up to the second floor, where a particularly heavily gilded set of doors were guarded by another pair of *cuirrassiers*, their swords drawn. He knocked loudly and at once threw them open, shouting "Le Comte de Persigny et Monsieur Slidell," pronouncing the latter's name as 'Slee-dell'.

The Emperor was seated at his desk and did not rise, but looked up and gestured towards two small brocaded chairs which faced him. He was an impressive looking man with dark hair brushed back from his broad brow and a large, somewhat curved nose, below which he wore a heavy moustache whose ends were twirled and waxed to fine points and a small goatee beard. He was dressed in a dark blue uniform jacket, much bemedalled, with heavy gilt epaulets and a purple sash across his chest. The Emperor studied his visitors for a minute, his dark intelligent eyes peering out from under hooded lids, before clearing his throat. He turned to his Minister.

"My dear Comte, it is always a pleasure to see you, although I must confess to just the slightest nervousness when you are away from your office and thus the reins of your Ministry are no longer in the hands of such a careful and experienced driver. I hope that France will not plunge into lawlessness during your brief absence?"

Persigny smiled at the compliment, but shook his head. "*Sire,*" he said, "permit me to introduce Mr John Slidell of Louisiana, the Commissioner of the Confederate States of America, resident in Paris."

The Emperor nodded. "Welcome, Monsieur Slidell, welcome to France ... and what is it that we may do for you?"

Slidell took a deep breath and launched into the offer of one hundred thousand bales of cotton – the same as Mason had proposed in his letter to Lord Russell, but which had been declined, reluctantly on the part of Russell, following a Cabinet meeting at the end of the previous week. He added that, were the Emperor to be interested, then French ships could bring goods of their choosing into Confederate harbours, without paying tax and then bring out the cotton themselves, thus greatly adding to the profitability of the voyage.

The Emperor was intrigued. Not only would the cotton be a godsend to his people, hundreds of thousands of whom were destitute and starving due to the shortage, but the profits would go towards financing his campaign in Mexico, which was a constant and serious drain on the Imperial exchequer. He thanked Slidell and expressed polite interest.

Slidell was gratified. He continued "and what is more *Sire*, when ... I say, when the Confederate States wins this war against the Federal aggressors, we will co-operate willingly with France in her ..." he cast around for the appropriate phrase, "... her Mexican campaign. Our 'friends' in the North, on the other hand are, as you know, keen to help Juarez by lending him money in order to block France's rightful ambitions in that region."

Napoleon frowned deeply at the reference to the Union loan to Juarez. He twirled the points of his moustache and looked out the window to where a fountain played in the middle of finely manicured lawns and artful topiary.

"It is clear to me", he said after a while, "that something must be done to end this ... dreadful and bloody war in which your country is currently engaged. And I find your proposal, with regard to the cotton ... most interesting. However ... thought must be given as to the appropriate timing for such an operation ... er, the views of the English and the Russians, of course, must be sought ... and so on. Nonetheless, you have my word that I will discuss our meeting with my Ministers with a view to making an early decision, the conclusion to which, I hope and believe, you will find satisfactory. Meanwhile, until our next meeting, let me leave you with one final thought. France has some of the best ship-yards in the world and our construction techniques are second to none. I believe that the Confederate States of America wishes to build a navy – is that not so?"

* *

Slidell and the Comte de Persigny met Bulloch in the lounge of the Hotel Meurice on the Rue de Rivoli. Slidell, who had not seen Bulloch for some months, was concerned at his appearance and asked solicitously after his health.

"Just tired," Bulloch replied to his enquiry. "Feeling my age and ... well ... let us just say that I would rather ... much rather ... be at sea, where the enemy at least hoists his own colours before opening fire."

"I see ..." said Slidell, who clearly didn't, but continued, "in any case James, we have good news. We had an audience with the Emperor this morning and we were ... warmly received." He turned to the Comte de Persigny for confirmation, who nodded his head and said, "most assuredly."

"He said that he was interested in the offer of the cotton and would discuss it with his ministers but that ... get this James ... he hoped that we would find the outcome of their deliberations satis-factory. There." He sat back beaming. "Oh, and there is more. He

190

actually invited us to build warships in France. Now what do you think of that?"

"Is that so?" Bulloch immediately became more animated, and to Slidell, more his old self. "That is a matter of considerable significance, because I fear that England s becoming increasingly hostile. I will write to Mallory at once, but as always, John, we labour under the same constraint – namely a lack of money. We are already committed beyond our current means in England and I fear that we will not be able to take advantage of the Emperor's offer unless we find a new source of funds."

Slidell leaned forward conspiratorially and said to Bulloch in a low voice, "have you ever met my daughter Mathilde's father-in-law, Emil Erlanger, who is the proprietor of the banking house, which carries his name? No? Well, you must. I will arrange it. He has a scheme which will enable us to raise a prodigious amount in Sterling and Francs, all of which can be applied to the purchase of ships and guns. He and I ..." Slidell looked around to make sure that they were not being overheard and lowered his voice still further ... "he and I are to visit Richmond shortly in order to discuss this scheme with Judah Benjamin. If he approves it, we would hope to float an issue of bonds some time in the New Year!"

XIII

London and Liverpool – October, 1862

❧ ❧

Rose opened the door to her sitting room and stood unmoving in the doorway, while she surveyed the room. Finally she turned and spoke over her shoulder. "McDermott – someone's been here. The window is open and I always close it before I go out."

She went back onto the landing and shouted over the banister. "Mrs P, oh Mrs P." A short, plump, smiling woman came out of a door below the staircase wiping her flour-covered hands on her apron. "Yes, dearie, is it some tea you'd like?"

"Not right now, thank you Mrs P, but tell me, has anyone been in my room since I left?"

"Well now you ask, there was this foreign gentleman, although I'm not sure as 'ow I would really call 'im a gentleman, if you know what I mean. 'E said that the landlord 'ad sent 'im to touch up some of the paintwork, what was chipped, so I showed 'im up to your sitting room. 'E dabbed at a few spots 'ere and there on the winder frame and went away. I stayed with 'im the 'ole time. I 'ope I did right!"

"Yes, Mrs P, that's fine, thank you. And yes, perhaps some tea would be nice." Rose smiled down at the retreating back of Mrs P and, turning back to McDermott, who was leaning against the door jamb, his pipe jutting from his clenched jaw said, "sounds innocent enough."

"Well, I don't like it," McDermott replied. Seems like an easy excuse for someone to search your rooms while you were out. And foreign too – could be that man who attacked you."

"Yes, and it could be almost anyone else. Don't forget, McDermott, you and I are both foreigners to Mrs P. Anyway, let's see if there is anything missing."

192

Rose went back into her room, noticing the faint smell of fresh paint for the first time. She shrugged and went across to close the window. She put her hands on the lower part of the sash but as she did so, she was roughly shoved out of the way by McDermott. "Don't stand in front of the ..." he managed to get out, before a bullet slammed into his forehead, knocking him backwards on top of Rose.

Rose heard three sounds distinctly and separately, although they were to all intents, simultaneous. The gunshot, which sounded like a door slamming, the noise of breaking glass and the nauseating dull thud of a bullet striking flesh and bone. The heavy .58 soft lead minie ball, hit McDermott just above the bridge of the nose on a slightly downward trajectory, continued through the lower part of the brain and flattened itself against the back of his skull, just above the first cervical vertebra. The force of the low velocity, but weighty projectile, which had expanded to the diameter of a half crown, blew away a section of McDermott's head the size of an apple and sprayed Rose with blood and grey brain tissue. The body, thrown backwards by the momentum of the bullet collapsed on top of her and blood coursed from the gaping fissure in the skull into Rose's face. She was winded to begin with, but quickly started wriggling and pushing at the body, desperately trying to get out from under the suffocating and inert weight of her former bodyguard. She became aware of a strange keening sound, but it was not until she had rolled free and crawled behind the sofa that she was able to recognise this as her own high pitched, but monotonic scream.

The door burst open and Mrs P entered at a run, stopping suddenly, her hands flying up to her mouth and her eyes bulging wide with the horror of the scene.

"Mrs P," Rose shouted, franticly wiping blood from her face with both hands, "stay away from the window ... McDermott's been shot, but I'm ..." she paused for a cursory personal inspection ... "I'm fine. Call the police – quickly now Mrs P."

By the time the police arrived, led by a superintendent in a tweed suit with a bowler hat pulled well down onto his ears, Rose had washed off the worst of McDermott's blood and was sitting in an upright chair staring at the corpse of the man who had died, undoubtedly saving her life.

The superintendent looked carefully at the wound in McDermott's forehead, walked across to the window, the shards of broken glass crunching below his hob-nailed boots and stared out.

"Bowman," he shouted over his shoulder, "come 'ere. You see that window up there. Yes that one, the open one. Get up there and see what you can find. It's my guess that that's where the shot came from. Sharply now."

He pulled up a chair and sat down near to Rose. "You alright Ma'am?" he said quietly. Rose nodded, her lips pressed into a thin bloodless line. "I'm going to have to ask you a few questions, if you don't mind. I know this has been a terrible shock, but if we're to have a chance of apprehending the perpetrator ... Now, let's start at the beginning." He pulled out a battered notebook, held shut with a rubber band and the short stub of a pencil, whose point he licked, before starting to write.

After several minutes of questions about the deceased and his relationship with Rose, the constable came running back in and whispered into the superintendent's ear.

"Is that so, by golly," he said, his eyebrow's rising, "we'd better get over there then." He stood up.

"What is it, Inspector?" Rose asked.

"Superintendent, Ma'am. Ah, there's been another killing. The owner of that room over yonder. Bludgeoned to death it seems. Almost certainly by our man, I wouldn't wonder. Now I've got to go across there, so I suggest you wait downstairs with your landlady and I'll be back as quick as I can. You won't want to stay up here with him, will you?"

✻   ✻

Shortly after his return from Paris a messenger arrived at Bulloch's lodgings with a brief note from Charles Prioleau suggesting that a meeting to discuss matters of mutual interest was overdue and please could Mr Bulloch call at their offices in Rumford Place, at his earliest convenience.

Bulloch had not been looking forward to this meeting, partly because he felt awkward about having been discovered in a situation which was open to some misinterpretation, with Prioleau's admittedly gorgeous and clearly promiscuous wife, but also because he was reluctant to discuss his and the Confederate Navy's financial affairs in any detail. Nonetheless, he felt that any further delay on his part would only serve to make Prioleau more suspicious and therefore he penned a short note stating that he would attend Fraser, Trenholm's offices at ten o'clock the following morning, if that were convenient, and sent it back with the messenger.

The next morning, at the appointed hour, he was admitted to the double-fronted Georgian building occupied by Fraser, Trenholm and was shown directly up to Charles Prioleau's office on the first floor. Prioleau rose and greeted Bulloch warmly with a firm handshake, offering him tea and coffee and enquiring most solicitously after his health.

"We have not met since that day when you escaped the clutches of the Customs' men by pretendin' to take the *Enrica* out to sea on trial" Prioleau began. "It was a fine ruse, Mr Bulloch, a fine ruse." He laughed and banged the desk top with the flat of his hand, bouncing his neatly arranged writing implements into disarray. "I would dearly have loved to have seen their faces when they discovered that you were not returnin' … it surely must have been a picture! And now I hear that Captain Semmes is devastatin' the Yankee merchant fleet up and down the Eastern seaboard and it is all down to you Mr Bulloch – you have been the author of this triumph. I salute you." He bowed from the waist, while remaining seated. "And let me tell you, I had a delegation here, just the other day, from Lloyds of London, who have insured many of these ships, to see if I could do anything to prevent further losses to their underwriting account. Why, the very cheek of it! Of course I sent them away with a flea in their ears. 'Gentlemen', I said, 'you have accepted premiums to insure others against various risks, including acts of war and now you are required to perform on your indemnities. That is your business. But, if you should find this business too rich for your blood then, may I suggest as an alternative haberdashery or millinery, both of which, I understand, can be highly rewarding, but are somewhat less risky." He laughed again, with Bulloch joining in. "I said that, I actually said that!"

"Now, Mr Bulloch," Prioleau wiped the tears of mirth from his eyes and drew his brows together," perhaps we should turn to business. I have invited young Mr Spence to join us here, but before he arrives perhaps you could help me by explaining, in some detail if you would be so kind, how the funds entrusted to you have been disbursed to date, and what funds still remain available to fulfil the further commitments which you have undertaken. This is only so that I may understand the dimension of any shortfall to see best how this may be covered."

Bulloch took a deep breath and began. He had been anticipating a question of almost exactly this nature and had prepared himself accordingly. Various items were rounded upwards and others, including 'incentives' given to fictitious officials, were inserted in order to arrive at a balanced ledger. Nonetheless he felt extremely uncomfortable in lying directly in this manner and repeated the promise to himself that, one way or another, the money would be repaid.

When he had finished, Prioleau nodded, looking up from the notes that he had been taking and asked whether receipts were available for the various items of expenditure. Bulloch flushed red. "Please do not take me wrong Mr Bulloch, I imply nothing," Prioleau interjected rapidly, aware that he had probably overstepped the mark, "this is merely the pernickety behaviour of a penny-pinching banker."

"In any case," Bulloch replied, "there are receipts for some items, but not for all, especially the ... ah ... inducements. Also, in some cases, the vendors of the guns and war materiel seemed reluctant to have their business dealings with ourselves too well documented. I'm sure you understand."

"Indeed. Indeed. So where does this leave us Mr Bulloch? To recap, you have around £22,500 on deposit with the Liverpool & County Bank, but need another £71,250 in the near future to complete the down payment on the Rams and a further £25,000, which will become due to Millers for the *Alexandra*, in the spring. Then, of course, you will need £93,750 when the Rams are completed, later in the year.

"That is correct. Laird has been, as always, very reasonable. Construction has already begun on the Rams in spite of his having received no down payment to date. Indeed, Hull 294, which I saw just a few days ago when I visited the Birkenhead works, is already taking shape, with her main timbers cut and laid out. But I feel that we must pay the money without delay so as to ensure his continuing co-operation. Miller is working for payment on delivery this time, but the *Alexandra* is well-advanced and will, he says, be ready by the due date. Then, of course, we have an opportunity in France to build further ships there" and Bulloch went on to recount the story of Slidell's meeting the Emperor Napoleon.

Prioleau nodded happily, proud of his own Gallic descent and pleased that France was an enthusiastic supporter of their Cause, while the English, whom he had never really liked nor trusted, pursued their own self-interested goals in a typically hypocritical and duplicitous manner.

"Upon reflection," Prioleau continued, twirling the ends of his moustache in a subconscious imitation of the Emperor, "I believe that Fraser, Trenholm can readily advance the further £71,250 that you need for Lairds at, say, four and a half percent per annum? Would that be satisfactory?" Bulloch nodded. "No doubt we will also find you £25,000 for Millers' somewhere, but as to the more significant amounts that you will require upon the completion of the Rams, not to mention what will be needed in order to commence shipbuilding operations in France, I suggest that we wait for the arrival of Mr Spence." As if on cue, there was a rap on the door and the tousle-headed James Spence was shown in, smiling broadly and radiating bonhomie as he waved his hat in greeting at the two seated men.

They discussed the war, the confused fighting in the West, the victories at Harpers Ferry and Second Manassas and then the terrible bloody day at Antietam, which led to Lee's withdrawal back across the Potomac into Virginia. Richmond was safe again, but then again, so was Washington. Meanwhile, the finances of the Confederacy continued to deteriorate, with the dollar falling to 2-1 to gold and the price of goods spiralling ever upwards.

"So," Bulloch concluded grimly, "it would appear then that I can expect little in the way of further financial support from Richmond."

"I would not wager on it," Spence agreed.

"Then if we are to take up the Emperor's offer of building further ships in France, we will have to hope that Slidell's plan to float some large issue of bonds is successful."

Spence frowned.

"This is the scheme hatched by Emil Erlanger, is it not? I have heard something of this, but from what I know, I would not have said that it carries a high probability of success. Do you know how it works?" Both men shook their heads. "Well, it is like this. You purchase a bond for £100, which carries a high rate of interest of, say, 8%. At that time cotton is, as today, ten pence a pound. Now, the bond is either redeemable at its face value – £100 – in twenty years' time or ... and this is the lure ... or it is exchangeable for cotton at a fraction of today's price, but only after the war is over and, needless to say, in Charleston or some such Southern harbour. So, d'ye see, it not only raises cash, but every buyer immediately becomes a Southern sympathiser whose one aim is to end the war as soon as possible so that he can lay his hands on the cheap cotton and sell it on at a profit. Good idea you'd say. Well, perhaps, but then again, when the war ends the price of cotton will go back down and so will the profit on the bonds. Why, only the other day, when Gladstone made his speech in Newcastle, cotton fell by nearly a quarter, as the brokers felt that the blockade would be ending any day. All tosh of course, but it cost some of the chaps on the Flags pretty dear I can tell you – and myself a penny or two," he added ruefully.

"What speech was this?" asked Bulloch.

"Why I am surprised you missed it, it was in all the newspapers. Here." Spencer took out his wallet and unfolded a cutting, which he handed to Bulloch. "Read it."

Bulloch glanced down the article. "Yes," he said, "I see what you mean. Listen to this. "… There is no doubt that Jefferson Davis and other leaders of the South have made an army. They are now making it appears, a navy." Spence reached over and patted Bulloch's back, who smiled in acknowledgement. "We may anticipate with certainty the success of the Southern States so far as regards their separation from the North."

"This is wonderful news," Bulloch beamed broadly.

"I would not celebrate quite yet, my friend." Prioleau added with a shake of his head. "There is much in English politics that we do not see and hear. I fear that this speech may have been a personal opinion rather than official Government policy."

"So then we are back to the Erlanger scheme," said Bulloch, exasperated. "You really do not think that it will work?"

Spence shook his head.

"I would not be so categoric. In any case, at the moment, it has not even received the imprimatur of Judah Benjamin. Let us see how it comes out. Investors are a greedy and fickle lot – so, who knows, it may just be the making of us yet."

Bulloch left Rumford Place in high spirits, pleased that the explanation as to his disbursements had been accepted – or so he hoped and believed; that he would achieve a further loan so that he could pay Laird the deposit on the Rams and that there was at least a chance, in Spence's considered opinion, that funds would become available from Erlanger's bonds for further ship construction in France. He whistled as he strode down the street.

He and Spence had agreed to meet later, for a night on the town, but not at the Castle Street gambling club, Bulloch had insisted, where, he explained, there had been an unfortunate incident.

"The Jew cheat you out of all your money did he?" Spence enquired, with a certain bitterness in his voice.

"Well yes and no," Bulloch mumbled, reluctant to go into any details. "In any case, I am sure that there are more salubrious places that we can patronise."

They agreed to meet later at Ribgy's on Dale Street at around eight o'clock and then they parted.

Shortly before the appointed hour, Bulloch was striding along Victoria Street in evening dress, the long cape which covered his tailcoat offering some protection against the chill of the night and a black silk top hat set at a jaunty angle on his head. He turned into Croshall Street and quickened his step to shorten the time spent in the relative darkness of the unlit street that crossed between the two gas-lit thoroughfares.

"Hello dearie, looking for a good time? Only thruppence to a lovely gent like you…" An ageing whore, burping gin, loomed out of the night and clutched briefly at Bulloch's cape for support, before he brushed her away and sent her reeling off into the gloom. Another drunk was sprawled across the pavement, comatose, his legs splayed, an empty bottle still clutched in his fist. Bulloch moved to step over his outstretched legs, but was surprised and annoyed when the drunk suddenly came to life, lashing out with his legs and tripping Bulloch up, so that he fell, sprawling full length down the curb. The fall knocked the wind from him, but he had no time to recover before a heavy weight landed on his back winding him further and pinning his arms to the ground. Someone grabbed him by the hair, pulling his head back and a lantern shone in his face.

"That him?" a gruff voice enquired.

"Yes, that's him. You know what to do". A face came down very close to Bulloch's. A face with a heavy gauze bandage across the nose and swelling around blackened eyes, with a split lip and missing teeth. "Seems you lose again, Mr Bulloch. Hwar, hwar, hwar." Then a blow from a lead-filled cosh smashed into the back of Bulloch's head and the light of the lantern and noise of the voices drifted away into a deeper and more impenetrable night.

The first awareness that returned to Bulloch was in the form of a pounding headache, that started at the back of his head and crossed over his skull to find a throbbing core behind the eyes. He felt his stomach contract and he vomited, continuing to retch bile long after its contents had been emptied. When he was able to open his eyes and assess the situation, he found himself to be lying on hard stone flags in a large empty room. The darkness was broken only by a feeble beam of light that came from a street lamp outside and shone dimly through the dirt-encrusted panes of a small window.

Bulloch tried to move, groaning with pain, but found himself tightly bound, hand and foot, with cords. He struggled, but could make no impression on the bonds that bit cruelly into his flesh. He tried to manoeuvre himself into a sitting position, but found that he could not rise because of the weight of the chains that had been wrapped around his torso. He felt a surge of panic as his mind began to digest the implications of the chains and the noise of lapping water that could be heard close by, beyond the walls of what Bulloch now perceived to be an empty warehouse.

"Help!" he wheezed. "Help! Help!" The cries sounded pathetically weak, coming as they did from his constricted chest. He had been heard, however, for a door opened at the back of the warehouse and three men with heavy boots entered. Bulloch could see that their trouser bottoms were tied with string and that they wore waistcoats and checked shirts, with bandanas around their necks.

"'E's awake," one said.

"Yeh, I kin see that," the other replied. They came across to Bulloch and bent down. When they came closer, Bulloch could see from in meagre light that their hands and faces were deeply engrained with coal dust as a result of years spent underground. "We 'ad to wait for you ter wake up on account of 'ow we was told to make sure you knew what was gonna 'appen to you." The miners looked at each other and smiled, showing several gaps in their teeth.

"'Ave you guessed then?" one asked.

Bulloch shook his head furiously. "Look" he said, "I don't know what you've been paid, but I can pay you more. I just want to get out of this. Please, you've got to help me."

"Oh no, we can't do that. Mr Ampleside, – 'oo you know – 'es the guv'nor of the mine where we works – or at least 'is dad is – 'es given us money – and a guarantee of our jobs for life, like, so we don't 'ave to worry abaht being laid orf, or nuffin like that nor being booted aht of our cottages, come the 'ard times, as they surely will. That's a powerful weight orf the mind fer working men like us."

"But, fust," said another miner, "we's gonna give yew a good kickin', like we wus told" and he swung his heavy boot at Bulloch's head, catching him on the cheek, which split open and splattered blood into Bulloch's eyes. He did his best to assume a foetal position, somewhat comforted by the fact that the chains protected most of the vital organs of his body, but aware that he could easily sustain lethal damage from the kicks to his face and skull.

The pain from the kicks was intense, especially from his knees and shins and from one kick to his jaw, which Bulloch felt break from the impact. After a while the miners stopped, out of breath and Bulloch gratefully yielded to unconsciousness, sinking into a deep pit, which was mercifully free of pain.

Later he came to, the pain from his various cuts and contusions crashing in like a wave and causing Bulloch to cry out. "Es awake again", one of the miners called out. "Good, let's finish 'im an' be away. Dawn's not far orf."

The three miners picked Bulloch up, staggering under the combined weight of a large man and the enveloping chains and carried him out through the door of the warehouse, onto the rough planking of the wharf. The gas lamps had been extinguished earlier and the moon had already set leaving the place in complete and inky darkness.

"Carn't see yer hand in front of yer face out 'ere" said one of the miners. "Mind 'ow yer go then," said another. "We don't want ter be joining 'im in the drink, nah do we? 'Ere we are – 'ere's the edge of the jetty. All together nah."

The miners started to swing Bulloch backwards and forwards, gathering momentum. "No, wait, please" he called out, but on the count of three they all let go and Bulloch was falling, twisting, turning in the air, a cry on his lips as he plummeted towards the dark river, which he hit with a mighty splash. Immediately he was dragged under by the weight of the chains and the cold water closed over his head as he sank.

The miners peered down over the edge of the wharf to where they could just see the widening ripples and a little circle of tell-tale bubbles. "That's it then. Let's be orf," one said and, muttering agreement, they walked quickly away, their heavy boots sounding loudly on the hollow planking and echoing in-between the dark deserted brick warehouses, which loomed over them, their barred windows mute witnesses to the act of murder.

As Bulloch entered the chilling water, his mind froze at the inevitable approach of its own extinction. It took some time, therefore, for it to register that he had hit the bottom very quickly after submersion. "Low tide," he finally thought and began to struggle into a sitting position on the mud and shingle which formed the riverbed close to the banks. He had little air in his lungs and already his heart was pounding and his chest heaving in desperation for oxygen. Once in a sitting position, however, he pulled his legs up to his chest and pushed with his bound feet, sliding himself backwards up the slope of riverbed, a little at a time. Once, twice, three times and yet still he had not broken clear of the surrounding water. His body's need for air was now all-consuming, but the possibility of life and the resultant rush of adrenalin powered his legs again and again until he felt the top of his head come out of the water and the sharp wind chill his wet scalp. Two more pushes and his face just came clear and he was dragging in lungfulls of air from extended lips, the wavelets pushing water into his mouth, which he blew out like a whale.

When he had recovered sufficiently, he pushed himself further out of the water, until his head came up against the planking of the wharf. He tried to remember the times of the tides and whether it was now rising or still falling but gave up after a while and devoted his energies to remaining conscious, aware that if he passed out he would surely drown. After what seemed an eternity, but in reality was less than an hour, he heard above him the footsteps of the stevedores arriving for work at six o'clock. He called out, aware of the weakness of his voice and his inability to open his mouth widely, from the fracture to his jaw. To start with, no-one heard him, but finally a voice said, "'ere, Will, I kin 'ear summat from down unner the dock. Quiet now. Just lissen." In the silence they could hear Bulloch's cries for help quite plainly. "Bloody 'ell, there's a geezer trapped down there. Come on you two – let's get darn and give 'im an 'and."

Bulloch was covered with sacking for warmth, taken back to his lodgings in a cart and a doctor was called. The doctor treated his cuts and bruises and set his broken jaw 'tutting' all the while. The police came and took a statement in which Bulloch swore that the assailants were unknown to him and that he could think of no reason for his attack. The inspector clearly did not believe him, because no attempt had been made to rob Bulloch, while every attempt had been made to silence him permanently. Nonetheless he was unable to extend his investigation in the face of Bulloch's intransigence and eventually he left and Bulloch collapsed gratefully back onto his stack of pillows.

Due to the soaking in cold water and his generally weakened condition, pneumonia set in, seizing Bulloch's chest in a grip of iron. His fever raged and again the doctor was sent for, dispensing opiates and expectorants and ordering additional blankets and constant care. His landlady, at her wit's end, sent a telegram to Mrs Rose Greenhow, whose visiting card she had had the presence of mind to keep. Believing her to be a friend of Bulloch's and desperate for assistance, she claimed that Bulloch was at death's door and that he had been calling for her, Rose, with every gasp of his fever-racked body.

The telegram was collected from Rose's old lodgings, which she had vacated after the assassination of her bodyguard, by one of her couriers. The man called daily to collect the post, arriving by the back entrance and then returning in a most circumspect manner, so as to avoid detection and pursuit. Rose read the telegram with mixed emotions, but found herself, nonetheless, quickly packing a bag and giving orders concerning a protracted absence. She took a cab to Euston station and boarded the express for Liverpool. Barely six hours after receiving the telegram she was knocking at the front door of Bulloch's lodgings. The landlady greeted her like a long-lost daughter, throwing her arms around her and hugging her before pulling her into the house and slamming the door against the damp autumn wind.

She showed Rose up to Bulloch's bedroom and then left to make some tea. The first thing that Rose noticed was the stifling heat in the bedroom. A highly banked coal fire blazed in the hearth and rolled towels were stacked against the edges of the window frames as draft excluders. The bed was piled high with blankets and quilts so that its occupant was scarcely visible, although his laboured breathing and the wheezy rattle from by the fluid in his lungs were clearly audible.

Rose approached and then stopped, her hand going to her mouth in shock. For in the place of the powerfully built individual, whose jocular manner and easy self-assurance shone from his large and prominently featured face, there, on the pillow, lay the death mask of an elderly man. Over the past week, Bulloch's cheeks had collapsed, his eyes had sunk back into their sockets and his skin had lost its usual ruddy glow, being replaced by a jaundiced pallor. Greying stubble covered his chin, while the swelling from his broken jaw and the bruises to his head and face were still livid and gave him a strangely mottled appearance.

"Oh my poor dear, what have they done to you?" she murmured, throwing off her coat and gloves and perching herself on the side of the bed. She picked up a sponge from a bowl of water and wrung it out before gently mopping his brow and wiping away the beads of sweat that were as much a result of the heat of the room as the fever. She called for Bulloch's landlady, loudly shouting "bring me hot water – lots of it – and clean, dry towels." While she waited, she threw off several of the blankets and quilts, wrinkling her nose at the rank sour odour that emanated from below the bedclothes. After a few minutes, Mrs Benson arrived at the door of Bulloch's room, puffing and panting under the weight of an iron bath full of hot water, the other end being supported by her niece, Sarah, a stupid girl with protuberant teeth.

Rose stripped Bulloch and carefully washed him, observed all the time by Miss Benson, while the niece was forced to turn her back on the proceedings at precisely the moment when the objects of her vivid, but uneducated, imagination were about to be revealed. With help from the others, Rose redressed Bulloch in a clean night shirt, shaved his chin and neck, brushed his hair and put him back into a bed with clean sheets. She then sent Mrs Benson and the goggle-eyed niece off to make soup.

Throughout all this Bulloch had been slipping in and out of consciousness, at times able to help by lifting himself, at other times inert and dreadfully heavy; sometimes muttering, almost coherently and sometimes silent except for the whistle of air through his locked teeth and the gurgle of mucus in his chest.

Rose made every effort to get Bulloch to take some of the soup when it arrived, but more often than not it would trickle out from the corners of his mouth and soak into the towel that she held beneath his chin as a bib.

Over the following days, Rose spent much of the time beside Bulloch, sleeping on his sofa at night and frequently being woken by his cries that sent her running across to comfort him, stroking his brow and holding his hand. As the days went by and his fever abated, so the periods of lucidity increased, as did the food he consumed and slowly his strength started to return, although he still remained so weak and debilitated by the fever that he could not rise from his bed unaided. At last Rose felt that he had recovered sufficiently for her to ask him about the events that led up his current condition.

Bulloch recounted the story, leaving out nothing except for the reason behind his beating and attempted murder. He confessed himself perplexed as to why anyone should want him dead, let alone in such a brutal and vengeful manner. Throughout his story, Rose was silent, shocked by the details, but also by the thought that was just occurring to her. When Bulloch had finished she took him by the hand and said:

"James, I know who attacked you – and why."

Bulloch sat very upright in bed, swallowing hard and replied, "You do?"

"Yes, I believe I do. I think that this is the same assassin, who has now tried to kill me twice." She saw a momentary flash of something like relief cross Bulloch's features before he said: "Twice, Rose? You said twice. When was the second occasion?" So, she recounted the story of McDermott's death and was pleased to see a build-up of the colour in Bulloch's face that would have presaged an outbreak of bad temper and foul language in the old Bulloch. 'He *is* getting better,' she thought and surprised herself by hugging him.

"So," she concluded, "it seems as if this man is an agent in the pay of the Federals after all. Even if Charles Adams was not lying, it is almost certain that Benjamin Moran was, the rat! He has been sent to wipe out the opposition in this Country and they have clearly decided that your activities single you out for a particularly gruesome end."

"Yes, yes, that must be it," Bulloch insisted, delighted at this highly convenient explanation, that had been handed to him on a platter. "Rose, you and I must certainly take very great care in the future," he added, "because these assassins are still on the loose and will undoubtedly try again."

"That is precisely what I was thinking," Rose agreed. "And what is more, rather than just waiting like rabbits for the hawk, I think that we should try to smoke them out and put an end to them. Finish them, as they would do to us. In fact, I have been thinking ... James, you and I should team up ... find some place together, where we can watch each other's backs and plan the destruction of these murdering swine. What do you say?"

Bulloch looked a little uncomfortable. "I think it is a fine idea Rose ... were it not for that other matter which has come between us." She nodded and looked down, unwilling to meet his gaze. "I have been thinking about that too, James. In fact I have had considerable opportunity to think over a great many things these past few days. I believe that I owe you an apology. I did search your rooms, which was wrong, and I spoke to you in a manner that was not only vicious and cruel, it was unforgivable. I had already decided that nothing would be achieved by passing this information on to Richmond, but I would now like to offer you an apology. I can only put my behaviour down to the shock of that first attack and the pain of my wounds. I hope that you can bring yourself to forgive me, for I feel truly ashamed."

Bulloch shook his head in disbelief. "Rose, of course you are forgiven. But you were correct, though, to upbraid me for what I did, which was indeed wrong. The money was to repay my gambling debts, as you said. I was foolish, I was drawn in little by little and, it now seems clear, I was cheated. But that does not excuse my conduct. It was unforgivable. However, I have always determined that I would repay the money as soon as I was able and so I shall, have no fear."

Rose put out a hand and stroked his cheek. "Then there is nothing between us any more," she said softly.

XIV

Liverpool and London – November, December, 1862

❧ ❦

With November and the shortening days that herald the approach of winter, came the first of the really cold weather, with freezing rain and flurries of wet snow. The sky assumed the colour of old lead and loured down on the people of Liverpool, who scurried from arch to doorway, their umbrellas held firmly at waist height by chapped hands, while sodden feet marched the slippery pavements or turned in rapid pursuit of lost hats, snatched by the sudden icy gusts.

Bulloch made slow progress in his recovery. The pneumonia left him short of breath while, from time to time, fits of coughing wracked his frame. The broken jaw set, but not completely straight, so that his bite was uneven and this caused him pain while eating. The remainder of the cuts and bruises healed well, although he had a long and angry scar high on his right cheek, just below the eye. In spite of this he regarded himself as having been thoroughly lucky. If Ampleside had not hired men who knew little of the sea and its tides to execute his revenge, then Bulloch would surely be dead. And then his rapprochement with Rose gave him great pleasure, but perhaps also just the slightest twinge of guilt in that it had been fraudulently obtained. He had, however, committed absolutely to himself and to Rose that the money would be repaid and that he would under no circumstances gamble any more nor risk incurring further debts.

What Rose, of course, did not know was that he still owed the Jew a further one thousand three hundred pounds. The dilemma was, however, whether to seek out the Jew and repay him or to assume that Ampleside had informed him of Bulloch's untimely

207

demise. After all, being dead could be a highly advantageous state and Bulloch was in no hurry to exchange it for one where his enemies and his creditors still pursued him.

His convalescence kept him, by necessity, mainly confined to his lodgings and, on the infrequent occasions when he ventured out, the bad weather enabled him to travel abroad with a muffler wrapped around his lower face. Rose stayed with him for the first half of the month, but then an urgent summons from Mason sent her hurrying up to London. She returned two days later and informed Bulloch that she would be going back to live in London, at a new and closely-guarded address. She urged Bulloch to come and stay with her there as soon as he was able as she was impatient for them start the hunt for the Yankee assassin, whom she firmly believed had murderous intentions on them both.

Bulloch promised that he would come as soon as he had recovered sufficiently and had visited Laird to check on the progress of his Rams. As her bags were taken down to a waiting cab, Rose, smartly dressed in a long maroon velvet coat which buttoned up to the neck and a small black bonnet, reached up to kiss Bulloch. As usual he proffered his cheek and was greatly surprised when she took his face in both her hands and pulled his mouth onto hers, sliding her tongue deeply into his mouth and running it slowly and lasciviously around his tongue. She broke away suddenly, her eyes bright and a fetching blush across her cheeks and ran for the door, pausing only to blow him a kiss as she left.

Bulloch was highly aroused by this deeply passionate kiss and sat on the edge of a chair fanning himself with his hand and breathing rapidly. And as he became aware, breathing clearly. The congestion in his lungs had abated. 'If that is what one kiss will do', he thought, 'making love to a beautiful woman would cure me completely!' He thought of Marise and then of the voluptuous redhead, whom he remembered as a highly charged and sensual lover, although the details remained unusually blurred in his memory. He was quite clear on one point however and that was that she would have benefited from a bath. Regretfully, both these ladies were to be found at the Jew's establishment and Bulloch was not prepared to risk a return to that venue, even on medicinal grounds. He looked out the window at the driving rain and occasional sleet and dismissed the idea of seeking a companion on the streets and instead poured himself another whisky and sat down in front of the fire. He took out his pair of matched Adams revolvers, his Colts, the Navy .36 and the Pocket Model .32 and proceeded to strip and clean each one, before loading them carefully and putting them back in the drawer. All except for the .32 which he slipped into the inside pocket of his frock coat, even as he hung it in the wardrobe.

* *

Charles Adams was clearly pleased, but also somewhat perplexed and, had he been honest with himself, just slightly worried. Instead of being rebuffed and rejected in his attempts to see Lord Russell, where his meetings were often cancelled or rescheduled at short notice on the flimsiest of pretexts, he had just received a note inviting him to present himself at the Foreign Office, at his earliest convenience, where Lord Russell was desirous of an interview. Again, instead of being kept waiting in the outer office by the haughty secretary, often for hours, he was greeted warmly by Stainforth, who showed him immediately into Russell's office.

Lord Russell was in an extremely bad mood. Three days earlier, all the senior members of Palmerston's Ministry had attended a Cabinet meeting, at which the Emperor Napoleon's proposal of a joint approach to the warring parties with an offer of mediation, to be accompanied by an immediate cessation of hostilities and a six-month suspension of the blockade, was discussed. Russell believed that this was a serious and sensible proposition, even though he suspected that Napoleon's motives might have been influenced by an offer of cotton similar to that he had received and France's need for cash to support its ruinously expensive Mexican adventure.

Palmerston, as usual, was wishy-washy and ambivalent, first pointing out the pros and then the cons, before passing the matter over to George Lewis, who went on and on about the South being in rebellion, about efforts to mediate being seen as an act of war and about the costs and unpopularity of fighting such a war, so far away and for such a worthless cause. What was that he had said? Some nonsense about it being cheaper to feed all the cotton workers on venison and turtle rather than fight a war with the United States. Utter balderdash! Still, for all that, his damned rhetoric had swayed the Cabinet against Napoleon's plan. When

George finally piped down and they all voted, it was 15-3 against, with only Gladstone, himself and old Westbury standing up to be counted. Surely everyone could see what Lewis was afraid of – the damned ironclads! What were they called? Oh, yes, Monitors – like the lizards. He was afraid that they'd float up the Thames and sink the fleet at anchor at Spithead. Show us up for what we really were – old fashioned and unprepared – and then Lewis would get it in the neck. Forced to resign, no doubt. And, as if it wasn't enough to be outvoted on such an important issue he, as Foreign Secretary had been asked to write the note to Napoleon explaining why Her Britannic Majesty's Government, after careful consideration, did not feel that the timing was appropriate, blahdy, blahdy, blah. And now, to make matters even worse, after this morning's article in the *Times*, which revealed that a vote on the Emperor's plan had actually taken place in Cabinet (no prizes for guessing who leaked that!) Pam had called him over and had literally ordered him to explain to Adams that it had *never* been our intention to support France and that the vote was nothing more than a mere formality. As he got up to leave Pam had added: "Johnny, do be nice to the man – very nice, if you can be."

Russell rose from behind his desk, his lips pulled back in a grim rictus that revealed his yellowing and crooked teeth, but which he firmly believed to be a warm and welcoming smile. He bowed to Adams and gestured for him to be seated at the fireside, instead of in his usual place opposite the broad and intimidating desk.

"You are well, I trust, Mr Adams?" he began. "Good, good. Filthy weather we've been having of late, eh? Still, I expect you get just as bad in New England, what?" He then lapsed into silence and contemplated the hissing of the damp coal in the grate. "D'ye see the *Times* this morning?", he enquired at last.

'Ah, so that is what this is about', Adams thought, 'the newspapers smoked them out and now they want to convey the official line to me. Well, let him sweat.'

"Yes, Foreign Secretary. There were a number of good articles and I particularly liked the 'Leader' – on Poland, I recall – very interesting. Also a good review of that new play that's just opened at the Criterion. I must try and get to see it."

Russell looked at him with undisguised annoyance. "No, not that. The piece about the Cabinet meeting – the vote on

Napoleon's proposal to offer joint mediation. Surely you saw that?"

"Ah, yes – now I recall. A well written piece."

"Be damned how it was wr…" Russell paused and gave his tetanic smile again … "well, anyway, we, the Cabinet that is, just wanted to assure you that … we are required to vote on such matters and that we would never have contemplated for one minute …" He paused to swallow the bile that was rising in his gorge … "acceding to such an outlandish request …"

"I am very glad to hear it Foreign Secretary, as will be both the President and Mr Seward. However, might I enquire, for the sake of completeness, as to the how the vote was split?"

"The balance of the vote? On no! Oh, dear me no. We don't publicise matters such as that."

"Is there any particular reason for your reluctance to divulge the balance of the vote, I wonder? Was it a particularly close thing, for example?"

"No, it was not!" Russell snapped. "It was … well, let us just say that it was 'overwhelmingly' against the proposition. I myself voted with the majority, of course… just thought you might like to know that." He breathed deeply, glad that this repulsive task was over.

'I wouldn't put a cent on you voting that way', thought Adams. He said: "was there anything further you wished to tell me?" Russell shook his head. "Good, well, thank you for your assurances, but now I have something to tell you. Do you remember the ship that was built at Laird's in Birkenhead and just managed to evade our clutches, slipping out to sea in late July? Yes? Well, the last I heard she had sunk or taken twenty-five merchantmen with many lives lost and millions of dollars in cargo and shipping gone to the bottom. And as a direct result the insurers have now trebled – trebled I tell you – marine insurance on U.S. merchantmen. They are all re-registering as British ships to avoid this! What do you have to say to that?"

Russell lowered his eyelids to hide the gleam of amusement and sucked on his teeth in contemplation. "How very unfortunate," he said after a while.

"I'll say it's unfortunate. It's damned unfortunate. And now, Foreign Secretary, I understand that Laird may be building more ships for the Rebels. Not that I can get you any proof at the moment. He's tightened up his security and only picked men are working on the new hulls, which are screened off from the rest of his yard. But when I do ..."

"When you do, Mr Adams, then we may discuss this further."

* *

Bulloch received a letter from Rose, which he read carefully, memorising the contents. He then held the letter just below his nose, savouring the faint scent of violets that emanated from the paper, before tearing it into small pieces and throwing them on the fire. He summoned Mrs Benson and sent her off to the post office with a telegram in reply, went into his bedroom and started to pack.

On his arrival at Euston station, he took a cab to Piccadilly, but jumped out while the cab was still moving, having paid the driver in advance and ran across the road, through the traffic and into the Burlington Arcade. He ran the length of the Arcade, his *porte-manteau* under one arm, holding his top hat with the other, apologising to the several fashionably dressed ladies whom he startled by the rapidity of his progress. Once out of the far side of the Arcade, he carried on into Cork Street, where he found another cab in front of the Burlington Hotel, which he immediately boarded. Looking out of the small rear window he could see no signs of pursuit and so relaxed back into the musty cushions, his heart racing and his breath coming in short gasps.

At Rose's new address, the door was answered by a tall thin man, with a drooping moustache, who regarded Bulloch with suspicion. After he had introduced himself however, the man stood back, nodding and called up to Rose with a strong Southern accent, "Missus Greenhow, the gennelmun yew is expectin' is heah."

Rose greeted Bulloch with a hug, took him into the parlour and closed the door. "Are you absolutely certain that you were not followed?" she asked, frowning, the tension clearly visible on her features."

"I am quite sure. You need have no fear on my account. I have considerable experience in ditching Yankee agents – indeed it is my speciality."

"Good," she said, relaxing, one of her warm smiles lighting up her face and returning to it the beauty and grace that had temporarily been masked by her concern. Bulloch slid an arm around her waist and pulled her to him, kissing her hard on the mouth, which immediately opened to his probing tongue. They remained locked in this embrace for moments, until Bulloch placed a hand on one her large breasts and squeezed it gently through the soft fine wool of her dress. She moaned softly, but then broke away. "Too much, too fast, Mr Bulloch," she said, holding him at arm's length, but with a seductive smile playing around her lips that conveyed the message that one day, soon, anything might be possible.

They dined at the Savoy Grill on brown Windsor soup, followed by poached fish and then a partridge, which had clearly been hung for several days. This was served with watery cabbage and boiled potatoes, which had acquired a coating of white fur. Finally, an apple pie arrived with the apples having disintegrated from the cooking and then a powerful stilton. "My God, James," Rose said with a look of disgust on her face, "the food in this country either has no taste or a terrible taste!"

"Hmmm", Bulloch replied, who had actually enjoyed his meal considerably. In comparison to the thin and often rotten rations produced by ships' galleys, which had been his stable fare for much of his adult life, this was truly a cornucopia. He assumed that the same applied to the English upper classes, who were sent away from home to boarding schools at a tender age, to be subjected to a cruel and oppressive regime that trained them perfectly for the rigours of campaigning in one of the far flung and less salubrious outposts of the Empire.

Instead, changing the subject, he asked Rose if she had thought of a way to trap the assassin. "Only by using myself as bait", she replied. "I could return to my old lodgings and go in and out, while staying away from windows, of course, until he showed himself".

"No". Bulloch was emphatic. "It's far too dangerous and I will not have your risking your life in this manner. Perhaps it is also a little too obvious. Instead, why don't we have the messenger who collects the mail, enter and leave through the front door and walk down the street, instead of making his usual dash from a carriage. The assassin will believe that enough time has gone by for us to relax and become careless. He will then follow the messenger to a new address, where I will be waiting. Sooner or later his curiosity will get the better of him and he will break in to see who is there. Then I'll kill him."

Rose nodded, impressed. "What if he is no longer watching? Nearly six weeks have gone by since the shooting. He may have given up by now."

Bulloch shook his head. "Unlikely. He seems to me to be of a most determined disposition. I doubt he will have given up, because what other leads to you does he have? He could watch the houses of other prominent Confederates in England, such as Mason or Hotze, hoping that you might be seen with them, but that would be a remote chance. No. He will be there somewhere, in a crowd perhaps, or on a roof-top, waiting patiently. I am sure of it."

On the way home in the cab, Rose was silent and pre-occupied. She parted from Bulloch in the hallway, complaining of a headache, merely brushing his cheek with hers, before climbing the stairs to her room. Bulloch went into the parlour to drink a brandy and smoke a cigar in order to ease his frustration, for he had heard the key turning in the lock of Rose's bedroom door with a very final click.

The next morning Bulloch rose late. He shaved carefully but still managed to nick his jaw. He swore and dabbed at the cut with a towel. Then he held both his hands out in front of him, palms down. They were steady. He took a deep breath and went down to breakfast. Rose sat at the table, staring into a cold cup of coffee, her eyes unfocused. "What is it?" Bulloch asked. Rose swallowed and replied, her voice hoarse with emotion. "I have only just found you and I don't want to lose you."

"You won't lose me and this is the only way. Trust me. Now, let me have the address of this house and the key to the back door. It does have a back door I hope?" Rose nodded. "And perhaps you could ask your housekeeper to make me some sandwiches and a flask of coffee."

"You should also take a lantern and a blanket," she added. "There is no furniture and it is quite bare. You are armed of course?"

"Always," Bulloch responded grimly.

*   *

Bulloch found the house, which was in the middle of a terrace of identical small houses in a narrow cobbled street in Chelsea. The daylight was already fading as he arrived and the lamp-lighter was igniting the last of the few widely interspersed gas lights, each of which weakly illuminated a small area around its base, accentuating the darkness between it and its neighbour.

He walked to the end of the row of houses counting as he went and looked up and down the adjoining street. Finding it deserted, he vaulted over the low wooden fence that separated the garden of the first house from the pavement. He then crossed over from one garden to the next, incurring the wrath of a sleeping dog, which barked furiously and snapped at his heels as he leapt the fence. At last he arrived at what he believed to be the right house. He slid the key into the lock, turned it, pushed open the door and entered, relieved that he had not miscounted in the dark. He quickly scouted the small house, drawing the shutters closed and fastening them on the inside.

Bulloch chose the back room in which to wait and positioned himself in the far corner, from where he could see through the open door to the foot of the stairs. Anyone entering the house through the front door would be out of his line of sight, but only until they decided either to proceed deeper into the house or to go up the stairs to the bedrooms. He took out both Adams revolvers and placed them on the rug in front of him, after checking that none of the percussion caps had become dislodged. Then he settled down to wait.

The darkness was so complete and so palpable that he could actually feel it pressing down on him like a physical entity. At every sound from the street outside, whether the footsteps of a passer-by or the rattle of wheels on the cobbles, he would start and pick up one of the revolvers, easing the hammer back with his thumb while holding the trigger depressed, so that there was only the very faintest of 'clicks' to betray his presence. As the hours passed, so he became sleepy, finding to his alarm that his head nodded and even occasionally slumped forward onto his chest in a momentary lapse of consciousness. Then there was the cold, which penetrated every loose seam and window frame of the house. He had wrapped his arms around himself in an attempt to keep warm, but still gave way to sporadic and violent fits of shivering. He blew on his fingers and pressed his hands into his armpits to prevent them from going numb and each time he did so he left the revolvers resting on his lap, with their handles facing outwards.

Finally dawn came, at around 8 a.m. Bulloch waited for one more hour before leaving the way he had come, giving a cheery 'morning' to the individuals whom he met in their gardens, usually on the way to or from their outside privy.

The following night Bulloch improved the conditions of his vigil with cushions and rugs, so that he was now tolerably warm and comfortable. Sleep remained his greatest enemy, but copious quantities of coffee and rests during the day enabled him to fend it off, until the dawn again cast thin strips of light through the cracks around the door, which soon crept down the passage to the point where they became visible from his corner location.

On the third night he was back in his corner, swathed in rugs, his knees drawn up to his chest, with his revolvers positioned either side of him on the floor, within easy reach. Time passed and Bulloch felt his head begin to nod. He stifled a yawn, but then suddenly froze. He heard no sound. Nothing disturbed the absolute stillness of the house and yet ... and yet something had changed. Then he identified it. He was just able to detect the merest hint of a whiff of garlic. Someone had entered the house more silently than he had dreamed possible and was, even now, either in this same room or just outside in the passage. But Bulloch was so swaddled in rugs that he knew that he would not be able to disentangle himself and grab the revolvers, without there being sufficient noise and delay for the intruder to have the advantage over him. So he sat very still and waited, breathing as shallowly as he could and only through his nose.

There was the faintest creak of a floorboard from the stairs, then nothing. Then another creak from above. Quickly, Bulloch threw off the blankets and removed his shoes. He shrugged off his coat and picked up the revolvers, which he cocked silently. Moving as quietly as he could, he went out into the hall and knelt down with his back to the front door. The intruder would have to pass within feet of his position as he came down the stairs. Bulloch hoped that, by kneeling, he would reduce the target area that his opponent would have and also be below the waist-height level of instinctive fire.

There it was again – the squeaky floorboard on the stairs. Bulloch raised both arms out in front of him and squeezed the trigger of the pistol in his left hand. In the muzzle flash he saw a figure, its face white in the sudden glare, astride the banister, not in the middle of the staircase, as Bulloch would have imagined.

Bulloch shifted his aim fractionally to the right and fired with the other gun, but as he did so, he saw the man drop neatly over the banister and into the passage below.

Bulloch rolled to his right just as the crash of his opponent's pistol sent a heavy lead ball slamming into the door where he had been only a split second before. A splinter from the shattered wood flew into Bulloch's face and lodged in his cheek, just below the left eye. Bulloch sprawled full length down the passage, simultaneously cocking and firing both his pistols. He saw the figure lurch, as if hit, and heard him cry "*Scheiss!*". When Bulloch fired again, it was into an empty passage. He sprang to his feet and ran towards the back door, which he could now see was wide open, and out into the garden where he paused, one revolver pointing to his left, the other to his right. He listened carefully for any sound while his night vision returned. Clearly the man had left by climbing over a fence and into a neighbouring garden, but which one? Bulloch decided that it would be the obvious route, which would take someone most quickly to the street and jumped the fence into the garden to his right.

By now, windows were flying up and lights were coming on in all the neighbouring houses. A head emerged. "Ere you down there, what's going on? What's all the rukus?" Bulloch said nothing, but continued at a run, vaulting each fence until finally he arrived at the end of the terrace. "Damn," he shouted, "damn, damn, damn. I've lost him."

Bulloch recounted the story to Rose, as she worked the long splinter out of his cheek and then dabbed his face with iodine, ignoring his yells. When she had finished she said grimly, "so we are back to where we started then?"

"No, not really," he replied. "I know that he is German and that he is wounded – again. There is probably quite a small German community here in London, which will be centred around one of the Lutheran churches. I will go and speak to the pastor, find out the names of his parishioners who are doctors and approach them to see if they have recently treated a man for gunshot wounds."

Rose looked impressed. "Why would they talk to you, though? Will they not protect one of their own against a foreigner?"

"*Ja, naturlich,*" Bulloch replied, "*aber ich bin kein Ausländer.* In fact," he continued, "I am told that I speak with a pronounced Schwabian accent. My Governess was German you see."

Rose nodded. Nothing very much surprised her about this strange man anymore. She took a deep breath before continuing, her knuckles white where they grasped the arms of the chair. "James ... you should know that he has killed Samuel".

"Samuel?"

"The messenger. The young man who answered the door when you first came here. You see I had Samuel act as the messenger and collect the mail from my old lodgings and take it to the house where you have spent these last few nights. You felt sure that he would be followed...and he was. You were right But I never, never thought that he would be killed...stabbed in the back. Its too awful James – I sent him to his death and I will never forgive myself." She got up and walked slowly and stiffly from the room.

Bulloch remained seated, his lips pressed into a thin line. He took the revolvers out of his coat and carefully began to clean and re-load them.

XV

Richmond — December, 1862

❧ ❦

It was over a year since Slidell had last been in Richmond and he was profoundly shocked by the change.

The streets were now crowded with soldiers, many of them wounded, some struggling down the sidewalk on new crutches, an empty trouser-leg flapping where once a leg had been, others sitting in dispirited rows on benches, the blind, the maimed and the limbless, taking in the thin winter sunshine. In the place of carriages and landaus, wagons carrying powder and shot hurried between the arsenal and the outlying batteries. Unsprung ambulances brought yet more wounded in from distant battlefields, their cries of pain audible to the passers-by each time an iron-shod wheel found one of the many mud-filled ruts or potholes.

Slidell sat silently, staring out the window of their carriage as it took them the short distance from the railway terminus to the Exchange Hotel. To his companion, Baron Emil Erlanger, the chaos and desperation of Richmond seemed a grim portent as to the eventual outcome of the war. But he shrugged and put the street scenes out of his mind, and concentrated instead on the proposal that he was here to discuss with the Confederate Secretary of State, Judah Benjamin, a fellow Jew.

At the hotel, a message was waiting for Slidell. He tore open the small envelope with a long and dirty thumbnail. "Ah," he said, "good. Benjamin has invited us to dine. He has taken a private room upstairs and expects us at around seven. Shall I see you there?" Erlanger nodded and disappeared up the stairs, preceded by several Negroes, who struggled under the weight of his many cases, all crafted from the finest matched alligator skins and fastened with sturdy brass hinges and locks. Slidell shook his head as he watched him go and then, running his fingers through his long and unkempt hair, departed for his own room.

Dinner had been a pleasant affair. They had drunk whisky before and champagne during, what had seemed to be, by the standards of Parisian cuisine, enormous servings of very plain fare, consisting of hunks of overcooked meat, swimming in greasy gravy, with mounds of fried potatoes piled on top. The conversation, however, had been better than the food, with Erlanger at his most amusing, enthralling the others with stories of Paris high society and the notorious sexual escapades of the *demi-monde*. The war was discussed at length, with Benjamin painting a relatively rosy picture, but warning that the armies were manoeuvring for another major battle even as they spoke. Both he and Meminger, the Treasury Secretary, bemoaned the fact that the value of the confederate dollar to gold had fallen to 4-1 and the relentless rise in prices caused by shortages of almost every type of commodity and foodstuff.

At last the plates were pushed away and cigars were lit. Slidell burped loudly, while Meminger picked his teeth with a long and dirty fingernail and Erlanger feigned to notice neither, his suave and polished exterior unruffled by the mild disgust that he felt for this coarse behaviour. At least Benjamin was a gentleman – and a jew; he felt that he could do business with this man. He tapped the stem of his wine glass with a spoon and, in the resulting silence, began.

"So, Gentlemen, my thanks go out to you for the excellent repast and now, with your permission, I would like to suggest that we get down to business. Perhaps I may be permitted to outline my proposal. Yes?" Heads nodded around the table. "Very well. In essence, it would be my intention to float a bond, denominated in both pounds Sterling and francs Français, listed on both national stock exchanges, with a par value of, say, twenty-five million dollars. The issue price is, of course, open to negotiation, but I would recommend around seventy percent to ensure the success of the emission. The bonds would be payable as to ten percent down and ten percent per month for the next six months and would bear interest at a rate of, say, eight percent per annum, payable half-yearly in arrears, on the principal amount. Now the key feature of these bonds – and what will distinguish them from all others that have gone before – is that the holder may, at his own volition, exchange his bonds into cotton at six pence per pound – which is, ah, let me see, twelve and a half of your cents – but only after the conclusion of this unfortunate war and in such of your ports as you may nominate. *Et voilà*, that is my proposal." He looked around. Slidell nodded enthusiastically, Meminger sucked on his teeth, looking perplexed, while Benjamin leaned back in his chair and blew a long thin stream of smoke at the ceiling.

"And what would your Bank's commission be for arranging this loan?" Benjamin asked finally.

Erlanger smiled. "A very modest five percent on all the bonds that we sell and a further one percent for acting as agent on the payment."

"I see. So, if I understand it correctly, we offer, not only the inducements of a very high interest rate and a low issue price, but also the extra benefit of buying cotton at twelve cents a pound, when it currently sells for slightly over twenty-one cents. Do you not think that this smacks a little of desperation?"

"I for one, do not." It was Slidell who interrupted. "People are greedy and I do not believe that they will look a gift horse in the mouth. And from our point of view, in Europe, the successful float of such a loan would be a sign of the market's confidence in our prospects for victory. Not to mention the individual investors who would become financially committed to our cause. And finally, we need the money to build more *Alabamas* – that is, unless Stephen Mallory has further funds available to send us." Meminger shook his head emphatically.

Judah Benjamin rose to his feet. "Your proposal is not without some merit. I will think it over and let you know tomorrow, if I may? Very well then, good night Gentlemen." He left as Meminger was calling loudly for another bottle of whisky.

*   *

The following morning Benjamin received Erlanger alone in his office. "I have given considerable thought to your proposal overnight and I have decided that we are prepared to proceed, subject to one or two minor amendments and further subject to final ratification by Congress, of course. First, the loan is too expensive. Far too expensive. Instead of eight percent interest, I propose seven percent and I would not wish to sell the bonds below eighty percent. Even then, the value for us in this flotation is more of a political nature than a financial one. Accordingly, the amount should be reduced to, say, fifteen million dollars."

Erlanger winced theatrically. "You are a hard man, Monsieur. Of course, you are the client and I must abide by your wishes. But, in all honesty, I must advise you that a price of eighty percent might jeopardise the success of the whole issue and, if your motivation is largely of a political nature, then the success of the issue must be your overriding aim. It would be a shame to take such a large risk for such a small amount. I propose seventy five percent."

"Seventy seven".

"Done. It has been a pleasure doing business with you, *Monsieur Secrétaire*".

＊　＊

As Erlanger strolled back to the hotel, the bells of the many churches of Richmond broke into a joyous peal. Slowly, but gathering momentum, cheering started, until all the soldiers and civilians who thronged the sidewalks or passed down the cobbled streets on horse, mule or wagon, were shouting and waving their hats in the air. Erlanger, caught up in the spontaneous euphoria of the crowd was swept along, laughing and cheering as he went, without the first idea as to the reason for such an outbreak of collective happiness.

He broke free from the throng and entered the hotel, fighting his way through the crowded lobby. Slidell saw him and waved exuberantly. "What is it?" he shouted, "what is happening, *mon ami?*"

"You haven't heard?" Slidell was bending over the smaller man, his mouth close to his ear so as to be heard above the excited babble of voices. "Lee's only gone and licked the Yankees again! But he's given them a real thrashing this time. Over twelve thousand casualties for them, and barely a third of that for our side. At Fredericksburg, on the Rappahannock. Now we'll see what those stick-in-the-mud Europeans have to say!"

XVI

London and Liverpool – January, February, 1863

  ❧ ❧

It was on Christmas Day that Bulloch decided to attend matins at the Church of St Anne and St Agnes on Gresham Street. He reckoned that the Christmas service at the leading Lutheran church in London would produce the largest congregation and, if not the assassin himself, then at least those who might be able to identify him or his whereabouts.

The day was overcast with low dark clouds scudding across the sullen sky. It had frozen the night before and the pavements were treacherous with ice, which had not melted during the early part of the morning, as the temperature remained stubbornly below zero. Bulloch had dressed warmly, finally pulling on a heavy tweed cape coat, which he buttoned to the neck. This he felt would protect him not only from the cold of the outdoors, but also from the low temperature likely to prevail in the austere interior of a Lutheran church.

In the event he was correct and, although the church was crowded, it was bitterly cold within. Bulloch took a seat at the end of a pew, exchanged a *"heiliche Weinachten"* with his neighbour and looked around. The congregation seemed for the most part comparatively wealthy, judging from their clothes and, from the many exchanges and greetings, Bulloch judged this to be a close-knit community, where strangers would be quickly noticed and treated with some circumspection.

In spite of his long absence from any form of organised worship and his lack of familiarity with the Lutheran creed he managed nonetheless to follow the service quite well, standing and sitting at the appropriate moments and even joining in the singing of "*Stille Nacht*," his deep baritone drawing approving glances from his neighbours.

At the end of the service, the officiating Minister took up his position by the door in the traditional manner, bidding his parishioners a 'Happy Christmas' as they thanked him for the service. Bulloch stayed on in the church, pretending to examine the architectural features with interest until all had left, except for the few who remained on their knees in prayer. As the minister re-entered the church, rubbing his hands together to restore their circulation, Bulloch approached him. "*Guten tag, Vater* ... thank you for a most moving service and for the sermon, which was highly instructive."

The minister looked pleased. "I have not seen you here before, my son, but you are very welcome. Have you only recently arrived in this country?"

"Just in the last few weeks, Father. I would have come to church sooner but my wife has not been well...you understand."

"Of course, my son. I shall certainly pray for her speedy recovery. But is there anything else I can do to help?"

"It is a small thing, but my wife, who speaks no English, wishes to visit a doctor – a German-speaking doctor. I was wondering if there were any among your congregation that she could consult?"

"Of course. In fact we have several doctors who are regular churchgoers. Perhaps I could recommend one to you?"

Bulloch thought quickly. "In fact, I would be grateful if you could give me the names and addresses of all of them ... my wife, you see, is very particular about her doctors." The minister frowned and looked unconvinced. Bulloch lowered his voice. "In fact, as some of her problems are of a ... ah ... feminine nature ... she is only happy to discuss them with a doctor in whom she has the greatest confidence and I would like to give her the opportunity of having a choice of whom she consults."

"I see," said the minister, looking embarassed. "Very well then, please come into the vestry and wait a moment while I write you a list of names, from which your wife can make a selection. I hope that she finds one who pleases her."

*   *

It was the fourth doctor on the list, a Manfred Schönbauer, who had treated the assassin for his most recent gunshot wound. Bulloch had explained that his nephew, a large and heavily bearded young man, suffered from bouts of recurrent amnesia. During these attacks he even forgot his own name and had recently gone missing from his sister's house. She was distraught with worry. Bulloch added, looking shamefaced, that the young man often found himself in trouble after his absences and that he had been known to react violently to the slightest provocation. In fact … and here Bulloch sat forward and lowered his voice in a confiding manner … on one occasion in the recent past there had even been a gunshot wound!

The doctor gasped. "Why," he said, "how extraordinary. Only three weeks ago I treated a young man – much as the one you described – for a gun shot wound in the shoulder. But he sounded as if he came from Berlin or somewhere in Prussia – not as yourself, who I would hazard a guess, are from the South?"

Bulloch suppressed a smile. "Indeed you are correct, I am originally from Ulm, but my sister married a Prussian, God rest his soul, and the boy was brought up in Fürstenwald on the Spree, which is close to Berlin."

"From Ulm, you say? How extraordinary! I am from Ulm. How delightful to make your acquaintance! Frankly, with your accent, I had thought you to be Austrian … or even Swiss, if you will forgive me. What did you say your name was? I must know your family. Where did you live?"

'Goddam it, how unlucky can you get', thought Bulloch. "Well," he said, "I left Ulm many years ago and my family are all dead so I doubt you knew them. I have been living in America for many years."

"Even so," continued the doctor, delighted at the thought of meeting someone from his home town, "I am much older than you and I am sure that I must have known your father. What was his name?"

"Er, Erich von Simsen…but he died shortly after my birth…in 'twenty-five."

"Von Simsen, you say…no, I don't think so." The doctor looked perplexed, "I thought that I knew every family of good standing in Ulm. Where did you live?"

"I really can't remember…we left when I was very young."

"Is that right?" The doctor frowned, all of a sudden becoming suspicious. "I tell you what…ask your sister to come and visit me herself. I cannot give out information on my patients to anyone other than next of kin. Oh, and ask her to bring two guineas – your 'nephew' hasn't seen fit to settle my account as yet."

Bulloch left, cross with himself, but cursing his bad luck. 'In future' he thought, 'I will invent the name of some small village in Bavaria and then we'll see if anyone comes from the same place!"

Later that day, at around five in the afternoon, Bulloch returned to the same address and looked up to see that the lights were still on in the doctor's surgery, but that otherwise the house was dark. Then he positioned himself in the doorway opposite, standing well back in the shadows.

After half an hour the lights went out. A few minutes later the doctor came out of the front door, which he locked behind him. Bulloch watched the doctor walk off down the street, carefully avoiding the puddles left by the recent thaw.

Bulloch waited until it was clear that the doctor would not be returning. He looked to see that there was no one around, then crossed the street with a purposeful stride and slammed the sole of his boot into the door just by the lock. The wood broke on the inside and the door flew open, banging noisily against the wall behind. Bulloch quickly moved into the house, shut the door and waited, holding his breath. A dog barked. Then nothing.

Bulloch climbed the stairs to the first floor, making as little noise as possible, tried the handle of the surgery door and was pleased to find it unlocked. He took a dark lantern out of the voluminous inside pocket of his coat and lit it with a match. Then he closed the aperture down to a small point, which gave off a very narrow beam of light that would be less visible to passers-by.

He held up the lantern and looked around to see if there was a chest of drawers or a cupboard that might contain the files and notes of patients. Nothing. He swore under his breath. Then, going over to the desk, he saw piles of coloured cardboard folders stacked against the wall. Hundreds of them. He groaned inwardly. This would take hours.

One folder sat in the middle of the desk, square to the edge of the blotting paper. He opened it and read:

17 Sept 1862. Gottrried Kurz. Bullet wound to left forearm. Twelve stitches. 5s 6d. Paid

10 Dec 1862. Same. Bullet wound to right shoulder. Operated to remove ball. Also removed cloth and bone splin - ters. All? Extensive damage to pectoral muscle and fracture to collar bone. Prognosis: severe danger of infection. 2 Guineas (to include opiates and bandages)
Note: Patient transferred to St Mary's, Paddington. Invoice unpaid.
Note: Visit from man claiming to be uncle?

Bulloch smiled broadly, closed the file, blew out the lantern and left.

✻   ✻

Bulloch delayed his visit to St Mary's so as to give Rose the good news that he had found the assassin and because he wanted to look around the outside of the hospital and to plan his escape in the event of pursuit. So it was two days later that Bulloch, wearing a stethoscope around his neck and carrying a black bag of the type frequently used by doctors, entered the hospital and rapped impatiently on the reception desk with the silver ferule of his cane. "I have come to see my patient, Mr Kurz. Please be so good as to show me where he can be found." Books were opened and shut and long lists were consulted and hummed and hawed over. After some delay, during which the drumming of Bulloch's fingers on the counter-top rose to a crescendo, the patient was located and a porter, dressed in a filthy smock covered with dark smears, was designated to escort Bulloch to the Lazarus Ward.

They walked down long echoing corridors, which were decorated with pea-green tiles that covered the walls to shoulder height, above which the occasional gas light struggled to dispel the gloom. The porter explained that only the most terminal cases were sent to the Lazarus Ward. "In truth, there's not many of 'em as takes up their beds and walks." He laughed with a wheezy gurgle. "Deary me no. Out feet first on a stretcher most of 'em goes, I kin tell you." Then suddenly, fearing that he might have offended Bulloch's sense of professional pride, he continued, "..although I expect your chappie will soon be up and about seeing as how he can afford a fine doctor such as your good self." He gave Bulloch an ingratiating grin, which displayed the black and rotting stumps of his teeth.

Occasionally they would pass a stretcher in the corridor with a sheet pulled over it's occupant's face. At other times, nurses with crisp uniforms carrying trays or bedpans, would pass in or out of unmarked doors, which they allowed to slam behind them with a noise that reverberated down the empty passageway. They went up two flights of worn stone stairs, before emerging at the top of the building, where the eaves met and the ceiling was only just high enough for someone of Bulloch's stature to pass upright. They entered the ward, and Bulloch stopped, feeling that he had just crossed the threshold that divided the land of the living from the outer boundaries of hell.

The ward had only a few small dormer windows, which were widely interspersed and which admitted little light from the overcast day through their grimy panes. Down each side of the ward were long lines of beds, whose occupants coughed, moaned, heaved and gagged in the extremities of their conditions. Bulloch took out a handkerchief and held it to his face to ward off the nauseating stench of faeces, vomit and decaying flesh.

He looked around in disbelief. Each bed had a small table and a chair between it and its neighbour. On some tables an untrimmed tallow candle smoked and flickered, while others were without light, which mercifully shrouded the condition of the patient from passing eyes. Some, the lucky few, were attended to by family or loved ones, while the majority, who had neither, were left to rot in their own filth until death brought a merciful end to their sufferings.

"Not what you're used to I'm sure," said the porter sympathetically. "We don't get many doctors in 'ere of your standing, I kin tell you – nor what you would call doctors of any type," he added reflectively. "Anyhow, that's your gent over yonder – in bed twenty three. Do you want me to stay?"

"Er, no," Bulloch mumbled from behind his handkerchief, "thank you very much for your help. That will be all," and, pressing a penny into the outstretched hand, he waved the fellow away.

Bulloch cautiously approached bed twenty-three. He saw the long unkempt black hair and the huge matted beard, which spread like a pool of dark liquid over the thin grey hospital blanket. For the first time, the enormity of what he was about to undertake, struck him. Bulloch had killed several times before – once with a sword – and he had shot several men with rifles and with pistols, during the Mexican war. But these had been in combat, during the heat of a battle, when the killing fever was on him and on all of those who fought with or against him. True, there had been the man whom he and Edward Anderson had thrown from the train, but that had not been a deliberate act of cold-blooded murder, while below decks on the *Oreto* he had fought in self-defence.

As he sat down on the little chair and undid the clasp on his bag, the figure on the bed stirred and, reaching out a shaking hand, pushed the hair back from his forehead. The face that was revealed was surprisingly finely featured, with a high curving brow and a thin, but long and straight nose. The skin was so white as to be almost translucent, reflecting the flame from the candle in the sheen of sweat that clung to his brow, while the black eyes stared from their deep and dark-rimmed sockets. He licked his cracked lips with the tip of his tongue and said in little more than a whisper, in German:

"Who are you?"

"I am the man who shot you."

The assassin closed his eyes. "And have you now come to finish the job?"

Bulloch nodded, mainly to steel himself to his purpose and answered, "Yes" in a voice almost as quiet as the sick man's.

"I see. You know that I am dying anyway?" He inched back the sheet that covered his shoulder and revealed the mass of stained bandages from which the unmistakable smell of putrefaction arose. "The poison has spread. There is no hope."

"So, if you are indeed dying, then you have no reason not to tell me the truth. Why did you seek to kill Mrs Greenhow? For whom are you working?"

The assassin's breath was coming in shorter and shorter gasps. "You must understand … ordinarily I would not … I am a soldier … I was with Sigel … I .. I was accused … I had to escape … I was told … if I killed her … I could start again. Pinkerton … Pinkerton was his name …" The voice died to a whisper.

"And if, by some miracle, you were to survive, what then? How could I be sure that you would not again make an attempt on Mrs Greenhow's life?"

"There is no chance at all that I will live … but … if God were to perform such a miracle, to give me a second chance … you must understand I ... I would be born anew, everything would be different." His eyes closed. Bulloch leaned over him and could just hear the sound of his shallow breathing. Bulloch allowed the scalpel to fall from his fingers back into the doctor's bag, which he closed with a click.

He pushed back the chair, rose and left the ward and the hospital and the sickness and the despair behind him without a backward glance.

Later that evening, after two or three whiskies at the Angel in Holborn, Bulloch arrived at Rose's lodgings, where he found her seated at her desk facing the wall, hard at work on her book. He paused in the doorway unobserved and watched her for a while, the sound of her scratching nib audible above the groaning of the embers in the grate and the hiss of the gas table-lamp.

The maid entered from the dining room and to Bulloch's surprise, stood behind Rose, reading over her shoulder. As she stood there, she started to gently rub the base of Rose's neck, lightly kneading the flesh with her strong rough hands. Rose moaned softly. Suddenly, as if some sixth sense alerted her to his presence, Rose pushed the maid's hands away and turned around.

"Well?" she asked.

"It is done."

She nodded. "And what did you find out?"

"Only that he was sent by Alan Pinkerton, who used to work for McClellan and that he will bother us no more. Now, let us not talk of this matter further. It is finished and must be put behind us".

Again she nodded, sighing deeply. "I think that will be easier for you than for me. Pinkerton has pursued me across the Atlantic. He hates me because I did not give in to him. I do not know that I will ever be free of him."

She stood up and crossed to where he stood, laying her warm palm against the side of his face, stroking it gently. She reached up and kissed him lightly, but on the lips – the kiss of a sister. "Shall we ever be lovers?" she mused aloud. "In truth I do not know but, perhaps, one day ..." She smiled and left Bulloch alone with the fire and his dreams.

*   *

Charles Prioleau swirled the dark red wine around the glass, pausing to peer into its ruby depths, which were clear against the pristine white backdrop of the tablecloth. He held the glass to his nose and inhaled deeply, savouring the intense bouquet, before raising it to his lips and sipping, allowing the wine to run slowly over his tongue before he swallowed. "Ah, what a fine wine … you spoil us James, you surely do. There are so many of your countrymen who have forsaken the wines of Burgundy and only drink their little Clarets … but this Echezeaux is really magnificent. 1851, if I am not mistaken?"

Spence nodded and raised an eyebrow to his butler, who advanced, decanter in hand. "Leave the decanter thank you Timmins, that will be all."

"Sir," replied the butler with a slight nod of the head and left, as smoothly and silently as a ghost, the door closing soundlessly behind him.

"How things have changed for you since we first met," Prioleau said after a pause, waving his hand to indicate the opulent surroundings, the heavy silver tableware and the stern-faced portraits that adorned the walls of the panelled dining room.

"Oh indeed, I must clearly acknowledge my good fortune. When we first met I was on the very edge of bankruptcy – the bailiffs were grouped around my door and the family…" he pointed at the portraits, "were at the pawnbrokers." 'And you,' he thought to himself, 'used my misfortune to get me to act as your agent.' But he smiled and continued, "Yes indeed, I have been very fortunate. My ships converted well to blockade runners and one of them has now completed eleven runs, you know. Of course we lost a couple, but I shared the losses with my partners and in any case, they had both paid for themselves many times over by then."

"And your activities on the cotton exchange also make you money, of course."

"Make us money, Charles, make us money."

"Indeed. But it is a fair exchange is it not? Fraser, Trenholm have a virtual monopoly on imported cotton and you have a monopoly on information as it pertains to the arrival and availability of said cotton. Makes broking in the forward market a little simpler I should believe?"

"You know it does, Charles and you are handsomely rewarded for sharing this information. Nonetheless it would be churlish of me to deny that I have profited from my association with your firm – and indeed with your Country. Your war has made both of us rich – and many others besides. But I sense that this is leading somewhere. Is there any way in which I can be of particular service to you at this time?"

"Only in one small matter. Benjamin approved Erlanger's loan you know."

"I had heard. What of it?"

"Well, it seems that there is a considerable weight of political support behind this scheme. The President himself is concerned that it should be a great success and that it should bring us a number of highly placed and influential supporters."

"And you would like my help in achieving this?"

"Yes, in the sense that you know the names of many existing holders of our bonds, who should be approached in order to seek their support for this issue. This information should be shared with representatives of J. Henry Schroder & Co., who will be bringing the loan out in London."

"So you are asking that I should not only divulge the names of my clients to a competitor, but also that I should encourage them to purchase an issue, which I believe to be fundamentally flawed in its conception?"

"As I said, James, I believe that you have benefited considerably from our association and will no doubt continue to do so in the future. I believe that this would be both the time and the manner in which to display your appreciation. Am I being unfair? Do tell me if you think so."

Spence studied the glowing ember of his cigar and considered the implications of what he had been asked to do. While he was undoubtedly reluctant to hand over a list of his clients, he was finding it harder and harder to sell Confederate Government Bonds and this issue had such a high rate of interest, combined with its other incentives, that he would in any case find it hard to compete with. And the commissions he earned from the sales of bonds were insignificant compared to the money he made from his cotton trading and from having access to the best cargoes for his blockade runners. He flashed his most engaging smile and said: "of course I'll do it. It would be both an honour and a privilege to support your Country and its noble cause." He raised his glass and toasted his guest.

* *

Bulloch packed and left London the next day, pausing at the Great Northern Hotel to indulge himself in a fortifying lunch of lambs tongue stew and plum pudding, together with a rather young *Côtes du Rhone*.

Bulloch was glad to return to Liverpool, having ensured Rose's safety and with their relationship as warm as it had ever been, even though it was somewhat less physical than he might have desired. However, having observed Rose and the maid in an unguarded and strangely intimate moment, he was no longer sure where her preferences might lie. The more he thought about it, the less sure he became until, becoming annoyed with himself at the futility of his conjecture, he swore and returned to more pressing matters.

In Liverpool he still faced the problem of Ambrose Ampleside, who believed him to be dead and whose vengeance he could expect to be re-ignited in the event of a resurrection. For this reason he continued to move around the city with a muffler in place across the lower part of his face and shunned restaurants and clubs, where he might be seen by Ampleside or anyone else connected to him. Bulloch frequented pubs and taverns too humble for the likes of Ampleside and hotels of lesser repute, whose food was just barely edible and whose dining rooms were frequented by minor businessmen or families of the lower middle-class, preparing for a sea voyage.

The weather remained icy cold and overcast, with little improvement as January moved in February. Early in that month Bulloch went to see Bill Miller in his offices above the warehouse at Toxteth. He was greeted by a new chief clerk, an elderly man with a few fine wisps of grey hair that curled upwards from his pate like smoke from the embers of a dying fire. "Do come this way, Sir," he said, his voice rising barely above a whisper, but sufficient to be heard in the office, where the loudest noise was the scratch of nib on paper. "I know that Mr Miller is expecting you."

Miller was his usual rumbustuous self, bouncing out of his chair and greeting Bulloch with a vice-like grip of his hand. "And 'ow are you then Mr Bulloch, well I 'ope?"

"Yes, thank you, Mr Miller, very well indeed," he replied truthfully, for the months since his beating had repaired the physical damage and he had recovered from the pneumonia with no lingering after-effects.

Nonetheless, Miller was quick to spot the fresh scar, high up on the cheekbone, still pink against the pallor of Bulloch's skin and the slightly tight movement of his jaw as he spoke. 'Well now, my lad, someone's given you a thumping and no mistake. I only wish it had been me,' Miller thought to himself as they sipped coffee from small bone china cups that seemed ridiculously fragile and insubstantial in the large scarred hands of the men.

'He's put on a lot of weight' Bulloch thought, 'why, he's almost completely round. I'll bet that if you took him to the top of a hill and let him go, he'd roll the whole way down again.' "How is business, Mr Miller?" he enquired politely.

"Bloomin' marvellous, thankee for asking! And it's all your lot's doing. I've commissions for ships stacked up so I can't even start 'em and prices have gone through the roof. I've got every available construction dock I can get with a hull in it, either new-builds or conversions. Blockade-runners, Mr Bulloch, blockade-runners," he explained seeing Bulloch's puzzled expression. "We ship anything from silk for dresses, to buttons, to shoes, to salt – and of course guns and uniforms when we can get 'em – and it's cotton and baccy on the way 'ome. I've taken shares in a number of joint-stock companies set up for just this purpose and we're making a pretty penny I kin tell you!" He laughed and sat back in his elevated chair so that Bulloch could admire the gold watch chain that looped across the broad front of his bulging waistcoat, the links seemingly heavy enough to lift an anchor.

"Well, I am glad for it, of course, and my country needs both supplies and a market for its cotton." It is just such a shame, he reflected that so much money was being made by such undeserving individuals. But then, such was always the nature of a free market, where capital ruled and those brave enough to take the risks made the profits. God forbid that it should be any other way, as the socialists and the trade unionists and their other fellow travellers, the democrats, would have it. "And how is the *Alexandra* coming along, Mr Miller? I trust that we can expect her to be ready for sea trials on time, in spite of all the other work that is keeping your yard busy."

"That goes without saying, Mr Bulloch. I'm a man of my word. If I says April, it won't be May, you kin rest assured of that! We'll go and have a look in a minute, but you'll see, we have the masts in their footings and the deck planking is down. The engine is in, but we haven't run her as yet, and everything else is on

234

schedule." He smiled broadly. "Now, Sir, when can I expect some payment? I've been generous to a fault with you, I 'ave, what with not asking for any up-front money, and with all the construction being financed by myself and so on, I'm going to be out of pocket when all's said and done. So what do you say?"

"On delivery Mr Miller, as agreed and not before". Bulloch paused for reflection. "Now, what really makes you so anxious to get payment? Is it just the cash outlay on your side, or have we had visitors again, asking questions. Hmmm?"

Miller looked like a small boy caught in the act of scrumping apples. He thought about denying it, but decided to tell the truth, even though it went against the grain to do so. "You're right" he finally admitted. "We've had snoopers – up from London with your lot in tow. And we had the Customs busybodies in here only last week. Course the good thing is that we've got a lot of ships under construction now – not like with the dear old *Oreto* – and there's American money in more than one of 'em. Northerners too, as it 'appens. I mean, why not? A profit's a profit, I say. Anyhow, it all makes a good smoke screen to hide behind, so they've got nothing to go on, eh! The Customs boys asked to see my books, but I told 'em, I'm an MP, I am and you can't go messing with me, oh no! Come back with a warrant and I'll show you me auntie's bloomers if ye want, but till then it's 'oh-ree-vwar'."

"And will they come back with a warrant do you think – and what would they find if they did?"

Miller shrugged his shoulders, which, as he had no discernable neck, gave the impression of his torso consuming the lower part of his face. "Yes, I think they will be back, but it will take 'em some little while to get the warrant. I'm 'on the square' with the Chief Magistrate, if you know what I mean – he'll slow things up as much as he can without looking suspicious and then he'll give us plenty of warning before the Customs boys arrive. They'll have to look at all the records for all the ships under construction, most of which are ordered by joint-stock companies with foreign shareholders on the register. Very hard to get to the bottom of, I should say. Now the *Alexandra* is I-talian, just like the *Oreto*, but ordered by an Asian trading group out of Naples this time. So, on the whole, I don't think we've got too much to worry about."

"But enough to ask me for some payment, so as to at least lay off a part of the risk?"

"You can't be too careful these days, can you Mr Bulloch?" He smiled menacingly.

Bulloch left Miller's office in a thoughtful frame of mind. The *Alexandra* was not a large nor a particularly important ship and the order had, to a large extent, been placed with Miller's so as to keep him honest and on their side. Even so, Bulloch would be very reluctant to see the *Alexandra* impounded, but he considered Miller's precautions to be the best that could be put in place and therefore he dismissed that situation from his mind. Not so the 'Rams' though, which were of much greater strategic importance to his Country in that they could, between them, smash the blockade and then steam up the Mississippi to relieve Vicksburg. He even had visions of them entering New York's East River and destroying the naval dockyards in Brooklyn. But before then he had to protect them from the vicissitudes of the British Government, which he believed to be weakening in the face of external threats from Washington. Local pressure was also on the increase from the many supporters of the emancipation societies that flourished, especially in the north of England and among the working classes and which had been much emboldened by Lincoln's Emancipation Declaration in January.

So with this very much at the forefront of his mind, he packed a small bag and boarded the train for London as the first leg on his journey to Paris.

Three days later, Bulloch was back in Liverpool, somewhat tired and disheveled. He washed and put on a clean shirt and caught the ferry to Birkenhead, where he walked to Laird's shipyard, marveling at the high wooden fences that surrounded a part of the dock and the heavily-built pug-uglies that stood outside the entrance to that area, arms crossed and muscles bulging.

Young John Laird found him surveying the fenced-off area and escorted him to the house and away from the hired thugs, who had noted Bulloch's interest and were on their way towards him with billy-clubs in hand. John Laird senior greeted him warmly and they discussed the progress of hulls 294 and 295. "We should have one ready for sea in July," Laird said "but I would advise you to mount the gun-turrets outside British waters. Anything we can do to reduce the visibility of their purpose is to be strongly recommended."

"Indeed," Bulloch replied "I quite agree. However, you should know that I have just put in place a scheme so as to distance myself and my Country as far as possible from these ships."

"How interesting! I hope that you will elucidate."

Bulloch produced a document from his pocket and unfolded it, pushing it across the table to Laird, who picked it up, after having precariously balanced a pair of *pince-nez* on the end of his nose. "Hmmm. My French is not that good I am afraid, Mr Bulloch, but this seems to be a Bill of Sale?"

"That is correct. Specifically it is a Bill of Sale between yourself and Bravay et Cie. of Paris, who have just purchased the Rams on behalf of the Pasha of Egypt. I have a banker's draft, drawn on Hoare's of London, who bank for Bravay, for ninety-three thousand seven hundred and fifty pounds. If you would be kind enough to endorse the bill on the back and make it payable to the 'Bee Company', I would be much obliged – and lastly just your signature on this receipt – so – stating that you have received payment for these ships, which you have sold as principal, subject only to one further payment of ninety-three thousand seven hundred and fifty pounds, which will become due upon their completion".

Laird looked at the documents, sucked in his cheeks, and scratched his head, but after some hesitation, signed in the appropriate places. "You seem to have covered your tracks admirably, Mr Bulloch, except for the original draft I received from you, drawn on Fraser, Trenholm."

"That is why I have asked you to endorse the bill to the Bee Company. They are one of the larger joint-stock companies who are engaged in blockade-running and they have an existing banking relationship with Fraser, Trenholm. It will seem that Bravay have paid you and you have passed on the money to your original client, the Bee Company. Needless to say, the proceeds of this bill will not end in their account."

Laird smiled as the penny dropped and the smile was echoed across the faces of his sons.

XVII

London and Liverpool – March, 1863

❧ ❧

The sun shone from an almost cloudless sky and a warm breeze stirred the daffodils, which had but recently burst from the earth in such profusion that visitors to London's parks stood in silent admiration at the carpet of gold. It seemed that all of London had thrown off their coats and scarves, donned their frilled bonnets or fancy waistcoats and had taken to the park for a stroll, blinking in the unaccustomed glare, much like a bear fresh from a long hibernation in a dark cave.

Two elderly gentlemen entered St. James' Park at the Whitehall end and sauntered slowly towards the Palace, gently swinging their canes to the rhythm of their steps. From time to time, other users of the park's finely gravelled paths would pause and raise their hats or being better acquainted, might stop for a few words while their companions made a small curtsey. On these occasions, however, the elderly gentlemens' demeanour was such that a prolonged conversation was not encouraged; indeed the scowl on the face of one of them sent the majority quickly onward about their business.

For a while both Lord Palmerston, the Prime Minister and Lord Russell, his Foreign Secretary, simply strolled, enjoying the sunshine and the warm air and refrained from discussing the American situation, which, if anything, became thornier and more intractable with each passing day.

Finally Russell broke the companionable silence and broached the topic that was in the forefront of both their minds. "I have received a note from Lyons, Prime Minister, sent at the request of Seward. He informs me – and I quote, 'that the departure of more armed vessels under insurgent-rebel command from English ports is a thing to be deprecated above all things'."

"What exactly is he trying to say, Johnny? You are better at this diplomatic mumbo-jumbo than I."

"In the note, Seward is merely informing us as to the extent of their concern as it relates to the ships that are allegedly being constructed in our yards, on the instruction of their Southern adversaries. However, the threat which he chooses not to refer to in writing, but which Lyons informs me is quite real, is that they may dust off their Privateering Bill, which Lincoln is quite prepared to push through Congress. This would give virtual carte blanche to their privateers to prey on neutral shipping, suspected of trading with the Confederate States."

"But we can't allow that, Johnny." Palmerston was shaking his head vigorously. A passer-by stopped to greet the Prime Minister and was brusquely dismissed with an impatient wave of a gloved hand. "I mean, it would be war. Without doubt. And think of the loss of trade. Good heavens, half the Party's got shares in blockade running companies and are doing jolly well out of them too, thankee very much! In fact," he lowered his voice, "I hear that Gladstone's quite heavily invested."

"Well, that's as may be, Prime Minister, but you are correct, of course, in saying that we cannot allow this. Especially as I have just heard that the Russian Atlantic fleet has recently put to sea."

"Good God man – headed for where?"

"Their destination is unknown at this time, although we will be shadowing them – at a safe distance of course. Regardless, it remains the case that the Tsar has no reason to love us – quite the contrary, in fact – and in any conflict between us and the United States, he would indubitably support the Americans. I suspect that their fleet putting to sea at this precise moment is no coincidence."

"Yes, yes, of course. So what can we do? The Foreign Enlistment Act, as written, gives us little scope to seize these ships that are being built in Liverpool – especially as the owners seem to be deuced cautious about covering their tracks and not arming them until they're well out of our waters. So what about an amendment to the Act then, eh? Stick in a provision which would enable us to impound any suspicious vessel, until the real owners showed up and said who they were. That should do the trick, what?"

"Yes, that could work," Russell grudgingly agreed, meanwhile considering how such a draconian measure could be watered down, restricted in scope, hedged about with provisos and generally rendered ineffective. An idea occurred to him. What if the amendment were to be voted down? The Ministry's coalition was shaky enough on the best of days and could hardly be expected to vote together, especially on an emotive and divisive motion. But how to make such a prosaic amendment both emotive and divisive? After a moment's reflection he said: "Let us give this matter to John Bright, Prime Minister. You will recall that he spoke well against Lindsay's motion last summer and is a strong proponent of the Northern cause. He will make sure that it goes through!"

*   *

Bulloch was lunching alone at the Mitre in Victoria Street, occupying a small table towards the rear of the dining room. From there he could see the entrance while he was, at least partially, screened from view himself by the etched glass panes of the partition that separated the dining area from the public bar. He had already consumed some tepid floury soup and was now waiting, without enthusiasm, for his chop. An elderly and very small lady entered by herself and swept across the bar, holding the skirt of her old-fashioned and heavily pleated black taffeta dress in front of her, as if to avoid the hem being trailed in the dirt. She came into the dining area and sat down at the adjacent table, which was laid for two. Bulloch regarded her with interest from behind his newspaper, not only for the fact that she was by herself in a public house, but also for the determined set to her jaw and the fierceness of her gaze. As she sat, she contemplated Bulloch for a minute with the small dark pebbles of her eyes and then looked away.

After a short interval her food arrived, as did Bulloch's chop, which was, as he had feared, mutton rather than lamb, tepid rather than hot and swimming in a sea of partially congealed fat. He ate two mouthfuls and then pushed the plate away, sitting back to light a cigar and finish his ale before calling for a coffee and the bill. However, at that moment, the old lady looked up from her plate and said: "we were told that you were dead. It seems that we have been misinformed. My son will be so pleased."

"I'm sorry, but I am afraid that you must have mistaken me for someone else," Bulloch said hurriedly, rising to his feet.

"Oh I don't think so Mr Bulloch – and it would be such a shame if you had to leave right away, when I have only just made your acquaintance".

Bulloch sat back down at the table and sighed. "Very well, Madam, but I do not believe that I have had the pleasure …"

"I understand that you've had the pleasure on many occasions Mr Bulloch – although not with me, more's the pity. But the squeaking of your bed-springs have kept me awake on many a night." She gave Bulloch a lewd wink, quite out of keeping with her stern and proper appearance.

"In which case," he said, blushing, "you must be Mrs Kopa. I had begun to doubt that you existed."

"You don't think that that fool of a son of mine could run the Club by himself do you? Hah! All he's fit for is misbehaving himself with our girls and extending more credit than he ought to … which reminds me Mr Bulloch, that although Jesus Christ's creditors were not waiting for him outside the tomb, when they rolled away the stone, I am very much in evidence at your miraculous recovery." She looked up. "Ah," she said, "here is Isaac now. Oh, Isaac, look who has come back from the dead – it is our own Messiah, risen again!"

Isaac Kopa stood completely still by the entrance to the dining area, his jaw open and hanging slack, with his tongue seeming very pink against the black of the surrounding beard. His eyes bulged. "Why… why … I was assured … that is … we were told that … you … were … dead." He sat down heavily, next to his mother.

"It seems, my dear" she said, "that we have been misinformed. Deliberately? I wonder… but no, I think not. Which means that Mr Ampleside does not know the truth either. Now that is interesting, because it raises some amusing possibilities. But first, you owe us one thousand three hundred pounds, Mr Bulloch. Can you pay?"

Bulloch grimaced. "Yes, I can," he said through clenched teeth. "But," and he paused for emphasis, "but I would strongly prefer that Mr Ampleside is kept in ignorance as to the state of my health."

"Pah!" the old lady leant across and rebukingly tapped him on the arm with her fan, "he will find out sooner or later. No, I have a better idea. You should write to him and tell him. Tell him that you are alive. Then you should tell him what you know about him and say that if anything untoward were to happen to you, then evidence would be sent to his father. Mr Ampleside lives in great fear of his father, Lord Fawkes, who has threatened to disinherit him on several occasions, on account of his gambling and … other habits, which he felt were bringing the family name into disrepute – although I for one fail to see how there is anything the son could do to make the reputation of that family any worse. The conditions of their coal mines, I've been told, make the salt mines in the old country look positively luxurious."

"But I know nothing about him – nothing at any rate that I can threaten him with, but I am very interested to find out what you know." Bulloch, leant forward and looked into the old lady's dark, expressionless eyes.

"Only that he murdered one of our girls, an Irish lassie called 'Holy Mary', because she gave him syphilis. He beat her to death with a lead-filled cudgel – in my house, if you please. Then he ran for it, leaving us to clear up after him. He was back a few days later, of course, with a large purse of gold coins, full of apologies and asking if we knew the names of any doctors who could be relied on to be discreet. So we gave him the name of this doctor, who turns out to have been playing poker with you the night you lost your temper and decked the honourable Ambrose. It seems that Ambrose had some cards up his sleeve and the doctor had nearly lost his practice as a result."

"He cheated?"

"That's right, Mr Bulloch, you had him beat fair and square. But it don't change nothing between you and me though. You still owe us the money and if you want our help you'll pay up."

Bulloch shook his head, angry but at the same time pleased. "Alright", he said, "go on."

"So anyhow, Ampleside goes to this doctor and got the mercury cure – best as it works anyhow – and we have the doctor's sworn testimony that he treated young Ampleside for syphilis. We also have the cudgel as well – with Mary's blood and bits of her skull on it and the red hair still attached. Horrible, it is too." She shuddered.

"Did you say red hair?" he asked, a sinking feeling in the pit of his stomach.

"Yes. Holy Mary had long dark red hair – and that white,

white skin that goes with it. A real beauty she was! What a shame!"

"And a large chest as well," Isaac interjected looking thoughtful – "but wasn't that Mary you left with after the game finished that evening?"

Bulloch had gone very pale. "I believe it may have been. To tell the truth, I was very drunk and she was not there the next morning, so I am unsure as to what, if anything …" he glanced at Mrs Kopa … "well, you know what I am saying."

"I think you should also visit this doctor Mr Bulloch," Isaac said kindly. "Best not to leave things too long."

"Yes, I think I will thank you." Then forcing himself back to the business in hand, he asked: "But, you are sure that this scheme will work?"

"Of course," Mrs Kopa replied quickly, "how could it not? He will be too frightened to risk exposure and, while he may suspect us of giving you the evidence, he would never dare to move against us directly. Oh, no, not with what I know about the local gentry, some of the town councillors, even an M.P. or two." She looked at her son who nodded and smiled happily, the edges of his mouth rising beyond the tip of his hooked nose, so that he looked to Bulloch like a vulture, perched on a rock, examining a carcass.

As soon as Bulloch returned to his lodgings, he removed his trousers and gave his penis a very thorough examination. It looked normal. He squeezed it all over. It felt normal – and he had experienced none of the problems urinating which were associated with such diseases. Relieved, he pulled up his trousers.

He picked up a pen and wrote:

Dear Mr Ampleside,
    You will know who I am when I tell you that the miners in your employ were unable to perform their side of the bargain fully in accordance with your instructions and that, as a result, I am still very much alive.
    Strange though it may seem, I have a strong desire to remain this way until God, in His infinite wisdom, decides otherwise, hopefully towards the end of my natural span of three score years and ten.
    In order to ensure my continued well-being, I am prepared to enter into an arrangement with you. The way it will work is this: I remain healthy and unmolested and you will never

hear from me again. Were, on the other hand, anything untoward to happen to me, then evidence relating to your recent and somewhat embarrassing illness, and to the quite bestial manner in which you repaid its communicator, will be sent both to your Father and to the Chief Constable.

In addition to the above, I also understand that you cheated during our game. While I am a foreigner in your country, I have nonetheless been here for long enough to understand that members of the aristocracy may well get away with murder, but to be accused of cheating at cards, by witnesses, would finish you. You will therefore repay each of the players that night their stakes – in my case that amounts to one thousand eight hundred pounds. A bank draft in my favour will be acceptable.

I am, etc.

Lazarus

It was late morning and the Long Bar was starting to fill with brokers and jobbers from the Exchange across the road. Young men dressed in the height of fashion with extravagantly cut and coloured waistcoats and the tallest of stove-pipe hats, jostled clerks and secretaries in drab and often shabby black coats for access to the bar. Behind this, men in aprons ran to and fro dispensing stout and porter, Madeira and sherry and hot cheese on toast, soft roes and fried oysters.

A young man approached their table, fighting his way through the packed bar.

"I say, oh I say!" he shouted, waving his hat.

Spence looked up. "At last," he said to the Commissioners, "here is Stanley Morton from Schroders – he will be able to let us know where we are! Sit down, sit down." Spence made a place at the table for the young man, who gratefully accepted the proffered glass of sherry and drank deeply.

"Well," he said, when he had fully recovered, "I expect you are keen to hear the news. First let me tell you that it is all good." The expressions on the faces of the three men changed instantly from anxious frowns to broad smiles. They looked at each other as if to say 'well, of course, I wasn't worried in the slightest'. "Now, on the level of subscription – or rather over-subscription. We have completed the count and, in round numbers, we have applications, with valid payment for ..." he paused for dramatic effect "... sixteen million pounds, which is more than five times the amount on offer."

"Wonderful news", cried Slidell, banging the table with the palm of his hand. "Champagne – bring us Champagne," yelled Mason, rising to his feet, his deep voice and Southern drawl carrying over the hubbub of the crowded bar and causing a sudden silence to fall as heads turned in his direction.

"That should be worth another point on the bonds," said the young man out of the corner of his mouth to Spence, who nodded thoughtfully.

When the Commissioners had retaken their seats, Morton continued. "Indeed, we have nearly three thousand individual applicants, mainly from England, but also some from as far away as Austria and, of course, more than a few from France and the Netherlands." He leaned forward and lowered his voice. "And I can tell you, confidentially of course, that we have received subscriptions from several prominent figures in the worlds of politics, finance and the law – including an application for ten thousand pounds from the Home Secretary himself, Mr William Gladstone. There – what do you think of that!"

"You have done us proud," Slidell said, slapping him on the back, with "hear, hears" echoing around the table.

"Lastly," Morton continued, "I should tell you that the bonds started to trade this morning, in their partly-paid form and, as news of the over-subscription got out, went to a premium of five percent to their issue price and are rock solid at that level."

Spence raised an eyebrow. "Rock solid? Or merely buoyed up for the moment by the bids of unsatisfied stags?"

"Well ... yes, I suppose you could put it like that." Morton looked around the table, quickly regaining his former exuberance as he saw the happy uncomprehending smiles on the faces of his American clients.

They sipped the champagne, which arrived in the hands of a flustered and heavily perspiring waiter in a grease-stained apron, and toasted the success of the Bonds, the Confederate States of America, President Davis and finally Emil Erlanger. "My word, but he has made a great deal of money from this," Spence said aloud, immediately regretting the statement, which sounded envious and shallow even to his own ears.

"I think he has deserved every penny", Slidell said pompously.

Mason, after a quick glance at Slidell asked Spence how much he thought that Erlanger would make, all told. Spence thought carefully and made a few quick calculations on his napkin with a pencil. "Somewhere around two and half million dollars, I shouldn't wonder," he said finally.

Slidell looked pensive and sucked on his teeth. Mason looked at him again and then asked: "How on earth could it be so much. The commissions are only five percent or so."

"Oh it's not the commissions," Spence replied, "or at least it is partially, but the major part of his profits come from the fact that he agreed an issue price of seventy seven percent with Benjamin, but the Bonds have been sold to investors for ninety percent."

"Doesn't that seem a little greedy?" Mason enquired, his eyebrows rising.

"I would have thought so," Spence said.

"On the other hand," Stanley Morton interjected, "the issue has been over-subscribed and is trading at a premium, even with an issue price of ninety percent, so it is hard to criticise the final result, or begrudge Erlanger his profit on such a well conceived and, if I may say so, well executed plan."

The champagne finished, the four rose to leave. Spence took Morton aside when they reached the Capel Court entrance to the Stock Exchange, and said: "I have received information that the other side has sent someone by the name of Robert J Walker over here. He's a wily old bird, who knows his stuff and he will no doubt try to sabotage the issue. If I were you I would keep my eyes peeled for any sign of bear activity, for it will surely emanate from him – oh, and I wouldn't push the price up any more if I were you, it will only make his job easier."

XVIII

London and Paris — April, 1863

❧   ☙

Pressed into the main part of the great hall, close-packed, shoulder to shoulder, scarcely able to move, stood a huge throng of cloth-capped English working men, the tumultuous noise of their excited voices breaking like waves against the wooden planking of the walls and washing up into the high vaulted ceiling of the auditorium.

Behind the milling masses, on row after row of hard benches and pews, were seated the shopkeepers, publicans and artisans, the union leaders and representatives, all of them bowler-hatted, bonneted, staunch and respectable.

On the stage that presided magisterially over the north end of the hall, a long deal table had been placed, together with a dozen or so chairs. These were occupied by the speakers and dignitaries, who, heavily bearded and resplendent in their top hats, lounged in attitudes that were reminiscent of the Disciples at the Last Supper.

A small man with slicked down fair hair and shabby but neat clothes, rose from behind the table and approached the dias with some diffidence. An expectant hush fell. He arranged his notes carefully and then looked up, the light from the many hanging gas chandeliers reflecting off his round spectacles. He cleared his throat.

"Fellow trade-unionists and working men, welcome. On behalf of the Emancipation Society, welcome to you all. My name is Josiah Wetherspoon and I 'ave the 'onour to represent the Manchester Cotton-Workers Union. Now, my members are as badly affected as any other group in this country, if not more so, by the current cotton shortage, which, as we all know, has been brought about by the war between the American States." He paused and adjusted his spectacles. A few cries of 'speak up' or 'louder' could be heard from the back of the hall, but otherwise the audience maintained a respectful silence.

"Our members 'ave endured and are enduring terrible 'ardship as a result of this war. Tens of thousands of men are out of work. 'Undreds of thousands more are on short time. Wages 'ave been cut by unscrupulous and greedy mill owners, anxious only for greater profit and, as a result, there is 'unger and starvation in our towns and cities. In Manchester alone, there are one 'undred and fifty thousand out of work. And for each of these there are crying 'ungry children and desperate wives. But do we say to Mr Lincoln, 'give up'? Do we say 'our suffering is too great'? No we do not!" A loud and prolonged burst of cheering and clapping exploded from the audience, many of whom were now on their feet.

"We say," he continued after the applause had died down and he could be heard, "we say, that your cause is just and your arm is strong. That you *will* prevail against the forces of injustice and greed that are arrayed against you. That it is the Lord's work you do in liberating our fellow men from the bonds of oppression – whether it be the factory worker that you free from the yoke of capitalism, or the Negro slave whom you free from the whips of the land owning classes. Each and every one of these are our comrades and our brothers, and we must rejoice in their liberation." Again the applause drowned out the speaker's voice.

"In January, after the Emancipation Proclamation had been published, we, the Manchester Cotton-Workers, wrote to Mr Lincoln to congratulate him on his achievement. He wrote back to us and, with your permission, I would like to read a paragraph or two from his letter." He took the letter from a cardboard file and, with great care, unfolded it and laid it on the lectern, smoothing out the creases with his palm. He cleared his throat again and started to read, the words themselves lending dignity and authority to his thin reedy voice.

"I have understood well that the duty of self-preservation rests solely with the American people; but I have at the same time been aware that the favour or disfavour of foreign nations might have a material influence in enlarging or prolonging the struggle with disloyal men, in which the country is engaged.

I know and deeply deplore the sufferings which the working men at Manchester and in all Europe, are called to endure in this crisis. I cannot but regard your decisive utterances upon the question as an instance of sublime Christian heroism, which has not been surpassed in any age, in any country. It is indeed an energetic and re-inspiring assurance of the inherent power of truth and of the ultimate and universal triumph of justice, humanity and freedom.

I hail this interchange of sentiment, therefore, as an augury that whatever else may happen, whatever misfortune may befall your country or my own, the peace and friendship which now exist between the two nations will be, as it shall be my desire to make them, perpetual."

As one, the audience rose to its feet cheering and applauding wildly.

Josiah Wetherspoon held up one slender hand the noise subsided. "I 'ave already spoken too long, and taken up too much of your time, for there are other speakers with greater knowledge and ability than are within my own feeble grasp. So, brothers, please join me now in welcoming our next speaker and very distinguished guest, the honourable Member of Parliament for Birmingham, Mr John Bright."

In the prolonged applause, John Bright, aglow with the fire and zeal of his message, took the podium. His eyes blazed and, with his arm raised, he launched into an attack on English middle-class complacency and hypocrisy, lauded Lincoln and the Northern States as liberators and democrats while condemning their opponents as evil men who, in enslaving their fellows, reduced them to no more than a chattels. He compared the Southern slave owners to English land and factory owners who, he maintained, were preoccupied only by the preservation of the class system and their desire for self-enrichment through the sweat of their down-trodden employees.

The audience again responded warmly to the speech, as they did to the ones that followed, by eminent trade unionists and Emancipation Society leaders. But around the hall there were those who received the socialistic dogma with less enthusiasm. Among these were several reporters, who were present from eminent newspapers, including the *Times* and also a lady whose dark good looks were only partly disguised by the shawl, which was draped over her head and shoulders.

Rose Greenhow had that morning received an urgent communiqué from her source informing her that John Bright, who was to propose the motion to amend the Foreign Enlistment Act the next day in Parliament, was to address a meeting that evening whose tone would be both strongly pro-North and anti-the land-owning classes, from whose ranks came the vast majority of the Members of Parliament of all parties. She had, in her turn, informed several journalists of her acquaintance. Some had been turned away at the door, but others were, even now, taking notes, often under the disapproving or even downright hostile gaze of their neighbours.

＊　＊

John Bright rose slightly later than usual, having found it hard to sleep after the tension and excitement of the previous evening and, still aglow with the warmth of the reception to his speech, sat down to a hurried breakfast of softly boiled eggs and sweet tea while he scanned the front page of The *Times*. As he read the leading article, his jaw swung open of its own volition and a small piece of egg-white fell out, landing unnoticed in a crease of his waistcoat. Wiping his mouth hurriedly, he rose from the table and ran out the front door to look for a cab. None could be found and he spent an anxious half-hour pacing up and down the pavement until his breathless footman returned at a run, preceded by a cab, whose driver just managed to whip his ageing horse into a trot.

The cab found its way down Birdcage Walk blocked by an entire battalion of Grenadier Guards, which marched with exasperating slowness the entire way down to Whitehall. As a consequence the debate had already started by the time that he entered the Commons chamber. He walked past the Government front bench, nodded at the Prime Minister and received in return a glare that would have frozen the blood of a reptile. John Laird, Member for Birkenhead had the floor. His calm gaze looked out over a packed house as he began:

"I would rather be handed down to posterity as the builder of a dozen *Alabamas* than as a man who applies himself deliberately to set class against class and to cry up the institutions of another country which, when they come to be tested, are of no value whatever and which reduce the very name of liberty to an utter absurdity."

He sat down to prolonged cheering and waving of order papers from both sides of the House. Bright was not called upon to speak.

The Speaker called for a vote on the motion. The members rose and, led by the Prime Minister himself, who had correctly identified the prevailing sentiment of the House, entered *en masse* through the 'no' door. The motion to amend the Act was dismissed by an overwhelming majority.

*   *

James Spence had telegraphed the anticipated time of his arrival and accordingly was expected when he arrived at the lavishly appointed offices of Erlanger et Cie on the Rue de Rivoli. Although the men had never met, Spence and his activities in raising finance for the Confederacy was well known to Erlanger. After a short while they were joined by Slidell and James Spence began to explain the reason why he had urgently sought this meeting.

"Gentlemen" he began, "I wonder if either of you have ever heard of Robert J. Walker? No? John? Very well then. By way of background, he was Secretary of the Treasury in the administration of President Polk, he is a banker by training and a self-made millionaire. As a result, he is very savy when it comes to matters financial. Now a Robert Walker arrived in England last week and it is no coincidence that, shortly thereafter, the Bonds met a heavy wave of short-selling, which encouraged some of the stags to take a quick profit and get out. As a result, the price quickly fell back to its issue level of ninety percent. Then – and I could scarcely credit this myself – comes the story of some eccentric Yank – beggin' your pardon, of course – who's gone up in a balloon and is scattering leaflets all over the City. It seemed funny at first, but then I heard what was in the leaflets. They're headed "Davis the Repudiator" and they go on to describe how your President Davis, back when he was the Senator for Mississippi in the 1840s, repudiated some State debt, which cost British investors upwards of ten million dollars."

"It's all nonsense of course and we will deny it," shouted Slidell angrily.

"Well, of course we will deny it, but I have checked and unfortunately it seems in the main to be true. Anyhow, this knocked confidence further, aided I may say, by some skilful short-selling towards the close and the bonds finished yesterday at a discount of four percent."

"Four and a half percent this morning," said Erlanger gloomily.

"Quite. Now, although you, Monsieur Elranger will certainly appreciate the danger, I should explain it to John here. You see, the Bonds are only fifteen percent paid at the moment and the next payment of ten percent is due on first of May. Now if the Bonds were to fall to a discount of, say, ten percent, then clearly no one would make the next payment and the issue would fail, leaving us with only what we have received to date, which, after Monsieur Erlanger's modest fees, is a mere one million three hundred and fifty thousand dollars. Unfortunately, even at the four and a half percent discount which prevails today, there could be some who feel that the next payment may be throwing good money after bad and will simply write the whole thing off as a mistake."

"So what do you suggest then?" Slidell asked, a worried frown on his face.

"I propose that we bull the issue, to counteract the bear sales of Robert J. Walker." He saw Slidell looking perplexed and continued. "We would go into the market and buy back a certain amount of the Bonds, using the subscription monies we have received to date. I spoke to the jobbers who work the Government's pitch, and they believe that one million pounds nominal should be more than enough."

"One million pounds?" Slidell cried, "but we only have one and a half million *dollars* so far – less, in fact. How can we do this?"

"Remember again, the bonds are only fifteen percent paid at the moment, so one million pounds would cost you less than one hundred and fifty thousand pounds – one hundred and five thousand pounds at today's price to be exact, which is around five hundred and twenty five thousand dollars. Now, the plan is that we will go into the market and buy noisily – badly – on behalf of several unknown but reputedly very rich and very astute clients, using several different brokers. This will frighten the bears, push up the price and restore confidence. Now, when the Bonds are back on an even keel – trading at above ninety percent – we will quietly unload the paper back into the market – hopefully at a decent profit. Ingenious, eh?"

"Ingenious, yes, but not exactly ethical, is it?" suggested Slidell.

"Perhaps not." Spence shrugged. "But it *is* legal and it is to counter short-selling against us, so what do you say?"

Slidell scratched his head in bewilderment and then ran his fingers through his hair. "We would have to get Mason's agreement of course ... but Emil, what do you think?"

"My friend, I think that it is an excellent plan, quite superb in fact and I believe that it should be most effective." He looked both happy and relieved. 'Of course,' thought Spence, 'the greedy bugger is still long himself and he will want to unload his position into our bid. I wonder which broker he will use, or if he will have the gall to do it himself. I must warn the jobbers to be on the look-out so that they can bid down for his paper.'

"Good," he said, shaking hands with both Slidell and Erlanger, "so we are agreed then."

*　*

Lord Russell had never seen the Prime Minister so angry. He stormed up and down his office, his face crimson, a large vein throbbing visibly at one temple. "The man is a complete liability. He is nothing but a rabid socialist, who cannot be relied on to curb his tongue, nor to exercise the merest hint of discretion in the interests of his coalition partners – or indeed his country. I tell you Johnny, this Bright's finished so far as I am concerned. The closest he will ever get to a ministerial position from now on is if he volunteers to clean out my privy!"

The Prime Minister fell silent for a moment and then his head swivelled in Russell's direction, the heavily lidded eyes cold and dark like the barrels of a gun. "It was you who suggested that we have Bright propose this motion – wasn't it Johnny, eh? Tell me, why did you do that?"

"As I explained, Prime Minister, he is pro-Federal and is a good speaker. I could hardly be expected to know that he would be making some rabble-rousing speech at a trades-union convention the night before he was due to propose the motion in Parliament *and* that he would have the bad taste to allow it to be splashed all over the front page of the *Times*, now could I?"

"Hmm." Palmerston regarded his old friend and political ally steadily from under his bushy eyebrows, a small kernel of suspicion still alive in his chest. "So now we are back to where we were. To recap, we have several suspicious ships under construction in various of our yards, we have the Americans threatening to precipitate a war if we let them out to sea and there is nothing we can do about it under the current state of our legislation. Would that seem fair?" He did not wait for an answer, but continued on. "And to make matters worse, the Federals had a go at Charleston Harbour the other day and were repulsed with a very bloody nose. Several of their vaunted monitors sunk by things called 'torpedoes', apparently. So if they weren't sensitive to matters naval before, they damn bloody well are now." He paused and then his face suddenly lit up as an idea came to him. "I'll tell you what we'll do. We'll seize one of these damned ships anyway and let the owners, whoever they may be, take us to court. That will show the Americans that we are serious in trying to stop this thing and if we lose, well, what of it? The rule of law, nothing further we can do, blah, blah, blah, and so on, eh what, Johnny."

Russell nodded. He felt that he could not oppose the Prime Minister in this – especially after Palmerston had nearly accused him to his face of selecting Bright on purpose to spoil the motion. The old boy was still as smart as ever and he would have to be very careful. "Well, Prime Minister, it is not a course of action that I would normally have recommended but, under the circumstances, it is hard to see that there are any viable alternatives." 'And, what is more,' he thought, 'I know just the ship – nearing completion, but not too big, nor too important, if she were to be tied up in the courts for some time.'

*   *

Bulloch was furious. He sat in Miller's office and listened to the little man, who was clearly both upset and nervous, explain how customs officers, together with local constabulary had arrived at his office, without warning, armed with the appropriate warrants. They had also insisted on visiting the Toxteth dock where the *Alexandra* was undergoing the final stages of her construction and had impounded the ship and seized papers relating to her ownership.

"It's not like the Chief Constable to let me down here," he mumbled, "what with us being feller Masons and all. This must have come from some real high-ups with a lot of political clout, I wouldn't wonder."

"That's as maybe, but where does that leave me? Without a ship it would seem."

"Well at least this 'asn't cost you a penny! I'm out twenty five thousand pounds – which doesn't put me in the poor-house or nothing, but it's a powerful lot of money, whichever way you look at it. I'm to blame though, generous to a fault I am, never should have taken this commission on without up-front cash ..."

"Oh shut up, for God's sake! Stop whining about your money. Let's sue them. You for the loss of your profit and I ... or the owners rather ... for the loss of the ship. Why not?"

"I'll tell you why not. Because the likes of them what's behind this don't do nothing without being sure of where they stand legal-wise before they start. And suing's a costly business. There's many a poor litigant what's gone bankrupt as their suit slowly ground its way through Chancery or Queen's Bench. And what did they get out of it in the end? Nothing, that's what. Just a lot of rich lawyers – the bloody parasites!"

"Well I'm not going to sit still and do nothing" Bulloch shouted, coming to his feet. He jabbed his finger at the strangely deflated Miller. "You may be happy to lie down and play dead, but I'm damned well not going to." And with that he stormed out of the office, past the rows of silent staring clerks and out of the front door, which he slammed behind him, causing dust motes to jump from the wall and hang motionless in the still air.

The next day Bulloch received a message from James Spence, inviting him to lunch at the Conservative Club. He arrived at one o'clock in a somewhat better frame of mind than on the previous evening, when he had sat in his lodgings and had morosely consumed the better part of a bottle of whisky by himself.

The reason for the improvement in his mood was a telegram from Rose, which said:

'DO NOT DESPAIR STOP COMMENCE LEGAL PROCEEDINGS IMMEDIATELY STOP YOU HAVE A STRONG CASE STOP THE GOVERNMENT DOES NOT EXPECT TO WIN STOP ROSE'

Bulloch immediately sought an appointment with F.S. Hull, who had previously advised him on the ramifications of the Foreign Enlistment Act. Hull confirmed the strength of their case, especially as this action came only days after the legislation that would have made the seizure legal had been defeated by a vote of the

255

House of Commons. Bulloch warned him that he himself would not be appearing as a claimant and would in fact have to take somewhat of a back seat in the whole proceedings. This did not seem to worry Hull, who only sought formal instruction by the actual claimants before proceeding to seek council's opinion, which, he had no doubt, would fully concur with his own.

*　　*

Bulloch was shown into the members bar, where he found Spence, who greeted him warmly. They drank small glasses of sherry before proceeding upstairs to lunch in the high-ceilinged dining room, whose sepulchral silence discouraged any conversation above a whisper. They ate steak, kidney and oyster pie, followed by a plum duff with custard, washed down by a rather nasty thin wine, described as a 'club claret'. After the dishes had been cleared and Bulloch was sitting back in his chair, puffing on a cigar and wondering how he could undo the top button of his trousers without attracting attention, James Spence leaned closer to him and in a low voice said:

"James, there is a matter of some importance that I wish to discuss with you." Bulloch nodded for him to continue.

"I don't really know where to begin …" Spence looked around the almost empty dining room for inspiration …"except possibly with an apology."

"An apology?"

"Yes. You see, I have felt for some time, shall we say, responsible … yes, responsible, for the situation you found yourself in vis-à-vis a certain gambling club and its semitic proprietor – not to mention his ghastly mother." He shuddered. Bulloch attempted to interrupt, but was silenced by a raised hand.

"On your first night in Liverpool, nay in this Country, what do I do? I introduce you to one of the most corrupt establishments north of Newmarket and, if that were not enough, you were decent enough to lend me five guineas to see me through a temporary pecuniary embarrassment." Spence had reddened somewhat and was now shifting uncomfortably in his chair. "And that is not all. I, ah, was at that time in debt to the Jew – indeed, to the Bank, to Fraser, Trenholm, to my suppliers, well, really to anyone and anywhere that would extend me a hap'worth of credit. And I was persuaded by the Jew that it would be in the interest of my prolonged health, not to mention what was left of my reputation, if I were to introduce new punters to his establishment. So you see, I really am directly to blame for your losses at the Club. I feel very badly about this, don't you know and I would very much like to do something to make amends."

Bulloch shook his head. "It is not necessary. I lost fair and square and I must carry the responsibility for my own actions."

"You don't understand, James." Spence was now staring fixedly at his own well-manicured fingernails. "You could never have won. Every game was fixed against you, except when they wanted you to win and that was only ever a small amount to encourage you to gamble further."

Bulloch thought of the poker game where he had also been cheated and started to become angry. What was it about these English? They seemed so uncommon civil on the outside, but underneath they were as twisted as a rattler, stealing, lying, cheating...

He looked at Spence, who was unable to meet his eye. 'Well, perhaps not all of them' he thought. Here at least was one gentleman. He put his hand on Spence's arm and noted the way he flinched, clearly uncomfortable at being touched.

"Don't worry," Bulloch said, "I'm not going to hit you, even though God knows you deserve it. But there's something about you limeys I just can't fathom and I've been far too trusting. So no hard feelings, feller."

"You are a brick, James and there's no denying it. But, I must make amends. You see, I have become rich – very rich in fact – as a result of my association with your Country and in particular with Messrs Fraser, Trenholm, who have been most helpful in my blockade-running activities. James, I wish to repay all your losses and I have with me a draft, drawn on my bank, Overend, Gurney for three thousand three hundred pounds which, after conversations with the Jew, I understand to be the extent of your losses. Here." He pushed a folded piece of paper across the table.

Bulloch picked up the paper, looked at it and then pushed it back.

"I cannot accept this. If I have any cause for complaint, it is against the Jew and indeed against my own gullibility and naivety. But thank you anyway, it is a very considerate gesture." He smiled warmly.

"Hmmm. Well," said Spence, picking up the draft and replacing it inside his jacket, "perhaps, then, I could introduce you to a situation on the Stock Market, whereby with limited risk, you could recoup your losses. How does that sound?"

It sounded good to Bulloch, who had only that morning received by messenger, a bank draft for one thousand eight hundred pounds drawn on Hoares in the City, but making no reference to the identity of the payer. He nodded for Spence to proceed.

Spence explained how matters lay with the Erlanger Bonds and the scheme to bull up their price. "So you see, you would go into the market just ahead of the start of our operation and buy, say, seventy five thousand pounds nominal, which due to the partly-paid or installment nature of the Bonds would cost ten and a half percent at today's price which is, um, a mere, seven thousand eight hundred and seventy five pounds. Now, assuming we are successful – and I have every reason to believe that we will be – the Bonds should move up in price by the amount of their discount, namely four and a half percent, to at least fifteen percent, which is the price at which they were issued. You will want to sell before the end of the month, so that you do not have to put up the next ten percent which is due on the first of May and I will make sure that there is a good bid for your paper when you do. And *voilà*, your seven thousand eight hundred and seventy five pounds will now be worth eleven thousand two hundred and fifty pounds – a profit of three thousand three hundred and seventy five pounds. Simple, eh?"

Bulloch thought that he understood. "The idea is fine but the only problem is that I don't currently have the initial seven thousand eight hundred and seventy five pounds."

"Why, you have no need for any cash at all," said Spence smiling and showing all his teeth. "As long as you buy and sell within the same account period, the bargains are matched against each other and all you need do is to collect the profit."

Spence and Bulloch parted outside the club's front door and agreed to meet again in two days time at the Capel Court entrance to the Stock Exchange, at 11 a.m. Spence left in the direction of Meyer and Greenwoods offices on Victoria Street, who were reputable brokers that he intended to entrust with the purchase of

Bulloch's bonds. Bulloch took a cab to Lime Street to catch the early afternoon train to London. He was suddenly very anxious to see Rose again.

He found Rose at home, working on her book and reluctant to be interrupted. Nonetheless she embraced Bulloch warmly and called for tea.

Bulloch observed her over the rim of his tea-cup and noticed the dark smudges under her eyes and her care-worn expression on her face. "What ails you Rose?" he enquired gently.

"Oh, no great matter," she replied, "I am perhaps a little tired, a little lonely, a little sad. Nothing of any great import. But it is nice to see you," she said, visibly brightening and squeezing Bulloch's knee, "and looking so well. Quite your old self … just a little more knocked about." She ran a finger over the scar on his cheek, "and perhaps, with a little more grey in your whiskers … which makes you look *very* distinguished," she added quickly.

"Rose, come to Paris with me," he said suddenly, unaware even of the thought that should have preceded the words, but continuing rapidly as he warmed to the topic. "Yes, indeed, for I must go there in the next few weeks to start commissioning ships from French yards. We have been told, at the highest levels, that we will be welcome as long as we have the money – and with this loan of Erlanger's we should have money aplenty. So come with me and together we shall see Paris, which many say is the most beautiful city in the world. You may shop for gowns in the very latest fashion, while I will better acquaint myself with the wines and brandies for which the country is so justly famous. So, what do you say my dear?"

Rose looked at him evenly, slowly becoming aware of the slight blush that travelled up from the high frilled neck of her silk blouse and of the faster beating of her heart.

"Why, James, what a wonderful thought. Yes, I should very much enjoy discovering Paris with you. The break, I am sure, will do me good and in any case, I have things to discuss with Slidell. Oh, James, when can we go? The sooner the better for me!" she said, clapping her hands with excitement.

"I have one or two matters of a business nature to conclude first – especially our suit against the Government for the seizure of the *Alexandra*. Our counsel, Sir Peter Rochester, has applied for expedition and expects a date for a hearing in the next week or so.

Hopefully in early May, when the weather will be warm, but not hot and the cherry blossom with be in bloom down the length of the Champs Elysées. Frankly, I cannot wait my dear." He kissed her lightly on the lips as he left, but did not seek to pursue the matter further, as he would have done in earlier days.

*   *

At 11 a.m. exactly, by the tolling of the bell of St Margaret's, Lothbury, Bulloch ran lightly up the steps to the Capel Court entrance of the Exchange and looked around for Spence. Minutes later he saw Spence emerge from the main door of the Exchange and come out onto the steps. Spence saw Bulloch immediately and waved him over.

"Good morning James. Let us go in quickly, because the fun is about to start. As a non-member, you are not supposed to gain admittance to the floor, but this is something you will not want to miss. Let us keep our fingers crossed that no-one notices you although you are not entirely an inconspicuous figure, if I may be so bold as to say." He looked Bulloch up and down, noting the man's height, accentuated by a stove-pipe hat in the best silk from Locke's and his girth, which was encircled by a bright red velvet waistcoat with turned back lapels and large brass buttons. "Oh well," he murmured, "never mind."

The two men walked quickly through the main doors, Spence smiling at the doorman, whom he evidently knew, as they entered. Bulloch had tipped his hat forward over his face, but raised a finger in salute to the other doorman, who nodded back.

Once inside they were in a lobby with a tall domed ceiling, which thronged with brokers and jobbers conversing loudly with one another. An open pair of double doors led onto the floor of the Exchange, which was equally crowded. Smartly dressed individuals conferred earnestly together while others crossed the floor at a fast walk to seek a word from another member, which was often answered only by a nod or the shake of a head. Papers lay strewn across the floor and the air was heavy with cigar smoke.

"Is there a meaning to this chaos?" Bulloch asked Spence, at a loss to comprehend the seeming pandemonium.

"Indeed" Spence replied, "it is really quite simple. You see the coves leaning up against the pillars and around the walls. Yes? Well they are jobbers standing at their pitches. They make prices. The brokers' men, blue buttons, are coming up to them with orders to buy or sell from clients. The jobber will only buy at a certain price if he believes that he can off-load the stock, pretty well right away, at a profit. Sometimes, however, he will 'go short' – that is, he will sell first and buy later, but only when he knows that he can cover himself – or to put in another way, buy back that which he has already sold, but at a lower price than that at which he sold it. D'ye see?"

"Yes, I suppose so," mumbled Bulloch, who clearly did not.

"Now, watch this." Spence caught the eye of a somewhat portly individual with a red face and nodded. The individual crossed the floor and raised his hat to one of the jobbers, a cadaverous looking man, dressed entirely in black, who was leaning up against a pillar by the entrance. They conferred briefly, then the red-faced individual raised his hat again and strutted away. Minutes later he passed close to Spence. "One hundred at ten percent," he said out of the corner of his mouth without stopping.

Another member approached the jobber, raised his hat, muttered something and then withdrew, looking pleased. Shortly after that, a third broker completed the same process. By now, however, the jobber was no longer looking so relaxed and nor was he reclining against the pillar, but instead was standing bolt upright, slowly moving his head from side to side as he surveyed the Exchange floor with slitted eyes. He called his clerk over to him, who wrote down some figures in a notebook. He then pointed out a broker across the floor, whom the clerk went to fetch. The broker and the jobber talked quietly to one another for a moment before the broker shook his head and left. The jobber looked angry, briefly, then shrugged.

A broker came up to Spence and handed him a note, then raised his hat and passed out of the doors. Spence opened the note. It said: "two hundred and fifty at eleven percent." "Aha," he said, looking pleased with himself, "it is starting to work."

During the next hour, the jobber was approached over twenty times by various different brokers, some only once, others on multiple occasions. By noon he was starting to look seriously worried. "He is now very short indeed and is beginning to feel that he has been caught in a bear squeeze. If he is lucky, Walker is

261

behind him the whole way, but somehow, judging from his expression, I doubt it. He does however have more than a week to go before settlement, by which time he must deliver what he has sold. These he must buy at any price."

Spence summoned the original rubicund broker, who had been one of the most active in the morning's proceedings. "So what are we seeing now?" he enquired.

"Well," said the broker, "he won't offer more than ten thousand pounds at a go and then its at fifteen and a half percent. He won't do size at any price. I'd say he's been taken well short."

"Very good." Spence was now smiling broadly. "Why don't you go and cheer him up a bit Mr Meriweather. Go and offer him seventy five thousand pounds at fifteen. See what he does." The broker scampered away. "These are your bonds this time James."

The broker returned. "Done," he said. "Are these down to you, Mr Spence?"

"For a client, actually" Spence replied.

"That will be me." Bulloch interrupted, looking pleased.

"You?" said the broker. "A client? Then he's not a member, Mr Spence? You shouldn't be bringing him onto the floor then, as you well know. Now, if you'll excuse me" and he left, walking slowly with as much dignity as his rotund figure would allow. He spoke to two other brokers, who were standing nearby and could be seen looking at Spence and Bulloch as he did so.

"Oh dear," Spence said. "James, I think you should leave right away."

"But I am enjoying this," Bulloch replied. No sooner had the words left his mouth than one of the nearby brokers suddenly shouted "fourteen hundred!" at the top of his voice. "Fourteen hundred!" picked up two other members, who could be seen pointing at Bulloch. "Fourteen hundred!" shouted a voice close behind Bulloch and a hand smartly knocked his new stove-pipe hat from his head.

Bulloch spun around to remonstrate with his attacker, but Spence already had him by the arm. "You are coming with me now," he shouted in his ear and hustled him out of the main doors, as the cries of "fourteen hundred" multiplied. Several members tried to jostle him on the way out, but his size deterred all but the most foolhardy, one of whom was sent flying as he attempted to block Bulloch's path.

On the steps outside, Bulloch turned to Spence, hatless, his hair blowing in the breeze and said, "James, I must apologise for my lapse, I do so hope that it will not make any real trouble for you."

"No, I am sure that it will not. Some will assume that you are the mystery client behind the buying today, but all this will only add to the scare that we have just put into Walker and his friendly bears. The Bonds are now back up to their issue price, you have just made over three thousand three hundred pounds and all for the cost of one of Locke's best toppers. Not a bad morning's work, eh?"

XIX

Paris — May, 1863

❧ ❧

The carriage turned onto the Pont Louis Phillipe just as the sun started to set behind the Ile de la Cité, its dying rays throwing the massive bulk of the Cathedral of Notre Dame into sudden stark relief, highlighting the great spire that thrust itself into the sky like a huge arm, pointing the way to God.

In the back of the carriage sat two people, a man and a woman, both in their early forties. She was wearing a hooped dress of burgundy silk with black bows down the front of the skirt and frogging across the blouse, in imitation of a military uniform, which was, she had been assured by the couturier in the Rue St Honoré, quite the latest fashion and inspired by the Empress herself.

The man was simply, but correctly dressed in a black tail coat and trousers from Savile Row, with a rigorously starched shirt front and high collar points that forced him to sit with his head up and back, and his chest distended.

Neither occupant of the carriage spoke and yet each was only too aware of the other; and in the moments when the carriage lurched on the uneven road surface and the two were thrown together and their thighs or shoulders touched, a current passed between them of almost shocking intensity.

Rose wore her mother's locket at her throat, which she fiddled with continuously, as she stared out of the carriage window, entranced by the drama and beauty of the city.

Bulloch, constrained by his collar, was unable to turn his head without at the same time turning his whole body. However, being reluctant to press himself against his companion in the narrow carriage, he thus found himself unable either to look out the window or, which he would have preferred, to look at Rose.

The carriage continued south into the Quartier Latin, an area of narrow winding streets, where the tall houses nearly met above them, and where the air was filled with the strange and exotic smells of the heavily spiced meat that the street vendors cooked on their portable grills.

At last they drew up in front of a house, whose grand pillars and ornately carved lintels set it apart from the more modern and functional buildings that crowded the remainder of the street. Torches burned brightly in sconces on each side of the massive front door, which was flanked by footmen in high-collared, brass-buttoned coats and white breeches. One of these ran to open the carriage door, dropping down the steps for Rose to alight, while the other preceded them into the house.

Once inside, they were in a marble flagged hall whose ceiling rose several stories to a glass cupola. Facing them was a broad staircase, carpeted with a rich deep pile. A servant politely enquired as to Bulloch's name, before leading the way up the staircase and opening one of the doors on the landing. He stood aside, allowing them to enter. Rose went in first.

"Why James, how really ..." she started to say, as she saw the table set for two in the middle of the room, with candles burning brightly in the candelabra and the setting of fine silver and cut glass on the starched damask cloth. She stopped suddenly in mid-sentence, however, as she noticed the red velour chaise-longue on the far wall, below a large and somewhat garish reproduction of Madame Recamier reclining on a similar piece of furniture and wearing no more than an inviting smile.

Rose looked at Bulloch, who suddenly seemed unwilling to catch her eye. She stepped across to a heavily lacquered screen that hid the far corner of the room and looked behind it.

"Ugh," she said.

"Why, what is it Rose? Do you not like the room? No matter, we will get another." Bulloch turned to the servant, attempting to hide his confusion behind a display of outrage.

"Does Madame not find the room to her satisfaction?", enquired the servant, who remained hovering by the open door.

Rose stared fiercely at Bulloch, noting his puce and sweating face and his downcast eyes and took pity on him. She sighed. "No, no it is fine, thank you".

"Then with your permission, Monsieur, Madame, I will serve the Champagne. It is one of the best Cuvées of 1852, which I am sure you will enjoy."

When he had left Rose turned to Bulloch. "Where have you brought me?" she demanded, firmly.

"I... I... only asked the Concierge at the hotel for a restaurant, which served good food and which had a romantic atmosphere. You must believe me Rose, I had no idea that we would be coming to a... er... well, whatever this place is."

"I will tell you what this place is," she said with a steely look to her eye. "This is a place where married men bring their mistresses so that they can make love to them over dinner. There is even a ... you know, one of those 'bee-day' things, behind the curtain. It really is so sordid."

"I am sorry Rose, I really am. I don't know what to say. I just wanted this evening to be perfect and now it is ruined."

Rose felt an almost overwhelming wave of tenderness and affection come over her for this man who, though so well-intentioned could be nonetheless so clumsy. She rose from her seat and kissed him lightly on the cheek, playfully ruffling his hair in a manner which she knew annoyed him.

"I know you did not do this on purpose. Never mind. No harm has been done. Let us just hope that the food is up to expectations, for in truth I am quite weak with hunger. And James," she said rapping him on the back of the hand with her folded fan for emphasis... "just do not get any ideas into your head about trying to use that... that sofa thing over there. I am quite immune to your charms." 'At least until I have had several more glasses of champagne', she thought.

They started with oysters in a rich cream soup, whose deep bowl was topped with a thin crust of pastry and followed this with turbot in a saffron sauce. The main course was a duck, stuffed with its own *foie*, in a much reduced sauce of wine and myrtles. Lastly, and to much applause, a *bombe* of fresh fruit ice cream and meringue arrived, flambéed in brandy, the pale blue flames dancing over its crust like the waves of the Caribbean sea.

They drank several glasses of champagne. Then they drank a crisp white Burgundy, followed by an inky claret and finally a sweet Sauternes. Rose looked at the chaise-longue and the chaise-longue looked at her.

At last Bulloch pushed back his chair, his face aglow and lit a cigar.

"What a capital meal. Truly the best I have had since I was last in Richmond," he said, sighing.

"It is true" she replied. "One becomes somehow numbed by English food so that one does not realise how ghastly it really is until you eat something actually good and then you think of all the grey and gristly meat with its cold greasy gravy and ..."

"Enough Rose, thank you." He held up both his hands. "Now we have several things to celebrate tonight. To enumerate: One;" he held up one finger, "I am here with you – that above all else. Two;" he held up the second finger. "The English court found in our favour that the *Alexandra* was seized illegally – as you said it would! And three;" he held up the third finger, "I made an investment on the stock market in London, which proved to be very rewarding and therefore I am able to give this into your safe-keeping." He undid a canvas belt from around his waist with an audible sigh of relief and dropped it onto the table, where it fell with a heavy thump.

"What is it?" she asked, intrigued.

"Three thousand pounds in gold sovereigns, each bearing the likeness of Her majesty, Queen Victoria. Exactly the sum that I 'borrowed' from the Naval funds entrusted to me. I would like you to keep it, until such time as it can be used in an appropriate manner."

Rose stared at the belt and nodded, more pleased that she could say. "So, in truth, we have nothing between us now," she said softly.

"Except for our clothes," he added, nonchalantly. She laughed and rose from the table, walking across to the chaise-longue, unbuttoning the front of her dress as she went.

After she had removed her dress, which she carefully draped over the back of a chair, she unfastened the belt that supported the stiff hoops that flared the skirt into a voluminous tent of material. Then she unlaced her corset, which she threw across the room, groaning with the relief that she felt in the release of her distended stomach. Bulloch sat and watched her silently, his face wreathed in the smoke of his cigar. She came across to where he sat and slowly undid the bows that secured the front of her shift, releasing her breasts, which she took in both hands and pressed up against his face as she straddled him, pushing herself firmly into his lap.

She started to undress him, while he sat, his face buried between her breasts, inhaling deeply. His tie, jacket and waistcoat came off easily and quickly, but how she struggled in vain with the myriad of studs that secured his collar and shirt. Finally she gave up and ripped at the front of his shirt, the studs snapping off and vanishing into the shadows. She stood up and pulled him across the room by the front of his trousers which she tugged down to his knees before they collapsed together onto the chaise-longue in a tangle of limbs and partially removed clothing. There they made love furiously but untidily until, both satiated, Rose, overcome by his weight, pushed him off her on to the floor where he lay, with his trousers around his ankles, panting like a race horse and laughing with glee.

On the way back to their hotel in the carriage, Rose sat on Bulloch's knee, her arms around his neck, gently kissing his cheek and licking his ear lobe, while he grinned to himself in the darkness.

The next morning Bulloch woke early, but lay still and quiet so as not to disturb Rose, content merely to listen to her breathing and to watch her sleeping features in the soft dawn light that crept through the window of her room. He loved the way in which her nostrils flared as she inhaled; he loved the way in which her eyes moved beneath her lids and the fine tracery of lines that emanated from their corners. Finally he could bear it no more and kissed her gently on the lips. She moved into his arms, pulling the hem of her night-gown up above her hips as she did so and kissing him with passion, all without opening her eyes, so that later he wondered if he had made love to her while she still slept.

The next week they spent most of their days and all of their nights together, marvelling at the imperial grandeur of Paris by day and dining and making love by night. In the months to come Bulloch would remember this as the happiest week of his life, when the war and politics left them alone and nothing intruded into their private world, while their affair ruled them with a degree of passion and piquancy that was all the more intense and surprising given the age and experience of the couple.

At the end of the week, with considerable regret, Rose returned to England and Bulloch called on Lucien Arman et Cie., the largest shipbuilder in France, where he commissioned four fast steamers, to be built along the lines of the *Alabama* and two ironclad rams, all of which he hoped to be able to pay for with the proceeds of Erlanger's Cotton Bonds.

XX

Paris and London – June, 1863

❧ ❧

For the diminutive John Roebuck, an audience with his Imperial Highness, Napoleon III, was both a source of great excitement and anticipation, as well as the cause of extreme nervousness. His anxiety to appear learned, grave, sober, trustworthy and dignified – attributes all well beyond his meagre capabilities – was such that great rivulets of sweat coursed down his badly shaved face, dampening the already none too clean collar of his shirt.

His fellow Member of Parliament, William Lindsay, sat as far away from him as was possible, given the intimate nature of the small sitting room in the Palais de Tuileries, and viewed his colleague with some distaste.

After a wait, which seemed interminable, the unctuous secretary returned and escorted the two Englishmen up the stairs and into the Imperial presence.

The Emperor received them politely, but did not invite them to sit; and so they stood, side by side, in front of his Louis XIV desk, which came up well beyond John Roebuck's waist, and waited to be addressed. The Emperor spent some time stroking his moustache so as to hide his smile because, as a man of no great height himself, he was particularly amused by Roebuck's almost dwarfish appearance. Finally he pulled himself together and welcomed the two parliamentarians. He asked politely after the health of Her Majesty and of his old friend Disraeli and then enquired as to what service he could be to two such distinguished members of the oldest and most highly regarded democratically elected legislative assembly in the world. This was all spoken in French and then translated into English by the secretary, with considerable flourish and some further embellishment.

Roebuck, warmed by the praise, puffed out his chest so that he resembled some old bantam cock and raised his finger in the air, preparatory to speaking, but was pre-empted by William Lindsay who thanked the Emperor warmly and then continued:

"You see *Sire*, in the past there have been many attempts to push Palmerston's Ministry into recognising the Confederate States of America, which God knows, they deserve, seeing as how they've battled their Northern brethren to a standstill over the past two years and more. Now for one reason or another, Palmerston has always found a way to avoid committing himself and, what is more, to avoid England committing herself. Now you, *Sire*, as a far-seeing and, if I may say so, deeply compassionate Monarch and as the ruler of one of the most powerful nations in the world, have in the past taken a more robust view than Palmerston and have even acted, unilaterally, to offer France's assistance as a mediator, in an attempt to find a solution to this dreadful and bloody conflict."

This was translated for the Emperor, even though he had understood it all, who nodded for Lindsay to continue.

"Now *Sire*, we – that is all right-thinking Members of Parliament of both parties and with the support of the majority of those in our Country who are deemed to be persons of influence – we feel that the time is now right for one more concerted attempt to make Palmerston stand up, not only for what is right, but for what is clearly in the interests of England, just as it is in the interests of France. So, we have come here today to enlist your support for joint recognition of the Confederate States, by our two countries – and if your support is forthcoming, we will immediately bring a motion before the House, which will force Palmerston to act."

Napoleon interrupted Lindsay to ask: "Why now? Why do you feel that you will succeed on this occasion, when in the past you have failed even to obtain a majority in Parliament and, as I understand it, have never even been close to convincing Palmerston to follow a course of action that would risk a war with the United States?"

"Well *Sire*, I, that is we, we feel that the military situation has changed markedly in favour of the South. After the very thorough beating that the Yankees took at Fredericksburg in December, there was this other battle just a few weeks ago – Chancellorville it was called, where they took another pounding. After that, Lincoln threw out their army's commanding general – Hooker I believe his name was – who must be the third or fourth they've been through. Can't seem to find one who can win, it seems. Then I hear that the siege of Vicksburg – that's in the West, on the Mississippi, you know – well, it's about to be lifted by an army under Joe Johnston while Lee himself has gone back up North again – into Pennsylvania – and will be putting himself between the Northern Army and Washington, if he can. He could end the war like that" and he clicked his fingers. "And then, *Sire*, there is the economic situation, which has worsened of late, what with unemployment in the cotton industry and rising prices. Working people in both our countries are starving, as I am sure you are only too aware. The end of this war would be a blessing for all of them."

Throughout all this, Roebuck's head was nodding so rapidly that the secretary began to fear that it might become detached, but he wisely kept his own council and added nothing to Lindsay's impassioned appeal, which he could see had been well received by the Emperor.

In fact the Emperor had used the time taken by the translator in which to formulate his response, which he now gave.

"Gentlemen, I must thank you for your visit and you, Mr. Lindsay, for your most eloquent and persuasive argument in support of a cause, which we both believe to be one that merits our most earnest support. You may return to your Country safe in the knowledge that France will act, as she has always done before, in the interest of humanity and with the very best of intentions. And now, if you will excuse me, I must wish you a good day and *bon voyage.*"

Lindsay and Roebuck left the audience chamber walking backwards, in accordance with strict protocol.

"What a magnificent man," muttered Roebuck as the door closed behind them, "and what a great speech, Lindsay. Damned effective too, I should say. We can be sure of his support then!"

"I wonder", Lindsay replied, looking thoughtful. "He's too much the diplomat for my liking, not much plain-speaking in him. Still, I doubt any of them calls a spade a spade much, so we must take what we got and push on, eh?"

The Emperor sat by himself for a while, stroking his beard and considering the matter further. It was complicated, much more complicated than those two politicians knew. Yes, he supported the

Southerners with his heart and admired their unequal struggle for *Liberté* and yes, he had approached the North with France's offer to mediate – and had been sternly rebuffed for his pains. However, on the reverse side of the coin, his troops had just taken Mexico City, Juarez had fled and he, Napoleon, had offered the imperial crown of Mexico to the Archduke Maximilian Habsburg, brother of the Emperor Francis Joseph. This would not only put a totally compliant ruler on the throne of Mexico, one who was beholden to him in all respects, but would also go a long way towards improving France's somewhat strained relationship with Austria-Hungary. Much was at stake. Lincoln, a long-time proponent of the Munroe Doctrine seemed to have acquiesced to this, quite justifiable, expansion of France's empire on the American Continent and, as a further gesture, Seward had written offering to allow French ships right of passage into Southern ports to take out the goods which they had bought, but had not shipped by the time that the war had begun. All this made him reluctant to act, overtly, in support of the Southern cause at this time. Behind the scenes, of course, any help that France could give to their war effort, through the sale of munitions or the construction of ships, he would be delighted to provide, especially as prices were high at this moment. But to actually join with Britain in recognising the Confederacy? No, he didn't think so. Not now at any rate... but perhaps, after he saw how Lee fared in Pennsylvania, after he could be sure which country would be on the other side of Mexico's long, long border...

Roebuck and Lindsay left Paris that morning and went directly to Calais by train, where they embarked on a ferry which covered the twenty five mile crossing to Dover in an astounding three hours. They spent the night at the Grand Hotel and left for London early the next day, now fully confident of Napoleon's support and intending to table the Motion for Recognition before the House that very afternoon.

As their cab crossed Waterloo Bridge, Roebuck pulled down the window in the door and put his head out to listen.

"I say, Lindsay. They're playing 'Dixie'. Well I'll be damned. If that's not a good omen, I don't know what is!"

Lindsay listened and was forced to agree. As the cab turned the corner into Parliament Square, a brass band could be seen on the green, while all about Confederate battle flags flew and a clown, on stilts, attired as a very sinister looking Abraham Lincoln, complete with a three foot high stove-pipe hat, leered down and scared children into fits of tears. Many of the onlookers had joined in the singing and one or two were dancing a jig to the music, while men in grey uniforms handed out leaflets, and stalls dispensed free roasted corn cobs to passers-by. Roebuck laughed loudly and waved his hat out the cab window, shouting "Long live President Davis!" and "Good luck to Robert Lee!" as it passed through the gates and into the Houses of Parliament.

XXI

Gettysburg, Pennsylvania 3pm July 3rd, 1863 (Third and last day of the battle)

～ ⹌

The Union cannon fire slackened and then died, relieving the grey-clad infantry from the deadly rain of incoming projectiles that had mangled their ranks while they lay, unmoving, in the edge of the woods that ran down the length of Seminary Ridge.

Their own guns, some one hundred and forty in number, maintained a sporadic rate of fire for nearly half an hour more, before building up to a deafening crescendo and then falling silent. To the infantry, the cessation of the bombardment brought blessed relief to their pounded eardrums and in the singing silence the calls of wild birds could be heard once more.

All down the mile-long line, officers could be seen rising to their feet and brushing down their jackets and trousers, adjusting their hats and looking at one another with small waves and relieved smiles. Commands were given, orders were shouted and nine brigades of three divisions – the cream of Lee's Army of North Virginia – some eleven thousand men in all, formed up and dressed neatly into line, each man touching his neighbour at arm's length.

At the word, the soldiers stepped smartly out from the woods, their bayonets gleaming in the bright sunlight, just as the last of the smoke from the artillery fire, that had covered the ground with a yellow pall, blew away in the light breeze and the sun broke through, shining brightly down from a cloudless sky. As they marched forward, through their own line of guns, the cannoneers, who leant sweating on their ram-rods or against the wheels of their pieces, stood upright and cheered, waving their hats in the air, with cries of "good luck men" or, "you whip them Yankees for us, boys, and whip 'em good."

And then they were out in the open and, for a moment, a great and powerful feeling of exhilaration swept over the men and imbued each and every soldier with a sense the greatness of their undertaking. For a while, too, there was no sound except for the noise of feet as they flicked against the corn-stubble or tramped the dry earth.

To the Union troops waiting on the opposing ridge, it was a magnificent and awe-inspiring sight, as that long grey line moved slowly forward like a breaker moves across the ocean.

And then the moment passed and the Union artillery lined up facing them along Cemetary Ridge and looking down on both flanks from Little Round Top and Cemetery Hill, opened fire and the first gaps began to appear in the Confederate formations. At this range many guns fired solid shot which whipped through the ranks, knocking men down like skittles or simply obliterating any soldier unlucky enough to receive a direct hit. Others fired explosive shells that burst over the massed ranks, raining deadly shrapnel down onto the men and causing terrible wounds from the jagged pieces of metal.

Above the noise of the guns, sergeants could be heard shouting "Close up, close up on the center," and as the gaps grew, so the formations shrank and as they moved forward, so the ground behind them was strewn, ever more thickly, with the dead and the wounded.

As they approached the Emmitsburg Road, they were nearly three-quarters of the way to the Union infantry, who waited patiently, eager for the slaughter to come, crouching down behind a low stone wall. But the line of men, which had started out over a mile from flank to flank, was now only five hundred yards wide.

In a dip before the road, the officers halted the men to dress them again into straight lines, which were constantly in need of redressing as the enemy guns, which fired canister shot at this range, poured a never-ending barrage of iron balls, a half-inch in diameter, into the packed mass of grey-clad troops, with awful effect.

At the road, the Confederate troops paused again to take down the two wooden fences that ran its length and then continued their advance.

In front, four hundred yards of bare field, devoid of any

shelter, slope gently up hill to the low stone wall, behind which a mass of blue clad troops now rise to their feet and pour a volley of rifle fire into the Confederates, thinning their ranks as if with a comb. At both ends of the Union line, which overlaps the advancing troops, regiments swing out of their positions so as to enfilade the attackers, firing into their flanks.

On the right, Pickett's two lead brigades under Garnett and Kemper have been savaged by the flanking fire from the guns on the Little Round Top and both Garnett and Kemper are out of the fight, one killed, the other mortally wounded. The commander of the rear brigade, General Armistead, forces his way through the press of men to the front and assumes command of all three brigades.

To his immediate front, the Union line is closer by some eighty yards, as the wall behind which the Union infantry has been sheltering dog-legs, before again continuing in a straight line. It is to this point that General Armistead has brought the remainder of Pickett's Division and now, in an act of pure heroism, he takes off his black plumed hat and places it on the point of his sword, which he holds above his head, rallying his men, and then he is over the wall at their head. The defenders at this point are Pennsylvanians and, in spite of the fact that they are defending their own State, they break and run, as grey and butternut clad troops, ragged, filthy and bearded to a man, swarm over the wall yelling like banshees.

For one brief moment, for one impossibly short instant, the charge is home and the battle is won. But then two fresh Union regiments came running down the hill from behind a clump of trees and Armistead and the three hundred of his men, who made it with him over the wall, are subjected to fire from three sides. Armistead himself falls mortally wounded in a hail of bullets and his men look around desperately for support. But there is none to be had. All down the line Confederate troops are in head-long flight, still under fire, and the battle is lost.

XXII

London and Liverpool – July, 1863

రా ⚜

Lord Russell sat at his desk, peering myopically at the *Times*, which was spread out in front of him and from time to time 'tutting' as some item in the article that he was reading caused him particular annoyance or distress.

The article in question covered the withdrawal of John Roebuck's motion for the recognition of the Confederate States. It was particularly scathing about the way in which Roebuck had purported to have the support of France for such a proposition, supposedly given by the Emperor himself, when diplomatic channels were quite unable to confirm that any such support either had, or indeed would ever be given.

Roebuck, who had brought the motion before the House alone, after his friend William Lindsay had decided that prudence demanded his presence elsewhere, had been put in the uncomfortable position where he had no alternative but to withdraw his own motion, after Disraeli and the rest of the Conservative party had refused to back him, their own colleague. Roebuck, being a man whose reputation and influence were no greater than his stature, had also been unable to garner any supporters from outside his own party and, as a result, had fled the chamber, almost in tears, to the jeers and catcalls of the assembled Members on both sides of the House.

Russell stared out of the window, tapping his fingernail against the wooden surround to his desktop. 'Why' he wondered, 'did the Confederacy seem unable to attract supporters of any real calibre? Why always the Roebucks and the Lindsay's of this world, whose lack of intellectual capacity was only equalled by their paucity of moral fibre?'

His musing was interrupted by the almost silent entrance of his secretary, who coughed lightly in order to attract the Foreign Secretary's attention. Russell looked up. "Yes, Stainforth, what is it?"

"My Lord, you asked me to inform you when Mr Adams arrived. He is now seated outside. Would you like me to show him in or shall I give him some coffee and ask him to wait?"

Russell looked at his secretary from under half-lowered lids and contemplated having Adams wait, just for his own pleasure and for old time's sake. But then he shook his head. "Thank you Stainforth, you can show him in now." He practiced a smile twice, so that his face muscles would be able to respond in the appropriate manner when Adams entered and then rose stiffly from behind his desk, twitched his cravat unnecessarily and positioned himself in front of the door.

"Why Mr Foreign Secretary, thank you so much for seeing me at such short notice, so very kind and you know how I do enjoy our little chats together." Before Russell was fully aware, Adams was into the room, talking like a Gattling gun and had already grasped Russell firmly by the hand and was leading him to the two leather wing-back chairs that flanked the fire-place, which now contained only a vase of flowers wilting in the mid-summer heat.

Adams seemed in a particularly ebullient and enthusiastic mood and altogether even more full of himself and annoying than usual. 'Typical damned Yankee', thought Russell, as he contemplated his guest with barely-concealed distaste.

"So, ah, yes, very happy to see you and all that. Now what can I do for you on this occasion, Mr Adams?" Lord Russell deliberately and obviously stressed the 'this', which was duly noted by his visitor.

"We'll come to that in just one minute my Lord, but first I would like to share with you the excellent news which I have just received by flying packet from Washington. News that is so fresh, that it is still hot, you may say!"

"Indeed. Pray continue."

"You had heard, of course, that Lee had invaded Pennsylvania with his rag-tag army and was, again, hoping to make some demonstration towards Washington?"

"Of course," but he thought 'yes, and that 'rag-tag' army has beaten yours at every major encounter, despite the smart uniforms and the new equipment that your men carry.'

"Well, last week General Meade met him at a little town called Gettysburg and they fought for three days. At the end, Lee was beaten and was forced to retreat, leaving behind over eight thousand dead or captured and with a further thirteen thousand wounded, by our reckoning."

"And how were your own losses?"

"Ah, well, they were unfortunately, very high as well. Possibly in the case of wounded, even somewhat higher…"

"A very bloody day, then. And tell me, was General Lee taken? Was his army destroyed?"

Adams shifted uncomfortably in his chair. "No, Lee escaped and he has re-crossed the Potomac into Virginia taking the remnants of his army with him. But he was beaten fair and square and he left the field to us."

"So you have regained all of Pennsylvania? My congratulations!" His sarcasm was not lost on Adams, who reddened, but nor was the seriousness of the situation lost on Russell. The Army of North Virginia, invincible in the field, had at last been beaten. While the North, with its vastly superior man-power and resources could swallow losses of this magnitude, a defeat such as this would be a body blow for the Confederacy's best and most experienced fighting unit, and thus for its own chances of survival.

Adams perked up suddenly. "But of course, that is not all! You will not have heard about Vicksburg either, which has fallen to General Ulysses Grant! The entire Mississippi is now a Union roadway and the Confederacy is cut in two! This is the end for them you know!"

'Damn the man, but he is probably right', thought Russell. 'And now I will have to put up with your arrogant and boorish behaviour while you crow about your victories. An intact United States is a disaster for us, but Palmerston, Lewis and the others are just too damn blind to see it, for in the longer term their navy will undoubtedly threaten British control of the high seas and the trade routes to our Empire. In a way, I am glad that my time is nearly over and at least I won't live to see it. But in the meantime, this calls for a shift in Government policy, unless I am mistaken and a somewhat more supportive posture towards the likely victor of this conflict.'

Adams had watched Lord Russell as these thoughts had crowded through his mind, seeing the flickering eyelids and the pursing of the fleshy lips and he had wondered if he were witnessing some change of heart, as the wily old politician sought, as always, to anchor himself firmly to the winning side.

"So," Russell spoke at last, "you are indeed to be congratulated. I only hope that now a speedy resolution can be brought to this perfidious conflict."

"Indeed, my Lord, we all share your sentiments. Now, it is particularly in regard to our mutual desire not to prolong this ... perfidious conflict ... unduly, that I wished to see you ... to ask your assistance. It is in the matter of the Rebel warships under construction at Laird's yard in Birkenhead, of which we have already spoken on many occasions. And before you ask, no, I have no positive proof that the ultimate owners are our rebel Southern States.

However, this is what I do know: first, that they are named the *El Tousson* and the *El Mounasser* and the French Foreign Secretary, De L'Huys believes that they are being built for the Pasha of Egypt – or so he says; secondly, while they are still being constructed in the utmost secrecy and behind high fences – which does not really jibe with the Egyptian story, by the by – one of my men has been able to gain admittance, albeit briefly. The ships are clearly men-of-war, having long iron piercing rams on their bows and are designed to carry two revolving gun-turrets amidships. One of them is nearly complete and will, I estimate, be ready to sail within a fortnight. Thirdly, Laird was paid by a draft drawn on Fraser, Trenholm, whose scurrilous activities are well known to us all, and although the draft was said to be backed by the 'Bee Company', a well known blockade-runner and war profiteer, this also makes very little sense, as the ships are slow, heavy and quite unsuited for that purpose. And lastly ..." and here Adams paused to draw breath ... "and lastly, my agents in Liverpool confirm that a ship arrived this week, apparently from Nassau, but with a large number of Southern gentlemen on board, who seem to be of a naval disposition. We believe that they are the crew of the *El Tousson*, arrived to take this ship back to American waters."

Russell had been listening attentively to this account and with growing admiration for the Union's spy network, which seemed able to gain access to so many sources of information that remained unavailable even to their British counterparts.

"I see, yes, I see," he said at last. "Well, we must clearly do something about this. I will today send a telegram to the Customs

Office in Liverpool requesting that they investigate the ownership of these vessels with the utmost expedition."

"But, my Lord, is that not exactly what you ordered just prior to the escape of the *Alabama*? I must tell you that these ships could smash our blockade or even retake the Mississippi for the Confederacy and although I do not believe that either of these events would change the eventual outcome of the war, they would certainly prolong it substantially and we cannot allow that to happen. Do I make myself clear, my Lord? We *cannot* allow that to happen."

"You make yourself perfectly clear Mr Adams," Russell replied, sucking on his teeth and wondering what on earth he was going to do now.

* *

Bulloch's landlady rapped on the door of his sitting room and put her head around the door, without waiting for an answer. "Oh Mr Bulloch, there's a gentleman here to see you. Says it's ever so urgent. A right proper gentleman, he is too. Shall I show him up?"

"Yes, Mrs Benson, if you would be so kind," Bulloch replied, wiping his mouth on his napkin and pushing away his dinner plates. He got to his feet and brushed the crumbs from his waist-coat. The door opened and John Laird senior entered, clearly quite agitated and red in the face.

"What is it, John?" Bulloch enquired without preamble.

"Bad news – we have Customs officials all over the shop. They've been there all day and I've only just managed to get away. Said I had to catch a train up to London – Parliamentary business and all that. They brought a camera with them, you know, and have photographed 294 and 295, paying particular attention to the rams on their prows. And they've gone through my papers – seemed to know what they're looking for too. They took away a couple of ledgers relating to our dealings. They've got warrants, properly filled out and signed by the Chief Constable – so, it's all above-board. That's the last time I have him to dinner though, I can tell you!"

Bulloch sat down heavily. "How much longer, John?" he asked.

Laird swallowed. "Two weeks. And then we will have to fit the turrets at sea, which is a dangerous operation. They'll be unarmed even then and you should expect that the Union Navy will be out in force."

"You let me worry about the Union Navy. Your job is to get these ships ready as soon as you possibly can. Dammit John, we stole the *Alabama* out from under their noses and we'll damn well do it again," and he punched the palm of his hand with his fist for emphasis.

*   *

Lord Russell sat in his office and read the report from the Liverpool Customs Office from beginning to end, carefully, twice. Then he read the conclusion out loud:

"and so, while there is a considerable weight of hearsay and circum - stantial evidence, we have been unable to find any proof, of a nature that would be sustainable in a court of law, that these vessels are either owned by or bound for the Confederate States of America."

He called in his secretary and dictated a letter to Adams, enclosing a copy of the report and concluding that, under the circumstances and, with much regret, he felt unable to take any more direct action, especially given the recent reversal on appeal of the case concerning the seizure of the *Alexandra*. He hoped that Mr Adams would understand, given that in both their countries the rule of law was pre-eminent and due process must inevitably be followed in order to avoid chaos and anarchy. Nonetheless, he expressed his personal regret and his fervent hope that further evidence might come to light, which would enable them to proceed in a more direct and robust manner.

'There', he thought, 'that should do it'. But he was wrong.

Within one hour Adams' written response was on his desk. Russell picked up the letter, holding it with the very tips of his fingers, as if the paper were impregnated with poison. He read, furrowing his brow as he did so. "Blah, blah, blah, expresses profound regret, blah, blah, blah." He paused and read the last sentence several times. "Now what does this mean?" he said out loud: *"It would be superfluous for me to point out to your Lordship that this is war..."* 'Is this a declaration of war or merely a statement of the facts?' he thought. Why would he use the word 'super-fluous' in connection with a threat to declare war between the United States and Great Britain? Surely no diplomatic exchange could be superfluous in such a context?'

Satisfied that this was not tantamount to an automatic declaration of war, in the event that one or other of the Rams were to be permitted to leave for the open sea, Russell nonetheless spent the rest of the morning worrying about what the reaction of the Federals might be under such circumstances. Even to send a diplomatic message, which contained a deliberate ambiguity referencing war, must mean that this was one possible option, which would seriously be considered upon the happening of the contemplated event. To put it another way, if he did not order the Rams to be seized, then he would be risking war. So, were these ships worth the risk? Adams did not believe that they would change the eventual outcome of the war, but he, Russell, was less sure. Breaking the blockade and giving the South free access to imported guns and munitions, while permitting cotton to flood into the starved markets of Europe would undoubtedly buy the Confederacy time, while such a major reversal for the North would probably affect Lincoln's chances of re-election in '64. A new President could mean a negotiated peace and the permanent division of the United States! But on the other hand, while he had been prepared to risk, or even precipitate a war with the United States in the past, he now acknowledged that such a venture could carry a very high cost, given the likely lack of support by the ever-fickle French and the possibility of armed intervention by the Russians, who still smarted from the Crimea. And that was not all. War with the United States would be unpopular in the Country and would be strongly opposed by the Prime Minister and the vast majority of his Cabinet colleagues. It could be the end of his political career and he was not sure that he was yet ready to retire to his estates and spend his time shooting pheasants and discussing crop rotation.

So the Rams had to go. He was sorry, but that was just the way it was. But if he could not legally seize the Rams ... then he could at least order them to be detained pending a full enquiry into their ownership! Yes, that would be the correct solution. He could always apologise afterwards, if necessary and if the courts ultimately ordered the ships to be returned to their owners, well, so be it. If not … he chuckled as an idea occurred to him… if these ships were tied in court for long enough, then the owners might very well accept an offer from Her Majesty's Government, to purchase said vessels. Not his department exactly, but he was sure that Sir George Lewis would welcome these modern and dangerous additions to Britain's largely outdated fleet. He rubbed his dry hands together and shouted loudly, "Stainforth, get in here – right away, if you please!"

*   *

It was three in the morning and dawn was an hour and a half away, even this close to the summer solstice. The moon was no more than a sliver, low in the sky, and the night was heavy and dark as the steam-launch gently bumped into the rope fenders and a sailor threw a line to a barely discernible figure waiting on the jetty, who secured it to an iron ring.

"Mr Bulloch? Is that you?" hissed the figure. "It is I, John Laird, junior."

Bulloch stepped onto the swaying jetty and grasped him by the hand. "Is everything ready?" he asked.

"It is. Now, follow me, as quietly as you can."

Bulloch beckoned to the other men, who waited on the launch. They came ashore, one by one, each carrying a bag or sack with his personal belongings. Quietly, in single file, they proceeded up the ramp and onto the dock, following the young man, who held a dark lantern, shuttered so that only a narrow beam illuminated the ground just in front of his feet. They came to a high wooden fence, in which was set a door, guarded by a burly night watchman in a bowler hat. Laird nodded to him and the door was swung open on recently oiled hinges. Before them loomed the bulk of one of the Rams. "Now get your men below," Laird whispered to Bulloch "and keep them out of sight. You should come up to the house with us and have breakfast. We will fire the engines and prepare for sea at first light, when the trial crew arrive. I will stay on board and keep them from going below decks. We don't want them tripping over your men, do we?"

Bulloch arrived at the house just as the sun rose, lifting his spirits immediately. John Laird senior, who was already wearing his sea-boots, greeted him warmly and they sat down to breakfast.

"You will be pleased to hear, James, that the *Dolphin* sailed from here at midnight last night, with the turrets on her deck. Her captain is a good man with considerable experience, whom I trust implicitly. He even knows that bay, by Kinsale, where you will meet tonight and has anchored there before."

"Very good. Thank you, John. As always, I am in your debt. For my part, the *Bermuda* has also sailed, with our guns and our supplies. I know that I am taking a risk arming 294 in British waters, but the Irish have no love for the English and from Kinsale I am but a few short miles to the open sea. Truly, I will be a happy man when I am sitting behind her thick iron plate with four loaded eight-inch rifled guns mounted in their turrets above me."

Laird laughed and clapped his friend on the back.

"Now tell me," Bulloch asked, "when did you let the harbour authorities know that we would be taking 294 out on sea-trials today?"

"Late yesterday afternoon. Just before they all went home for the night."

"And did they seem unduly interested?"

"Not at all. I sent William who said that the Harbourmaster merely noted it in his book and was grumpy at being delayed on his way home."

Bulloch nodded. "Good. So let us keep our fingers crossed that all goes smoothly today. But, even assuming it does, I have to say John, that I fear very much for 295. We should certainly expect further legal interference from the authorities and I think you should also double the guards in case some attempt is made to destroy the ship."

"You should have no fear of anyone harming any ship in my yards – but as to what the Customs johnnies might do next..." he shrugged. "In any case there is nothing more we can do about it now," he said, pulling out his gold fob watch and flipping open the cover. "It is time ... let us proceed to the dock and board 294."

By the time they arrived, the Ram was making steam from her squat funnel and her deck was a hive of activity. The dock had been flooded and the high fencing had been removed from the river-end. As they boarded, the dock gates swung open, and the passage was clear to the river and on to the sea.

Bulloch gave the order to cast off. Her engines came slowly to life, vibrating the wooden deck under their feet and her screws began to turn, stirring the dark oily water beneath her keel. She moved slowly forward out of the dock and her blunt prow above the vicious iron ram eased gently out into the river.

Half her length was already beyond the mouth of the dock when Laird gasped and grabbed Bulloch by the arm. He pointed down the wharf to where a large steam launch had just moored and a company of red-coated marines, carrying rifles, were spilling out onto the shore. Bulloch could clearly see their Captain assist the fat Collector of Customs out of the launch. The Collector, who held a roll of papers in his hand and had a large cigar clamped between his teeth, looked down the wharf to where 294 was manoeuvring into the river, saw John Laird on her deck, recognised that the ship he had been sent to detain was about to escape and opened his mouth to remonstrate, forgetting about the cigar, which fell to his feet. "Dammit!" he said. Then, taking a megaphone from the Captain, he shouted: "Oh I say, Laird, come back. I must speak with you – don't leave!"

Laird cupped his ear with his hand, miming his inability to hear. In actual fact, he had heard nothing at all, because Bulloch had given the order for 'full speed ahead' and the noise of her engines had risen from a steady throbbing to a rapid hammering. 294 gathered speed, leaving a white line of churned water in her wake, and headed directly out into mid-river so as to get beyond range of the Marines' rifles as quickly as possible, before turning down-stream and heading for the sea.

"That was a close call," Bullock shouted to Laird, who nodded back at him, looking grim, his jaw clamped shut and his lips pressed together in a thin line.

After a while, 294 slackened speed and Bulloch visibly relaxed, shrugging to ease the tension from his cramped shoulder muscles. He smiled at Laird, who still looked worried and was about to say something to him when a lookout shouted down to the deck.

"Ships ahoy. Signalling us, Captain."

Bulloch seized a telescope and ran to the prow. He put the glass to his eye and focussed it. Two large warships, some two hundred yards apart and heading up-river directly towards them, sprang into view. The leading ship had signal flags flying, ordering them to heave to.

"Damn," Bulloch shouted, "damn, damn, damn." He ran back to the wheel. "Make full speed ahead", he ordered and again 294 surged forward, heading directly for the warships, which were getting closer by the minute.

"You must heave to," Laird shouted.

"Damned if I will – we're going through them," Bulloch yelled back.

The warships had slowed and Bulloch could now see that they were new sixty-gun steam frigates. The ships turned slowly until they were positioned one directly astern of the other, across the river, and then came to a complete stop. With a noise that was audible even over the clamour of the engines, all the starboard gun ports on both frigates slammed open simultaneously and the ugly black snouts of their cannons protruded from the dark recesses behind.

"They mean to fire on us," Laird shouted, "you must stop – they will sink us!"

"Hard about," Bulloch ordered, but as the Master span the wheel Bulloch looked astern to where the steam launch with its contingent of marines, all with rifles at the ready, was coming up on them fast and the fight went out of him.

"Stop all engines," he ordered, "heave to." Having given the order, he slumped down onto the deck, rested his back against the mast and took no further interest in the proceedings.

* *

"I am finished here," he had told Rose after his release later that day, "and they have made that very clear. In the nicest, politest, most English way possible of course, but the message is unmistakable. We have become a political embarrassment – and that is not all. There was even a vague suggestion that I might be in some way involved in the untimely death of our friend Miller. Had you heard?" Rose shook her head. "Apparently he was found early this morning, seated at his desk, with his throat cut. It seems that someone had used a straight razor on him. Now, no one is going to mourn Miller's passing, but he was an MP and so there will be an investigation and all this means that I must go and soon. But where to – that is the question."

"Why, France of course, my dear."

"Will they have me?"

"If you have money and you intend to spend it, then yes of course. A Frenchman has three organs of thought. His wallet, his stomach and his penis – and of these his wallet reigns supreme."

"Well, that is fortuitous, because even though the Erlanger Bonds plummeted in price after the news of Gettysberg and there will be no further instalments coming from them, I still have some five hundred thousand pounds in hand. Enough to pay for all the ships I ordered from Lucien Arman back in May." He frowned. "Not I fear that they will make much difference in the long run. With Lee beaten I believe that it is now a matter of time only."

"Hush now. Don't talk like that." Rose held up an admonishing finger. "We must all of us persevere, no matter how bleak the outlook may be. And you shall go to France and build your ships," she finished sternly. Rose suddenly looked down at her fingers, reluctant to meet Bulloch's gaze. "And should you like it if I were to join you in Paris?" she asked after a pause. "You see, Mason has been recalled," she hurried on, "and President Davis thinks that I may be of more use on the Continent. He wants me first to return to Richmond for a short while, but after that ...". But she was unable to finish as Bulloch had grabbed her and held her so tightly that for a moment she was unable to breathe.

289

XXIII

Off Cape Fear, North Carolina – September, 1863

❧ ❦

The storm had closed in shortly after the *Condor* had left the safety of the shallow waters around Bermuda, heading due west for Wilmington. The high seas and strong winds caused her to pitch and toss with an awful corkscrewing motion, first diving into the trough of a wave and then rearing back out of it, rolling to one side as she climbed the crest of the next wave.

The *Condor* was a purpose built blockade-runner, long and narrow for speed and low in the water to avoid detection. Loaded down as she now was with munitions and supplies of all types, she sat even lower in the water. Dangerously so, for the waves that broke over her deck ran freely into her holds, soaking the precious cargo, in spite of the hatches, which had been covered with canvas and lashed down tightly. Each time she rolled in the swell, her side paddles spun furiously as they were lifted clear of the water, causing the engines to scream in complaint.

The Captain was on deck, secured to the short stubby mast by a thick rope around his waist. He had a glass to his eye, and was looking out across the rolling waves for any sign of the long white line of foam that would signal the edge of the reef. Occasionally he would turn and look behind him to where the Union warship, just visible each time it crested a wave, remained in dogged pursuit.

'Hell,' he thought, 'I have no choice. I must attempt to cross the reef. If I wait, the flooding in the holds could take us under or she could lose an engine and we would broach in this sea – or the Yankee could get close enough to fire on us. Damn this storm.'

He was still staring out forward when the *Condor* gave a lurch and with a sickening grinding noise, slowed and finally juddered to a halt, flinging the Captain against his rope belt. Immediately he knew what had happened. The waves and the high seas had obscured the line of the outer reef, which they had struck and were now held fast. It would only be a matter of time before the *Condor* broke up in the waves that smashed relentlessly against her hull. An ashen-faced seaman emerged from the companionway.

"Captain, captain, there's a great rent in her hull and she's taking water into the number one hold!"

"Then pump it out, damn you!" he shouted back. "That Yankee will get us all off alive, but we have to buy the time for him to get here. So pump!"

The Captain was confident that they would be rescued, but the loss of the *Condor* meant the loss of his share of the profits, not to mention the money he had invested in his own personal cargo – the silk bales and cases of perfume which filled his own cabin. 'Damn everything,' he thought again.

The next out of the companionway was the passenger they had picked up in Bermuda. A strikingly beautiful woman, with thick dark hair, by the name of Mrs Greenhow. A widow, as he understood it and one with whom he had hoped to become better acquainted, after they had arrived safely in Wilmington harbour and he was lording it about town, flush with cash.

"Captain," she shouted, "have we struck the reef?"

"I fear so Ma'am, but you have no need to fear … that Yankee warship over yonder will take us all off before she breaks up. We've lost the ship and her cargo though, for sure!"

"But Captain, you don't understand. I cannot be taken by the Yankees. They will imprison me, at the very least. I must get off this ship before they arrive. Can I be rowed to the shore?"

The Captain looked at the waves and at the shore, which was barely visible over a mile away behind a curtain of driving rain. He shook his head. "Too risky Ma'am. Much too risky!"

"I'll pay." she said, stamping her feet in exasperation. "I'll pay in gold."

"In gold you say?" He looked around and beckoned two burly seamen who were holding tight to the shrouds for support.

"Men," he said, "this lady needs to get to shore, bad like. She'll pay you in gold, if you row her."

The men looked at each other and then at the sea. One shook his head. "How much?" the other said.

"Fifty dollars."

"One hundred. In gold. In advance."

"Very well," she said. "Wait here." Within a minute she was back with a small carpetbag and a number of small gold coins clutched in her fist. "Are you sure?" she said to the first sailor, who had seemed the more reluctant of the pair, holding out the coins on the palm of her hand. "Oh, alright then" he said, eyeing the gold "but let's be quick about it."

The long boat was lowered and the sailors jumped from the side of the *Condor*, which had heeled over when it became stuck on the reef. They timed it for when the small boat rose on a wave and the distance from the deck closed to a mere two or three feet. Rose mistimed the jump and landed heavily on one of the sailors, who pushed her roughly onto the bench amidships, where she crouched between the two oarsmen. They pushed off.

"Good luck Ma'am," the Captain yelled, his hands cupped so as to be heard over the wind.

The small boat turned for the shore. The Captain continued to watch as the distance increased between them, his stomach knotting each time he lost sight of Rose and the seamen as their boat went into a trough, only to be relieved as the frail craft rose again, climbing up the face of the next wave.

And then they were gone. The Captain desperately searched the sea for any sign of the boat, hoping that he might have taken his eye off them for a second and would at any moment see them again, well ahead and closer to the shore. But no. The boat had vanished completely, swallowed up by the towering seas, undoubtedly smashed to pieces and its occupants drowned.

*   *

It was the corporal of a foot patrol who found her the next morning. The storm had passed, the winds had died and the sun had come out on a warm and balmy summer's day. All down the beach, small waves lapped at the detritus which the storm had thrown ashore – spars, ropes, barrels – and the body of a woman, who lay face down at the edge of the water, her long dark hair spread out around her like a shawl. Occasionally a wave larger than the others would lift her slightly, rocking her head, before retreating down the beach and leaving her further from the sea than before.

The wreck of the *Condor* was still visible, although the ship had broken in two during the night and only her bow section, as far aft as her smoke stack, was left, still firmly grounded on the reef. The afterdeck, her side-wheels, engines and stern had been swept away. Of the Yankee warship there was no sign.

The Corporal, having fought at Chancellorville and Gettysburg was no stranger to death in its many guises. But he found himself strangely unwilling to disturb the corpse of this woman. Nonetheless, he steeled himself and rolled her over onto her back, marvelling at her beauty, even in death and the alabaster skin of her face, to which a few strands of damp hair clung untidily. He brushed back the offending hair and called for his troopers to fabricate a stretcher, on which they would carry her body the three miles inland to Wilmington.

When the stretcher was ready, he lifted Rose and gently lay her down on it. Then he lifted the long, loose skirt of her dress so as to place it on top of her legs and to prevent it from dragging along the ground as they carried her. Immediately he felt the extraordinary weight of the cloth and bent down to look for its cause. Turning over the hem, he could see that many round objects had been sewn into the inner lining. Intrigued, he ripped open a small area and gasped as a stream of gold coins poured out onto the sand. He picked one of them up and examined it, reading the inscription around the portrait of a stern faced young woman, whose hair was tied severely back in a bun: 'Victoria R. Dei Gratia'.

"Hey fellas!" he shouted to his men, "come on over and have a look-see what we got here!"

EPILOGUE

Liverpool — January, 1901

~ ~

A particularly stormy gust of wind rattled the panes of the small window and the old man stirred uneasily in his narrow bed. A middle-aged woman with dark hair tied back in an untidy bun looked up at the doctor, who held the old man's wrist, taking his pulse.

"Is he awake?" she asked.

The doctor shook his head. "Very unlikely. I have just given him an injection of morphine for the pain and he is now in a deep sleep. Really my dear, it is for the best. He is really quite comfortable ."

The woman dabbed the corner of her eye with a small handkerchief, which she then pushed into the cuff of her cardigan. She sniffed. Then she lent forward and stroked the old man's forehead, smoothing the thinning grey hair across his scalp.

"How long?" she asked.

"It is impossible to say. Not long. Hours maybe. Not days. The cancer is very advanced and you can see how shallow his breathing is. It will be painless though." He took the woman's hand. "You should reflect on the fact that he has had a long and active life. He has had five children. In the end he was reconciled with Harriet, your mother, and has made a good life here in Liverpool. He is a hero to many and he will be remembered. That is more than most of us can say. I doubt that he had many regrets."

The woman looked over the head of the doctor to where an oil painting hung, just above the fireplace. The painting depicted a naval battle, where two rather old-fashioned looking ships fought, the smoke from their cannon partially obscuring their outlines. In the water were broken masts and spars to which clung desperate looking seamen. In the background a small yacht could just be seen.

"Perhaps one." she said.

In the old man's deep narcotic-induced sleep, he was young again, strong and vigorous. He stood on the deck of a seventy-five foot, three-masted steam yacht and lightly held on to the rail as the *Deerhound*, as sleek and fast as her name implied, ran before the wind.

"Look," he said, pointing towards the mouth of Cherbourg harbour, barely a mile distant, "she's coming out. Now we'll have some sport."

"I hope you are right James. The *Kearsarge* seems every bit her equal." Bulloch looked at John Lancaster, the owner of the *Deerhound*, with an expression that on another face might have been considered quizzical. On his it merely registered surprise.

"You forget, John, I built her. She's fast, she's got a seven inch rifled Blakeley and Semmes, much though I don't like the man, is a good captain. D'ye know that he's taken sixty-six prizes in under two years. And he's had half the Union fleet on his tail. I sometimes wonder if I could have done that much better myself."

He cocked his head to one side and frowned in concentration. "Dixie…?"

Lancaster listened carefully. "Why so it is … now who …?"

"It's coming from that French frigate over there … do let's go in closer, John."

The *Deerhound* tacked and ran for the mouth of the harbour. As they closed they could see the *Alabama* clearly, just rounding the outer defences, under steam. At anchor just outside the harbour was a French warship. Down the length of her deck, crowded against the rail, stood the entire ship's company, cheering and waving their hats in the air, while on the poop deck the band played *Dixie's Land*.

The captain of the *Alabama*, standing to attention in full dress uniform on his quarterdeck, raised his hat in reply as they passed. The *Deerhound* sounded her klaxon and Semmes turned around, catching sight of the yacht for the first time. He raised his telescope to his eye and examined the two men standing side by side on the deck. Bulloch waved. Semmes, ignoring him, snapped his telescope shut, picked up a megaphone and begun shouting orders to his crew.

About three miles to the North, just outside French territorial waters, the *Kearsarge*, a three masted steam sloop of some one thousand five hundred tons, lay at anchor. Her captain, John Winslow, a devout Christian, stood hatless in the morning sun, reading to his assembled crew from a prayer book. A lookout atop the mizzen mast suddenly cried: "The *Alabama*, it's the *Alabama*!" Captain Winslow immediately slammed shut the prayer book and gave orders for the *Kearsarge* to get under way. The steam capstans groaned and began to turn, the anchor chains rattled across the deck and down into the chain lockers and steam began to pour from her funnel. Minutes later she had turned North East and was heading out to sea and away from the *Alabama* at her full eleven knots.

Semmes watched this manoeuvre through his telescope and was puzzled. 'He can't be running', he thought to himself, a worried frown knitting his brows. 'It may be a trap though. He may be luring me out to sea where another Union ship is waiting. But I can't afford to run either, or he will give chase. No, I must fight him here.' Relieved that the decision had been taken, he gave the order for full speed ahead and set off in pursuit, followed at a safe distance by the *Deerhound*.

The *Alabama*, whose copper bottom was fouled by a thick growth of weed and barnacles, could no longer outpace the *Kearsage* as she might have once done. Instead she followed at a slower speed, her Captain pacing the quarterdeck and staring impatiently through his telescope every few minutes. After less than half an hour he saw the *Kearsage* turn full about and steam back towards the *Alabama*. "My God," Semmes muttered out loud, "she means to stand and fight."

"All hands to stations – run out the starboard battery!" he yelled, peering forward at the *Kearsage*, which was now easily visible to the naked eye. The three thirty-two pound broadside guns ran out, their crews positioned at the ready, the master gunner holding the firing lanyard. Both pivot guns swung to starboard.

"Mr Kell," Semmes turned to his First Lieutenant, "keep your distance. We have the advantage of range and I can see that she is trying to close on us." The *Alabama* veered a few points to port and as the two ships came abreast a mile and a half of water separated them.

Semmes gave the order to fire and with a roar the thirty-two pounders slammed back against their restraining ropes and thick black smoke obscured their view of the other ship. The pivot guns fired seconds later. Then the smoke was whipped away in the breeze and Semmes was able to see the solid shot of the broadside guns hit the water short of the *Kearsage* and then rise into the air and clear the mast tops. One shell tore through the shrouds, sending broken spars crashing down on to the deck. The other, from the rifled Blakeley, struck the wooden sternpost, sending out a shower of lethal splinters, but failed to explode.

At this point the *Kearsage* turned hard to starboard, seeking to close the gap and bring its heavier but shorter range guns into action.

Semmes saw this and ordered the *Alabama* also to turn to starboard. The two ships then circled each other like weary prize fighters, the one seeking to close the distance, the other to maintain it. The *Alabama* fired two more broadsides. The gunners had refined their aim and Semmes was delighted to see the heavy shot smack into the *Kearsage* full amidships. Delight soon turned to dismay as he trained his telescope on his opponent only to find that she had suffered almost no damage. By staring fixedly at the points of impact of each shot, he was able to discover the reason for this – she had lengths of heavy chain hanging thickly down her sides. She was ironclad!

Semmes felt a knot of worry form in his stomach. Quickly he gave the order to raise the elevation of the guns again. He approached Lieutenant Kell. "We cannot sink her, so we must board her. Give the order for the men to arm themselves but to stay below until further notice. We will close on the *Kearsage*."

"But Captain…" Kell looked worried. "We will take terrible punishment before we get close enough to board."

"I know, but there is no other way. May God preserve us."

So the dance continued, but now it was the *Alabama* who sought to close the gap and the *Kearsage* seemed to allow her to do so until Captain Winslow was sure that she was within range of all his guns and then he gave the order to open fire.

Immediately a shell exploded on the *Alabama's* deck, throwing the port pivot gun onto its side, crushing a gunner underneath and spraying shards of hot metal around the deck with awful consequences. Sailors with terrible wounds from the jagged projectiles fell to the deck screaming while others lay silent, blood pouring from their broken bodies. Other shells tore into the *Alabama's* hull ripping large holes in her side.

She returned fire and the Blakeley's shells could be seen impacting on the *Kearsage*. One tore through her smokestack, another sheared off the engine room hatch, while a third exploded on the quarterdeck, killing one sailor and injuring two more.

The men of the *Alabama* cheered, but the eleven-inch Dahlgrens of the *Kearsage* were now within range and shot after shot ploughed into her sides. One shell hit the *Alabama* at the waterline and penetrated her hull, exploding in the engine room. The ship shuddered and Semmes, sensing that the wound was mortal, put his hand on his Lieutenant's arm. "A damage report if you will Mr Kell."

The Lieutenant ran off and reappeared moments later. "The good news, Sir, is that the fire is out. The bad news is that we are taking on water faster than our pumps can handle it. We are sinking, Sir."

"Thank you Lieutenant. Give the order to raise the white flag and prepare to launch the boats. We will abandon ship at my command."

Bulloch had watched the engagement with mounting dismay. The *Deerhound* had positioned herself a mile or so to the *Kearsage's* port side and as a result Bulloch, who knew nothing of her chain mail, cursed the inaccuracy of the *Alabama's* gunners.

"Look John," he shouted, "Semmes is letting them sink my ship!" Then he saw the white flag run up her mast and even as it did so, the *Alabama* started to settle by the stern. Bulloch stood silently as the two remaining ships' boats pulled away from the stricken ship and other members of the crew threw themselves into the sea and started to swim.

Slowly the *Alabama* settled further in the water, stern first, the bow rising high into the air. The main mast snapped with an audible crack. Then, for a moment, she was perpendicular, before she sank quickly, her proud bow vanishing last, lost beneath the waves.

Bulloch stood and watched, hat in hand, tears blurring his vision. Then he took a deep breath, roughly dashed the back of his hand across his eyes and shouted for the Captain to pick up survivors.

The *Deerhound*, flying the Union Jack, was a neutral ship in international waters. The *Kearsage* could not have fired on her and Captain Winslow watched in impotent fury as she cut across his bow and raced towards the *Alabama's* crew, who waved from the water.

Semmes sat in the stern of a cutter and was rowed towards the *Deerhound* by twelve uninjured sailors. The *Deerhound* had already reached the swimmers, and its crew together with Bulloch and John Lancaster, were leaning over its side pulling shivering and, in many cases, bleeding men from the water. The cutter with Semmes at the helm, pulled up to the *Deerhound's* side, the oarsmen ignoring those in the water.

"Make way, make way there", shouted Semmes, angrily pushing past the seated rowers and clambering up onto the deck. He was about to step over the rail when he found himself confronted by a large and angry man, who grabbed him by the front of his uniform jacket.

"And where do you think you are going?"

"Ah, Bulloch, it's you. Let me pass then."

Bulloch looked carefully into Semmes' eyes. "You know Semmes, I never did like you and now you've gone and lost my ship. Wait your turn."

Bulloch released Semmes' jacket and gently pushed with the flat of his hand. Semmes let out a cry and, with his arms cartwheeling, fell backwards into the sea with a splash.

The middle-aged woman, who had been looking at her sleeping father, suddenly saw him smile and wondered where his dreams had taken him.

THE END

Historical Note
and Apology

꙰   ꙫ

I believe that some readers may wish to understand the dividing lines between fact and fiction in this novel. This is not easy, because I have well and truly muddied the waters in this respect. However, I will endeavour, in a few paragraphs, to describe the major aspects of invention and to point out where real events or dates have been altered in the interests of the plot.

First, as a generalisation, all the major characters in this book are, or rather were, real people and all the *major* historical events are correct as to their dates and, in most cases, details. Needless to say, almost all the dialogue is invented and in many cases, particularly with lesser-known individuals, I have simply guessed at what might have been appropriate opinions for characters of that type at that time.

This having been said, I must now confess as to the elements of fiction which I have created in this book. In doing so I feel a little like one of the many Chinese who, during the cultural revolution, were forced to make a public admission as to their counter-revolutionary and non-conformist views, prior to accepting their punishment. I can only hope, for my part, that I will not, as a result of my confession, be sent to a distant province for re-education.

Where do I start? Well, I suppose with James Dunwoody Bulloch – where else? Right up front, let me say that he was a very brave and resourceful individual and a great patriot, from a good Georgia family and was in fact the uncle of Theodore ('Teddy') Roosevelt, who became President of the United States in 1901. At the start of the war his property and business were in New York and he neither owned a house in Savannah, nor slaves, but as was so often the case, he felt that his ties to his birthplace were stronger than to his place of residence, and thus decided to fight for the Confederacy.

The events such as the sailing of the *Fingal*, the building of the *Oreto/Florida*, the escape of the *Enrica/Alabama* are, to a very large extent, accurately described as is Bulloch's role in these events. The incident involving the seizure of 294 is not, however, both because it occurred two months later that I have it, in September and because she was never even permitted to leave the dock, but was hemmed in by armed marines and a gunboat. 294 and 295 were ultimately bought by the British Government and named the *Scorpion* and the *Wyvern*.

Bulloch's wife Harriet (who neither left him nor went mad) and his children – five in total, were in fact in Liverpool with him throughout this period. As a result I very much doubt that he was a heavy drinking, philandering gambler, as I have portrayed him. Indeed, he is even supposed to have been a somewhat staid individual, much given to correct manners and behaviour and I am quite sure that nothing could have been further from his mind than the misappropriation of Confederate Navy funds. The costs of the ships, the permanent shortage of money and the saga of the Erlanger bonds are all accurate. Not so the random acts of violence, in the railway carriage and in the hold of the *Oreto,* which are both fictional.

Although Rose Greenhow was in England at the same time as Bulloch and it is quite possible that they met, their love affair is again a total invention.

After the war, James Bulloch stayed on in Liverpool because he was one of the few Confederate officers who would not have been granted amnesty and would have been put on trial. He became a British citizen and a successful cotton broker and died in his daughter Martha's house in January 1901. Bulloch is buried in Toxteth cemetery, together with his wife Harriet, two of his sons, Henry and James, both of whom sadly predeceased him and his daughter Martha, who having been born in 1865, lived until 1947. The inscription on his tombstone reads – "an American by birth, and an Englishman by choice." 'By necessity' I would have thought would be more accurate given the robust nature of his patriotism. Should there be descendants of Bulloch's alive today, I apologise to them unreservedly for many of the deeds which I have portrayed their grandfather or great-grandfather, committing. In my defence I will only say that I have tried to write him to be a sympathetic character, who is weak but repentant, proud but humbled and essentially kind, brave and honest. His actions in support of a cause in which he believed passionately are not widely known and in bringing these to the attention of the public, albeit in a somewhat bastardised form, I hope that he will achieve a measure of the fame which he justly deserves.

Next, let me turn to Rose Greenhow, one of the Confederacy's most famous spies. The details of her passing information on the Union troop movements prior to First Manassas are true and she is credited with playing a vital role in securing the ensuing victory. The details of her receiving the plans of the defences of Washington, Pinkerton's pursuit of the Captain and of her arrest are also largely true. Where fiction rudely intrudes is in the person of Pinkerton, who, though by his own admission finds Mrs Greenhow a fascinating and attractive woman, did not attempt to use his position in order to seduce her. Hence the entire sub-plot of the German assassin, Gottfried Kürz is all fictional. Rose's death is accurate: she did drown, weighed down by gold coins, but their origin is unknown. The description of the Old Capitol building is also highly exaggerated. It was previously a lodging house where Rose lived for part of her childhood and conditions there, when it was used as a prison, were not unreasonable. I have also changed the dates here somewhat, as she was confined in her own house with other suspected female spies until January of 1862 when she was sent to the Old Capitol building from where she was released in June of 1862, but did not go to England until later that year. The precise reason for her extended visit to England is not known, although she is supposed to have been engaged on some sort of secret mission. Lastly, while Lily Mackall is known to have had a crush on Rose, I have no reason to believe that this manifested itself in any physical manner. Again, my apologies to any living descendants of Rose Greenhow, although I have somewhat less to apologise for here than in the case of James Bulloch or, for that matter, Allan Pinkerton.

Of the minor characters, I have a (relatively) clear conscience in the cases of Stephen Mallory, President Jefferson Davis, Edward Anderson (although I have really combined his role with that of Caleb Huse, the Confederate Army purchasing agent in England), Charles Adams, Lord Palmerston, John Slidell, James Mason, John Bright, William Lindsay, John Roebuck, Emil Erlanger and His Imperial Highness, the Emperor Napoleon III.

Pinkerton, as I have already said, is guilty neither of what today would be aggravated sexual harassment nor of conspiracy to commit murder. On a separate point, the Captain whom he identifies passing information to Rose, is only believed to have been a Captain Elwood. Pinkerton merely refers to him as Captain 'E' in his own book.

Lord John Russell, who became Earl Russell in December 1861, is accurately portrayed as regards most of his actions, but I am sure that I have exaggerated his machiavellian deeds in providing William Lindsay (a member of an opposing political party) with information and using John Bright's speech at an emancipation meeting on purpose to discredit his motion – although it did actually have this effect. Nonetheless he did fear a re-united United States and his actions do support the thesis that he was at least a covert supporter of the Confederacy.

William Cowley Miller is the next victim of my overworked imagination. He did exist and his firm built both the *Oreto/Florida* and the *Alexandra*. However he was neither an M.P. nor the vindictive and unpleasant individual that I have portrayed him to be. Above all he was not murdered and, for all I know, he may well have been six foot six inches tall.

James Spence did raise money for the Confederacy, but I do not believe that Prioleau (or anyone) used his debts to persuade him to do so. I have also exaggerated his role in the 'bulling' of the Erlanger Bonds (an event that is otherwise quite accurately depicted) and his blockade-running and cotton-broking activities using inside information are complete fiction.

Charles and Mary Elizabeth Prioleau are abused insofar as she never (to my knowledge) enjoyed a sexual liaison, albeit interrupted, with James Bulloch and nor therefore was she beaten by her husband for this or any other offence.

As regards the Lairds, Bulloch goes out of his way time and again in his memoirs to stress their ignorance as to the true purpose and true ownership of the *Enrica/Alabama* and the fact that they believed the sale to Bravay & Cie of Paris to be a valid arms' length sale. I find this very hard to believe.

There may well be those who will criticise the way in which I have taken real people and events and have altered them at my whim to suit the vagaries of the plot of my novel. 'How would you like it if this were to happen to your forebears?' they will ask. I would point out to them that Isaac Kopa, whom I disparagingly refer to as 'the Jew', was in fact an immigrant from what is now Northern Poland, but was at that time Eastern Prussia. Upon his arrival in England in 1851 he changed his name to Isaac Summer. He was my great-grandfather. However, although he was actually living in Liverpool during the period of this book, he did not own a gambling club-cum-brothel in Castle Street. Unfortunately. Had he done so, the Summer family inheritance which came down to me might have been considerably greater than it actually was.

Julian Summer
May, 2006